Nantucket
Red Tickets

Books by Steven Axelrod

The Henry Kennis Myteries
Nantucket Sawbuck
Nantucket Five-Spot
Nantucket Grand
Nantucket Red Tickets

Nantucket Red Tickets

A Henry Kennis Christmas Mystery

Steven Axelrod

Poisoned Pen Press

Copyright © 2017 by Steven Axelrod

First Edition 2017
Large Print Edition 2017

10 9 8 7 6 5 4 3 2 1

Library of Congress Catalog Card Number: 2017938959

ISBN: 9781464207143   Large Print

Poisoned Pen Press
4014 N. Goldwater Boulevard, #201
Scottsdale, Arizona 85251
www.poisonedpenpress.com
info@poisonedpenpress.com

Printed in the United States of America

To Charles Dickens,
who told the best story first.

Acknowledgments

The usual thanks to William Pittman, the real police chief of Nantucket, and his dedicated team of uniformed officers and detectives. All errors and exaggerations in the story (as well as the poems) are entirely my fault, and have nothing to do with them.

I also want to thank the diverse group of friends and colleagues whose generosity over the years has allowed me to remain on Nantucket: Gregg Nosiglia, David Goodman, Jane and Jock McLeod, Anne Strain, John Copenhaver and Suellen Ward, Ginger Andrews, and of course my late mother Gloria Goforth, who owned the house my young family lived in for a decade. Beyond those kind souls I have to thank Annie Breeding, the obvious inspiration for Jane Stiles, who for the last eighteen years has been the best reason of all for staying here.

"You will be haunted," resumed the Ghost, "by three spirits."

Scrooge's countenance fell almost as low as the Ghost's had done.

"Is that the chance and hope you mentioned, Jacob?

"It is."

"I—I think I'd rather not."

"Without their visits," said the Ghost, "you cannot hope to shun the path I tread. Expect the first tomorrow when the bell tolls One."

"Couldn't I take them all at once, and have it over, Jacob?"

—Charles Dickens, *A Christmas Carol*

Contents

Part One
Christmas Stroll

Chapter One

The Ghost of Christmas Past

Nantucket, November 1997

It had all started with the Winthrop deal. They had a chance to buy the building next door on Main Street, expand the business, and become a serious force in the town's economy. It was a once-in-a-lifetime opportunity—property values would never be this low again. The island's marathon of development was just beginning.

If they didn't buy the building, someone else would. Blum liked to say that Main Street real estate was gold, but in fact, it was more valuable than gold. The world had vast supplies of that shiny mineral; piles of it filled the vaults in the Federal Reserve building and Fort Knox. But store-frontage on Nantucket's Main Street? That was a limited resource, like the eighty-thousand-dollar bottle of 1858 pre-phylloxera cognac in his liquor cabinet.

Coddington didn't get it. "Nantucket is finished," he liked to say. "They've ruined this place. They've killed the Golden Goose." It was never exactly clear who "they" were—immigrants from various countries, tourists, developers, millionaires and billionaires, or all of them together.

• • ● • •

Jackson Blum stared down at his partner's corpse, clutching the murder weapon in his hand, chanting silently, "I am not a killer, I am not a killer, I am not a killer."

He gaped stupidly at the gun—he didn't even remember picking it up—and then dropped it like…like—he remembered, years ago, carrying his old French bulldog outside to do his business and the ancient creature releasing a turd directly into his palm. This gave his stomach the same queasy twirl of disgust and horror. He staggered back a few steps. Throwing the gun down was pointless. He had to pick it up. He couldn't leave it here. And he had to bury the body. The bullet lodged in that skull would match his pistol if it was ever dug out, if the corpse was ever found.

He should dig it out himself. He shuddered. That was grotesque, unthinkable. To puncture Ted Coddington's skull with his penknife? Was that even possible? And then burrow into the brain, gouging and pulling the interior as if he was scooping out a pumpkin? No, no, no, absolutely not. He could barely stand to look at the body; he dreaded moving that surly inert weight—dead weight, that was the term—shoving it into a shallow grave.

The rasping engine of a motorcycle snapped him alert. He was far out of sight of the Madaket Road but a dirt track ran through this wedge of moorlands. If someone were to drive by…

He stood frozen in place as the Harley growl faded away toward town. He was safe for the moment. But the urgency remained. He was lucky in one way: along with the yearly series of off-road driving permits that decorated the rear bumper of his Ford Excursion, like a line of commemorative stamps in a binder, testifying to his seniority on the beaches of Wauwinet and Coatue, he stowed the legally required boards, towrope, and, most importantly, the shovel. So he had the tool he needed to bury the body.

But it would take time. And he had no alibi for his presence here—he had rushed out of the store fearing the worst, after Coddington bailed on their meeting with the Winthrop people. Coddington had sounded crazed and shaky on the phone and Anna had no idea where he'd gone. She was off-island—she had answered her cell in Pain D'Avignon. And she wasn't worried, not yet anyway. Coddington liked his long walks on the beach and his solitary bike rides in the moors.

Blum clenched his fists and his jaw in a motionless seizure of self-disgust. He should never have called Anna. His neutral inquiry would look suspicious in retrospect. If she'd picked up on his worry and guessed he was cruising the island searching for her husband, that would be worse than no alibi—it was the anti-alibi! A virtual confession of guilt. I found your husband on the afternoon of the day he was planning to wreck all our plans for the business....

And he happened to be dead!

And he happened to have my gun in his hand!

With one of my bullets in his brain!

Anna had overheard some of their arguments. The loudest and most combative one had broken out at 21 Federal on a busy Saturday night with the bar packed three-deep and every table taken. Chick Walsh himself had escorted the two of them out the door. Slim, elegant Chick Walsh—the least likely bouncer on the whole Eastern Seaboard. But they had submitted to the controlled rage on Chick's face and stumbled out like chastened schoolboys being marched off to the principal's office.

So there would be plenty of witnesses to testify at the murder trial.

"You were dining at the restaurant 21 Federal on the night in question, September twenty-first, 1997?"

"That's right."

"And you heard the defendant arguing with Mr. Coddington?"

"I'll say!"

"Just answer the questions, please."

"Sorry. Yes. Yes, I did."

"And did Mr. Blum threaten Mr. Coddington with bodily harm at that time?"

"Yes, he did. He said, 'It would be easier just to kill you.'"

"So Mr. Coddington was in fear of his life?"

"Objection! Calls for a conclusion."

"Sustained."

"I'll rephrase that, Your Honor. Did Mr. Coddington do or say anything on that occasion that made you feel he might have feared for his life?"

"Yes. He lurched back in his chair, knocked it into my wife's chair, in fact. She was sitting with her back to their table. And he shouted, 'Get away from me!' I thought Mr.—the defendant—I thought he was going to attack Coddington right then and there."

Oh, yeah, that would go over well. That was a first-class ticket to Cedar Junction. Go directly to jail. Do not pass go, do not inherit your business from your dead partner. Blum squirted out a high-pitched laugh, clamped it to silence. He sounded crazy, even to himself.

He had to take charge. This was a manageable situation. That was what he did best. That was how he had made his fortune—managing situations, finding solutions and implementing them. Problems seemed hopeless because you took them up all at once, in a single unwieldy slab. They had to be deconstructed, broken down into bits, and the bits taken care of, one at a time.

The first bit: bury the body.

This was Land Bank property—"forever wild," as they liked to say. No one would ever find the grave and Coddington's disappearance would remain a mystery—was he a middle-aged runaway? Had a secret crime from his past come back to haunt him? Had he eloped with an old lover, disappeared into the Witness Protection program, slipped away to join a monastery? All that stuff happened. People did those things and more. People went crazy. People snapped. Anything was possible.

As long as they never found the body.

That was the conundrum—it buzzed around his head like angry yellow jackets: if he dug a grave and the grave was found…Blum wasn't faking anything, he wasn't trying to cover up a murder, but that was how it would look.

Bodies don't bury themselves.

Still, leaving the body where it was, in full view of any stray hiker or birder was foolhardy, idiotic—with a bullet from his gun lodged in Coddington's brain? Absolutely not.

He crashed back to his car, lifted the tailgate, grabbed the shovel, and trudged back. With the first stab of metal blade into soil he realized the chore he'd set for himself. The ground was a tangle of roots and vines, pitted with rocks of all sizes. He stamped down hard on the back of the shovel with his boot, felt metal cutting the webbed gristle under the surface. He lifted the weight of dirt, flung it aside. He had thrown out his back the year before, after the big blizzard, perversely determined to shovel out his own driveway—refusing to pay off some money-grubbing teenage hustler.

This would be much worse.

"The whole plan is crazy!" Coddington had shouted at him that night in the restaurant. "It's financial suicide. You're digging your own grave! And mine, too."

The words came back at him now. Was he doing that? Burying both of them in the moors? It certainly felt that way. How had it all happened? He was a business prodigy! *Forbes* magazine said so! *The Wall Street Journal* called him a visionary in their profile last year! He'd spent hours watching the sycophantic little geek from the paper scribble down every word he said. Days.

And what if that fawning punk could see him now? Visionaries were supposed to anticipate the future, grasp events taking shape before everyone else.

He kicked the nose of the shovel into the ground again.

He hadn't seen this one coming.

Or was it that he'd seen it perfectly well and just didn't want to look? Denial, that most despised human weakness, the puny foible he ridiculed in others—demanding that his wife have that lump checked (it turned out to be benign), that Coddington investigate that ominous whistle from his car's engine (yes, some belt or other had to be replaced and it was a good thing they did it before that old Volvo broke down on the highway!).

Well, he hadn't been in denial about Coddington's suicidal tendencies. No one could have predicted this act. The people who talked about it rarely did the deed; and the actual depressives kept things buttoned up so much that even their closest friends were surprised when they found the body, baffled when the read the note.

The note!

It was probably sitting on Coddington's desk at home right now. It was only a matter of time before Anna walked in and saw it: one of those pale blue envelopes he used for personal correspondence, with her name scrawled across the front.

Coddington would never confess the real reason—but somehow he'd still make it sound like everything was Blum's fault, evil Jackson Blum who had turned poor Coddington's life into a nightmare. She'd buy it, too—people committed suicide for a million different cockamamy reasons, and Anna had always hated Jackson anyway.

Thinking about it as he jabbed the rusty shield of the old gardening spade into the hard ground, sweating through his shirt even after he'd pulled his jacket and his sweater off, he realized that Coddington's suicide note was his insurance policy of last resort. Better they should never find the body, never know what happened; but if they ever did, the dead man's last message to the world would go a long way toward clearing Jackson of a murder charge.

He made the list in his head: finish the grave, clean up, get the suicide note, take the gun home and stash it back in its box. He couldn't just ditch it, unfortunately. It had significant value—a Ruger Standard, one of the first ones ever made. The certificate it came with and the serial number on the barrel made it worth thousands of dollars to the right collector. But that had nothing to do with the weapon's real worth. The gun meant too much for him to just dispose of it like a hunk of trash.

Blum's father had brought the pistol back from Germany after the Berlin Airlift—the gun nestled in its red box with the black griffin logo. That gun—it looked a little like a Luger—lying in the dirt at his feet. An ordinary, semi-obsolete handgun, but priceless. His father hadn't left him much. In fact, beyond the Ruger and a pile of unpaid debts, there was next to nothing. Some letters, some handmade furniture, his great grandmother's wedding ring that Marjorie still wore. The gun was his legacy and to Blum's father it symbolized the war—the bombing runs and then the food runs during what he always called Operation Vittles. Dad's whole growing up, in fact. Blum's father became a man during those years and this gun was the totem of that passage. He couldn't just throw it away. And he wouldn't have to. He had never mentioned the Ruger to anyone except Coddington and Marjorie—who, as his wife, couldn't testify against him, even if she wanted to. The Ruger fired standard rounds, and the .22 was the most common bullet in the world. If they ever found the body, they'd just assume the gun had been stolen by scavengers. People wandered the moors with those metal-detector wands all the time, looking for just this kind of loot.

He slagged another load of soil to the side of the pit, felt something shift in his back. He was going to be crippled tomorrow.

His head was spinning, but his plan made sense. Coddington would disappear. People would wonder why, they'd make crackpot guesses about where he went. Everyone loved a mystery. Unanswered questions fueled the Nantucket gossip mill like big dry hardwood logs on a fire. The enigma would keep them warm for years, like that town where everyone disappeared one morning, what was it? The Roanoke Colony, right. Coddington's vanishing act would be like that. No muss, no fuss, lots questions, no answers. That's how Coddington would have wanted it. He just wasn't thinking straight. Well, that had always been Blum's job anyway.

One more spadeful and he was done. It didn't need to be a deep grave. Good thing, because Blum was wrecked. He stood panting, leaning on the handle, letting his heart rate normalize. How had he gotten into such lousy shape? He used to be an athlete.

When he caught his breath, he rolled Coddington into the narrow trench and starting filling it in. The question would remain: how had

Coddington gotten buried? But some eccentric Good Samaritan might have taken on the job. That was possible, wasn't it? Nantucket people did Quixotic things all the time—like opening the ponds to the sea—Steve Scannell had done that with Sesacacha Pond a few years before—one guy and shovel, clawing a channel out of the barrier beach! Burying some random corpse was nothing, by comparison. You couldn't just leave the body out in the open, but you didn't want problems with the cops, either. That made sense.

But if the cops somehow connected Blum to the burial…No, no, they wouldn't, they couldn't. How could they? He was going to give himself a panic attack. He paused, took a couple of deep breaths.

Then he went back to work, filling in the trench. He cut his wrists while ripping the coarse shrubbery to cover the mound of fresh soil. His hands were filthy, so were his clothes. He looked like he'd been rolling around in the dirt, like some burrowing animal, like—

Like a rat. Jesus Christ. Rats!

He was maybe a mile and half from the dump here. Nantucket had more rats than people, and ninety percent of them lived in that trash paradise. They'd smell the decomposing body. They'd come for the fresh meat. That was what they did. That was their job. This grave wouldn't last a month unless he could keep them away.

The endlessly multiplying complications overwhelmed him. He thought he might scream, or break down crying, or vomit. Or all three. And the complications assaulting him now were just the ones he had happened to notice. What about all the other ones he hadn't thought of? This was impossible.

He stood still, letting the icy north wind buffet him.

Rats. He caught some stray scrap of memory about rats. A family of them had taken up residence in his father's vintage Buick Roadmaster while it was in storage at a local garage. They chewed through the wiring, shredded hoses and belts, nested in the engine block. What had Dad done about it? Peppermint oil? Blum remembered something about peppermint oil. But that hadn't worked. How was Blum supposed to remember this stuff? He'd been…what? Maybe nine years old at the time? That was thirty years ago. They were still living in Schenectady, in the old house on Union Street. The place probably didn't even exist anymore. Still, his dad had figured something out. Some Old World folk remedy.

But what?

Blum felt like a green recruit in an old war

movie, holding onto an enemy grenade, paralyzed, waiting for it to go off in his hand.

Throw it, get rid of it, think!

"Even rats know this crap is poison!" That's what his dad had said. Poison, poison—what could be such a terrible poison? What crap was he talking about? Blum could feel his brain bulging with thought, pressing against the smooth walls of his skull like water freezing in a full bottle. Something was going to crack.

Then he gave up, sagged, opened his eyes—relaxation that was somehow a final exertion of the will. And the answer snapped open like a jammed window.

Tobacco!

That was it. And not just any tobacco—chewing tobacco. The smell kept the rats out of the engine block. It would keep them away from the grave. So Blum needed chewing tobacco, cans and cans of chewing tobacco. Ten cans? Twenty? As many as he could find and as fast as he could find them.

One more item on the to-do list.

First, the suicide note. Then the snuff. What an appropriate term! Then back here—mix the shredded leaves in with the loose dirt, get back into town and start making up a good explanation for how he'd spent his afternoon.

Details, details. The Devil was in the details, that was what everyone said. He was never sure what that meant, but now he knew. The Devil was hiding in the details, physically hiding, camouflaging himself like a ferret in a leaf pile, fangs bared, ready to strike.

Blum strode to his car, javelined the shovel into the back. Thinking of the tobacco gave him hope. He had a good eye for detail. Nothing got past him. That was how he had nailed Coddington in the first place.

•••••

It hadn't been just a matter of analyzing the business ledgers—some routine act of forensic accounting that any bean counter could have managed. Blum had also noticed the tiny details of behavior—the irregularities in conversation and hand gestures and eye contact. But everything was connected—the odd uncomfortable pause, squeezing the thumbnail with the fist, eyes flicking sideways...they were far more revealing than some small discrepancy between absorption costing and cash flow.

Blum had gotten the feeling that there was more to Coddington's resistance to the Winthrop deal. Coddington seemed nervous, not cautious—jittery and scared, when he should have been calm and prudent.

Gradually it had dawned on Blum: Winthrop wanted to audit the business before the closing, and Coddington didn't want them examining the books.

What was it? Tax-dodging, embezzlement, fraud? What was he hiding? Drugs, hookers, gambling debts? And how was he doing it? Claiming withdrawals as advertising expenses, overstating net income? Or was there a whole other set of books to conceal the profits he was skimming? The possibilities were endless and Coddington had the necessary skills for fraud—he had studied to be a CPA, though he never passed the exam.

Blum was no accountant but he knew where his money was going and where it was coming from. He knew their vendors and their customers, their creditors, and their charge account customers. He knew who paid late—mostly the richest of them. One noted orchestra conductor who had inherited a giant house on Cliff Road and married a copper heiress, still hadn't paid for a set of Callaway Big Bertha irons he'd signed for at the beginning of last summer.

The point was the ledgers would be full of familiar names. They were as close as Coddington would ever come to an autobiography, measured in accrued interest and invoices paid. Best of all, Blum could poke around all he wanted and no one had to know. Whatever he discovered could stay private.

He had gone into the store early that Sunday morning, and pulled the ledgers. The store used a computer spreadsheet program, but Blum insisted on keeping hard copy double-entry books. He no longer trusted computers, after losing a year's worth of data with one crash.

The accounting tablets were a pleasure to read, and his cramped little office was warm and cozy on an autumn morning. The ledgers sat on a wooden filing cabinet tucked under shelves that rose to the ceiling piled with ski sweaters and shoe boxes. One desk held the desktop PC. Blum pulled a chair up to the other one, a scarred antique walnut keyhole printer's desk he'd purchased years before at one of Rafael Osona's auctions.

The store was quiet; the town was quiet. The only sound was the dull thunder of the old furnace and the occasional car rattling up the Main Street cobblestones.

He found what he was looking for in the first five minutes.

The company was called Spindrift LLC, and Coddington had been authorizing monthly payments of seventeen-hundred dollars into their account for the last eight months. The first entry dated from March tenth.

Blum rocked his old wooden chair on its back legs, pushing against the edge of the desk. What happened in March? Had Coddington purchased some small property? This could be a mortgage payment. Or installments on some debt. How did it work with book-makers? If you got in over your head, could you arrange some sort of installment plan, like with the IRS? Could this be back taxes? Or was there some windfall Coddington had been hiding, some giant cash haul he was laundering through this dummy corporation one month at a time? If so, he hid it well—no ostentatious purchases, not even a new car. Coddington was famously stingy—a voracious reader, he didn't even buy books. He would happily tell anyone willing to listen that he was outraged by the price of hardcovers and happy to wait a month to borrow any title he wanted from the Atheneum.

No, no—Anna would have mentioned a cash real estate transaction or a trifecta win at Suffolk Downs. She would certainly have upgraded her wardrobe. So no sudden influx of cash. Anyway, real estate sales were listed in the newspaper, filed at town hall. And the gambling idea was far-fetched, too. Coddington had never shown any interest in the gambling sports. He thought horse-racing was cruel. And he hated casinos. After one business trip to Las Vegas, he had memorably called it "the vampire city"—sleeping in its own dirt by day, and rising at sundown to suck the blood of its victims. So no gambling wins to hide, no gambling losses to pay off.

Blum stood and stepped out of the office into the shadowy store, pacing between the shelves, straightening the displays. The merchandise made good company.

What other vices could Coddington have? Drugs? But he couldn't imagine that dealers used payment plans, and anyway, didn't the prices always go up? But maybe Coddington was using prescription drugs—Percocet or Vicodin. That would be a price-stable monthly purchase. How much of that crap would seventeen-hunded a month buy you? Way too much, that was Blum's guess. Coddington didn't act like he was doped up, but Blum's father had never seemed drunk, either—despite the fifth of cheap Scotch he drank every day. He proudly referred to himself as a "functioning alcoholic" until the day the booze killed him. Maybe Coddington was the same way. But prescription meds required a doctor, and doctors needed a reason to write a script like that. Had Coddington hurt himself last March? Thrown out his back, taken a fall, suffered an accident of some kind? Nothing came to mind. In fact, Coddington had always been fit and agile, insisting pompously on the benefits of his dirt-road bicycle excursions, and gloating over his skills on the paddleball court. He had even started "juicing," reducing various vaguely nauseating combinations of vegetables into muddy sludge and gulping it with a lip-smacking glee that Blum found implausible at best.

But he was nimble, you had to give him that. Just the other day, Blum had taken Coddington and Anna out to lunch at Boarding House with Anna's sister, Irena, and the girl had tripped over an uneven spot on the sidewalk. She pitched forward and, before anyone else could even register the physical event, Coddington had caught her arm and saved her from a nasty fall. It was almost as if he'd been watching her, expecting an accident, waiting for it. Or maybe he was just studying her for more obvious reasons.

Irena was a stunner, far better looking than her older sister, as so often happened, at least in Blum's experience. But she was clumsy and careless, which might explain Coddington's wary eye. She had caused three fender-benders since arriving on the island last January, and she was always knocking into things, dropping things.

"I am having a war with the inanimate objects," she had told him once, after slipping on an unpadded rug and tipping over a lamp. "I think the objects are winning."

You couldn't be annoyed when she flashed that lovely smile. Coddington had mentioned it more than once. "It lights up a room," Blum had admitted. Ted went further: "I would say it lights up the world, dear boy. Sunrise over 'Sconset Beach." But so what? Outlandishly beautiful things naturally provoked comment.

Still, thinking back, something had struck Blum as odd that afternoon, walking away from the restaurant. Coddington had held on to Irena's arm for a little too long, as if he was reluctant to let her go. It was probably just an extra measure of concern, but there was something else, something about the date. The timing of it all snagged him, like brambles on his sleeve.

Irena had come to Nantucket just after New Year's, and three months later, the money flow began—the perfect incubation period for a romance, especially a forbidden one. Irena had come to Marjorie's birthday party early in January, single and shy, barely able to speak English. Coddington had chivalrously set himself the task of stage-managing her entry into local society, finding her a job and an English tutor, a car and a place to live, coaching her on the written section of the driving test.

"Everyone else has the right of way!" she had laughed. "It sounds just like Lithuania."

Blum had race-walked back into the office, reached the desk in two strides and yanked open the ledger. He wanted to see the entries again, in black and white. They were so obvious—the amounts and the schedule of the payments told the whole story.

Coddington was paying rent, and he was doing it in secret. He was leasing himself a little love-shack, meeting Irena there for "late lunch" afternoon delights. The upstanding Catholic family man was cheating on his wife, and he was doing it with her sister. Could it be? Was it even possible, from a practical point of view, in a town this small? Would Coddington take the risk? He preened himself as an upright "pillar of the community," a church deacon no less, proudly intolerant of other peoples' foibles, casually assigning slots in hell to an acquaintance caught drinking on a Sunday or taking a payment in cash to hide money from the IRS.

Could he really be committing adultery? It was almost incest, too—that made it so much worse. At least, it felt like incest, banging your sister-in-law. Incest-in-law? Something like that.

Blum shook his head, amazed and amused. He'd had to find out for sure.

The surveillance had taken one week. He followed Coddington for a couple of days before he located the house, tucked away at the end of a dirt road in Tom Nevers, an area far from the social hive of the island. Coddington was famously oblivious when he was driving, and routinely offended friends and colleagues who waved to him as their cars passed in the street, so Blum had no problem trailing him, up Milestone Road to the old naval base turnoff, but had to watch and drive past as the big Volvo station wagon hooked a right onto an unpaved side road. Even Coddington might notice another car chasing him down some dead-end dirt track.

Blum came back the next day and started scouting the houses. He found no obvious clues— he couldn't identify a car by its tire tracks, for instance, and there was no telltale scraping of paint where Coddington might have brushed against a fence post. The houses themselves were blank and anonymous—gray shingles, weathered cedar trim, semi-attached garages. Some had curtains, others had shades, but there was nothing distinctive about the window treatments, at least from the outside.

Blum eliminated three of the ten houses— there were toys in their yards. He couldn't imagine that Coddington had a whole other family going out here. That was too crazy. Another house featured at Ford F-350 pickup and a pair of sawhorses in the yard, straddled with three-by-five planks. So, some carpenter. Coddington was anything but.

That left six houses. One of them was being used as a barracks for construction workers—he counted seven cars in the dirt in front of the place and saw several young guys going in and out, different ones each time—sawdust-caked, paint-spattered, figure-piped with plaster. Maybe they worked for the contractor with the Ford pick-up.

There were five houses left, and short of actually stepping up and knocking on the doors, Blum was stumped.

That changed the following Sunday. He drove by in the late afternoon. At the last house on the road, he found a prayer card from St. Mary's Church floating in a muddy puddle near the split-rail fence. It was easy to imagine how it got there: a windy day, a forty-mile-an-hour gale honking out of the northeast, the card on the dashboard, lifted out of an open window.

And Saint Mary's was Coddington's church.

He glanced at his watch—almost four o'clock on a blustery afternoon. The neighborhood looked deserted—no kids playing in the street, no one working in the yards. Coddington's secret house was tilted toward the others, which meant you could park in the back without anyone seeing your car. Was someone parked there now? He couldn't tell, but the narrow dirt road allowed no other hiding places. To investigate further without being seen, Blum would have to drive around, himself. Coddington spent Sundays with his family—there was no chance of running into him. What about the girl, though? Did she live here? It was a waste of a solid rent check if she didn't. But the place felt deserted, almost abandoned, in the late afternoon sunlight.

Blum drove to the back. He saw spaces for three cars but the yard was empty.

He killed the motor and listened to the wind. It pushed at the car like an animal, a cat rubbing itself against a chair leg.

He sat still for a moment, hands on the wheel. He was no thief; he didn't even like the idea of trespassing. But of course he was already doing that, with his car parked on the property. And the fact remained: the inside of this little bungalow could contain all the leverage he needed to get Coddington on board with the Winthrop deal.

Blackmail, in other words. But Blum refused to see it that way. Knowledge was a commodity and so were secrets. The truth remained pristine. If you possessed a fragment of it that others did not, you could build a fortune on it. Think about the Comstock Lode. It had started out as a gold mine. Prospectors found it difficult to wash out the fine gold because of this peculiar dense sludge that clogged the rockers. Very annoying! Until one man grasped the fact that the sludge was silver. Pure sulphuret of silver! And that's where the vast wealth of that enterprise came from. Not the silver, but the ability to identify the silver. This was no different.

Whatever Coddington was doing out here, those actions constituted the truth. Blum hadn't contrived or manipulated that truth, any more than Comstock had transmuted base metal into the seventy thousand tons of silver of the Ophir Bonanza. You didn't create the truth. You discovered it. You recognized it.

And you exploited it.

Blum pulled himself out of the car on the surge of resolution. He found the house key under the welcome mat—that was a good way to make him feel welcome!—and let himself in. He knew what he was looking for, a short catalogue of incriminating items. It didn't take long to find them.

The front door opened onto a big kitchen— no front hall, no mudroom. Fake wood cabinets, rusty electric stove, old GE fridge. No cooking smells, no dishes in the sink. The place presented as impeccably tidy, but the clean counters made it seem vacant—a stage set. He snooped the shelves, found cans of beans and boxes of instant rice, a tin of oatmeal, and a jar of Nescafe instant coffee—the first item that matched Blum's inventory. Nescafe was Irena's brand—how often had she claimed it tasted better than the real thing?

The kitchen widened into an open plan, under-furnished living room. An old couch and two worn leather armchairs pointed at a big Sony Trinitron TV; generic Nantucket art fair pictures on the walls—cobblestone street scenes, Sankaty Light, sailboats. A vase of dying irises on an end table.

Irises—Irena's birth flower.

He checked the bathroom next—nothing there except the plush toilet paper favored by new money and the poor. Old money people bought the single-ply Scott tissue that demonstrated thrift and common sense, scorning ostentation and display. This small item was consistent, if not conclusive—Irena was an immigrant striver, drawn to any hint of luxury—from the fancy car (Range Rover was her ride of choice) to this tacky triple-ply "facial tissue."

The shag carpet in the bedroom was another clue. He had heard Irena extol it as a luxury item! Blum supposed a lifetime of grimy bare floors had warped her judgment. Then there were the pillows on the bed—way too many pillows, branded pillows from Nantucket Looms and Erica Wilson, and a blue lace neckroll very much like the one he and Marjorie had given Irena for her birthday. She had complained about never being comfortable reading in bed.

That would have been enough, but Blum recognized the clothes in the closet, also. The short dresses that showed off Irena's legs, the fur-collared coat she had brought with her from Lithuania.

Blum stepped back and sat down on the bed. He had been ninety-five percent sure of what was going on—hell, it was more like ninety-nine percent. But, oh, that last one percent! It meant more than the other ninety-nine put together.

It meant everything.

He stood up, thinking hard. He needed some token of his discovery. He opened the drawer of the nightstand and saw a litter of Avanti condoms—the newest thing—made by Durex, some English company. They weren't even going to be commercially available for another year, but Coddington had connections with the importer. He had bragged about all of this over drinks at Boarding House one night. It was so typical of the man—he had to have the best and the newest of everything. And if it happened to be English, whatever it was, so much the better. Like the Taylors of Harrogate tea he had shipped from Great Britain every few months, which tasted no different from Lipton's, as far as Blum could tell. Boasting about details that made you feel unique was a mistake—they set you apart, put the spotlight on you, made you vulnerable. This little condom was as incriminating as a fingerprint.

Blum took it, and one of the irises, and let himself out of the house.

• • ● • •

He chose his moment carefully. Anna was shopping off-island the following Monday afternoon and Coddington would be upstairs in the refinished attic, fiddling with his Lionel trains. The hobby had always struck Blum as useless and reductive. The tracks wandered among a series of excruciatingly tended molding clay and papier-mâché landscapes—forests and mini-mountain ranges, cluttered little dollhouse towns. Blum could understand the plodding satisfaction of constructing this scale-model world; he could grasp the "collect them all!" pleasures of assembling the trains themselves, car by car. But once all of that was finished, once you owned the toys and laid all the tracks and constructed all the landscapes, there was nothing left do but watch the trains run in circles, signals chiming, draw-bridges opening and closing forever, without even the occasional derailment, station fire, or avalanche to break the monotony.

Still, Coddington loved his little railroad world.

Blum could hear the faint whine and clatter of the train from the foyer of the big house on India Street. He had come in through the open front door—Coddington never locked it—and paused a moment before starting to climb the stairs. He wasn't sure what to say and he wound up saying nothing. Instead, he placed the flower and the condom on the tracks, between the filigree forest and tiny town.

Coddington stopped the train. "What the hell—?"

He strode around the giant plywood plank table that held his Lionel dream world and then stopped, staring at Blum's offering.

"What the—how did you—? Oh, God."

A perfect progression: bafflement, understanding, despair, one, two, three—in about as many seconds. Blum couldn't have asked for more.

"You can't tell Anna."

"Actually, I can. Nothing would be easier. Some might even say it was my moral obligation. My responsibility, as her friend."

"You're not her friend! You've always hated her."

Blum smiled. "Well, there's that."

"Please, Jack. I don't know how you found out—"

"Spindrift LLC. You left the trail, and it was

much better marked than the average road leading into a New England town. But then…they want people to get lost. Maybe you don't. Maybe you wanted to get caught."

"Jack, no, that's crazy. You can't do this. It would kill Anna."

"You should have thought about that before you started fucking her sister."

"I couldn't—that was…it was beyond my… it—…we couldn't help ourselves. We tried. I swear, we tried."

"For a week?"

"I'd met her in Lithuania. Anna and I used to go back to Palanga every year. It's a resort on the Baltic…kind of like here. A summer town."

"Lots of chances to see the sister in a bathing suit."

"Or…not. There is a naturist beach in Nemirseta that Irena loves."

"Naturist? Nudist?"

"Ah—yes."

"How did you manage to—you know…not give yourself away?"

"I kept my eyes on my wife."

"Smart man. I always say—cellulite makes the best birth control."

Coddington crumpled the flower, stuffed it with the condom into his pants pocket. Then he started the train again. It passed through the covered station and headed up through a tunnel the mountains, emerging a few seconds later to cross an exquisitely rippled blue-glass river.

"I can't stop," Coddington said, finally.

"I'm not asking you to."

"Then…what? What do you want?"

"Sign the Winthrop deal."

The train completed another circuit. "Then this goes away?"

"I don't want to hurt you, Ted. I don't care about your love life. Every marriage has a secret or two. I just want to grow my business."

Coddington stopped the locomotive, cutting off the whining and the clickety-clack. The new silence felt like a gust of air from an open window. He set the control down. "But you'll always know. That's the thing. You can't…un-know it."

Blum shrugged.

"You'll always hold my life in your hands. Your soft, spoiled, manicured little hands."

"At least we'll know who's in charge from now on. That will simplify things."

Coddington exhaled a long breath. The spirit seemed to go out of him with the stale carbon dioxide.

"They have a notary. We can sign the papers in their office tomorrow."

But of course he never showed up for the meeting.

They all waited for an hour and finally agreed to reconvene the next day. Blum drove home to check his answering machine—and erase any messages, if necessary. God knows what Coddington might have said if he'd been drinking, and if Marjorie was home, standing near the little box when he triggered it from his cell phone, that would be one more problem to deal with. No, he had to do it himself, by hand, when he was certain he could listen in private.

Marjorie was out, she had left a note—something to do with volunteering at the NHA. That was a lucky break. There was no message on the answering machine, but Blum's Ruger box sat open and empty in the middle of the desk. Coddington had taken his gun.

He recalled Coddington scoffing at someone's suicide attempt, months before—how pills were for cowards and attention-seekers. "A cry for help? They should just try *crying for help*. They'd be astonished at how quickly people respond. It's all pantomime, Jack. If they really wanted to kill themselves, they'd put a bullet in their skull. That's a guarantee—Greg Norman, with a two-inch putt."

So was Coddington planning to commit suicide? Could Blum's threat have thrown Ted so completely? Well, he certainly wasn't capable of murder, and as far as Blum knew, the man had no interest in target practice.

But suicide?

Things tilted out of control so easily. He remembered cooking in the old Cliff Road house, with baby Martin in a bassinet on the counter, rocking himself to sleep. Then somehow he had tipped himself off the ledge and crashed to the kitchen floor. In the endless silence before the first outraged scream, Blum was sure the boy was dead, murdered by Blum's negligence, by an instant's criminal distraction—he had been separating eggs into a metal bowl. One irretrievable moment would poison his life forever, destroy his marriage, scatter his friends, render him a pariah, and rightfully so—and then Martin shrieked out his belated protest, and the world was set right.

But not this world. Not now.

Unless—if he could stop Ted somehow, intercept him before he committed the final act. Was that even possible? Coddington had at least ninety minutes' head start. He might be hesitating, though. He might be paralyzed with indecision. The notion of suicide might be romantic, but the feel of that metal ring against your temple, the bullet behind it one finger-twitch away...that was something else entirely. That was reality, and

Coddington had never excelled at reality. If he had snagged himself between the impulse and the act, there still might be time to stop him, to save him.

If Blum could find him.

Blum closed the gun case, put it away on the top shelf of the closet and hurried out of the house. He had a pretty good idea which spot Coddington would choose for his last stand.

The Coddington family had owned a parcel of land in Madaket, twenty acres around Long Pond, purchased for a few thousand dollars at the turn of the last century. Ted's father had left the property to the Land Bank. The decision had outraged all four of Ted's siblings, as well as his five cousins. They had been planning to sell off the land for yet another west-end subdivision, and expected a giant windfall—millions and millions of dollars to split up among themselves. None of them needed the money. They were all millionaires anyway. It was perverse, pathological, like all greed, like Blum's greed, or so Coddington had carped, simply because Blum had wanted to expand their business. He had endured Ted's lecture on this subject far more times than he cared to count.

The kids had contested the will, tried to get the old man declared incompetent, but Ted and quite a few others (including Pat Folger and Ed Delavane, Sr.) had testified in his favor. The will stood, and the land "went to waste," as Ted's cousin Marian had complained, bitterly and at great length, at the funeral and then at the graveyard, where Ted, furious and fed up, had finally slapped her face.

There was a stand of oak trees on that "wasted" land, where Ted's father had wanted to be buried. But he had died in a scalloping accident, drowning in Madaket harbor when his waders filled with water and the swift tides took him out to sea. The body was never found, and the funeral plot was never used.

Until today.

So here he was, and there they were.

Ted buried by the elm trees, Blum leaning against his car, still trembling from the exertions of the burial. "It is what it is," Ted had liked to say. "This is what I know"—his other pet phrase.

It is what it is.

Well, this is what I know, Ted: your life is over and my day is just beginning. I've got a grave to scatter with tobacco, a gun to put back in its case, and a suicide note to get rid of. I've got a lot to do and not much time to do it. You've got nothing to do and all the time in the world.

So who got the better deal?

Ted had already answered that one. He couldn't go on, and Blum couldn't quit. He couldn't even rest. Every second counted now.

He was pushing himself upright when he heard the engine note of a truck.

He froze with panic. He was filthy, covered with dirt from the burial, his hair standing up in all directions, eyes wild, his face bright red from hard exercise. He must look insane. What could he say? What possible excuse could he—?

The black Ford Ranger came around a bend in the dirt road—old Ed Delavane's boy, Billy. Of course it would have to be someone he knew. But people were oblivious, especially young people. Billy probably had girls and weed and surfing on his mind. Blum sucked in a solid bulge of air, pushed it out through his teeth.

Just act natural.

He lifted an arm to wave, and Billy slowed down. "Hey, Mr. Blum! Are you okay?"

"Fine, Billy—fine. Just took a bit of a tumble back there."

"You need a lift to the hospital?"

He forced a smile, a deranged clown rictus. "I'm just going to drive myself there. I think I sprained my ankle. Nothing to worry about."

"You sure?"

"I'm fine! Enjoy your day."

"Will do. Take care of yourself now."

He accelerated off, the fat tires dragging a cloud of dust behind the pick-up. When it was out

of sight, Blum climbed into his own car. He sighed
as he keyed the ignition. That moment could have
turned out worse. Billy would probably forget the
whole incident by New Year's.

Onward. With the body buried, his first stop
was Coddington's house.

The place was overheated as usual, and impeccably neat, as if "staged" by real estate agents: not a
book out of place, not a pillow unfluffed. The only
sound was the low rumble of the furnace, and even
that cut to silence when the house registered the
thermostat's preferred seventy-eight degrees.

Blum took the stairs two at a time, opened the
master bedroom door and saw the note propped
against the bed's outcropping of lace-trimmed
pillows. No envelope, just a single sheet of stiff
vellum with Coddington's flattened, almost illeg-
ible handwriting trailed across it.

Dearest Anna,

As you know I have been dread-
fully unhappy for a long time, since
before we met, in fact. Life has come
to feel like an overwhelming burden
with no purpose or meaning, just
effort, endless effort without joy or
reward. I'm tired. Every day I have to
haul this weight onto my back and

start walking again. I used to feel there was some destination, some end point. Now I just walk in circles. I'm lost. I cannot do it anymore. I'm sorry if this hurts you. I know you wanted to help me. The true tragedy of life is how little we can really do for one another. I hope my absence will help you, and ease your burden. After a while, I'm sure it will. Be strong, as I could not.

Ted

What a con artist! Of course, if he had been able to tell the truth about Irena, he wouldn't have had to kill himself in the first place. You had to admire the guy. He did the deed to protect the people he loved and this note finished off the job perfectly. It played on the mystery of the suicidal personality. How could you argue with a scrupulously hidden despair? It only made you look lame and oblivious. Playing the emotional chess of suicide, this was a brilliant checkmate. All Anna could do was nod and pretend she understood him.

He folded the note carefully and slipped it into his coat pocket. If the body was ever found, if the bullet was ever matched to his gun, he had proof that Coddington had killed himself, written in the man's own hand. It would be embarrassing, of course, old rumors would resurface, all the suspicions about why he did it, and why he used Blum's weapon, and who buried him, and all the rest…but the letter would stand: his last ditch get-out-of-jail-free card. And he might need it at any time—now or a dozen years from now.

There was no statute of limitations on murder.

And make no mistake, that was what they'd be coming after him for. Cops loved a murder case. They wouldn't care that it was a "cold case"—they liked things cold, the way a gourmand liked his potato and leek soup cold. Mmmmmm, vichyssoise. They'd slurp it up and lick the bowl clean when they were done. His bowl—his life. But not with the suicide note in his hands. That would stop them. Coddington's last will and…. The thought pounced softly, a cat's paw pressed to the string of his thoughts.

Coddington had always threatened he might change his will, leave his share of the business to Anna. "That would fix you!" he liked to gloat. "You'd be living in my world then! Fighting with her all day long! She'll have a thousand reasons not to do anything you want to do! One long miserable argument, all the way to the bankruptcy court."

Of course, he had been joking, "kidding on the square." But—

Blum tore out of the bedroom, down the hall to Coddington's home office.

The door was closed. Was it locked? He couldn't get it open. Then it unstuck from the jamb and he stumbled inside. The new will dominated the empty desk, drawing the eye like the intricately garnished sliver of swordfish on a plate at some fancy restaurant.

Coddington's last offering. Choke on this meal, partner.

Blum crossed the room in three steps and picked up the document—a one-page handwritten codicil, signed but not notarized. Of course it wasn't notarized, the ink was barely dry. It must have been written at the same time as the suicide note. Blum skimmed it. Just as he feared—Coddington had decided at the last minute, one of the last minutes, to leave controlling interest in business to his dithering arbitrary bitter ignorant willful wife. The Widow Coddington.

Not anymore.

Sorry, Ted. This document dies with you.

He crumpled it into a ball and jammed it into his pants pocket. Then he left the office, shut the door behind him, and took the stairs two at a time. He paused at the front door, glancing quickly out the sidelights. The street was empty, for the moment. He let himself out, walked without haste to his car, climbed in, and drove away.

Mission accomplished. But there was much more to do.

• • ● • •

He purchased the tobacco in four different locations, including the island's new tobacconist, a business Blum knew was doomed, along with the video store, and perhaps even the basement music shop that was already shifting away from cassettes to CDs.

He took a long shower after he was done mixing the snuff into the Madaket soil, scrubbing his hands raw. No one saw him on this trip, though he had to crouch in the bushes briefly when a group of birders traipsed past, heading for Long Pond.

He wasn't quite in the clear, though.

It turned out that some nosy neighbor had seen his car driving up to Irena's little lovenest, and then studied the big SUV as he drove away. It must have been a memorable event—they didn't find too many Range Rovers slumming at that end of the island, though it had only been a matter of time until Irena convinced Coddington to buy her one. Coddington himself had always driven that beater Volvo. Typical Old Money—he would no more have driven an expensive car than he would have flashed a Rolex watch or paraded his wife in a mink coat.

The neighbor had talked to Irena, which explained her showing up at the office that afternoon. Blum was still buffed, fresh and fragrant from his shower, feeling like a new man, or at least a better one. The guilt had washed off with the dirt. Coddington had committed suicide because he was suicidal. His life became unmanageable because he could no longer manage it. A comforting cadre of tautologies, but they had the ring of truth. Had Coddington really expected to cheat on his wife— with her sister, of all people—and get away with it? Actions had consequences. Blum wasn't responsible for the consequences! He merely expedited them.

It sounded good, but Irena was not convinced.

She burst into his office, wild-eyed, furious, potentially violent. Fortunately she was unarmed. More fortunately, his secretary had taken the day off and the office was empty—though anyone on the street could have noted her arrival.

"Where is he?"

That was her greeting. "Hello, Irena. Have a seat."

"What happened to him? What did you do to him?"

"Irena—"

"Tell me what is going on or I will start to scream!"

"Irena, please—"

"What have you done?"

"I've done nothing. I assume you're talking about Ted, but—"

"You are blackmailing him. You were snooping around the Tom Nevers house."

"I admit I may have dropped by, but—"

"How did you find out about it?"

He had no intention of detailing his detective work for her. "Did it ever occur to you that Ted might have told me about your little lovenest? He needed—" Past tense! Correct that lapse! "—*needs* to confide in someone."

She coughed out a disgusted laugh. "And that's you?"

"Is it so hard to believe?"

"What do you want of him? Money? Or just cooperation?"

"I want nothing from him."

"Liar!"

"Excuse me?"

"You found out about us. You knew you could destroy us both if you told Anna. You were going to be holding that over him forever. Ted couldn't stand that. He couldn't live with that."

Blum reached out to touch her arm. She

flinched away from him as if he had some contagious disease. "Irena…"

"Get away from me!"

He had to get her hysteria under control. He stepped back and spoke softly. "I'll tell you what probably happened. I did go out to the Tom Nevers house. And Ted figured out I'd been there, just like you did. He realized that you can't keep secrets in a small town. It's not practical. You'd have to be a master spy to make all the arrangements. You'd have to be shrewd and ruthless and clever. Ted is the opposite of those things. He's artless and sentimental and pedestrian. But lovable, I grant you. And pragmatic enough to read the writing on the wall. He knew it was over. Gossip is like good news and Chinese takeout. It's no fun unless you share it.

"Listen, when times got rough, Ted often talked about driving onto the boat and driving off in Hyannis and just not stopping. 'There's a whole continent out there, Jackson,' he said to me, once. 'A man could hide out and never be found, start over and give himself a second chance. Just by stepping on the gas and ignoring the rearview mirror.'

"Okay, it was just a fantasy, and most of us have felt that way one time or another, living in this fishbowl. But I think that's what he did. You could probably find him if you wanted to. Look in the places he loves—Key West, the Adirondacks,

Telluride. He didn't sign on with the Witness Protection program. Hire a detective. Track him down and bring him back. His family owns a tract of land on the coast in Nova Scotia. No roads, no electricity. His dad built a cabin there, before World War II—on the cliff over the sea. Ted might have gone there. The point is, he panicked. He's probably already regretting it. He may come back on his own. Starting over from scratch is overrated."

Irena just stared at him.

"What?"

She shook her head, more sad than angry, now. "I used to think you lied for gain—to get things people wouldn't give you if you are telling the truth, But this is not true! You like to lie. You enjoy to do it! You'd rather lie than tell truth! And I know why. It is so you can control! Like now. But it won't work. Not with me."

"That's ridiculous! Why would I lie if—?"

She laughed. "Why would I lie? That's what all liars say!"

Blum stepped back and held up his hands, a gesture of surrender that was meant to slow her down. "Now wait a second…"

"I know what happened! You blackmailed the only man I have love in my life, and so he killed himself and damned himself to Hell for eternity just to save me and to save Anna from learning the truth and hating me forever! That's what happened."

This was too much. "Hell? Really? I know Ted goes to church, and being a deacon makes him feel important, but—"

"He was devout! He took confession every week! His faith meant everything for him. He knew Hell was real and so do I and you sent him there with your sick greedy schemes, and I can't wait for you to join with him! And you will. Believe me, you will."

It was like a curse. It was frightening. Her twisted scowl made it real, and Blum had no answer for her. He was speechless for once. It didn't matter, though, because she spun around and stormed out of his office, slamming the door behind her so hard that his antique topographical map of the island rocked off the wall and crashed to the floor, cracking the glass.

She knew how to make an exit, he had to give her that.

And she was smart—tough and cunning in a way that Ted had never been. She had figured it all out, but Blum knew she'd never tell anyone. She was as invested in the lie as he was. If Anna ever found out, Ted's death and damnation would be for nothing.

Blum had taken his tongue-lashing; he might

have even deserved it. But he was safe now. Ted was gone, the new will was waste-paper, the Winthrop deal was as good as done. The rapids had been scary—a regular class IV thrill ride! But he had managed not to capsize, and it was nothing but smooth water ahead. They'd mount a halfhearted search for the body soon, but they weren't going to find it.

With any luck, they never would.

Chapter Two

Cold Case

Nantucket, December 2017

    I stood in the damp snow, staring down at the skeleton, listening to Lonnie Fraker's cell phone play "Hark the Herald Angels Sing." Pat Folger had pulled the bones from a basement excavation at the edge of the moors in Madaket. He stood next to me as the forensic anthropologist kneeled over the remains.

    The guy was named Shepherd Rollins. When I called State Attorney General Dave Carmichael for his advice, he had laughed and said, "You got a horseshoe up your ass, Kennis. My bone guy is on Nantucket right now. The best part is, he thinks he's on vacation."

    My impression was that Rollins was happy to get away from his family for a few hours. When I gave him the address, he said, "Ten minutes."

Lonnie answered his phone. "I don't know. I have no idea. I'm working here, honey, all right? Yeah, as soon as I can."

"Go home, Lonnie," I said. "We've got this."

"Yeah? It's my kid's birthday."

"Go."

"Thanks. This stuff give me the creeps anyway."

"Toscana was working here for twenty minutes when the bulldozer dug this up," Pat said. "I sent everybody home for the day. People get shaken up, they start making mistakes. You know? And I thought—is this a crime scene now? Could anything be left to—for you to, you know—to figure out what happened? Like on *Cold Case*?"

Rollins straightened up. I could hear his knees popping. Too many tackles? He had the bulky look of an ex-high school football star. "Well, there's not much, fellas. But we do have some scientific traction—hard tissue histology, skeletochronology. I can tell you right now, this man has been dead for more than ten years."

"This guy? You can determine the sex from the bones?" I asked.

"With adults, yeah. You don't get any significant sexual dimorphism until adolescence. Which is not a problem we have to deal with much, thank God. Anyway...the first indication is bone size. Men generally have bigger bones and this was a big strapping guy. Also, women have a larger subpubic angle to the pelvis. For childbirth. And the female forehead is more rounded. No, this was a male, all right. But we're at least a decade too late for a lot of other markers."

"Like what?"

"Well, see, in the first ten years postmortem we have access to forensic entomology techniques—we can pinpoint the age of the skeleton by the insect communities that colonize it, like the fish at a coral reef. Eventually the boom times are over and the insects move on or die out. But bones last much longer. This could be a Wampanoag Indian, for all we know."

"We have to be able to narrow it down a little more than that," I said.

He nodded, chewing at his inner cheek. "Well, Chief Kennis, that's the good news about this skeleton's lost decade. We've developed some remarkable new techniques in forensic anthropology. We can analyze the morphology of the auricular surface of the ilium—that's this area down near the pelvis. But people age differently and after a while basic wear and tear makes any clear estimate difficult. These bones look pretty much the same after fifty, whether you're sixty or eighty. No, it's the teeth that give us the answers."

"Right," I said. "Matching the dental work for a positive ID."

"That's part of it. But not every victim has a good set of dental X-rays for comparison, and in a case like this, where you may be talking about twenty years-plus in the ground, those records could be lost or sitting on some obsolete media—floppy discs, remember those?"

"So what else can you do?"

His face lit up. I guessed he didn't get to talk about his favorite topic very often, or to such an attentive audience. I could imagine his wife sitting down to dinner after a hard day, saying "Please, Shep—not the dead people's teeth again! I'm trying to chew my food here."

He took a breath. "Okay. Layman's terms. The teeth are held in the sockets by periodontal ligaments, attached to the dental cementum on the tooth's roots. The cementum is the material we study now, to determine the age of the remains. The closer you get to the chronological bull's-eye, the fewer missing persons reports you have to wade through. Am I right?"

"Absolutely. And cementum helps you figure it out?"

"Yeah, because it's laid down in annual bands. You know the tooth erupts at a certain age, you count the bands, and you have a pretty good idea of the age at the time of death. It's just arithmetic, once you have the material in front of you. Plus there's more. Under polarized light microscopy we can see two bands of cementum generated every year—a dark one in the winter and a light one in the summer. So we know the season of death as well."

"Wow."

"It's a complex field involving a great deal of abstruse research, and we've had detailed commentaries and peer reviews in the major journals, but the gist of it is—well, I have to say you summed it up pretty well right there, Chief…wow!"

His enthusiasm was faintly alarming. I looked away, at the big house next door, closed up for the season, batting-boards covering all the windows. The heavy plywood protected the house from the harbor winds, burglars, and nosy neighbors. But this morning they also seemed to be protecting the old mansion from the vision of death lying on the ground next door. The house seemed willfully blind, and I envied it. Despite Rollins' gusto, there's something deeply unsettling about a skeleton. Looking at it, you're looking at yourself without the temporary mask of flesh, the structural truth of human mortality. I made a fist and felt the linked bones curling together: dead man walking.

I pushed away the morbid ruminations. "How long will it take to get those results?"

"That's a good news, bad news story, Chief. The bad news is that cementum analysis can take anywhere from three weeks to three months, depending on staffing and backlog. But the good news is we don't necessarily have to rely on it in this case. This guy had a lot of dental work done—probably locally—and we should be able to expedite those results, because we're looking at a murder."

Pat Folger took a panicky step back from the bones, as if he'd seen them move. I ignored him and addressed Rollins. "How can you tell?"

This was probably the man's all-time favorite question, and he crouched beside the skeleton to answer it. He tipped the skull up gently with his pen. "See that?"

There was some sort of indentation visible through the mud. He wiped it clean with a finger. I moved to stop him, but this was no ordinary crime scene. There was nothing left to contaminate.

Pat was squinting down past Rollins' pointing finger. "Some kind of hole?"

"It's a bullet hole," I said. "Small caliber. Maybe a .22."

Rollins stood, mildly irritated at my intrusion. "I was going to point out the beveling diagnostic of perimortem ballistic trauma…. But, yes. Simply put, this is a bullet hole, and given the likely caliber of the bullet, I suspect we'll find it inside there, rattling around like a dried bean in a maraca, rifling intact. It'll match some local gun, and you'll have your killer."

"Assuming you can find it, if the killer is still here," Pat said. "A lot of people moved away since the nineties. You'd have to check the real estate sales records all over Vermont and South Carolina and even Costa Rica. That's where most of my friends went. Cashed in and got out. I've been thinking about doing that myself. I own a house down there. I could sell my place here along with my business, go down there and live like a king. From Tamarindo all the way down to Quepos. People are buying inland, too. San Jose, San Marcos."

I sighed. "That's a lot of ground to cover."

"But you still have those dental records, right?" Pat said. "You can at least figure out who this guy was. Is there some central database for that?"

Rollins slipped his pen back into his pocket. "I wish there was. No, you're going to have to go to every dentist on the island, and get their records going back twenty years, if they still have them, especially the X-rays. Then it's sort and compare."

"The Cape, too," I said.

"Excuse me?"

"A lot of Nantucketers use dentists on the Cape. My ex-wife does. Hyannis, Brewster, Orleans, Sandwich. All those towns."

Pat grunted, an animal exhalation of hopelessness and disgust. "Jesus. Forget it. That's crazy."

"No, Pat," I said. "It's police work. We're ants. We just keep going. We'll get every crumb from the picnic if you give us enough time."

"Yeah, well good luck, Chief. Tough job."

I shrugged. "We do all right."

"And some of us are trying to help out, any way we can."

Pat's son had been hooked on OxyContin a couple of years ago, and he'd been crusading against opiates ever since. He's been known to step over the line. "We don't need vigilantes, Pat."

He smiled. "No vigilantes, Chief. Just concerned citizens. Showing their concern."

"And their citizenship."

"Right."

We studied each other in the freshening breeze. Rollins broke the silence. "People say to me, 'How can you look at bones all day?' I tell them, 'I love looking at bones. I just wish the days were longer.' It's like…we all keep secrets, you know? And when everything else is gone, the skeleton is still keeping those secrets. This one's got more than most. Who killed him, and when and how and, most of all, why? That's what keeps us going, right, Chief? The why."

I nodded. "You got it, Shep."

Rollins shook Pat's hand. "I guess we're done here. Call any time you have more questions."

"I have a question right now," Pat said. "How am I going to get this goddamn skeleton out of here?"

"Normally, we take it apart, box it, remove it from the site," Rollins said.

"We should have an ambulance here in a few minutes," I added.

"I'd keep running that 'dozer for a while, though, Mr. Folger," Rollins said. "We want to be sure this is an individual grave."

"Jesus Christ! Are you saying this is some kind of mass burial? Like some serial killer's been dumping bodies here…?"

"Anything's possible. But even if that were the case, this is clearly the most recent victim, the one closest to the surface, so those…activities…ended a long time ago. I don't think you have to worry about an active perpetrator, Mr. Folger. But dig down a few more feet before you bring your crew back, and check with Chief Kennis. We need to certify the site."

Pat snorted. "That sounds like fun."

Rollins grinned. "Speaking of fun…I'll be happy to perform the lab analysis of the remains. Unless you have someone…"

"No," I said. "We have nobody. That would be great. If you're sure you have the time."

"My wife is always pleased when she can get me out of the house. Especially while we're on vacation. She loves vacations and I hate them. If I get to work the whole time, it's the perfect compromise."

We shook on it, my hand swallowed by his big dry paw, and he folded himself into his Prius to drive home and explain his new working holiday.

"I better get busy," Pat said as we watched the big man drive off. "Make sure this fella doesn't have any friends down there."

"Call me when you're done."

"This better not be some Indian graveyard, like in that horror movie, with the tree breaking the window to grab that kid. All I could think about watching it was, they're going to have to reframe that whole casing! Not to mention the landscaping work."

"You might not be the best audience for a horror movie involving real estate, Pat."

"Guess not. Move along, Chief. I'll call you."

I drove back to the station, explained the case to my detectives and settled in to wait for the dental X-rays. The downtime was convenient, as it turned out. The next day I had a less significant, but much more urgent missing persons case on my hands.

Santa Claus had disappeared.

Chapter Three

Finding Santa

I was house-hunting when I got the missing persons call. I had been hoping for a day off.

Christmas Stroll had begun—the first weekend in December, and traffic was as bad as July. The terrible drivers were out in force. "I want to arrest all of them," I said to Jane Stiles.

She had the driver's side window open on her truck. The unseasonable air streaming in felt like late September or early May. "I'm not sure you can do that, Henry. Most of them aren't even breaking the law."

We stopped at the five corners stop sign on York Street. Three cars caravanned through the intersection like a little train, gliding from Sparks Avenue along Pleasant Street, heading for town.

"That's what I'm talking about. Piggybacking through the stop sign. That's supposed to be one car at a time. You take turns. It's worse at the rotary. I counted six of them just now. The last one—that BMW—he was probably out by Moors End Farm when the first car in line got there. And we just sat watching the parade go by. I bet that BMW guy pushes to the front of the line at Bartlett's, too."

"At least he's not texting."

"Like his kids."

"I bet it was them giving me the finger when I stopped for that old lady yesterday."

"And how about the parking lot people? They're the worst. I can't arrest them, like you say, because the law is unwritten. But everybody knows the deal—parking spaces are a lottery. If someone is loading their groceries into the back of their car as you're driving by, *you lose*! Keep moving. You don't force a line of cars behind you to wait five minutes so you can have the spot."

Jane nodded. "You could get out, flash your badge, and yell at them."

"I might just do that next time."

"You should."

"And look at these people." Two bikers on ten-speed cycles veered in front of us. "We paid five million dollars for our bike paths on this island, your lordships—so use them! But you're too good for that, with your spandex and your toe-clips, you're so far above the three-speed plodders and the kids with the training wheels, so you deserve to share the road with the cars. Except, sorry, you don't! You block traffic, you're a danger to yourselves and others and your smug Tour-de-France attitude just makes you look like a bunch of clowns. Get over yourselves! Start using the bike path or we'll start drug-testing you!"

Jane laughed. "Go Chief!"

She hit the brakes. "This is the worst," I said. "Look at this." Two women in yoga outfits were pushing a pair of baby carriages down the middle of Pleasant Street. "Use the sidewalk, Super Mom! Let's parse that. Sidewalks are located on *the side of the road* for people *walking*! That would be you."

"I think the uneven pavement disturbs the babies."

"Right, we can't have that. I saw one overgrown toddler being wheeled around using a cell phone. I'm serious."

"Well, those brick sidewalks make texting impossible."

"And we can't have that."

"It's all about the kids, Henry."

"Yeah, like the Christmas trees on Main Street—with all the paper decorations by the middle-schoolers. Then it rains once and you've got a disgusting soggy mess, like someone toilet-papered the trees. Every year it's the same way."

"But the children get to express themselves." Jane said sweetly.

I love sarcasm. "You are a nasty, mean-spirited little Grinch! How did I ever find you?"

She leaned across to kiss my cheek. "Just lucky, I guess."

We were driving into town to get a key from Killen Real Estate. Like so many people on Nantucket, our lives were ruled by the exigencies of the housing market. I knew divorced couples who still lived together because neither one of them could afford to move out, even if they could track down a year-round rental, which was almost impossible anyway. Jane's situation was a common variation: her elderly landlord, who had leased her the cottage behind his house for almost twenty years, had died suddenly a few months ago and left the whole property to some right-wing think tank. They would sell it off to some dot-com millionaire who would no doubt bulldoze both structures, clear all the brush and scrub oak to the Land Bank property that edged the harbor, and build some sort of trophy compound. Jane would get booted as soon as the probate cleared. The old man had no immediate family left, and Jane had nursed the private fantasy that he might leave the place to her. They had grown close over the decades, but that wasn't the Yankee way, and somehow Jane had always known it.

Other Nantucket women, and some men, had forged temporary romances of convenience with elderly millionaires. Those people were set for life now, if quietly stigmatized for it, though perhaps they deserved their reward for the months, and sometimes years, of arduous caregiving that preceded the reading of the will.

Jane could never have played that game. So she was looking for a new place to live, and it looked like she had found one.

The house on Darling Street was never listed with a rental broker; no ad ever appeared in the *Inquirer and Mirror.* Nantucket locals had their own way of putting a roof over their heads. It was all done by word of mouth, friend to friend, family to family. State Police Captain Lonnie Fraker had grown up on the island with Jane, and their families had been close for more than a hundred years. Their grandfathers had fished together before World War II; their great grandfathers had run a thriving ice business on the old waterfront. Despite various falling-outs over the decades, the settled lawsuits and forgotten fist-fights, the island was finally too small to sustain any grudge into the next generation.

Lonnie's father was supposed to have had a long-running affair with Jane's mother, but the liaison went extinct, the scandal was hushed up, both marriages survived, and the rumor eventually calcified into one more fragment of the town's fossil record of ancient gossip.

None of that had kept Jane and Lonnie from becoming friends, though she had her own problems with his half-brother, Todd. She had broken Todd's heart, but she broke a lot of hearts in those days, and Lonnie had just laughed it off. He said Todd always needed to have his heart broken by somebody, and if it hadn't been Jane it would have been somebody else. In fact it was somebody else quite a few times afterward, and Todd was probably still having his heart broken by willowy blondes, no matter what he was doing or where he wound up. No one had heard from him in years.

Lonnie and Jane stayed close. They went to different colleges, but they both wound up back on the Rock. Nantucket had a gravitational pull on its natives; only the angriest, saddest, or most ambitious kids achieved escape velocity. Jane and Lonnie, like most of their friends (the odd math genius or movie director aside), hit the top of their parabolas and dropped back home: an easy fall and a soft landing.

Lonnie enjoyed Jane's Madeline Clark mystery novels. He helped her out with the factual details, and allowed her to tag along with the State Police whenever she wanted. He knew about her housing problem without being told because of a tangled string of hearsay. The estate was selling the old man's sailboat, a twenty-four-foot Mystic Alley Cat that hadn't been in the water, or even out of its plastic shrink wrap, for the better part of a decade. A friend of a friend of Lonnie's drove out to Polpis for a look, and soon the word got out. Lonnie knew what selling that boat meant for Jane: the whole estate was on the auction block, the eviction notice was in the mail—and he knew exactly what to do about it.

His uncle's old house on Darling Street was in limbo with six heirs fighting over it, trying to raise the money to buy each other out and going to war over various knickknacks and trinkets, as well as more valuable items like Tony Sarg paintings, Tiffany silver, and first editions. The scuffle could go on for years, and in the meantime, Lonnie talked them into renting it out for three thousand a month year-round. Even with the uncertainty of the arrangement, the house was a bargain. Still, Jane couldn't afford it.

That's where I came in.

I was living in a cramped apartment I referred to as a "lifeboat" after my divorce ("All it has to do is float," I liked to say.), which had become more of an issue every year as my kids got older. I couldn't afford to move any more than Jane could—but splitting the rent on Darling Street with her was a workable arrangement. Of course that meant moving in together. Was I ready for that? Was she? Was her little boy? Were my kids? The whole thing seemed rushed, risky, frantic, premature, potentially catastrophic.

But the house was available, and Lonnie could only offer it as an exclusive for one day.

Now or never. That's how Nantucket real estate rules our lives.

"What the hell," Jane had said. "At least let's take a look."

Of course she knew I'd love it. She'd spent half her childhood in that old saltbox. And it stood on one of the prettiest streets in New England, the modest crossbar of an "H" between two larger streets leading into town, shaded by ancient maple trees, the houses lined up even and straight, like books on a shelf.

It was a slow day at the cop shop—no news from Rollins yet—only an odd DUI and family dispute; someone had stolen the food set out for the AA meeting at the Congregational Church; and two girls had shoplifted a pair of sweaters from Murray's Toggery Shop. Nothing that needed my urgent attention.

So we decided to take a look.

Number 12 was the only house on the short straight street that hadn't been renovated. If the

Fraker kids ever got together, settled their differences, and sold the place, it would undoubtedly get the full treatment: lifted up on pilings so a new basement could replace the low ceilinged catacomb—barely more than a crawl space, that had sufficed since the 1850s. The new lower level would feature a couple of guest bedrooms, an entertainment center, a tiled climate-controlled wine cellar, maybe even a screening room—that was how the new money hijacked these old museum pieces into the twenty-first century.

They'd replace the kitchen, too, no doubt, carting the olive green appliances and the ancient gas stove to the dump and leveling out the floor. The wide boards tilted drastically now, as we strolled uphill to the pantry closet.

"People love houses like this or they hate them," Jane said.

I turned, taking in the heavy beams that crossed the lumpy ceiling, the wavy antique glass in the twelve-light sash of the big sunny windows, the deep-set sink whose enamel had mostly worn away, the Harbor Fuel tide calendar from 1987 tacked to the cracked plaster wall.

I ended up facing her again. "Love it."

She hugged me. "Let's look upstairs."

The second floor had three bedrooms, and a little office that we could convert into a fourth.

From the back bedroom, you had to pass through the middle bedroom to reach the big square landing that formed a sitting room at the top of the stairs. That meant that the middle bedroom was also a sort of corridor, with much less privacy for its occupant. I saw a sibling battleground in the making. I mentioned it to Jane.

"Sam can take the middle bedroom. He won't care."

We ducked into the master under the low lintel designed for the height of a different century's occupants: queen-sized bed, built-in bookshelves—and a fireplace.

"Does it work?"

"Totally."

"We may never go outside again."

"Sounds good to me."

She stood on her tiptoes for a kiss and for a minute or so we both forgot about the house. When we came up for air, the place felt like home.

"So?" Jane asked.

"Let's do it."

"Move in together? That's kind of big for a snap decision."

"Snap decisions are the best. Ask any detective. People who tell you not to trust your first idea should really think twice about that."

Jane exhaled on a grin and shook her

head—the closest I was going to get to a laugh. I took it. She walked to the window, and looked down at Darling Street. "What will your kids say?"

"We get our own rooms! That is literally all they care about. Getting away from each other."

"Then we're going to do it?"

"Call Lonnie."

Before she could grab her phone, my own cell rang: the dueling guitars that spark the opening of "Me & Julio Down By the Schoolyard."

It was my assistant chief, Haden Krakauer: police business.

I finger-swiped the screen. "What's up?"

"It's Santa Claus," Haden said. "He's missing."

Homer Boyce had never shown up for rehearsal.

"What does he need to rehearse?" I asked Haden as I walked into town to Jackson Blum's sporting goods store on Main Street. Blum had been sponsoring the Santa show since long before I arrived on the island. "All Homer has to do is sit down and say yes when some kid asks for a new bike."

"It's more complicated than that. He has his lines. He can't just promise the moon to these kids. And he has to deal with the crazy parents and the photographs, and the kids who start crying, and the hostile ones, and the smart asses who want to know how he gets everything done in one night, and what he does for families with no fireplace or whatever. Last year he had kids on his lap texting. How do you deal with that? Some kid almost put his eye out with a selfie stick."

"So they coach him."

"Yeah. Blum is kind of a control freak and he wants everything to go just right."

Apart from the occasional chamber of commerce gala or Maria Mitchell fund-raiser, I had managed to avoid Jackson Blum since my arrival on the island six years ago. Snippets of overheard conversation at those parties made me glad to keep my distance. He had a "Greatest Hits" of abrasive quotations.

To some poor sap he'd bought out and fired: "It's the free enterprise system, Larry. I was freer and more enterprising than you were." To a reporter from the *Inquirer and Mirror*, pleading for a brief interview: "You want five minutes of my time? Do you have any idea what one minute of my time is worth? You're talking six figures."

I was surprised he was even hosting Santa in his store. His idea of Christmas decoration was a single wreath on the door and some green and red ski parkas in the display window. But apparently his wife insisted. She ran the Toys for Tots program and she ruled him with the threat of a Draconian divorce. She'd take half of everything if she left, and she always had one foot out the door. Or so the Nantucket rumor mill claimed.

Blum was waiting for me by the bleached-oak counter that held the cash register and various high-end trinkets: Swiss Army knives, compasses, leather credit card holders. He was a big man, but he had that odd deflated look that fat people get when they lose a lot of weight. He looked insubstantial somehow, and also as if he might pop back to his old weight, fully inflated, fast as an airplane life jacket, if he so much as nibbled a candy bar. Late fifties, thick black hair, obviously a dye-job, and horn-rims that made him look like a professor who coached the wrestling team.

"Well, it's about time," he said, ready to grapple right now—sweep my feet out from under me and take me down to the pickled oak floor until I pounded it and gave him the win. I extended my hand to shake; he glanced down like it was an elephant's trunk poking through the bars of a cage. "Sorry. I'm fanatic about germs."

"Maybe I should wear surgical gloves next time."

He stared at me. "Good idea."

Time to downshift. "So what's going on, Mr. Blum?"

"We have a missing person on our hands, as I explained to your assistant chief. And the toys are missing also. I wouldn't be surprised if Homer stole them."

"Excuse me?"

"The Toys for Tots. My wife's crusade. Only the best for the Box Car Willies who slither up here with their greedy little palms out. Lionel train sets, GUND and Steiff stuffed animals, Xbox systems, two handmade dollhouses with all the furniture, die-cast model trucks and sports cars, you name it. A bunch of classic Barbie dolls from the 1960s. Giant LEGO and playmobil sets. All gone."

"And you think Homer Boyce stole them?"

"They're gone and so is he. Does that sound like a coincidence?"

"Well, Homer is a sixty-one-year-old gay man who works crossword puzzles for fun and spends his weekends restoring his 1969 Volkswagen bug. He has no children. He wouldn't be my first-choice candidate for toy thief."

"Yes, but there's a story going around town— you may have heard it. Homer certainly did."

"About the toys?"

"Apparently the idea is that something valuable's hidden among them somewhere. Taped to the bottom of something, or stitched inside or camouflaged somehow—I have no idea. But it's turned the Toys for Tots into a nasty mercenary scavenger hunt. You try to give back to the community and something like this happens! No good deed goes unpunished."

That struck me as a danger Blum didn't have to worry about much.

"Does this story include a theory about who planted the hidden treasure?"

"One of the donors? Some devious self-styled Robin Hood? The manufacturers? It's pointless to speculate. There's no treasure. No one slipped cocaine into the flavor straws or gave Barbie a twenty-four-karat necklace. The whole idea is patently absurd. But it makes foolish people do foolish things, and I have to deal with the consequences. Now Homer is gone, and he took the suit and the toys with him. He's the Anti-Santa Claus!"

"Mr. Blum...?"

A chubby balding little man in his mid-forties stepped out from the stock area. He saw me and recalibrated, but it was too late to retreat.

Blum glanced at him, instantly irritated. "What is it, Arnold?"

"Did you think about what we discussed earlier, Mr. Blum?"

"No. I didn't need to think about it."

"But, Mr. Blum, no other store is going to be open on Christmas. No one goes shopping on Christmas. Everyone's at home with their families."

"Which, I suppose, is where you want to be."

"Well—I mean—sure. Of course I do. Don't you?"

"What I want or do not want is manifestly none of your business."

"I know, I'm sorry. I just meant—"

"Your children will respect you for working hard to support them, Sprockett. You're the breadwinner! You might remind them of that when they're gobbling your bread."

"Yes, okay, I see, but…could I at least have the morning? No one leaves home on Christmas morning."

"And so you'd have nothing to do here? Is that it? Rattling around in an empty store while your children eat Christmas cookies? Is that it?'"

"Well, yeah, I mean—"

"There's a sheet posted on the stockroom wall. Tell Chief Kennis what it says."

He shot me a pleading look but there was nothing I could do, except leave, and I needed to stay a little longer.

"It's a list. Twenty things to do when…when there's nothing to do."

"Thank you. Like marking everything down for Boxing Day."

"Right. Sure, of course."

"And cleaning. Deep cleaning—the baseboards are filthy."

"That's true. I've been meaning to get to that."

"Well, Christmas will be a perfect opportunity. You'll have the store to yourself, as you just pointed out."

"Right."

"You'll get a jump on the big sale."

"Yeah."

"So that's settled."

Arnold Sprockett—I put the pieces together. Jane had told me about his son.

"How is Nat doing, Arnold?' I asked.

"I—he's...well, we're not really sure right now. It's wait and see, I guess."

"Well, send him my best. I'm sure the team misses him."

Sprockett smiled. "Not as much as he misses the team, sir."

"Well, let's hope he comes back for next season. That'll be his senior year, won't it?"

"Yeah. That's when the college scouts come sniffing. That's when you find out the future."

He looked pinched and miserable. I could tell whatever news he'd received after his son's brutal knee injury hadn't been good.

"Well—one future," I said.

There was no humor in his crooked smile. "Right. One future out of many for a small-town kid with a C-plus average and a college fund paying the mortgage."

Blum had heard enough. "Chief Kennis is looking into the missing toys. Any thoughts? Any clues?"

He shrugged. I think he was glad to change the subject. "Real crimes don't have clues."

"They do, actually," I said. "We've solved crimes with clues as small as a cigarette butt under a bed—or a dry suede jacket."

This caught Sprockett's interest. "A dry suede jacket?"

"It was raining where the killer claimed to be that day. The perfect alibi, until it wasn't."

"So you might really catch whoever this was— who stole the toys?"

"Sure."

"By…finding clues."

"It's possible."

"That's enough, Sprockett. I'm not paying you to socialize with the police."

"Right—no, of course not."

He retreated into the back of the store and Blum stepped toward me. "At the moment, none of that matters. The toys were all donated nd the whole circus is my wife's vanity project. ner Boyce is my Santa and he's got the suit. cAveety tailored that outfit for him. Funny story. Joe took one look at Homer and said, 'Forty-eight waist.' Homer was shocked. 'I wear size forty pants!' he said. 'These clothing companies size pants to make their customers feel better,' Joe told him. 'I don't trust the label, I trust what I see. Anyway, let's find out. The tape measure never lies.' Joe was right, of course. Quite the wake-up call for that useless little blimp! The suit was perfect when Joe finished—a bespoke costume from a Savile Row tailor, fitted at substantial expense. Homer committed to wear it. I need to find him, and I have…" he checked his Apple watch "…less than twenty-four hours."

"Why don't you ask Siri?" I suggested.

"You can laugh. Until some little computer chip replaces you. They already beat us at chess and *Jeopardy*."

"Well, until they can beat us at *Clue*, I'm not worried."

Blum frowned. "Just find Homer, Chief Kennis."

I tipped my head with that half-smiling eyebrows-raised inhale that serves as a shrug for the face. "I'll see what I can do."

"Why does that not make me feel confident?"

I met his tough-guy stare. "Because you don't know me."

That was the best exit line I was going to find

so I gave him a mock salute and started to make my exit.

"One more thing, Chief."

I turned at the door. "What?"

"I hear Pat Folger dug up a skeleton out in Madaket, yesterday. Any developments?"

"That's police business, Mr. Blum. How do you even know about it?"

"David Trezize, at the *Shoals?* I ran into him at the post office. He was gloating about his scoop! I pointed out that *The Boston Globe* and *The New York Times* probably weren't that interested in some bones dug up at a rural jobsite. When they started excavating for the dump back in the eighties, they found plenty of bones. It used to be Wampanoag burial ground! No one cared. I think the *Herald* ran a little squib about it on page ten. So David's victory dance was a tad delusional. He beat out *Yesterday's Island!* Get that boy a Pulitzer."

Yesterday's Island was a free paper that catered to the tourist trade. There was some good writing between the ads, but I wasn't going to waste time defending it to Blum. I was more interested in *The Shoals.* "How did David know anything?"

"He has contacts on the police department. I ′umed you were one of them."

"Not this time. And whoever talked to him ′t have."

"Well, it's bound to be in next week's paper. So I suggest you all get your stories straight."

I shrugged, and pushed open the door. "Thanks for your time, Mr. Blum. I'll let you know when we find Homer."

My first stop was his house. There's a thin line between going missing and simply refusing to answer the door. He could be hiding out or he could be lying on his bed with a stomach full of vodka and valium. He certainly had reason to be depressed, and even more reason to avoid Jackson Blum.

Homer's little fabric shop on Main Street— one of the last holdouts from the old Nantucket days of Buttner's, and Robinson's Five-and-Ten— was about to close its doors. I had never known the glory days of a more casual and rustic Nantucket, but I was very familiar with F&S Fabrics, on West Pico Boulevard in L.A., the shop on which Homer had modeled his own. My ex-wife had bought all the material for the dresses, slip covers, and curtains she stitched together in our little Westwood condo, and we had spent many hours roaming the endless cluttered rooms, fondling bolts of Egyptian cotton and merino wool.

Homer used to brag about his store, "This is the only place on-island where you can still buy a thimble!"

No longer. That's what Amazon is for.

Jackson Blum had purchased most of that side of Main Street from Stephen Karp and he was making Karp look like Habitat for Humanity. He doubled the already sky-high rents and demanded a fifteen percent cut of his tenants' business. No negotiations, no splitting the difference, no grace period: put up or shut up, yes or no, you were good for the money or you were gone.

Homer couldn't afford it, and no bank would give him a big enough loan.

So he was gone.

The store looked like a missing tooth in the jaw of Main Street right now. But a high-end jeweler from Chicago was supposedly negotiating for the space. Just what Nantucket needed—another high-end jeweler.

I pulled into Homer's driveway off Fairgrounds Road. His old Volkswagen was nowhere to be seen. I got out, strolled around the house. The shades were down. The place had an abandoned feeling. I knocked on the door—no answer. I checked under the shingles, found a key, and let myself in. The place smelled stuffy—dust and unwashed laundry. But it was neat enough—no bodies, no signs of struggle. And no sign of the missing toys.

The rugs were vacuumed, the bed was made, ⁿ was on the toothpaste and the toothbrush ʰlamp. Homer had started out the day at home, and he still had some home-pride. Another sign: the place was warm. The furnace cycled on as I stood in the living room. The house was vacant, not uninhabited.

But Homer wasn't hiding out here. He wasn't traveling, either. His suitcases were stacked neatly in the bedroom closet.

I stepped back outside and replaced the key, with a smile: the shingle was marked with a scratched X—typical Nantucket home-security.

One of his neighbors, an older woman wearing a red flannel shirt under denim overalls and clutching a garden trowel, stumped around the corner of her house as I walked to my cruiser.

She hoisted the trowel. "Planting the daffodil bulbs for next year. Feels like spring! A little odd for December, but I'm not complaining." She stuck out a glove caked with potting soil "Bessie Tarhouse, glad to meet you."

I shook her hand. "Chief of Police Kennis."

"I know you. Everybody knows Chief Kennis! You're on TV, you're in the newspaper. You're everywhere—underfoot like knapweed. And here you are in Homer Boyce's driveway, Mr. Big Shot Henry Kennis, all the way from Los Angeles, California! Some people say you brought the big city with you. More crime than ever since you washed ashore."

"I hope that's just a coincidence. The crime I've come across seems to be mostly homegrown."

She shook her head, frowning. "That mad bomber fella was from away. Far away."

"True."

"Some kind of Southern red-neck cracker crazy. Wasn't he?" I nodded. "Well, those boys scare me more than any Muslim I ever met! And I've met some."

"I bet you have."

"You do that. Take long odds and win some money."

We stood quietly for a moment. A UPS truck rumbled by. "I was wondering if you'd seen Homer today."

"Well, as a matter of fact, I did. He was loading bottles and plastic and trash bags into the back of that little car of his, and he brought out his Santa suit, too."

"He took it to the dump?"

"It sure looked that way."

"It's not his suit."

"I don't think he cares about those details, Chief. He said, 'I'm done. This is going to bulky ∖ste, and that's where I belong, too.' Check that ⌐umpster. You may find them both!"

⌐anked her and took off. I liked the fact that ⌐ talking. He might have told someone at our coyly named "Environmental Park" where he was going.

It turned out that he took the suit to the take-it-or-leave-it shed, and he did exchange a few words with Carol, the tough, funny woman who supervised the scavenger's paradise at the far end of the landfill. The suit was gone, scooped up less than ten minutes after Homer dumped it onto the big used clothes table.

"Horst Refn took it," she told me. "He got into a fight with two Jamaican ladies. I had to break it up, almost kicked them all out. Civil behavior mandatory—that's the rule. We even put a sign up. I thought it should have said 'Civil behavior appreciated,' you know? That would have been more civil. And we'd be setting an example."

She had the twinkle in her eye I always enjoyed.

"Horst Refn?" I asked. "The Theatre Workshop guy?"

"I guess he wanted it for the Christmas play."

"I'll have a talk with him after I find Homer."

"Do you think Homer's all right?"

"Did he not seem all right?"

"He looked like he hadn't slept in a couple of days and when I went through the Santa suit pockets I found his wallet and his cell phone. I ran out of the shed waving them, but he was driving away

He stopped for a second and said, 'Keep them. The phone is due for an upgrade.' He seemed to think that was hilarious—him getting an upgrade on anything."

"Can I take a look?"

She ducked into her shed and emerged with an old leather wallet and a Nokia flip phone. They both had a sad and battered look, as if they'd given up, along with Homer.

"I'll get these back to him," I said, "and figure out what's going on."

"Think you can help?"

"I don't know. I'll try."

"Give him a little of the old Christmas spirit!"

"Sure."

She smiled. "Maybe he'll take the upgrade."

I drove back to town, working through the few facts at my disposal. Wherever Homer was hunkered down, it had to be a place where he didn't need cash, credit cards, photo ID, or an easy way to stay in touch. The Yacht Club? He was still a legacy member, though far behind on his dues. I pulled over and made a call: they hadn't seen him since the summer. One of his friends managed the ᵈ Coffin House, but Homer wasn't there and 'y knew nothing. He sounded authentically ᵈ. "I've been calling him, but it just goes il."

Homer was a deacon at the Congregational Church; he even had a small office there. It seemed like a practical place to hunker down. There was a small kitchen in the warren the Theatre Workshop rented for costume storage and dressing rooms, though apart from church functions it was mostly used to set up snacks and coffee for Alcoholics Anonymous meetings.

My morning report: someone was stealing the food.

Got you, Homer.

I parked behind the church and pushed through into the cluttered backstage area. The place was deserted, though reindeer heads, bits of sleigh under construction, and other props were piled on a big central table, along with a jumble of elf costumes. I tracked through the corridors, past several rooms functioning as costume closets. I noticed the Santa suit hanging in the first of them.

Homer's office was closed and locked.

I rapped on the door. "Homer! This is Chief Kennis. I know you're in there. People are worried about you and we need to talk."

"Go 'way." His voice was muffled and slurred. I hoped he hadn't been drinking.

"I have your phone and your wallet."

"Keep them."

"This is nuts. You can't stay in there forever

"Long enough."

"For what?"

"For whatever I want to do that's none of your business."

"If you're talking about committing suicide, I have the legal right to kick this door open and stop you."

"Then I'm not."

"Your Santa suit is hanging down the hall, in case you want to use it tomorrow."

"Thanks anyway."

"Let me in, Homer. This is ridiculous."

"Am I under arrest?"

"No, of course not. I just want to talk."

"Fine."

He unlocked the door and let me push it open. He had the look of a party house on the morning after: squalid and disheveled. His hair was sticking out at all angles; he hadn't shaved in at least a week; and his shirt was spotted with—what? Wine, grease, spittle? Maybe all of the above. I chose not to investigate. He wore socks and his big toes protruded—they had obviously cut their way out. The nails were long, yellow, and sharp. The room ˈk of booze, body odor, and cigarette smoke. ˈng was illegal on church property but that ˈeast of Homer's problems. I thought of ˈn-spirited suspicions, dismissed them as absurd. Homer was many things that morning, but a cunning thief reaping his yuletide windfall was definitely not one of them.

I looked around. He sat down on his desk.

"So what's your plan, Homer?"

"Well, since you asked…I'll be drinking vodka, smoking American Spirits, writing hate mail about Blum to the *Inky Mirror* and repeat-dialing Alan's number until he picks up. With time out for naps and bathroom breaks."

I picked a topic out of the verbal mess, lifted it with two fingers. "I thought you and Alan were solid."

"So did I."

"But…"

"He lost thirty pounds, spent most of my money on a new wardrobe from the Ralph Lauren store, and ditched me for some pretty boy who shall remain nameless. Armand Flynn. Ooops."

"That won't last."

"And I suppose he'll come crawling back?"

"He might."

"Let him try."

"You might want to grab a shower and a shave, just in case."

"I don't think so. He's not coming back. Why would he? I lost my store. Which means I los my job. I'm losing my mind! I'd walk out on m

I wish I could. Does that sound like suicide talk again? Don't worry, Chief, I'm way too much of a coward for that. Another attractive trait for my grindr profile."

This was taking too long. "So, no Santa this year?"

"I'd scare the kids away."

"Any suggestion for a replacement?"

He grinned. "You, Chief. You'd be perfect."

He was right. I grabbed the suit on my way out.

Chapter Four

HackAck

My phone "Me and Julio"ed as I walked out of the church. I draped the cumbersome red suit over one shoulder, reached into my pocket and silenced the guitars. "Kennis."

"Chief, it's Shep Rollins. I have some news for you. Can we meet somewhere?"

"I'm on my way back to the station."

"Do they serve lattes there?"

I had to smile. "Not yet."

"How about the Handlebar Café—it has all five-star Yelp ratings."

"Five minutes."

I poked the end-call, slipped the phone back into my pocket, and manhandled the suit into the backseat of my cruiser—silly hat, ridiculous white beard, fur-trimmed red boots, and all. Wearing that costume for a long morning in Blum's overheate store was a grim prospect. But the kids might be fun.

Rollins had two lattes in front of him when I walked into the little coffee shop. With its scattered bookshelves and low tables, groups chatting on the low-slung armchairs and kids working on laptops, it always reminded me of a student lounge at Oberlin College. All it needed was a ride-board and an extracurricular sign-up sheet.

I sat down. "How's your drink?"

He grinned. "Perfect. That little blonde is the best barista in the world and I watched her teaching the Eastern European girl how to add the steamed milk. Which is not easy. You have to learn how to do stuff, you know? Everything is a skill. People don't realize that."

I lifted my latte; there was a perfect milky fern laid over the darker foam.

Rollins saw me notice. "Nice, huh? I got a heart."

I shrugged. "The really good baristas do portraits. But it costs extra."

He took the joke seriously. I suspected he did that a lot. "I'd pay for it. A work of art created to destroyed. Like those Renaissance painters who frescoes on the unprimed walls. They knew res wouldn't last. They just wanted to do

"Like you."

"I enjoy the process. It's interesting. Take your skeleton, for instance. I dug out some of the fillings—all amalgam…silver fillings, you'd call them, though the main ingredient is mercury. Nothing but mercury can actually bind the copper, tin, and silver together into a strong enough filling to last. And they do. They're still recommended for the back teeth, where people grind the molars together. The new resin composites are stronger, but that's just in the last ten years or so. So, I thought—no news here. You know, standard old-school dentistry and good solid workmanship. Could be anyone. Then I removed the amalgam and I saw the scoring around and inside the tooth. They used an erbium YAG laser to ablate the caries and modify the enamel—sorry, to get rid of the decay and prep the tooth for the filling. The laser etching is like a footprint. Can't miss it—like you guys could tell the brand of sneaker some perp was wearing by the tread pattern. Am I right?"

"Yeah, probably if the ground was soft, but I'm not sure what—"

"What I'm saying is they didn't start using the erbium laser until 1997. So now you have a cutoff date. This guy was killed within the last twenty years."

"So, he's not the missing link."

"Sorry, Professor. They found that guy last year in a cave outside Johannesburg, '*Homo naledi*'. Check it out. Apparently they buried their dead... and did a better job than your killer!"

I drained my coffee. It was tepid, but sipping hot coffee would have just slowed me down. I wanted to get moving. "This is great stuff, Shep."

"And it was a winter murder. Remember I told you about the dark cementum?"

"Right." I was sure I had jotted it down in a note somewhere. "So, is that it?"

"Well...for hard evidence. But the combination of the laser work and the amalgam makes me think this guy was an early-adapter, an outlier."

"A geek."

Rollins laughed. "Exactly! Someone like me."

I drained the last of my coffee and stood. "Thanks. You've been a real help."

"No problem. I'm going to do the dental X-rays myself. I've gotten attached to this guy."

We shook hands. "Let me know if you find anything interesting."

He grinned. "I always find something 'teresting."

I pulled out my phone as I left the Handlebar 'hinking—the skeleton dates from twenty who can tell me about twenty years ago?

I called the station. Barnaby Toll picked up, after a while.

"Nantucket Police. Can I help you?"

"You let the phone ring five times, Barney. I need you to pick up on the second ring. It shows respect."

"I…uh, okay. Yes, sir. I was in the bathroom."

"No, you weren't. You were texting someone." The guilty silence told me I was right. "Leave the cell phone in your locker, Barney. Anyone who wants to call you can wait a couple of hours."

"What if there's an emergency?"

"They can reach you on the department landline."

"Okay."

"Can you get me Kyle Donnelly?" He was the detective on watch that morning, and just about to head out. He liked working the graveyard shift but he'd be eager to get home, and not happy about one more assignment before he could climb into bed.

"Quiet night?" I asked when he came on the line.

"Couple a DUIs, fight at the Box, the usual."

"Can you get me Ted McGrady's contact information?"

"Ted McGrady?"

"He was the chief before me."

"You hired me. I never met the guy."

"But we must send his pension checks somewhere."

"That's handled out of Boston by the State of Mass."

I blew out a breath. "He lives in Maine, somewhere. Can you run a search on him?"

"Right now?"

Then the obvious solution hit me. "Put Haden on the line."

Haden Krakauer was my assistant chief. He'd lived on the island all his life, joined the NPD at twenty, and he'd been McGrady's assistant chief for more than a decade before I showed up. A lot of people thought he should have gotten the top job when the old man retired. Haden wasn't one of them.

"Camden, Maine," Haden said when he picked up the phone. "I'd give you his e-mail but McGrady doesn't do e-mail. No Facebook page. Which is crazy for a guy doing PI work. I'll text you his number. He doesn't text, either, by the way. He told me once, he likes his text *ink on paper*."

"I know how he feels."

"So what's this about?"

"The skeleton. The murder happened in the last twenty years."

"Rollins figure that out?"

"Yeah."

Haden chuckled. "You big-city boys."

"Not me. Not anymore."

"Whatever you say, Chief. But McGrady's the right guy to talk to. He never forgets a case. One time we were following someone on Milestone Road—pulled them over for erratic driving, turns out they were totally bombed at one in the afternoon. Just before we hit the flashers, Ted said, 'Weird—that license plate number is exactly the same as this drug dealer I pulled over in the city when I was still a rookie. Huge bust. Must have been ten pounds of coke in the trunk. Of course, those were Jersey plates.' How he kept all that crap in head, I'll never know."

"He was old school."

I disconnected, climbed into my cruiser, and drove out to one of my favorite parking spots—across from the old windmill, beside a miraculously undeveloped meadow at the top of South Mill Street. I pulled in next to the split-rail fence, opened my texts, scrolled to Haden's text of McGrady's number, and tapped it.

"McGrady Investigations. We set things right."

"Were you sitting on it?"

"Excuse me?"

"That's what my family always said when someone an answered the phone too fast."

"Kennis?"

I wasn't surprised that he recognized my voice. McGrady didn't miss much. He had noticed the nimbus of pale skin around my wristwatch at my swearing-in—and said "You can wear the Rolex again, Kennis. Put that Timex in the drawer. You're the police chief now."

He had instantly recognized that pale ghost of a more impressive predecessor. It turned out to be a good metaphor—for years, taking over the NPD after his storied reign, I felt like an inadequate cheaper replacement, myself.

"That's right," I said.

"You still out on the Rock? Bet you are. Call out of the blue like this, I'd say you were looking to rummage around in the archives."

"That's what you call your memory?"

"That's what my wife calls my memory. As in, *Oh God, here we go, another trip through the archives.* Always looking ahead, that old girl. I'm a little more nostalgic. But she spent thirty years trying to get us up here. Terrified I'll decide to go back."

"Any chance of that?"

"We get the *Inky* every week, Kennis. I keep up with developments."

"So you're not tempted."

"It's not the place it was, even when you got there. I've been following your career. Seems like you have more crime in the average month than we had in a decade. The only thing that doesn't change is the style. In my time they spend five million dollars building a swimming pool and make it six inches too short for competition. Nowadays they paint the bottom half of the Unitarian Church, spend eighty thousand dollars putting up a staging—and don't bother to paint the top half. Eighty thousand dollars for a two-tone church."

"Don't tell me you left the island to get away from human stupidity."

He chuckled. "Can't be done, son."

That was one of McGrady's catch phrases back in the day, his standard response, whether it was to an unlicensed driver with a lapsed registration asking not to be handcuffed for the ride to the station, or a teenager in jail overnight for a marijuana bust requesting a box of Downyflake donuts for the munchies.

"So, was it just your wife wanting to get away?"

"Naah, we owned some property up here. When we sold our crappy little house on Helens Drive, we built this place—ten thousand square feet and lots of extra bedrooms for the grandkids. Plus you can't beat the view of Penobscot Bay."

"It's a little cold for swimming, though."

"Like I ever had time to go to the beach! That's the real reason I quit. I was working too hard."

"Sounds familiar."

"But you love it. And I didn't any more. Still paying attention?"

"Trying to."

"So what's your problem this morning? I know you didn't call to chat about real estate."

I described excavating the skeleton in Madaket, and laid out the initial moves we'd made to identify it—the bone histology, tooth analysis, and the laborious sifting through twenty-year-old dental records, on- and off-island. "What I'm looking for now is some anecdotal evidence. Something happened twenty years ago and it wound up with a body in a shallow grave. Does any of that jog your memory?"

After a few moments of silence, McGrady said, "Well, there was the body that went missing from the funeral home. That was memorable."

"Tell me."

"It was Billy Delavane's Uncle Brandon. Crazy old drunk. Jacked so many deer out of season he was running a goddamn butcher shop out of his house—big walk-in freezer, hooks for the carcasses, you name it. I would have arrested him but he made the best venison sausage I ever ate. Anyway, he died and the burial plans kicked off a classic family feud. See, his wife was a devout Catholic. She wanted him to have a proper burial—the wake, the funeral liturgy, the Rite of Committal, the whole nine yards. That didn't sit right with the Delavanes. They knew he was a heathen who wanted to be buried in the Nantucket dirt, no ceremony, just some good stories and a bottle of Bushmills Twenty-one for his family, a few old friends. That meant stealing the body, and somebody did just that. Broke the lock on the bulkhead door, in and out, no witnesses, the night before the open-casket viewing. Everybody figured it was Ed Delavane, but he and Billy alibied each other and Ed's girlfriend backed them up. Case never went anywhere, but the wife sued the funeral home. The Delavanes didn't participate in the suit, which I thought was interesting.

"Ed said, 'It worked out fine for Brandon.' The crime was a misdemeanor in the state of Mass at that point, anyway, and the funeral home had plenty of evidence for the theft. I seem to recall they settled out of court, and the widow moved away. Betsy something. She had run for Selectwoman five or six times over the years, trying to expand the dry Sunday laws to restaurants. That was her whole platform—prohibition! My feeling was, good riddance. Anyway, if it really is old Brandon Delavane out there in Madaket, you might find traces of formaldehyde in the dirt. They were pretty far along prepping him at the funeral home—the body was snatched the day before the open-casket showing. Get a soil sample and keep me posted."

I hung up and sent Haden's nephew, Byron Lovell, to dig up a soil sample. It was worth a try.

I had another mystery waiting for me when I went to pick up the kids at school. Tim was in trouble.

"You have to go to Bissell's office," he said to me as the crowds of newly liberated teenagers pushed past us into the parking lot.

One of the kids, a handsome Hispanic boy of fifteen or sixteen, stopped for a second against the rush of bodies like a tree in a landslide. He was staring at Caroline as she rolled toward me, in the middle of a crowd of her friends. The boy's wingman whispered something to him and pushed him. The group of chattering, texting girls reached him.

This was his moment.

I watched the scene, pinned and transported, remembering my own high school mortifications. The boy stepped forward, reached a hand out to touch Caroline's shoulder as she saw me and let the pack of girls move away. The boy lost his nerve and fled, running down the less crowded hallway past the glass walls of the basketball court, cutting and juking past the occasional student or teacher like he was running a kickoff back through the Boston Latin secondary.

He was a natural sprinter. He looked familiar to me, but I couldn't place him.

"Dad!" Tim shouted. "Hello! You have to see Bissell. Right now."

I turned to him, trying to catch up. "What?"

"He cheated on his English midterm," Caroline announced.

He spun on her. "I did not!"

"His cross-grade poetry class."

"Dad—"

"Go to the car and wait for me. Both of you."

I stalked through the big glass doors to the wide main lobby and into the school offices. I nodded to Bissell's secretary, Alice Damaso, and she gave me a helpless shrug that said, "I deal with this crap every day." I returned the shrug on my way past.

Bissell perched behind his desk, trim and pinched, with his usual blazer and bow tie. His hair looked more real than the last time I saw him; maybe he had finally splurged on implants.

"What's going on?"

He looked up from some paperwork, set his Montblanc pen aside. "Why don't you tell me, Chief Kennis?"

"You're accusing my son of cheating. That's all I know. Well, that's not quite all. I also know he needs to cheat on a poetry exam about as much as you needed to plagiarize your last article in *Pedagogy Review*. I mean—who else would write a polemic about bringing back corporal punishment?"

"You read that?"

"I read everything that might affect my children."

"Then you know my philosophy. Spare the rod, spoil the child. It's in the Bible."

"No, it isn't."

"Excuse me?"

"They need better fact-checkers at *Pedagogy Review*. That's a quote from Samuel Butler. A poem called "Hudibras." I think you could relate. It's about a pompous blowhard who turns out to be a hypocrite and a clown. And whatever the nuns who rapped your knuckles with their rulers might have told you, the poem has nothing to do with beating school children into submission. Hudibras' girlfriend wants him to prove his love by flagellating himself. Here's the quote. Hold on." I had memorized the poem a long time ago. I couldn't remember the bulk of it anymore, but the key stanza had always stuck in my mind. I recited:

> *If matrimony and hanging go*
> *By dest'ny, why not whipping too?*
> *What med'cine else can cure the fits*
> *Of lovers when they lose their wits?*
> *Love is a boy by poets stil'd;*
> *Then spare the rod and spoil the child.*

Bissel pursed his lips so hard his eyes squeezed shut. "Well, Chief. That's very impressive. All the more tragic then, that your son not only fails to share your love and knowledge of poetry, but feels he can cheat with impunity to hide his ignorance."

"I guess. Except that didn't happen."

"You're absolutely sure?"

"I know my son."

He sighed. "If I had silver dollar for every deluded parent who has stood in my office making that plea…well, realistically, I could probably afford…what? Let me see. The down payment on a nice little bungalow on the Cape somewhere? Nantucket would still be out of my price range."

"You're saying I'm deluded?"

"I'm saying that you suffer from one of the two most common delusions of our benighted species. We believe our children are faultless. And that we are the only good drivers on the road. But with all the traffic accidents and miscreant children out there, someone has to be mistaken."

"My son didn't cheat."

"Then how do you explain the copy of Mr. Springer's test answer sheet we found in his locker this afternoon?"

"You're saying he stole the answers and kept the evidence?"

"He's an incompetent thief. But that may be his saving grace. Perhaps he wanted to get caught. This may be a cry for help."

"Or a setup."

"So someone is framing your little boy? Come, come, Chief Kennis. This is hardly some nefarious intrigue among big city criminals. It's a simple case of cheating, common as athlete's foot. And with a similar cause—a lack of cleanliness, rigor, and discipline."

I felt a cramp of rage—this insufferable little prig had real power over my children. Why did the wrong people run everything? I had always wondered that. Maybe it was because only the wrong people wanted to. I tried to be an exception to that rule, but then again, I had never schemed and campaigned to become Nantucket's police chief. The job became available at the perfect moment. I'd been fired by the LAPD for writing a tell-all true crime book. My wife had vacationed on Nantucket since she was a child and wanted to get her own children away from Los Angeles. Retreating to the East Coast felt like the right move, so I interviewed by Skype with the head of the Board of Selectman, Dan Taylor, and the departing chief. I was fighting a cold that day and I recall acting curt and dismissive of village life in general and the need for a strong resort town police presence, in particular.

"There's plenty of crime here, Detective Kennis," I remember Dan Taylor snapping.

"I'm sure I can handle it," I said.

"And how might you do that?" asked Ted McGrady. The retiring chief's jowly face held a spark of shrewd, amused intelligence. Even on the computer screen I felt the pressure of those glacier blue eyes.

I said, "By paying attention."

McGrady laughed and turned to Taylor. "I like this guy."

Taylor was off-screen but I could hear his snort of dismissal. "Yeah? Well, I don't."

I got the job, and judging from our phone call, McGrady seemed to remember the whole interview verbatim, but things hadn't changed much between me and Dan Taylor since my arrival—or between me and Bissell. We'd been locking antlers ever since I first arrived.

"I want to see the paper," I said now.

"Excuse me?"

"The answer sheet you found in Tim's locker."

"And on what authority do you claim to make that demand?"

"On what authority did you break into my son's locker in the first place?"

"I had reason to believe Tim had committed a serious infraction of school discipline. I have the right to investigate NHS property. It's in the charter."

"Which you rewrote when you got here."

"The new rules passed on a Town Meeting warrant and had the full support of the Selectmen. The school was falling apart, discipline was a joke, the children had no respect for the instructors, and the instructors had no respect for the administration. It was chaos. That's why I was hired in the first place! And I've made a difference, Chief. I run a tight ship. Everyone agrees."

Everyone hated him, but he was proud of that. "Are you going to show me the paper, Simon?"

"Can you tell me any reason at all why I should, Henry?"

"Apart from the fact that I might be able to find out who really stole it?"

"Apart from that. Since we already know."

"In my job I assume people are innocent until proven guilty."

"I have proof."

"You have a piece of paper. And you're going to give it to me."

"You still haven't told me why."

I set my palms on his desk and leaned over it. "All right. You're going to give it to me because you want to maintain a good relationship with the NPD. As a man with two DUIs on his record, a man who's one sloppy lane-change away from losing his license and one scandal away from losing his job, I assume you can appreciate that."

"Are you threatening me?"

"I'm giving you a reality check. We both want the same thing. Let's work together." I pushed off from the desk.

"Fine," he said. "You can have the paper. But it won't do you any good." He touched his intercom. "Alice, can you bring in the Cross-Grade English midterm answer sheet for Chief Kennis, please?"

She walked in a moment later, paper in hand. Alice was a slim, attractive Brazilian woman who always studiously overdressed for the job. Today she wore a knee-length hunter green dress set off by half a dozen bracelets, a jade necklace, and a silk scarf in her hair. She winked at me as she came in—she had the paper ready instantly because she knew Bissell was going to cave, and she knew I knew she knew. I turned away from Bissell and smiled at her.

"Found it," she said to him.

"Just give it to the chief. I'd like to get some work done today."

I took the paper, silently cursing myself for not carrying an evidence bag. But I would have had to have folded the paper twice to fit the sheet inside, so maybe it was just as well.

In front of the school, in the slant parking lane, Tim and Caroline were standing in front of my cruiser. Tim was trying to juggle with three hacky-sack bags he'd found in the take-it-or-leave-it pile at the dump. Caroline, shivering with annoyance at his clownish performance, stared down into her phone, swiping across the screen frantically.

"What's wrong?" I said to her.

Tim answered. "The car is locked."

"Oh, sorry." I thumbed the key and the locks popped with a quick bleat from the car horn. "Carrie?"

She glanced up irritably. "What?"

"Something wrong?"

"I only got twenty likes on my last selfie," she moaned.

"Everyone hates her," Tim added helpfully.

"They do not!"

"Twenty seems like a lot," I said.

"But they're not sharing them, Dad! And the comments are bad. The comments are all like "so cute" and "pretty" and—and nothing personal. Nothing like…I mean, I got a haircut! Okay? And no one even…I knew I shouldn't have taken that stupid part in your girlfriend's play!"

I was not following this at all. What did Jane's Christmas play have to do with some classmates' failure to notice Carrie's new hairstyle on an Instagram feed?

"I'm not sure…" I began.

"I've missed every important social event for the last two weeks! I missed Patty's party and the winter dance and the beach cleanup and a million yearbook meetings—"

"So, if—"

"And no one's sharing my selfies! Don't you get it?"

"Well, I'm not sure I really—"

"Abby Miller got fifty likes and tons of comments and everyone's sharing her pictures. Abby Miller! And she's new. I thought everyone hated her."

"Maybe she's a novelty. Flavor of the month? It'll pass."

"Not if I keep doing this stupid play. It's six nights a week for three weeks, Dad. I'll be a total pariah by the time it's over."

"Yeah, but—you knew that when—"

"Plus, I'm playing Santa's daughter. Ugh."

"But she saves Christmas!"

"Right."

"When her lazy brother won't get off the Internet long enough to pitch in and help."

This extracted a hard-won smile. "I like that part."

"I'm off the Internet, now," Tim said. "I'm learning to juggle."

Her look of stunned disgust and contempt ended the conversation. We got into the car and I ran down the schedule as we pulled into the traffic. "I want you guys to see the new house, then I'll drop Carrie off at rehearsal before we go home."

"We were going to go driving," Tim said, with a muscular whine of tween outrage. "Jane said we could borrow her truck."

Carrie shoved him. "Why don't you leave Jane alone? What's wrong with Dad's car?"

"It doesn't have a stick shift! You can't learn to drive on an automatic. Obviously. That's not even driving. With an automatic, you're just a monkey turning the steering wheel. That's what Jane says."

"Well, if Jane says it, it has to be right."

"Shut up."

"You shut up."

"Both of you shut up!"

We drove in a familiar seething silence to Darling Street, but the argument was forgotten once they got inside the house. They ran up and down the stairs, opened every door, even checked out the attic.

Tim said, "This is great!"

Carrie said "Can I have the big room?"

And the deal was done.

Ten minutes later, I was winding up the crooked cobblestone street that led to the Congregational Church parking lot. Caroline asked me to walk her inside. I thought that was a little unusual—she generally avoided being seen with me at all costs. Tim and I shared a quizzical glance, then I got out of the cruiser, leaving it parked next to the Theatre Workshop's battered Ford Ranger.

We walked down the steeply sloped parking area, around the corner of the church to the back doors. Piles of sawdust recorded the frenzied set-building of the last few weeks. I thought of my carpenter friend Billy Delavane. He would never have left a mess like that behind.

Inside, Carrie took my arm to stop me. "I saw some weird stuff on HackAck this morning," she said. HackAck was a gossip website some local geek had set up for his friends—one more way of keeping track of each other, organizing the high school hierarchies—like the Instagram rituals that were driving Caroline crazy. These kids were going to fit in very nicely to the surveillance society we were building. They liked it. When I rhapsodized about the pre-Internet privacy era they looked at me as if I'd been talking about cranking the car engine with a wooden handle.

"What did you see?"

"Lots of things. People were talking about rigging the Red Ticket Drawing."

"Really? Did they mention how they planned to do that?"

"Dad."

"Hey, it was worth a shot. So there's no information at all? None of the good stuff?"

"It's probably just kids trying to look cool. There was one thing, though. On one of the threads. Somebody wrote 'It takes two.' Whatever that means."

I nodded. "It makes sense. You'd need two people for a scam like that. It wouldn't even be that hard. One person works at a store and palms a ticket instead of putting it in the store's collection."

"But how does that make it the winning ticket?"

Realistically, there was only one answer. "The second person has to be the one drawing the tickets."

Carrie squinted at me. "I think you deal with criminals too much, Dad. You're starting to think like one. Besides, Alana Trikilis is home for the holidays. She's drawing the tickets and she'd never cheat. Her dad is Town Crier."

The position of Town Crier had started in the early nineteenth century with an authentic purpose—public announcements and warnings needed to be shouted in public, accompanied by a handbell. Town Criers served as fire wardens and lookouts for arriving whaleships. They even declaimed the news headlines. But the job degraded over time, with local businesses using that bell-and-buffoon combo to announce sales and specials.

These days, the Town Crier, dressed in Colonial

garb, rang in a host of chamber of commerce-approved celebrations: Daffodil Day, Christmas Stroll, and the lighting of the Main Street Christmas trees, among others. He also served as master of ceremonies for the Red Ticket Raffle.

The Christmas Eve drawing had begun in the 1980s as a Nantucket Chamber of Commerce scheme to lure Christmas shoppers back to the island, hoping that the chance to win five thousand dollars might offset the higher Nantucket prices and make the required two-and-half-hour boat ride to Hyannis—and Kmart and Marshalls and the Cape Cod Mall—seem less of a necessary ordeal and more of an gratuitous slog. The idea was that every participating merchant would hand out a Red Ticket when you spent twenty-five dollars. You collected the tickets as you did the rounds of local shops, and on Christmas Eve the whole town gathered on Main Street to hear the winning tickets announced by the Town Crier. The tactical venality of the event had mellowed over the years into a casual open-air party, more of a chance to see old friends and catch up on gossip than anything else—which was exactly the way Sam Trikilis liked it.

And he loved to play his part, Pied Pipering the crowd behind him. bellowing "Hear Ye! Hear Ye!" Sam was almost comically honest. He hadn't charged some of the hard-luck customers on his trash route for years. He was a snoop. If he noticed a couple of collection agency envelopes in your rubbish, he'd put you on the freebie list. If you asked about the bills you weren't getting from him, you'd hear his favorite catch-phrase, "No trouble, you're on my route."

He could no more conspire to rig the drawing than he could eat the garbage he hauled. Carrie knew it and so did everyone else. She tilted her chin and raised her eyebrows with the pursed lips that made her position clear: case closed. "It's just stupid kids making things up."

"I guess. Still, I'm going to be keeping an eye on Alana Trikilis. In case something happens to her."

"Dad!"

"It doesn't have to be something terrible. A half a valium slipped into her soda at lunch. She'd still be asleep when they drew the tickets."

"This is sick."

"So the real person to look at is the next in line. There must be some kind of understudy lined up. Don't they usually have the Junior Miss Pageant winner draw the tickets? She's the one to watch, if something happens to Alana."

Carrie crossed her arms and shuddered. "This is horrible. I don't want to talk about this anymore. Nothing is going to happen to Alana! Besides, the person who stole the ticket couldn't win—it would be too suspicious, having a winning ticket from her own store. And the person drawing the ticket couldn't win, either. There'd have to be three people involved—not two. So that wrecks your two-person theory. "

"You'd make a pretty good detective yourself." Two little kids—elves no doubt, like Jane's little boy, Sam—pushed past us, accompanied by their parents.

"I saw something else on the site," Caroline said, when we were alone again. "I think it was about drugs."

"What about drugs?"

"I don't know, they never come right out and say it. Everything's kind of in code, like they say 'kibbles and bits' for Ritalin and 'smoothies' for Oxy and…there's tons of things. 'Doing laundry' means—not just drugs—it's anything you don't want your parents to know about."

I had to laugh. "That's the code? Doing laundry? The one activity no kid is ever going to engage in voluntarily? That's going to fool absolutely no one. Why not call it 'summer reading' or 'cleaning my room'?"

"No, but this is serious. Supposedly, there's a ton of Oxy coming onto the island and this guy, Surfslider, wants to sell it all at once. Just kind of offload the whole shipment, and he's looking for some kid or group of kids who can take it off his hands."

I pressed my hand to her shoulder. "How much are they talking about?"

"I don't know. It might not even be true."

"Surfslider? This guy is a surfer?" I had friends who surfed; Billy Delavane might have an idea about who "Surfslider" was.

"I don't know, that's just what he calls himself, people never use their real names on HackAck unless they're in a special chat room. And this was, like—for everyone. Like taking an ad out in the newspaper—I mean, if anyone ever read the newspaper."

"Thanks, Carrie. Thanks for the heads-up."

"Can you do anything about it?"

"I can try." I thought of Frannie Tate, my old girlfriend, who was now high up in Homeland Security with a boyfriend at the NSA. They could probably root out this "Surfslider" during their morning coffee break, with or without an FISA warrant. But that was exactly the kind of law enforcement I hated the most. I preferred feet on the ground, person-to-person policing. The NPD had built up a good network of contacts in the community. I'd put the word out, see what happened.

But as it turned out, I didn't need to. I saw the drug deal going down less than half an hour later.

Chapter Five

At Tom Nevers Head

We picked up Jane's truck—a note told us she was inside writing and the keys were under the front mat—and headed out to the old Navy base. Tim was throwing one of his hacky-sack footbags up with his left hand and catching it with his right. "Look Dad! Polish juggling!"

I laughed, but I couldn't quite let it go by. "That's actually kind of politically incorrect," I told him.

"Come on, Dad."

"No, seriously. You studied Madame Curie in science class, right?

"Sure. She discovered radiation."

"Close enough. She won two Nobel prizes. Her maiden name was Sklodowska. There are just way too many brilliant Poles for those jokes to fly. There are lots of them you never study in school—like Joseph Rotblat—he's the scientist who walked away from the Manhattan Project. For some reason he thought making a world-killing weapon and giving it to a bunch of politicians was a bad idea."

"Fine. Polish people are super smart. So who can we use for jokes?"

"How about…generic stupid person?"

"But that's mean to stupid people."

"True."

We drove in silence or a while. "There's got to be some group it's okay to make fun of, Dad."

"How about rich kids?"

"That's good! So we need a rich kid joke. How many super rich kids does it take to screw in a light bulb?"

"None? Their nannies do it for them?"

"And their parents give them self-driving cars as a reward and then tell them what great little drivers they are."

"Right. While they sit in the backseat playing *Grand Theft Auto* on their iPhones."

I gave him a high five. "You can definitely get away with that one."

"Yeah. Rich kids suck."

We drove along.

"So," I said finally. "Mr. Springer thinks you cheated on the midterm exam."

"What?"

"That's what Bissell wanted to talk to me about."

"That's stupid. They should accuse me of cheating on my algebra test. I should have cheated on my algebra test. Ms. Albertson said I created a whole new system of mathematics."

I laughed. "Sounds good."

"Except it doesn't work."

"Right."

"She was pretty nice about it."

"She's nice."

"Yeah."

"So what happened with the Cross-Grade poetry? Your mom thought you shouldn't even take a class with all those older kids."

"They're okay, except for Dave Prescott."

Dave was the Whalers' quarterback. "What's he doing in a poetry class?"

"He needed a gut class to bring his marks up."

"A gut class? I guess he didn't know Fred Springer too well."

"Nope."

"They found the answer sheet for the midterm in your locker, Tim. You think Dave put it there?"

"Maybe. Or he had someone else do it."

"But why you?"

"Well, Jake Sauter's on the team. They're friends."

Jake was a bully who'd been tormenting Tim since seventh grade. I'd gotten into a fight with the boy's father a few years ago. Pat Sauter was a grown-up version of his son, designed to make a dismissive father think twice about advising his kid to stand up to bullies. Sauter had almost killed me that afternoon, I was pretty well banged-up going in to the brawl, and he probably would have finished the job if a group of stalwarts—including Tim himself—hadn't come to my rescue. The thought that junior might still be plotting against Tim struck me as grimly plausible. I wasn't sure exactly what to do about it, though. I touched the side pocket of my coat. The paper itself might hold some answers.

"Speaking of Mr. Springer…" Tim started.

"Oh, God. What now?"

"He wants us to bring in a Christmas poem."

"There aren't any good Christmas poems. Unless you think of 'A Child's Christmas in Wales' as free verse."

"That's too long anyway, Dad."

"Yeah." I thought for a few moments, as we came around the last turn and the ocean rolled out beyond the summer fairgrounds. "'River' is kind of a Christmas poem." He looked blank. "Joni Mitchell? I wish I had a river I could skate away on?"

"What is that?"

I squashed a quick surge of irritation—this gap in his education was my fault. "I need to play you some Joni Mitchell," I said, and started singing. "It's coming on Christmas, they're cutting down trees, putting up reindeer singing songs of joy and peace—"

"That's a song, Dad. If I could bring in a song I'd just use some old Christmas carol."

"Right, sorry. So what are you going to do?"

He hesitated. I sensed it coming before it arrived—like that pre-impact, hip-to-pavement that you feel in the first split-second when you slip on the ice. "That's kind of what I wanted to talk to you about."

"Okay."

"I told him you'd write one."

"Tim—"

"You're a poet! You've been published and everything!"

"In four little magazines that pay with copies."

"I said you'd do it."

"He accused you of cheating and now he wants me writing-to-order for him? Great. Can I do his laundry, too? How about the ironing? I'm good at pleats."

"Dad…"

"Well, ordinarily I'd say no. But you're in luck this afternoon. I actually had an idea for a

Christmas poem the other day. So I'll donate it to Mr. Springer. Plus I'll figure out who tried to frame you for cheating. He can get the full use of my talents. How's that for playing Santa?"

"Pretty good."

"And I'm actually playing Santa tomorrow.'

He stared at me. "What?"

"Oh, yes. Homer Boyce bailed on it."

"They can't find anyone else?"

"I volunteered."

"So you're really going to do it? I mean... the whole thing? Kids on your lap? Ho ho ho?" I nodded. "With the red fat suit and the beard?" I nodded again. He gave me the verdict. "Carrie is going to kill you."

I shrugged. "Finding new ways to embarrass the children is an essential part of any parent's job, son. Wait until I dress up as a giant bunny for the big Easter egg hunt." I almost laughed at the genuine panic on his face. "Just kidding."

We reached the wide open array of fields and parking lots fronting the ocean. The town held the annual demolition derby here, and the carnival set up on the bluff every July. In between, the place was mostly deserted—perfect for learning to drive. There was even a steeply canted section of road that led down to some disused garages. It made a stress-free arena for getting into gear on a hill.

I had mastered these same skills at the crest of La Cienega Boulevard, where it tips over onto Sunset in West Hollywood. I always felt like the car was going to pitch-pole on that unforgivingly vertical street, invariably with a Maserati or Bentley idling an inch from my back bumper.

Tim had it easier. He could roll backward onto the flats with no one behind him and nothing to hit, no worries. He had had done that several times, stalling out Jane's old Ford Ranger in the process, and he was just getting the hang of the clutch, letting in the gas as he released the pedal, when I said, "Drive up to the top again and cut the motor."

"What's going on?"

"I just want to see something."

He got us to level ground above the ramp, killed the engine and set the brake. "Dad? What is this?"

I patted his knee. "Police work."

He twisted around to look out the windows. "What's happening? I don't see anything."

"The dark green Hummer, stopped next to the dinged-up Chevy Cobalt. Anything strike you as odd about that?"

"Maybe they're just asking for directions."

"Could be. But I don't think so. They've been there too long—since we started down the ramp last time. Directions are like 'you passed Old Tom

Nevers Road. It's your first paved right on the way back.'—thirty seconds, tops."

"Old friends?"

"In a Hummer and a Cobalt? Not on Nantucket."

"So, that means the Cobalt guy is selling drugs?"

"No, I think the Cobalt guy is buying drugs."

"From some dude in a Hummer."

"It's possible. Remember that shooting in Madaket last month?"

"Not really."

"Shots were fired on Madaket Road, just past the dump. The purported victim, one Gary Pressman, claimed it was an attempted carjacking."

"Why would you jack a car on Nantucket? Where would you go?"

"I wondered that myself. He said it was two Jamaican kids and one of them flashed the gun at the Chicken Box a few nights later. We picked him up and he told us the Madaket incident was a drug deal gone wrong. The guy was overcharging for prescription Vicodin. The kid thought he was getting ripped off. An argument ensued and the gun went off. No one was hurt. No drugs changed hands."

"The guy selling the Vicodin was the guy in the Hummer?"

"Himself. Or anyway, that's what they said.

Mr. Gary Pressman, of Nantucket and Newport, Rhode Island. Member in good standing at the Sankaty Head Golf Club and the Nantucket Yacht Club. His grandfather was Commodore there. Old Nantucket money. He lives in the family house on Tuckernuck."

"And he's selling drugs?"

"According to Alfred Bailey, of Nantucket and Kingston, Jamaica, now serving two years at Barnstable Correctional."

"Did anyone believe him?

"You mean besides me? Take a guess."

"So what did you do?"

"I waited."

"For what?"

"For this."

Tim stared at the two cars, the wisps of exhaust scattering from their exhaust pipes in the sharp wind. I took out my binoculars and a pad, scribbled down the license plate numbers.

"Are you going to arrest them?" Tim was getting excited.

"Not today."

"Why not? They're right there!"

"Well, I could only get one of them, and I'm not interested in the buyer. The seller has nothing on him now but cash and Gary Pressman always carries a roll of cash—twenties and fifties. I asked him about that after the incident. He said it was a family tradition. 'Whenever my dad had a problem, he'd just peel off a twenty.' That's what Gary told me. 'It's usually a fifty now. A Nantucket five-spot, as they say.'"

"What a jerk."

"All the more reason to have solid evidence before I arrest him."

We watched as the two cars peeled away from each other and then drove off back along Tom Nevers Road.

"Well, they got away," Tim said.

"Not for long."

Tim lapsed into his oddly persuasive John Travolta imitation. "That's a bold statement, my friend."

I might as well admit it, I had let him watch *Pulp Fiction*. He was going to watch it anyway; it was his best friend Ethan's favorite movie and Ethan was basically unsupervised most of the time, with an absentee father and a mother who worked two jobs. I made the practical decision—keep Tim's introduction to Quentin Tarantino at home, where I could hover, pointing out that lowlife criminals I had encountered in Los Angeles were almost never as entertaining as Vincent Vega and Jules Winn-field, that slaves never actually went to war against plantation owners, and most important—that the

U.S government never donated Nantucket real estate to an ex-pat Nazi…although that last notion sometimes struck me as disturbingly plausible. And it wasn't just me. I remember Mike Henderson walking out of a screening of *Inglourious Basterds* at the Dreamland saying, "I think I painted that guy's house!"

"Wait and see," I told Tim now. "I'll get Pressman. Probably before the New Year."

But I had other criminals to root out first. I dropped Tim at home and drove to the station.

Shepherd Rollins was waiting for me, with a manila envelope in hand—the skeleton's dental X-rays.

"You've been busy," I said.

"It beats one more trip to the whaling museum. Or tramping around Squam Swamp, reading those markers. As if I didn't know that red maples thrive in wetland soils! Anyway, you're lucky—a pal of mine lent me his equipment."

"You have a dentist pal on Nantucket?"

"We met at a conference on digital impression scanning last year. Fascinating stuff."

I sensed a major tangent hurtling toward me. "So tell me what you found on the X-rays," I said.

"The—oh, right. Sorry. Well, there are some very interesting variations in tooth morphology. If you can find a proper array of ante-mortem dental records, the search is on!"

"I'm sure my detectives will be thrilled to hear that."

"I know it's a lot of work, but productive—if you stick with it. Here, look, I can show you a few things to look for."

I walked him into one of the ground floor conference rooms, and he pulled the photographs for me, laying them out like tarot cards on the big table. "Basically, you're looking for a these three anomalies. If you find them grouped together, you'll have a solid ID on your victim. The teeth don't lie." He pointed down at a little fang resting against one of the molars, inside at the gum line. "That's a talon cusp. Very unusual! Combine that with these two impacted wisdom teeth—see, right there, both of them still buried in the alveolar bone? And this diastema in the front teeth—the gap between them? Taken together, they're as unique as a fingerprint. All your men have to do is sort through the radiography for the diastema. Once they find it, they can check for the talon cusp. It only takes a few seconds. The impacted wisdom teeth should clinch it."

"Sounds good."

"Let me know if you find anything."

"I will."

He shook my hand. "Good hunting!"

I called Kyle Donnelly and Charlie Boyce into my office, filled them in on the case and showed them the X-rays. They didn't share Rollins' enthusiasm, but I hadn't expected them to. I said, "Each of you take two ambitious uniforms and start going through the files of every dentist here and on the Cape who's been in business since the late nineties. I want to identify this man."

Kyle shook his head. "That's a lot of work, boss."

"What else have you got going on?"

"Someone's dumping old furniture in the moors. And a lot of these off-island deer hunters are bagging above the limit."

"That can wait."

"We're still looking for the drug dealer, Chief," Charlie said. "We have a big-time supplier and he's in the wind right now."

"No leads?"

"Not so far."

"I may have one. But I'm going to follow it up myself. Meanwhile, you guys can help solve a murder."

"A twenty-year-old murder," Kyle sniffed.

"Doesn't matter. And you know it. The killer could still be around. He could have killed again. There could be other bodies buried in the moors. Let's take this one off the books."

Downstairs, in our new forensics lab, Monica Terwilliger, obese but light-footed, bounced up to greet me and wished me an early Merry Christmas. I told her what I needed and she plucked the Poetry midterm answer sheet out of my hand.

"Back in a sec," she said.

While she took the prints, I wandered the suite of rooms, admiring all our new toys—photo tables and fuming chambers and evidence-drying cabinets.

Twenty minutes later she was back. "All done."

"What have we got?"

Okay…I pulled four clear sets of prints. I ran them all through the IFIAS database. One was Mr. Springer, the English teacher. The second was Alice Damaso—she works at the school. And the third one was you!"

"How about the fourth one?"

"No hits anywhere. Sorry. Not even UCIS. Of course they don't fingerprint kids under the age of twelve. And some of these kids come here as babies."

"So it's not an adult immigrant, a criminal with an arrest record, or someone in the military."

"Or law enforcement. Plus…it's a pretty distinctive lift, at least this thumbprint is. Take a look." She handed me a blow-up of the latent. It looked like a regular fingerprint to me. She leaned in. "See that little whorl inside the central loop?

That's called a 'peacock's eye.' Very distinctive. Uncommon on any finger. On the thumb? You just hit the jackpot. If you ever come across this individual's prints again, that is."

"Right."

"It's a start."

"Absolutely. Thanks, Monica. I have to think about this."

"You just keep thinking, Butch. That's what you're good at."

Movie quotes! There was no escaping them today. I gave her my best mad grin on the way out, jabbed my finger at the ceiling and shouted, "Bolivia!" Though maybe I should have said, "Who are those guys?!" since, despite my boasting with Tim, I still had no solid evidence of anyone's involvement in anything—the toy thieves. the test-cheaters, the Red Ticket scammers, the drug dealers, and whoever had capped the Madaket skeleton all those years ago…they were all doing just fine, despite my best efforts.

On the way out I stuck my head in Haden Krakauer's office door. "Hear anything about a load of opioids hitting the island?"

He looked up from his computer. "Nope. But I'll check with my peeps."

"Peeps?"

"My people, Chief. I have people."

"But mostly they're birders."

"True."

"And birders are not high-incident opioid users."

"Also true."

"But it never hurts to stay alert."

He gave me a mock salute and went back to his computer.

I stopped by Sam Trikilis' house on the way home, to give him a heads-up about the possible Red Tickets scam, and to warn Alana about the risk she was running. A heightened level of awareness might prevent her from taking a drink from a stranger on Christmas Eve. The attempt to rig the drawing might be an empty rumor, or it might involve some sort of complex plan I hadn't figured out yet. You do what you can.

"Never gonna happen," Sam told me.

"Well, that's good news."

We were standing in his big messy kitchen. He poured himself a mug of coffee and extended the French press to me. When I shook my head he set down the pot. "I used to be addicted to booze. Now I'm addicted to work and coffee."

I smiled. "Do they have a support group for that?"

"Nah. We're all working too hard. For all the good it does us. One of my customers, some summer person up on Cliff Road, she asked me when I was going to retire. Can you believe that? I told her, we don't retire on Nantucket. We work till we're dead!"

I patted his shoulder. "Just—"

"Look out, right? Like that elevated threat level sign at the Steamship Authority. They never change that sign. Middle of February, high summer, doesn't matter. The threat is always elevated. Like my blood pressure."

"Between us, it's only until after the drawing. Okay? The chamber of commerce will horse-whip me if I screw this one up."

Alana stopped me at the front door, and took my arm. "Can I talk to you outside for a second?" We stepped out and she closed the door behind us. "I'm worried about Dad."

"What's going on? Is he sick?"

"No nothing like that. He says he should get sick, just to get some of his money back from Blue Cross. But that's the thing. The money."

"Does he need a loan?"

"What? From you? No. That wouldn't help. He's going to lose the house, Chief. He doesn't have any savings and he's two months behind and it's not the first time and they're really cracking down now at the bank and half of his customers he doesn't even charge anymore, and…Grampa died but the will's still in probate and I guess Dad thought it would come through in time, but the lawyers go back and forth and there's so much paperwork and the executor—my Aunt Judy—she doesn't seem to care how long it takes, so…it's—I don't know what we're going to do."

"How much does he need?"

"I don't know. Five thousand dollars? It might as well be a million. And he has to act all jolly while he presides over this stupid raffle and some rich jerk with a wad of tickets wins all the money because they just bought a car at Don Allen. It's not fair. I saw Nathan Parrish at the drawing one year, and he had a million tickets and a whole computer printout so he could keep track of them, and I said, 'Have you decided which charity you're going to donate the money to, if you win?' You should have seen the look on his face! Like it had never occurred to him. And those are the people who win! It makes me sick."

"Well, Nathan Parish is in jail now, if that's any comfort. And some people do give the money to charity."

"But no one's going to give it to us."

"No."

"Dad will probably have to move off-island. Where is he going to go? What's he supposed to do? Start over at age fifty-five in some strange town?

Move in with his brother Bob in Toledo? He'd rather shoot himself."

"I'm sorry. I wish there was something I could do."

"Why does this stuff always happen at the holidays?"

"I don't know."

"Me, either. I didn't mean to trap you like this...I just—I needed to vent, I guess. We'll be okay. Things will work out somehow. I'm going to stop worrying until after Christmas."

"Good idea."

We stood for a moment. I decided to shift the subject. "How's life in Hollywood?" She had moved out to Los Angeles at the end of the summer.

"It's good. I get to sit around and draw all day. And in my free time I do more drawings. I just did the storyboards for one of Jared's scripts. He thinks it will help him sell it, if people can visualize the story."

Jared Bromley had struck out for California at the same time Alana did. I often wondered if they'd get together. "He making any progress?"

"Too soon to tell. I'll keep you posted, though."

I gave her a quick hug. "Do that. Listen, your dad's a great guy. I've got his back."

She pulled away gently and spoke to the gravel driveway. "That's nice, but I don't think that's enough. He's being attacked from all sides, you know? Not just the back. From the front and left and right and above and below, and he's stopped fighting. I feel like he's given up. That's what I hate the most."

There was nothing more to say. I left her there and walked back to my cruiser. I could feel the irony of the season. I'd be wearing the Santa suit tomorrow, but that didn't mean I had anything in my bag that could help anyone.

Chapter Six

Grace Notes

I couldn't even get my son a dog, which would have made me an instant household Santa Claus. But it was out of the question for a lot of reasons. My ex-wife, Miranda, a real estate agent, hated dogs. They ruined the resale value of houses, including the house I was about to start renting. They destroyed the finish on antique floors and left hair on every surface.

We lived separately, of course, but Miranda's canine ban meant that I'd have no easy place to kennel a dog if I had to travel; and it would create one more black mark against their mother in the children's eyes. I was meticulous about my verbal neutrality, resisting all temptations to mock or insult Miranda—not even the occasional eye-roll or sigh escaped my vigilant self-mastery. Part of that truce involved maintaining a united front on child-rearing issues. Getting a dog in the face of her strident objections would have knocked down our cautious balancing act, like that Nantucket Whalers wide-receiver, pushed out of bounds last season, who reeled into a teetering pyramid of cheerleaders.

Not a pretty sight.

Then there was the work involved. My mother had let me have a dog when I was a kid, and even let me think that I was doing most of the maintenance. When I got older she told me the truth. Most of the day-to-day efforts of pet ownership had fallen to her, and would inevitably fall to me the same way, regardless of my kids' good intentions.

I didn't have time for a dog. People said a puppy was as much work as a new baby. That was a nice experience for the childless, but I'd been there and done that. Twice. And a dog was never going to grow up into someone more interesting, or take care of me in my old age, which, as my mother liked to say, "starts next week."

"But the good news is—no college tuition!" Tim said to me in the kitchen that Friday night, as I threw dinner together.

"And no freaking out when they're driving at night for the first time."

"Dogs do want to drive, though," Carrie pointed out. "They always sit behind the wheel when you leave them alone in a car, looking sort of hopeful."

The spaghetti was ready. I dumped in the

sauce I'd been heating on the stove (Silver Palate Thick and Sassy, FYI), and pulled the garlic bread out of the oven. The salad—mescal greens and a casual olive oil balsamic vinaigrette—was already on the table. As we sat down I said, "We can have the chocolates Carrie got from her secret admirer for dessert." The tin from Sweet Inspirations had been left on her homeroom desk.

"I'm not opening it," she said. "It gives me the creeps."

"Carrie has a boyfriend, Carrie has a boy-friend," Tim chanted, though with a sly smile, to distance himself a little from the childish taunt.

"No, Carrie has a stalker," she corrected him. An idea struck her and she turned to me. "You could get fingerprints off the tin and find out who it is."

"Well—"

"You fingerprinted Tim's answer sheet."

"Did you find anything out, Dad?" Tim chimed in.

"No matches," I told him. "And no unofficial snooping for you," I said to Carrie

"But it would be educational, Dad. I'd learn about police procedure. And we could bond!"

"I'll think about it."

"Yay!"

"I didn't say I'd do it."

"But you always wind up doing the thing

when you say that. It's Daddy code. So you can cave without looking bad."

"You shouldn't have told me that. Now I have to say no."

"Uh huh. You look even worse if you say no now—'cause you're trying to look like you're not spoiling us, when you totally are. So it looks like you're ashamed of yourself. If you say yes, it shows you have rules, even if they're weird lame rules."

Tim grinned. "Checkmate!"

I shrugged and said what any father would have said at that point. "Eat your dinner, smart-ass."

"So you'll check the prints?"

"What do you think? I've been checkmated."

"Yay!"

"I think you have good rules, Dad," Tim said.

"Well, thank you."

Carrie blew out a contemptuous breath. "Suck-up."

"You should try it sometime," I said. "Suck-ups go far in this world."

She gave me what must have been her idea of the perfect suck-up's smile. "Okay, Dad! That's a great idea. You're so smart. And worldly!"

"Eat."

We attacked the food in silence for a while.

"Any news from your Instagram account?" I asked Carrie as we cleared the table.

"I hate all of them. They're such bitches!"

"Carrie!"

"Well, they are. They've basically forced me out of the Accidentals, and I sing better than any of them. Well, except for Bessie Trott."

"Forced you?"

"They just make it horrible to be there, so…"

"Can't you talk to Mrs. Brock? She ought to be able to—"

"Dad. Forget it. She needs a cluestick. She wouldn't know what was going on if you—I can't even…anyway, no one wants Mrs. Brock on their side! I might as well just check out of school forever."

"So what are you going to do?"

"I don't know. Obviously. Nothing I guess."

I ran the water and starting piling the plates in the sink. Tim spooned the leftover pasta into a Tupperware bowl.

"I have an idea," I said

"Oh no."

"Kill them all. Like in *Heathers*?" said Tim. "But we could make the murders look like accidents! Like in one of Jane's novels."

"She only did that once."

"But it was really cool."

"Maybe, but I have a real idea."

"I'm going to hate this," Carrie said.

"Look, this cool group with the Instagram feeds, that's like—ten girls, tops. Right?"

"I guess."

"So there are lots of other girls in your class. They're not cool and mean and fashion-forward or whatever, but they do exist."

"Yeah, so what?"

"And I bet some of them can sing. They probably didn't even try out for the Accidentals because they knew it was hopeless and your Instagram pals would make their lives miserable."

"So I'm supposed to be friends with a bunch of gleebs?"

"Gleebs?"

"Dorks, dweebs, losers—whatever."

I rinsed a plate and handed it to her to dry. "You," I pronounced, when we were each holding a side, "are a hypocrite."

She snatched the plate away from me. "I am not!"

I was loving this. "You are. You are a total hypocrite. 'Dad, you say recycling is so important and then you just stuff a plastic milk bottle in the garbage. Dad, you say you care about pollution and then you drive the biggest gas-guzzling car on the planet.' Etcetera." It was her favorite line of attack, had been since she hit puberty. "Let me just add, you say it's terrible for girls to ostracize each other, and that's exactly what you're doing yourself."

We washed dishes in silence for a while. I knew better than to press my advantage. Carrie had a lot to think about and even Tim knew enough to stay out of it.

"So what would a non-hypocrite do?" she asked finally.

"You know what's odd? There's no word for that in English. For—non-hypocrite. Makes you wonder."

"Yeah, but anyway—"

"Hold auditions. Start your own singing group. I even have a better name for it than the Naturals or the Accidentals—the Grace Notes! What do you think?"

She nodded, putting away the last plate. "Well, it is a good name."

"Who knows—maybe some of those gleebs might turn out to be pretty cool themselves."

"You could call it the Gleeb Club," Tim said. "A glee club for losers!"

Carrie squinted at him. "We get it. Dad's name is better."

I kept my poker face. Unlike the fat hapless patriarch of Jane's Christmas play, I was doing all right—keeping peace among the elves, mediating the reindeer pecking order.

I might turn out to be a pretty good Santa Claus after all.

Chapter Seven

The Ghost of Christmas Present

"Take care of yourself, Mr. Sprockett," said the orthopedic surgeon, rising to shake Arnold's hand. Kuhn, that was his name—Anders Kuhn, the top knee man in Boston, supposedly, head of the Department at Brigham and Women's Hospital, almost a celebrity after that article in *Time* magazine about his revolutionary approach to ligament repair. Not to mention that "Forty Under Forty" piece in the AMA journal that Dr. Lepore had shown him. Tim Lepore had a passion for surgery and he knew the field—much more so than the average Nantucket GP. His quiet "Kuhn knows his shit" spoke volumes.

Arnold rose also, clearly dismissed, and took the slim balding doctor's hand, a strong grip for such a flimsy-looking fellow, and said, "Thank you" to the thick glasses. A blade of light from the open window glared against the lenses. Arnold couldn't see his eyes.

Why did people always say "Take care of yourself" at moments like this? Maybe it was because you both knew they weren't going to take care of you, and the gentle kiss-off made them sound sympathetic.

Arnold Sprockett was tired of sympathy. Sympathy didn't help. In fact, this was the dark secret of tragedy and loss, sympathy just made things worse. Your show of pity marked territory; it planted your flag on the happy side of hazard. It gloated: "This happened to you not me. I turn my head and your calamity disappears, while my charmed life continues, undisturbed."

That was what had made Dr. Lepore's brusque "Your son may never walk again without crutches. Anyway, his football days are over" so refreshing. Lepore respected him enough to assume he could cope with the truth. Lepore wasn't watching Arnold's son, Nat, from a distance, calibrating his own good fortune with the instrument of Nat's pain. Lepore was on Arnold's side. Lepore actually cared, which was more than Arnold could say for the famous and prominent Dr. Anders Kuhn.

The renowned surgeon had a keen interest, but not in Arnold's son, not in any individual patient. They were anonymous, interchangeable, the raw material of the work itself, the tendons he could repair, the techniques he could devise. That was what mattered, along with the publications, the publicity, the prestige. And of course, the money. Those big checks from the insurance companies. Can't forget them! Those his-and-hers Beemers and the summer house in Montauk don't pay for themselves.

Unless you win the lottery. That was what Arnold needed, he thought to himself as he trudged down the caustically overlit hospital corridor, his shoes squeaking on the polished linoleum, announcing his arrival at each room packed with someone else's misery, at the nurses' station, at the elevator, the big metal space deep enough for a gurney, with framed notices telling him to cover his mouth when he coughed and advising him of his patient's rights in tiny print that no one ever read anyway, like the tiny print on his insurance policy that might as well have said "No claim by you will be paid."

He had chosen the highest possible deductible for the smallest possible family premium, because he couldn't afford it at all, but the State of Massachusetts said he had to carry insurance or he'd be penalized on his taxes. Besides, who really believes they're going to get sick? Who organizes their life around some unknown random catastrophe?

Smart people, that's who.

People whose kids play high school football, people who know the risks, who do the research, who face the facts. Arnold never won that particular staring contest. He blinked, he looked away first. Arnold blinked now as the doors opened onto the hospital's luxurious grand hotel lobby, the perfect façade for people like him, who preferred the illusion, with its three-story glass atrium and elegant seating areas. You could linger there procrastinating for hours before riding down to the narrow two-tone corridors and cramped waiting rooms of radiology, cardiology, oncology, all the ologies of managed mortality.

He was lucky not to be ill, not to be caught in this beeping antiseptic web; he knew that. Crossing the big lobby, stepping out into the brisk December air, felt like a daring escape, a wild bolt to freedom. Invisible fingers seemed to snatch at him as he scurried away. They hadn't snared him this time! But he was trapped just the same. The deductible on his family insurance policy was sixty-five hundred dollars. It might as well have been sixty-five thousand.

He didn't have it. He couldn't pay it.

Which explained that chilly little fare-thee-well as Kuhn closed out their consultation. Why had he even discussed his financial problems with the doctor? Was he expecting a loan? Or could he simply not keep his mouth shut? He had no filter, no self-control. The skinny little man with the big glasses wasn't a priest or a friend or even a counselor. Bemoaning his pathetic circumstances was unseemly, degrading, pointless. But the doctor had given him some pretty good advice, after all.

Take care of yourself. Take care of your son.

Be a man. Man the barricades. Man up.

Walking aimlessly away from the hospital, away from the river, on Francis Street turning into Tremont across Huntington Avenue, he felt panic squeezing his skull, the headache he had damped down with three aspirin raging again, spiked by panic and despair.

He tucked into the hood of his NY Giants sweatshirt but the wind pushed it off, twice, three times. He knew the bulky cover-up made him a pariah in Boston, but that was fine with him. Some big guy on the boat had glanced at the NYG logo and sneered, "Get a real team." Arnold had smiled and replied, "Eighteen and one." That felt good. That was about the only thing that had felt good for quite a while. The wind bared his head again. Fine! Let his ears freeze—what did it matter? He was an animal with a trap-bitten paw, clamped and helpless. But the fox crippled by the metal jaws would at least be spared the additional misery of self-recrimination and guilt.

He had seen the question in the doctor's eyes—how could he have not known something like this might happen? The actuarial tables were available online. Common sense rendered them superfluous anyway. The school certainly knew the liabilities, and they'd been very careful to limit their exposure. Arnold had to sign away his right to sue them before Nat could even be fitted for a uniform.

Somehow he found himself walking past Fenway Park. Nat had such disdain for baseball. He had never shown the slightest interest in Little League. Only football had ever mattered to him, staying up late on Sunday night after two other games, when he was only eight years old, falling asleep in front of the television, no matter how hard he tried to keep his eyes open.

No doubt there was a football metaphor that summed up this situation. Nat could find it for him. That was how his mind worked—"Time to punt it, Dad" when a sale at the store wasn't drawing customers. Or when he'd let Nat run the store last Memorial Day weekend, and then showed up unexpectedly, just as things were getting out of control—"Ah, I get it! The old flea-flicker!"

Well, Arnold was on his own forty-yard line today, two minutes left in the fourth quarter, and a touchdown behind. A wild card game that could put them into the playoffs. "They're controlling their own destiny," that's what the announcers liked to say. He had to take control of his own destiny somehow. He needed a Hail Mary—a long bomb into the end zone, and then a try for the two-point conversion. They could still win by one point! Eli could do it, he'd done it before. Two minutes was plenty of time.

Sixty-five hundred dollars. There had to be a way to scrounge sixty-five hundred dollars. It wasn't even that much money, really. If he finally gave up and sold the old '91 Volkswagen Vanagon, rusting in the backyard for lack of a new exhaust system, he could probably get twenty-five hundred, even with the coolant leak. People loved those vans. His own mechanic had offered him two grand for it, the last time he worked on it. Call it two thousand, then. What else? He had priced Carol's antique Gorham Chantilly Service for eight—four-piece place settings. A few years ago it been worth nine hundred dollars. So, maybe a thousand, now? There was no monogram, the appraiser said that was a good thing. So that made three thousand dollars with the van—thirty-five hundred to go. He had some Stephen King first editions, a signed copy of some J.P. Marquand novel, and a copy of the 1930s *Moby Dick* with Rockwell Kent's woodcut illustrations. It was only worth five hundred dollars on Etsy, but it was priceless to Arnold. His father had bought it the day it came out. Arnold had slipped it out of the house before the bank assessors could find it. The creditors took everything else, including the Steinway piano and the statuettes of Napoleonic generals (Ney, Turenne, de Saxe, Massena) that had stood guard on the mantelpiece for as long as Arnold could remember.

Arnold yanked himself back to the present. The rest of his rare book collection—he might clear another thousand there, if he got lucky. So, four thousand dollars. They could have a yard sale, but it was the wrong season and most of their stuff was junk anyway.

He was still twenty-five hundred dollars short. They kept a pathetic thousand dollars in the savings account—that would take the bill down to fifteen hundred.

That was where he hit the wall.

There was his family, and Carol's family. But her parents had their own medical expenses and Carol's sister was always asking Arnold for loans. It was tough making ends meet as a social worker, and although she was running a program now, it didn't seem to make any difference. Philadelphia was an expensive city.

His parents were dead and the whole estate, such as it was, had been sucked up by the creditors. All but the Melville! And Arnold's brother, Ted, had helped them dodge the credit card vultures. "Those are unsecured loans. Just ignore them," Ted had scoffed. And he was right. They threatened court action, but Ted showed up for the hearing, and the lawyers had folded when he asked for documentation. Of course there was no documentation—those debts had been bought and sold so many times they were just names on a spreadsheet. "I should run up some new credit card debt and do this again," Ted had gloated.

Now Arnold was wishing he had. Instead, Ted had made reckless investments—hydrogen-fusion energy companies, outer space tourism start-ups. He was always "ahead of his time," but that wasn't going to help Arnold right now. When they last spoke, Ted had been looking for seed money to develop a product that, as far as Arnold could tell, was basically an "all food groups" hard candy for people who didn't have time to eat.

Worst idea ever, and it certainly hadn't made Ted into a millionaire with fifteen-hundred dollars to spare. Or fifteen dollars. Or fifteen cents. So, family was out.

He thought about his friends. Why didn't he have more of them? Why didn't he have any rich ones? Rich people were stingy, rich friends were reluctant to cross the "charity line," as Ted called it (his own rich friends had never ponied up a dime).

But Arnold was willing to beg. The money wasn't for him. It was for his son. That had to make a difference. But there was no one to ask. Everyone he knew was scrambling, just the way he was.

A credit card advance? He was maxed out.

A scratch ticket? Make me laugh.

A smash-and-grab convenience store heist? But he knew he could never pull that off. He was a coward, and a bumbler. There were other crimes, though, white-collar crimes. He considered embezzlement but the sad fact stared him down. He'd be caught. Jackson Blum's computers kept track of every transaction at the store, down to the penny, and Blum studied every day's take, marked down in a big ledger he kept in his desk with the words "BEAT YESTERDAY" embossed on the cover in gold. Arnold cashed out the store every evening—if he was ten cents off calculating the receipts, he'd hear about it. He supposed he could skim some money off the top if he were smarter, but were he smarter he wouldn't be in this position. No, he was stupid and shortsighted and he'd been functioning on some kind of crude day-to-day survival terms, only paying his taxes after every extension expired, taking out a third mortgage to pay off a fourth credit card, ducking, dancing, dodging, waiting for something to change.

Well, something had changed at last—a very

small something: the cruciate ligament in his son's knee. Not exactly the change he'd been hoping for.

Waiting at a red light, he added up his financials.

He still needed fifteen-hundred dollars.

And he needed it fast.

"The sooner we can perform the operation, the better the chances for a positive outcome," Kuhn had said before Arnold had blurted out his money woes. "Ideally, we would have had your boy on the table the afternoon of the incident. Of course there's nothing to be done about that now. But every moment counts."

And how long was a moment, exactly? Ten seconds? A minute? Five minutes? And how many of these moments remained before Nat's injuries became inoperable? Arnold wanted to know. The clock was ticking, the little red digital readout in his head blinking its way to zero. He could see the digits so clearly, the prissy engineer's efficiency of them, only the necessary little dashes changing, one at the bottom swinging up to turn the zero into a nine, a single replacement turning the nine into an eight—no wasted pixels, smooth and elegant where his life was a mess, but counting down just the same.

How did fund-raisers raise funds? They talked to rich people. Nantucket was squirming with rich people, bulging with them, but that didn't help Arnold. He didn't sip Dark 'N' Stormies at their cocktail parties, or eat lunch at their clubs. He didn't sail, he didn't play tennis, he didn't fish. He never played golf or bocce or croquet. There were paddleball courts somewhere mid-island but that was another club he had never joined, along with the health club and the garden club.

He was a clerk. He took those people's money and wrapped up their bathing trunks or their baseball mitts and handed them the change. He wasn't even human to them. If Blum replaced him with a robot, no one would even notice. Or they might actually prefer it! And Blum would do it if he could.

Blum! If you like irony, here was a good slice of it: the only authentically wealthy individual he'd ever known well enough to ask for a loan was Blum himself—his boss, who wanted him to work Christmas Day and hadn't given him a raise in two years. Still, what could fifteen-hundred dollars mean to Blum? Nothing. But it could help Arnold so much; it could rescue an innocent boy's future. That had to be a different category of expenditure—true charity in the season that celebrated it. The Santas in front of department stores collected for the Salvation Army. *The New York Times* had its Neediest Families donation drive. That was the Christmas spirit at work.

Well, this year the Sprocketts were one of Nantucket's neediest families. How could Blum not see that? How could he not want to help, when helping would cost him so little? He was always holding forth about efficiency and cost-effectiveness—what could be more cost-effective than this?

Fifteen-hundred dollars for a boy's future.

Arnold stopped walking, leaned against a parked van, and let the crowds jostle past him. This was a bad idea. This was a worse idea even than his brother Ted's all-food-group candy. Anyway, he had one more possibility, one more shot to take.

No time like the present.

He pushed his full weight onto his feet and starting walking back to the hospital.

• • ● • •

Althea Rose McCandless was the deputy administrator for Ambulatory Registration and Financial Counseling at Brigham and Women's Hospital. Arnold had spoken to her on the phone several times, but she had been brusque and impatient, listing forms he needed to fill out, websites he needed to visit, documentation he was required to obtain, before they could even have an intelligent conversation about the disposition of his son's medical treatment.

The whole process had begun to feel like

some distorted nightmare version of *The Wizard of Oz*—from "We're Not in Kansas Anymore" to "Follow the Yellow Brick Road" to "If I Only Had a Brain"…followed alarmingly by "Bring me the Broomstick of The Wicked Witch of the West" and "Surrender Dorothy."

He had pretty much given up on "There's No Place Like Home."

Still, he had completed the forms and gathered the necessary documents. He had turned them in and waited. He had made phone calls and left messages and waited for answers. He knew the suitable quotation for this phase of the process: "Pay no attention to the man behind the curtain."

Enough. It was time to confront the man behind the curtain, or in this case the lady. He was going to make his final plea in person.

He didn't have an appointment and he wound up sitting for two and a half hours in Althea Rose McCandless' big uncomfortable waiting room, perched on a plastic chair, leafing through old issues of *Golf Digest* and *Field & Stream,* reading articles on fly-fishing and putter technology. His mother was right—she used to say he'd read anything just to keep his eyes moving, scooping up the words. "You'd read the back of the U-Haul truck that ran you over," she said once. And he had read plenty of them, sitting in traffic—"Mom's Attic—Extra Space! Secure Tie-Downs, Rub Rails, EZ Load Ramp!" Why did he remember stuff like that? Though he had to admit, the phrases had a certain rhythm, a certain swing. He was chanting the U-Haul truck copy to himself, like a mantra, when they finally called his name.

He stood up stiffly—the chair had strained his back, and using his rolled-up sweatshirt as an improvised lumbar support had proved only partly successful.

Inside her cramped office, Althea Rose McCandless loomed above a cluttered desk strewn with forms, binders, an out-of-date computer monitor, and the remains of her lunch in a plastic box. Her hair was braided into tight perfect cornrows, which together with the matching hoop earrings and silver necklace and sharply tailored blue business suit jacket and white blouse, belied the air of disorganization broadcast by her desk. Arnold had read somewhere that a messy workspace was actually more productive. In any case you wouldn't question Althea Rose McCandless about it. Borderline obese, she carried her weight with authority and style. It was a provocation, a threat—like a Sumo wrestler's belly. You knew he could knock you on your ass with it—a blow from a medicine ball. Althea's bulk was armor, too, all the fashionably swathed heft of her, an unbreach-able redoubt, her narrowed eyes the gun slits in a bunker. By contrast, the fat white women waiting with Arnold on the plastic chairs had just seemed baggy and defeated.

Arnold felt old and flimsy as he eased himself down into the chair across from her.

"So what is the problem, Mr....Sprockett?"

"Arnold Sprockett, yes."

"Your insurance forms are all in order. I see you've been paying your premiums in a timely manner. That's more than I can say for some people."

"Yes, right—thanks...but it's the deductible. I was hoping—"

"Mr. Sprockett, I'll be frank with you. Insur-ance is just a form of legalized gambling. You bet you'll get sick. The carrier bets you'll stay healthy. We load the dice with actuarial tables and research. We analyze rates of disability, morbidity, mortality, fertility, and other contingencies, along with the effects of consumer choice and the geographical distribution of the utilization of medical services and procedures, and the utilization of drugs and therapies." She smiled to soften the jargon. "It's not unlike the way racing touts study the horses. The result, for insurance carriers, has been the Resource-Based Relative Value Scale. It's a lot of number-crunching and statistics, but it works.

That's how these companies stay in business! By contrast, all you have to go on is your bank book and a hunch. You just roll the dice, close your eyes, and pray."

"Yes, well—"

"And this time the dice came up snake eyes. Am I right?"

"Um, I—yes, I guess so. That's one way to put it."

"Yes, indeed. And it looks to me like you have to lay your hands on some six thousand, five hundred dollars."

"That's the thing, Ms. McCandless. I think I can get all but fifteen hundred dollars of it, and I was hoping that we could find some—accommodation, some plan, I guess, some payment plan where I could—"

She was shaking her head as he talked. "That's just not possible, Mr. Sprockett. I think you know that. The terms are stated quite clearly in the policy. The deductible must be paid in full in advance of treatment. That's just the rule."

"But I—"

"Most people set aside their deductible as part of their savings plan, so they'll be prepared for these eventualities."

"Well, I didn't."

"Clearly."

"So, I mean…there's no credit option…like the Care Credit card that dentists offer, or　?"

She turned sideways to him, clicking away at her computer keyboard. "I see you abused your privileges with Care Credit. Your account was turned over to collections fourteen months ago."

"I paid that off!"

"Well, congratulations, but once the lender has sold the debt, the eventual disposition of the liability makes no difference to the offender's credit rating." She smiled. "That ship has sailed, Mr. Sprockett. But the good news is, your standing doesn't make any difference today, since no such remedies are available in any case."

"Great."

She shrugged. "One less thing to worry about."

"So, there's nothing I can do?"

"You could borrow the money."

"I can't. I've already borrowed every penny I could possibly—"

"Or sell something. Some family heirloom. You must have something of value you could bear to part with."

"How do you think I scraped up the five thousand dollars? I'm tapped out, Ms. McCandless. I'm selling everything—and I can't bear to part with any of it."

She sighed. "Well, then. Let me suggest this.

Set aside a small amount from your weekly paycheck—say fifty dollars? Simply by doing that, you could have the whole amount saved in roughly ten months' time."

"But I don't have ten months! Nat needs the operation now."

She settled herself in her chair. "I'm not sure what you want me to do for you, Mr. Sprockett."

"Could you lend me the money?"

"If I could, I'd have been doing that very thing for years, and today I'd be as broke as you are."

He realized he was sitting forward. He eased back and blew out an exhausted breath. "It's just… it seems so…so arbitrary, somehow. I mean, if I had the money I'd just have it, you know? I wouldn't even think about it."

"But you don't. So you think about nothing else."

"Yeah. It' so random, and yet…There's nothing you can do, everything's like—set in stone."

"Tell me about it, mister."

"Hey, I didn't mean—"

"I know what you meant. And that's all right. We all got to do the best with what we was given. When my boss tells me I got to do this and do that, I tell him I don't got to do nothing but stay black and die."

"I wish I felt that way. My life is just a big pile of all the things I have to do."

"Then do the most important one."

"Excuse me?"

"Get up out of here and go to the place you most don't want to go and do the thing you most don't want to do. I don't know where that place is or what that thing is. Only you know that. But you best find it and do it, and do it right quick. Your son needs you and time's wasting."

"Yes, Ma'am."

She laughed out loud. "Now he calls me Ma'm! That's a good sign." She levered herself up and extended her arm across the cluttered desktop. He stood and shook her hand. "You go do what I say."

"I will." Her hand was bigger than his, warm and soft, but her grip made him wince. "Thank you."

They stood for another second then she tilted her head at the door. "Time's wasting, Mr. Sprockett."

He left her office knowing his plan—his last resort. He was bewildered by how fast he had gotten there. It should take longer to reach the end. Better to stop thinking about it. Thinking wasn't going to change things one iota. Iota—the ninth letter in the Greek alphabet, which no one ever noticed, the smallest letter, too, synonymous with the insignificant since Biblical times, the perfect term for Arnold himself.

Nothing had ever made him feel quite as insignificant as the prospect of asking Jackson Blum for money, but there was nowhere else to go now, and no one else to ask. Blum was Althea Rose McCandless' place and person, the dreaded destination, the doomed request. Or perhaps not doomed after all. That was Althea's real message. He decided to take a whiff of hope from her broad serious face and her X-ray smile, breathe in some optimism, let it fill up his chest like the icy Boston air rushing along Francis Street after the overheated lobby.

Yes, he was insignificant. But that could be a good thing! If he made himself insignificant enough, Blum might have mercy. Blum might help him.

After all, it was almost Christmas.

Chapter Eight

Inspector Claus

I was worried when I moved to the island from Los Angeles that life on Nantucket would be uneventful to the point of tedium. Not my most astute prediction. I'd faced killers and pornographers, drug dealers and arsonists. I'd saved the Boston Pops concert from a bombing and watched a seventy-million-dollar mega yacht sink without a trace.

By now I was just hoping for a respite. No such luck.

But I was juggling things pretty well until the armed robbery.

I started the day at the station, running another set of fingerprints. The Whalers' quarterback, Dave Prescott, had been arrested the year before, shoplifting a sweater from Murray's Toggery Shop. When we brought him in he had an ounce of weed in his pocket, along with some rolling papers. It was early November, the height of the football season and the school swept down on us like an old-fashioned New England blizzard, and, like a blizzard, it covered everything up and slowed everything down. Coach Alan Brock—the music teacher's husband—made it clear to the Selectmen, who made it clear to me, that Dave Prescott was not going to be prosecuted. The drugs disappeared and Murray's dropped the charges.

The Whalers didn't have a particularly deep bench, and the backup QB hadn't thrown a pass since Pop Warner. That gave Dave Prescott something like diplomatic immunity—a minor envoy from the sovereign nation of Big Time Sports, able to park where he liked and litter with impunity. If Prescott parlayed his scholarship to Notre Dame into a Heisman Trophy and a slot in the NFL, Nantucket would have another star to brag about. Meanwhile, the Selectmen, the school, Prescott's parents, and the NPD were busily working together to assemble a classic spoiled-brat turbo jock who would no doubt assume cheating on a poetry exam was his right and privilege.

He had walked away from the incident at Murray's clean, but we did get his fingerprints. I ran them against the test answer sheet.

No match.

Well, that made sense. He'd have someone

else do the dirty work. But who? I called the school and got the roll-call list for Tim's poetry class. One name stood out from the list of fifteen kids: Hector Cruz. I hasten to add this had nothing to do with his Hispanic name. I respected those kids. They had been dragged here from Mexico or Ecuador, dumped into an alien world, with both parents working—most of them had two or even three jobs, putting out a lot more energy and ingenuity than their complacent local competition. I remembered sitting at Lola Burger one summer afternoon, having lunch with Mike Henderson, whose painting contracting business was struggling against the low bids and fierce industry of the newcomers. As we watched the rotary traffic, we saw two Hispanic guys on bikes, each one holding one end of a forty-foot extension ladder.

No truck? No problem.

"See?" Mike said. "I can't compete with that."

The kids were on their own a lot of the time—no tutors, no nannies. Thank God for the Boys & Girls Club. But they did all right. On top of everything else, most of them were bilingual, which was more than I could say for my own children—or myself. Hector Cruz was probably reading Frederico Garcia Lorca and Pablo Neruda in the original.

None of that mattered to me. What mattered

to me was football. Hector was on the Whalers—a tight end who Jane Stiles had pointed out to me at one of the home games. I had never cared much for football until I met Jane, but she loved it, any form of it—pro football, college football, arena football, high school football…she even played the Madden video game and was getting Tim hooked on it.

She had won me over to the NFL, but Whalers games remained a duty I tried to shirk. I always made sure to have a fully charged Kindle with me in the stands, but on this occasion, Jane had roused me from my book.

"He's totally free! He's in the clear! Are you blind? There's no coverage on that kid! What the hell? You throw a screen pass? Air it out! HE'S IN THE END ZONE! Jesus, Henry. What the hell is going on out there?"

What was going on? A tight end named Hector Cruz was never getting the football.

"He hasn't had a touch since the West Bridgewater game."

He was a stocky kid, with a crew cut and big ears. He was deceptively fast, though, running clean routes and usually twisting free, waving for a pass that never came.

He was the most likely accomplice in Tim's poetry class. A kid like that would do almost anything to get on the quarterback's good side.

I e-mailed Bissell to send me a picture of Hector and when I opened the attachment a few minutes later I recognized him instantly.

This was the boy who had approached Carrie in the school lobby and then chickened out. He fit the Hispanic profile in one way, at least: he probably came to the country before the age of twelve, so no fingerprints. I checked with INS. The Cruz family paperwork dated from 2007. He would have been eleven when they arrived—just under the wire.

I had a hunch I'd find his fingerprints on that tin of chocolates from Carrie's mystery admirer. If they matched the prints on the test sheet, I'd be closer to my answer. Not quite there, though—I'd still need a verifiable print for Hector, and he was nowhere in the system.

As a cop you were often in this position: knowing something you couldn't quite prove. In a big city with a grown-up who had committed a real crime, the next step would be obvious—take what I had and sweat a confession out of him. But this was a small-town kid and a minor infraction. The situation called for a more delicate touch.

How to get Hector's prints? That was the question. An idea occurred to me but I didn't have time to act on it.

I had a Santa suit to put on.

•• ● ••

Millie Graham was walking up Blum's driveway when I arrived that morning. She ran a crew of house-cleaners, but Blum insisted she clean his mansion herself. It was a compliment and an insult at once, praising her, but snubbing her girls and increasing her workload. Blowing him off wasn't an option. As Millie often pointed out, she didn't have enough customers to pick and choose.

I had been friends with the Graham family since I first arrived on the island, but the affection between us had been clouded lately by the death of Millie's son, Oscar. I had attended the "nine night" memorial service and eventually solved the boy's murder, but none of that had brought us the mythical "closure" we had been taught to expect. I could have let the man behind Oscar's death drown, and I suspect Millie wished I had. It wouldn't have helped, though. I would always be a bitter reminder of her darkest days.

Still, she managed a smile this morning. "Hey, there, Chief. Lovely weather."

"For April! But this is December."

"You're going to be sweating in that Santa suit."

"Tell me about it."

"At least you don't have to come back here and clean this place twice in two days!"

We stopped at the front door while she pulled her keys out of her purse. "You were here yesterday?"

"Yeah, but I had to spend all my time cleaning up that boy's room. Looked like two dogs been fighting in there. But I know it was them boys, though. I spent three hours cleaning the bathroom, scrubbing blood out of the grout with a toothbrush! I tell you, Chief, I never seen such a mess. He lets those kids run wild."

I went on-point, a bird hound set to spring when he hears the goose splash down. "Blood? Really?"

"They were just roughhousing and it got out of hand. That's what Max told me."

"Roughhousing with who?"

"You know, that gang of his, Dave Prescott and the others. That Dave! Sylvester calls him the Boy King of Nantucket. Strutting around like he does. Max takes him in hand, though. Most of the time."

"So…they got into a fight?"

"That they did. And I'll bet you diamonds to dog shit it was about girls or money."

I laughed. "Diamonds to dog shit? I thought it was dollars to donuts."

"Well, Chief, you got to adapt. This is Nantucket. We got five jewelry stores and nobody minds the leash laws."

She let us in. The house had a rumpled look to it, cups and plates and a small saucepan piled in the kitchen sink, pillows and throw blankets from the couch on the living room floor, a coat slumped in a pile below its hook in the front hall. I hung up the coat as Millie tidied the living room. I was checking out the kitchen sink when Blum came downstairs, his arms full of a plastic-draped Santa suit. He'd had it dry-cleaned—hopefully he'd gotten the smell of Homer's cigarettes out of the fabric.

"Let's get this over with," he said by way of greeting.

I gave him a hearty grin, to shame his absurd distemper. "Merry Christmas!"

"Spare me."

I wanted to get upstairs. But how? Perhaps I could play on his home pride. "Do we have time for a quick tour?' I asked. "I'd love to see the house."

"Especially Max's room," Millie said. She winked at me, but Blum missed it.

"Why not? Max needs to get his ass out of bed, anyway. Oh, and Millie? We've talked about this before. Do not leave the vacuum cleaner handle leaning against the wall again. Not if you want to keep cleaning my house. I expect that kind of thing from your people, but not from you." She started to speak, but he raised a hand to cut her off. 'You know better than that."

Chastised, Millie scurried away. Blum turned back to me. "Come on, time is money."

"Is it, though? Wouldn't everyone be rich if that were true? We all have the same twenty-four hours every day."

"But most people waste them, Chief. They're not productive. They're lazy. I make money every second of every day."

"Your investments do, you mean. Your money has an excellent work-ethic. How about you?"

"Look around you. I do fine."

He led me upstairs. Max was in the shower, but if I knew Millie there'd be no evidence of his brawl left between the tiles. His room looked like he'd been tearing it up in his sleep—clothes scattered, bedding twisted, dirty plates piled in the corner, an ashtray full of brown resinated nubbins of rolling paper—roaches. Max had been doing a lot of weed, and the room smelled suspiciously floral. It seemed like a pointless subterfuge if you weren't willing to empty your ashtrays. I shook my head: Millie worked mornings, so this mess represented a single afternoon and evening of teenage entropy. I thought of Carrie and the chaos she left in her wake. It was like living with a cyclone.

A pair of bowls anchored the cluttered desk, one full of coins, the other one heaped with Max's collection of marbles. I felt a quick spark of connection—I had been obsessed with marbles as a kid, and launched an apocalyptic fight with my mother (the worst one of my childhood) when she threw them out as if they were trash just before my fifteenth birthday. Most of them were used (some quite well used) with the predictable moons, chips, and flakes. But I had some real treasures, too, including a Christensen Agate Banded Transparent that someone probably wound up selling for close to a thousand dollars, at least if New York City trash collectors took the active interest in their merchandise that Sam Trikilis did.

I glanced over Max's collection—nothing special: some pretty core swirls and branded opaques, a Lutz or two, and a funny little Sulfide with an off-center whale floating inside—nothing mint or even near-mint. I was turning away from the bowl when a tiny alarm went off in the back of my mind, like the beep of a low battery fire alarm through a closed door. What's wrong with this picture?

"Chief? You want to take a look at the master bedroom? We just installed a whirlpool tub in the bath."

"One second."

I put my back to Blum, reached over to the bowl and plucked the piece I wanted from the bowl. If I saw it, Max would too. It was a small miracle that he hadn't noticed anything yet. Chalk it up to all those doobies.

Blum stepped toward me. "Chief?"

"Let's go," I said. "You're right. We're running late. Time is money."

I took the Santa suit from him, thinking that Blum's "time is money" axiom probably didn't carry much weight at the North Pole, where a fat guy with perversely low-tech transportation managed to deliver billions of presents on five continents in one night. Santa had time management figured out.

• • ● • •

This was the setup. A drive out to Wauwinet, followed by fifteen-minute boat ride down the length of the harbor back to town. I disembarked and walked from the town pier to Blum's with a crowd of kids and their harried parents behind me. Blum had the store arranged with a huge chair draped in red silk and fake white fur. The suit was cumbersome and the fake beard was itchy, but the walk was fun.

Listening to the toy requests tamped my mood down a little. Girls wanted *Frozen* merchandise—dolls and ice castles—despite the movie being more than two years old. Some kids wanted toy smartwatches; the more ambitious ones requested the real thing, along with ominous-sounding toy drones and quadricopters. A lot of grown-ups on the island had real drones, and Blum was one of them. What else? Some kids still wanted LEGOs and playmobils, but a shocking number asked for iPhones and tablet computers.

"We don't make those at the North Pole," I informed one particularly irritating ten-year-old girl wearing a black leather motorcycle jacket over a striped dress with matching leather bows.

"So do you, like, outsource them, or what?" she said.

I sighed. "Right. The elves can only do so much."

I'd been working for about two hours, and the line was still out the door, when Barnaby Toll rushed in and pushed his way to my chair.

"We got an emergency, Chief," he whispered. "They're robbing On Island Gas and they took two hostages."

"What?"

"Charlie Boyce is on the scene, but he's never had to deal with this kind of stuff. He's scared."

I thought for a second. "Okay. You're taking over here."

"Wait—what? No, are you kidding? I can't—"

"Come into the back with me, you can get changed."

"But, I can't—I don't know—How am I—? What are you supposed to do?"

"Just ask the kids what they want and tell them to be good. For goodness sake. I'm not handling hostage negotiations in a Santa suit. Come on." I stood up. "Hold on, everybody. There's going to be a short delay."

We left the grumbling behind us and dodged into the stockroom where I had left my clothes. We changed quickly. It was a relief to disentangle myself from the folds of bulky fabric. The suit that had been too big on me looked like a red tent on Barney, but that was okay. All he had to do was make room on his lap and promise every kid who climbed up there anything they wanted. I knew he had political aspirations—he often talked about running for Selectman.

This would be good practice.

Chapter Nine

Hostage Negotiation

My cell phone went off as I drove toward mid-island—Dan Taylor calling me. "I want total security on this," the Head Selectman was shouting when I touched the steering wheel to open the bluetooth line. It was as if I'd caught him in mid-argument. He didn't even need me to join in anymore. After seven years, he knew my side of every argument. "Radio silence, do you understand me, Kennis? News blackout. Minimal backup, no sirens. No chatter on the police band. You send six cars to a bar fight. Not today! This isn't happening. Not in my town. Not on the busiest shopping day of the year."

I didn't have time to parse that outburst—to mention that a stickup at On Island Gas, across the street from the busiest and most profitable Stop&Shop supermarket on the Eastern Seaboard (almost doubled in size after a year-long renovation) with a parking lot full of people with smartphone cameras, would be impossible to keep secret. The "police band chatter" horse had left the barn, and—FYI—I never sent more than three cars to break up a bar fight.

Also, Nantucket wasn't his town. Not yet.

There were three cruisers parked around the pumps when I pulled in, past the crowd of gawkers, all of them hoping for a selfie with the gas bandits, no doubt. I wondered how the infinitely calibrated sarcasm of Carrie's cool group might respond to a posting like that. "Sweet! Your sweater matches his gun! Totes Bonnie and Clyde LOL."

The official presence at the crime scene: A patrol car with officers Randy Ray and Bob Coffin leaning against the hood and my chief detective, Charlie Boyce, using his own ride, a mud-spattered Jeep wrangler. The last car, a perfectly maintained canary yellow nineties vintage Opel Manta, belonged to my new junior investigator, Karen Gifford. The daughter of a wealthy island family, she had surprised them all by choosing law enforcement as her career. She was smart and eager and felt she had a lot to prove—a good combination, from my point of view.

The car that caught my eye had nothing to do with the police. It was parked behind the new

Cumberland Farms, next to the filling station—a very familiar Chevy Cobalt. I'd run the plates after Tim's driving lesson at Tom Nevers. The vehicle was registered to Stoller Construction, but the insurance was listed for Mike Stoller's son, Mike Jr., who had gotten his Junior Operator License at the end of the summer. Another football player, second-string special teams.

Maybe he was just picking up a microwave hero and a soda at Cumbie's, but the Pressman connection made me doubt it. If the suspected drug deal Tim and I watched at the old Navy base had gone south because the money was short, a quick smash-and-grab at a local gas station might seem like an easy solution, especially if you'd gotten a few too many concussions from those punt return tackles.

Karen came around her cruiser as I approached, a tall girl with short black hair, wide-set eyes, and a tight incision of a mouth that could startle you when she smiled. But she used that smile sparingly, and never at work. All those teeth and dimples would make her look unprofessional. I knew the feeling—I'd spent my first two years on the LAPD frowning. I'm not sure it had much effect on anyone else, but it made me feel better.

"There's two of them," Karen said. "No ID on them yet."

"One of them is named Mike Stoller."

"He—wait. How could you know that?"

"I don't know it. Not for sure." I tilted my head toward the Cumberland Farms parking lot. "But that's his car over there, and I've had my eye on him for a while. Jock, not quite good enough for a college scholarship. Oxy user. Probably started for the pain. Advil only takes you so far."

She stared at the reflecting glass of the station office. "Maybe he works at Cumbie's."

"Maybe."

"Or just shops there."

"The thought occurred to me."

Charlie walked over. "Bullhorn?"

"No. We're supposed to keep this quiet."

He nodded toward the growing crowd at the fringe of Sparks Avenue. "Really?"

"Well, we do the best we can."

"So what do you think?"

"Best to wrap it up quickly. I'm going in."

Karen stepped back, stared at me eye-to-eye. She was exactly my height. "Chief, I'm sorry, but that's a really bad—"

"Shhhhh." I held up one finger. "I'm not sending either of you in. And Dan Taylor won't volunteer. Just a guess."

Charlie smiled at that. He stood still, watching us both. "You sure about this, boss?"

"It's a couple of kids. If you hear gunshots, feel free to storm the place."

Charlie turned to Karen. "He's kidding."

"No, he's not."

I pulled them both toward me in a quick embrace. "You're both right. Now stay alert and let's get some work done."

I walked through the office door, into a blast of warm air scented with new rubber and old gasoline. A big white kid, two smaller Jamaicans. Probably neighbors—the Stollers lived on Essex Road.

"Hey, Mike," I said, "too bad about that touchback." He stared at me blankly. "In the Holbrook/Avon game. I thought you had that one for sure." Jane had described the game to me, a memorable loss because of the escalating missed routes, tipped passes, bungled running plays, penalties, and injuries that made it a standout calamity in an unhappy season.

Stoller obviously didn't want to be reminded. "I slipped."

So it was him. "Football in the rain," I commiserated. "Tough for everybody."

He was clutching a Springfield XDs .45 ACP—a small lightweight gun, smooth to conceal—just an inch wide—and easy to shoot. But those 45-caliber bullets could do some serious damage. He swung the gun to point at me. I hated that. You've probably never had a loaded gun pointed at you, or looked into that black metal ring that needs one twitch of a finger muscle to ruin your life or end it. I have, too many times. It ages you. It kills you in small ways, even if the gun never discharges.

But of course you can't let any of those feelings show. Especially with a drug-tainted, hormone-addled adolescent punk like Stoller.

"That gun cost more than you'd ever make on this robbery," I pointed out.

"Says who?" His voice was thin and brittle, puddle ice that cracked when you stepped on it.

"Look it up. That's about five hundred dollars, new. I doubt there's half that in the cash register."

"A hundred and fifty-four bucks," the attendant said. A heavyset guy in a Toscana sweat shirt and jeans, late fifties, balding, just wanting to get things back to normal.

Yeah, well. Join the club.

"But it doesn't matter because you didn't pay for the gun. It's your dad's, right? Swiped out of his gun safe. Nice work, getting the combination. Though I doubt Dad will give you extra points for that trick."

"Shut up!" He spun back on the clerk. "Give me the money. Now!"

"Mike," I said. "You haven't thought this

through. If you take the money you'll be arrested within the hour. We know your address, your car's parked in front of Cumbie's and even if you found a clean vehicle, or managed to steal one, there's nowhere to go. We have the boat docks and the airport covered. Unless you're planning to swim to Hyannis, you're stuck here. But you got lucky today. We want to close this incident down and forget about it. So that gives you a choice. You're a minor, this is a first offense. Put the gun down and come with me. I'll book you at the station, but those records are sealed. You'll get six months' probation and a second chance. But if you touch that money you're going to jail. And if you pull that trigger you'll be tried as an adult. You'll wind up in Walpole with the adult population, and you don't want that."

Okay, I exaggerated a little, there. He'd have to kill someone to be tried as an adult in Massachusetts. But Mike didn't know that. And I have poetic license—at least in my day job. Getting one for your actual poetry requires a road test.

Mike looked from me to the clerk to his silent Jamaican friends—and back to me. His little caper had already failed, because of the silent alarm they'd installed a couple of years ago. You pushed a button under the counter and the alarm registered at the police station, which was less than a minute away, disregarding traffic. And my cops loved disregarding traffic.

"Okay," Mike said.

He handed me the gun, and it was over. I used the phone behind the counter to call Charlie's cell. No police band, no walkie talkies. "Get in here," I said when he came on the line. "We're taking them out the back."

I walked around to the front after Charlie took the kids away.

"What's next?" Karen asked.

"Crowd control."

We walked past the two rows of pumps to the street. The patrol officers had the lookie-loos contained but they weren't going anywhere. Didn't they have Christmas strolling to do?

I addressed the crowd. "Nothing happening here, folks. Couple of kids playing a prank. It takes more than a water pistol and an attitude to scare an old Nantucketer. Right now, Chester in there has a wet shirt, a story to tell at dinner, and a gas station that's losing money because you're all blocking the entrance. So move along. Go back to town. The stores are serving hot cider."

As the group dispersed, picking their way back to the Stop&Shop parking lot through the traffic on Sparks Avenue, Karen stepped up to me.

"You are a liar!"

"What can I say? I was married for twelve years. You develop skills."

David Trezize separated himself from the throng and strolled up to me, against the outgoing pedestrian tide. I should have known he'd be there. David ran the upstart local paper and he rarely missed a story. He used social media, always tracking dozens of Snapchat and Twitter and Instagram, Facebook, and Reddit accounts, all of them flagged for keywords like "robbery," "assault," and "domestic disturbance." He wasn't likely to overlook a small circus like this one.

"Hey, Chief," he said.

"David."

"Hey, Karen."

She turned to me. "Are you talking to the press?"

"She's still mad because I blew the whistle on her Nantucket Food Pantry bake sale, back in high school. Mr. Bargusfelder…was that his name?"

"Argusfelder," Karen said.

"Right. This guy was the caretaker for a couple of hundred houses—though how that even works, I still have no idea. I guess he did a drive-by every now and then. The twenty-twenty test. It looks good from twenty feet away, at twenty miles an hour. Anyway, he kept all the money from the bake sale and gave the Food Pantry canned goods he looted from his customers' houses."

"He was broke. His wife was sick."

"He was a crook! One of the food bank women—Dottie Clutter, she was a friend of my mom's—she noticed when he brought in a haul of canned abalone and escargots and chestnuts and foie gras, and God-knows-what other expensive crap. She knew no one at school contributed that kind of stuff. I heard her talking to my mom—"

"You eavesdropped on the extension!"

"Yeah. We still had a landline in those days. So I started poking around."

"And got Mr. Argusfelder fired," Karen finished for him.

"He deserved it. He was a dick. I dropped my pencil during a math test and he wouldn't let me pick it up. Seriously. He said, 'It can't fall any farther'—whatever that was supposed to mean. I didn't think a hole was going to open up in the floor. I just wanted to finish the test. Then he gives me an incomplete. Worst teacher ever. And a crook."

"David has always prided himself on his balanced and unbiased reporting," Karen said.

"Very funny. Am I biased? Fucking right, I am. I go after the crooks and liars. I want to see justice done. You want to know the 'he-said-she-said' with that Argusfelder story? 'Guilty' and 'Great job!' The 'he' was that judge that sent that bum to prison. 'She' was the school superintendent who gave me the Good Citizenship award. I still have the pin! Balanced reporting. Forget balanced reporting. Balance is for acrobats."

She slipped him a sarcastic half-smile. "That could be your new slogan." She turned to me. "The kids all hated him after that. Mr. Argusfelder was such a sweet guy. The rich people never missed the stuff, the Food Pantry customers got some treats, and Mr. Argusfelder could afford all those trips to visit his wife at Mass General. It was a win for everyone, until David wrecked it. The rumor was, that's why the family moved to New York."

"My dad got a great job. But I was happy to go. Most kids dread changing schools. I had to go take summer classes to catch up. Dalton was a real school. That was a shock. Didn't matter—I was thrilled to get away from this place. I swore I'd never come back."

"But you did," Karen said. "People always do."

David put his back to her. "So, what really happened, Chief? Did that kid have a gun?"

"Just a toy, David. It was a harmless prank. A false alarm."

"Why don't I believe you?"

"Because you're smart. And that's also why

you're going to leave this alone. When I have a real story, I'll tell you. I always do."

That mollified him but I wanted this particular real story more than he did. Why were the kids robbing the station at all? I had my suspicions but I wanted them confirmed.

I asked Stoller myself, half an hour later. He sat across from me in the main interview room. No filming or recording, no lawyers. After a quick cup of coffee with the judge, the prosecutor, and the court-appointed defense counsel, Mike's probation hearing was set for the new year—that is, after the holidays—and we all agreed to release him on his own recognizance, if he agreed to take a guilty plea and talk to me before we cut him loose.

"So—why?" I asked him. "What was so urgent you needed that hundred and fifty bucks today?"

"I didn't know that was all he had. I heard there was a grand in the register."

"Why? It's all credit card transactions at that place."

"Oh, yeah. I didn't think of that."

This kid didn't think of much. We were getting off-topic. "Why did you want the money, Mike?"

"Come on."

"Drugs?"

"It's December on Nantucket. What else are you going to buy?"

"Books? A Netflix subscription? Season tickets to the Boston Ballet?"

"Yeah, right. But I already got that stuff."

That tricked a laugh out of me. He laughed, too, startled by my reaction. Then we settled back. He pushed against the edge of the table, setting his chair on two legs and rocking a little.

"Who were you buying from?"

"I can't tell you that."

"Really? You're that scared of him?"

"I never said him."

"Him or her."

"Right."

"So, what do you think this person would do to you?"

"People like that—they have their ways."

"Like what?"

"He'd send somebody. He can afford to pay."

"Or she can."

He smiled. "Right. He or she."

I sat forward, rested my forearms the table. "Let's do this, Mike. Then we can both go home. I'll say a name and if it's the right name you just sit there and say nothing, and then if anyone asks you can say you said nothing and you can say that under oath. Because it'll be true. How about it?"

He grinned. "I'm not saying a word."

"Atta boy." He watched me, waiting. I let

him wait a few seconds, then gave him the name. "Pressman."

He said nothing.

"Gary Pressman."

Still nothing. I scraped my chair back and stood up. "Thanks, Mike. You're free to go."

Chapter Ten

On Tuckernuck Island

It was time to pay a visit to Gary Pressman. I didn't have enough evidence for a warrant, but if he really did have a massive supply of opioids in stock out there on Tuckernuck, I needed to stop him from selling it. I'd done my research on the guy. Without judicial authority, guns, or handcuffs, I still had a few tools at my disposal—intimidation and persuasion, shaming and praise, threats and deception. The trick was to use them all at once, like Lyndon Johnson in the Senate cloakroom, manhandling a critical vote from a cringing colleague. It was as much performance art as police work: Good cop, bad cop, fatherly cop, flattering cop, cool cop, crazy cop, crooked cop—all the cops rolled into one.

I couldn't arrest him, but I might just confuse him into submission.

I called Karen Gifford into my office a few

minutes later. Her family had a house on Tucker-nuck and she knew our pilot fish island better than anyone else at the station. Haden Krakauer went over once a year for the Christmas bird count, but apart from those grueling three-night stays in houses with no heat, the little island was as foreign to him as to most Nantucketers. I knew he'd feel somewhat miffed to be excluded from the excursion—he had seniority, after all, as well as a long-standing friendship with me. I thought of Barton Manges, the cinematographer for the first of the only two movies my father ever directed. Flying to New York for location shooting, I sat next to my dad, and got the window seat, no less. I never thought about it, and evidently neither had my father, but Manges took the seating arrangement as a devastating slight. He always sat next to the director on the plane.

My dad just shrugged. "Now he tells me."

Much in the same way, Haden had gotten used to being my wingman. But I wanted him at the station when I was gone, and I didn't like showing up in a gang at Pressman's house. It was a two-person job. Karen and I made a less-threatening couple. And I thought she might learn something.

"No problem," Haden said when I laid out the plan. Which meant there was a huge problem. It was like dealing with my kids. And, as with them, often the best way to deal with a problem was not to.

"Great!" I chirped, and got the hell out of there.

"So how do you get out to Tuckernuck?" I asked Karen when she was seated in my office with a cup of coffee. "Do you have a boat?"

"My family does. I hitch a ride with a scalloper. Or just call the Pereiras. Sal and Joey Pereira? They pretty much have a monopoly on transportation, to and from. My dad let someone bring over some parts for our generator back in the nineties. He wound up feuding with Sal for a decade over it. They're pretty touchy over there."

I nodded. "How many people actually live on the island?"

"I don't know—maybe ten families? Sal and Joey live there year-round, and Gary. A couple of kids stayed out there last winter. Some kind of project for college. But that's about it. Tuckernuck people don't like visitors. It's not exactly a tourist spot. You show up and everybody knows it. This time of year the scallopers'll drop the dime on you. The Land Bank was going to buy a big piece of property a few years ago, but the homeowners got together and outbid them." She laughed, a rueful chuckle. "No way that was ever going to happen.

They don't like strangers and they don't like people traipsing around their land."

"So what do they like?"

"Privacy. And quiet. Tuckernuck is like—Nantucket, a hundred years ago. That's what they like."

I nodded. "It sounds pretty good."

"You'll see for yourself. Let me just call Sal. He'll meet us at Jackson Point. Normally, he charges a hundred dollars for the trip, but he'll take us for free."

"Because I'm the police chief?"

"Uh, no. Because he has a crush on me. Sorry."

It was windy and cold at Jackson Point—officially named the S. Byron Coffin Boat Landing—and a thin sleet had started spitting out of the northeast. Sal kept us waiting for ten minutes and I wandered around the dirt circle that faced the boat ramp with Madaket Harbor gray and milling beyond it and the houses that dotted the shoreline trailing east beyond that. The summer moorings had been pulled, the scallopers were finished for the day, and the houses were boarded-up for the winter—a bleak vista. I said as much to Karen and got one of those spectacular smiles for my trouble.

"Heaven," she said.

A dark spot on the dirt caught my eye. "Do people park here?"

"No, that's another sore spot. The Pereiras

don't like to see cars here and none of us want people staying overnight on Tuckernuck. It's not a campground."

I was still studying the patch of dirt. "I don't recall any complaint calls."

She coughed out a little laugh. "We don't call the police. We deal with these things ourselves."

"That sounds ominous."

"Just bring a can of fix-a-flat if you plan to leave your car here. Or make that a jack and a spare. We cut the sidewalls."

"'We,' Sergeant Gifford?"

"By 'we' I mean 'they.' And by 'they' I mean 'the alleged perpetrators,' which, by the way, I always thought would be a great name for a street gang."

"A Tuckernuck street gang?"

"Right. All we need is a street."

I pulled my Swiss Army knife and an evidence bag out of my coat pocket, and kneeled down over the stain on the dirt. A useful law enforcement tip: always carry a Swiss Army knife and some evidence bags—and not just when you're dropping in on a suspected drug dealer. You never know when some evidence is going to turn up.

"What is it?" Karen asked.

I cut around the stain. "It looks like an oil leak. So somebody was parked here for a while. And drove away with their tires intact."

I slipped my hand under the loose pancake of dirt and nudged it into the plastic bag. As I stood up, sealing it, Sal's battered but sturdy scallop boat nudged up to the landing. I scrambled aboard as Sal offered his hand to Karen. He was a short stocky tree stump of a man in an old barn jacket, jeans, and heavy rubber boots. When we were headed back out to open water, he looked me over and shrugged dismissively. "Washashore."

"I've lived here for almost ten years," I protested.

"Rounding up from seven," Karen smiled. "Salvadore Pereira, this is Police Chief Kennis."

"I know who he is, girl."

We shook hands. His grip was crushing. "Ted McGrady had a real handshake."

Ted was a favorite topic among the old Nantucketers I ran into. I gave Sal the consensus before he could deliver it himself. "I'm sure he was better than me in every other way, too."

I got a grudging smirk, as if he was tasting some new food he wasn't quite sure about—quinoa or seitan. He kept hold of my hand, squinting genially. Maybe all this newfangled food didn't taste so bad after all.

"I dunno. You did all right rounding up them bombers. I knew Fizzy Krakauer didn't have shit to do with all that. And you put away Eddie Delavane. Good riddance to that prick."

"Fizzy" Krakauer. I was definitely going to use that one on Haden, the next time I saw him. Fizzy. Did he drink too many beers as a kid? Or dump Alka-Seltzer in the Summer House pool? I needed to investigate this.

Sal jabbed a finger east. "See that channel between Jackson's Point and Little Neck? That'll take you to Hither Creek and just past it to the Madaket Ditch. My grandfather caught herring in the ditch right up through the fifties. The Indians dug it with the first settlers, believe it or not. The Wampanoags got to fish in it, so them fucking English thought they were giving the redskins the deal of the century. Funny, but Indians didn't see it that way. *Thanks for letting use our own land, assholes.* It was a great spot, though, back in the day. Herring used it on their spring spawning run, saltwater to fresh. No herring anymore. No Wampanoags, either. Them days is dead as driftwood."

He settled in to steering the boat and Karen walked me to the stern. Barely audible over the growl of the engine, she said, "He must really like you! I haven't heard him talk that much since he delivered his father's eulogy. And that was ten years ago."

Sal navigated around East Pond, past the seven rocks, gliding over the shoals. The tide was high and the trip was easy, but the rain picked up and we were all soaked to the skin by the time the Pressman house on its little bluff drifted into view.

As we approached, someone appeared in the backyard, sprinting for the trees. He must have seen us coming and fled out the back door—a man of middle height, with an awkward running style, wearing a gray hoodie with the New York Giants football team NYG logo on the back in dark blue. Brown pants, running shoes of some kind, no visible wristwatch, Caucasian, slightly overweight, late thirties or early forties—that was my best-guess inventory in the six-second window before he disappeared. I glanced over at Karen.

She shrugged. "It's the uniform."

I nodded. "Profiling goes both ways."

"Except they can't stop and frisk us. Or shoot us."

That struck a nerve. "My cops don't do that. I have zero tolerance for that crap. I can fire anyone for any reason at any time without consulting anyone and I will. But I haven't had to because my cops know they're here to help and I don't hire bullies."

"Okay, okay—sorry, Chief. But that guy looked scared."

"Yeah—because he was doing something wrong and we were about to catch him."

The house had its own dock. Sal tied up at

the dock and we walked ashore over the weathered planks, then across the hard-packed sand, to the swath of dune grass and that fronted the house. Pressman came out and stood waiting for us on the big back porch, looking slim and Brooklyn hipster in skinny jeans, basketball sneakers, a lumberjack shirt, and an unbuttoned striped cardigan. He was sporting a perfect stubble, wire-rimmed glasses, and a pork-pie hat. Sitting next to him, banging his short tail on the weathered cedar decking, was a Portuguese water dog. Except for his big stubby head he looked like an unclipped poodle. But I knew better. Water dogs weren't as smart as poodles—some people I knew weren't as smart as poodles—but they were a hell of a lot nicer.

"Stay right there," Pressman said. "Bailey is a trained attack dog."

"No, she isn't," I said.

Sal laughed. "Are you kidding? She licked a burglar to death a few months ago."

"Hey, Sal," Pressman said. He nodded to me. "Chief Kennis. And Karen Gifford, throwing a perfectly good education to waste."

"You sound like my mother."

He grinned. "Girls always say that. I should start sounding like their fathers."

"You'll have to get a PhD in Linguistics to pull

that one off, Gary. And it wouldn't work, anyway."
She shrugged. "No issues. Sorry."

He shrugged. "I'm out of my league. What
the hell, come on in. It's a little rustic out here, I
know. My father installed a gas generator and a
composting toilet, but until the sixties, the family
got by on a kerosene stove, hurricane lamps, and
an outhouse."

I couldn't resist. "So—no cable?"

He looked at me as if I'd inquired about an
ant infestation. "No. We don't have cable television
on Tuckernuck. Thank God." He pushed open the
door and swept his arm toward the house. "Come
in and get dry. It's freezing out there."

I stepped into the big high-ceilinged living
room and walked over to the moor-facing picture
window at the far side. Bailey followed me and
shoved her muzzle into my open palm. Quite the
attack dog. I roughed her up behind the ears and
got her tail thumping again.

The house looked out along the rocky coast
of the little island. Pressman stepped next to me
and pointed toward the water. "Nice fishing on
the striper flats, Chief. Good entertainment if you
don't have a TV."

Closer by, I took in the Tuckernuck moors,
cut with dirt roads, dotted with gray-shingled
unpainted houses, most of them at least a hundred

years old. No power lines, no construction crews, no cars; at this time of year, no people. Just the sandplain grass, the huckleberry, and scrub oak. And, according to Haden Krakauer, the owls.

"It's a time machine," I said to Pressman.

"No. It's the big island that's the time machine—a straight shot into the future. H.G. Wells would have had a good laugh—the Morlocks and the Eloi. Of course, our Morlocks work above ground. And they haven't started eating us. Yet."

"I seem to recall the Eloi were weak and feeble-minded."

"Touche. But they didn't have to deal with our problems—development, immigration—"

"And drugs?"

"Oh, yeah. Drugs are the worst of it."

"Poor Eloi. Well, if you can't beat 'em, join 'em. Right, Gary?"

"Excuse me?"

Time for my LBJ move: threaten, flatter, and ambush and deceive. I put my arm around his shoulders and pulled him close to me. Unfortunately, I didn't tower over him as Johnson would have. But the abrupt physical intimacy would still be weird and unsettling.

"Your family goes back a long way around here, Gary. The name means a lot. You've got it all—memberships at the Yacht Club and Sankaty, two-digit box number in the Main Street Post Office. House in 'Sconset, this place. You're on the board of the Basket Museum and the Theatre Workshop. It would be a pity to lose all that. Disgrace your family, turn yourself into a pariah, not to mention the jail time. You'd be catnip to those lifers at Walpole."

"What the hell are you talking about?"

Threat and flattery were working well.

I turned him loose. He was rattled. I decide to ambush him next.

"I think we saw one of your customers leaving the house when we arrived."

"He—I…what? No—that wasn't—he's just a friend."

"So he came all the way out here just to chat."

"I'm starting a business. I'm looking for investors."

"Really?"

"I have some land in town, I want to open a bowling alley. We haven't had one on-island since 1983. I was born in '82, so I missed out."

Sal had walked over to join us. "It never made any money, kid. Robert Young kept it open for years out of pocket. Like—community service. And that was in the days before kids sat around with their video contraptions all day long."

"We have Wii bowling now," Karen added helpfully.

"It's a lot of square footage for not much return. You really think people are going to give you money for that?"

"Invest money. It's an opportunity."

"Right. Opportunists always talk about opportunities."

"Who said that?"

"Me. So who's your investor?"

"I think he'd like to remain anonymous for now."

"Well, he's one of six Giants fans on the island. He shouldn't be too hard to track down."

"Good luck. He got that sweatshirt from the take-it-or-leave it pile."

"He gets his clothes at the dump? That sounds like kind of a red flag for an investor, Gary."

"Then you don't know New England, Chief."

"He's right about that," Karen said.

This was going nowhere. Time for some deception and persuasion.

"Let's cut to the chase, Gary. I know what you're doing out here. I have a signed confession from Mike Stoller sitting on my desk and he's willing to testify against you. I hit one number on my speed dial, you're going back with me in handcuffs and you're going to be sitting in jail until your trial."

"Bullshit. I'm not going anywhere and if you did arrest me I could make bail in five minutes."

"No, you couldn't."

I parked myself on the windowsill, my back to the view. I inventoried the big room while he absorbed my answer.

The place hadn't been touched since the seventies—barrel-back lounge chairs, wicker magazine racks stuffed with old issues of *Time, House Beautiful,* and the Orvis catalogue; nubby sectional couch with some kind of leather patchwork pillows; walls hung with mirrors and nautical paintings and ugly rectangular multi-frame picture holders with family beach snapshots turning pink in the oval displays. I could see into the dining room, dominated by a Danish modern glass table and steel-tube chairs. There was even a bean-bag chair in the corner. It looked like someone had thrown a leather sheet over a cross-legged Buddha with a tiny head.

Karen stepped over to sit in its lap.

"Don't do that!" Pressman barked at her. She straightened up as if she'd broken a vase. "Sorry," he said. "But that's a collector's item. A Sacco bean-bag designed by Piero Gratti and Cesare Paolino. 1968. They have one in the permanent collection at Museum of Modern Art!"

"Sorry."

"No problem. I just—I feel like a curator here

sometimes. Or one of those guards who won't let you take pictures."

We were drifting off-topic. "Too bad it's not a paying job. You're out of money, Gary," I said. "No donations to the NHA or Maria Mitchell this year. The Boys & Girls Clubs came up empty too. And I know why. You dumped all your money into the stock market just before the crash, and pulled it out before the bull market began. You've been running on fumes ever since. You got cut out of your father's will and you signed a pre-nup with your ex-wife. That's a perfect storm. There's just this house and it goes to the Land Bank when your grandmother dies."

"How—how do you know all this?"

"It's all in the public record, Gary. And you live on Nantucket, which, as far as I can see, makes the NSA surveillance program look like a pair of kids with two Dixie cups and a string."

"I don't have to put up with this! You don't have a warrant."

"No, but I could get one in ten minutes. You don't want that, Gary. Just show us where you keep your stash and we'll work something out."

"Stash? I have no stash."

"Really? You want to do it this way?"

"Search the house. Forget the warrant. Do what you have to do and get out."

So we did.

Bailey followed us around as we unzipped the couch pillows, pulled up the rugs and tested the floorboards, looked behind the picture frames and the mirrors, checked every closet, drawer and cabinet in the house. He had a dusty old wide-body TV—I opened up the back and checked inside— ditto the toilet tank, oven, and every decent-sized container in his refrigerator. I searched the chimney flue with a flashlight, tapped the beams to make sure they were solid, pulled the curtains and the curtain rods. We opened every book on the shelf fat enough to hold drugs in a rectangle of cut-out pages, and probed the interiors of his stereo speakers.

While Karen tossed the attic, I went outside, opened up the generator housing, searched the bulkhead doors, and worked my way down into the basement. I opened every trunk, tackle box, and paint carton down there, along with every rust-rimmed can of paint and five-gallon tub of joint compound. I poked behind the furnace and the boiler, investigated the heating ducts, tapped the walls for hollow spaces. All I got for my trouble was a face full of cobwebs and a nasty chill.

Back inside, Karen's face told the same story. The house was clean.

Except, I knew it wasn't.

There was nothing I could do about my

hunch, though. Pressman had already extended himself well beyond the requirements of the law and, after this fiasco, no judge would even consider issuing a warrant.

"Anything else I can do for you folks?" Pressman asked. He knew I knew the drugs were in the house somewhere, and I knew he knew it. But I was stumped. He'd beaten me, at least for now.

"No thanks," I said. "I appreciate your cooperation."

He offered a cordial fake smile. "Any time."

"I may take you up on that."

"I look forward to it."

Enough. I turned to Karen. "Let's go."

Bailey followed us out of the house and down the porch steps. "Bailey!" Pressman shouted. The dog ignored him. I stopped and got her to sit. I kneeled down and she licked my face. Pressman stormed out with a collar and a leash. "What the hell?"

I set my cheek against her big warm jowl. "We're putting our heads together on this one, Gary," I said.

"Very funny." He attached the collar, clipped on the leash, yanked Bailey away and dragged her inside.

Karen watched them go. "You just made a friend."

"Yeah." Sal stared at the house. "And an enemy."

Chapter Eleven

Surfsliders

"Know your enemy," Sun Tzu suggests in *The Art of War*, and though I had no particular desire to be pals with Gary Pressman, a little more information on the guy couldn't hurt. There were some facts I couldn't retrieve from county records or the Internet. For instance—was he using the name "Surfslider" on the HackAck website? If so I'd have one more scrap of evidence for a possible indictment.

To find out, I decided to check with my own favorite surfslider, Billy Delavane. Stepping onto dry land at Jackson Point, I was right in Billy's neighborhood. I asked Sal to drop Karen off at the town dock and climbed into my cruiser alone. The big SUV undulated over the dirt road puddles and deep "Thank you, Ma'am" craters of Maine Avenue. I had almost arrived at Billy's low-slung shack when

I had to back up and go around the other way. The last bend of the road had disappeared, washed into the sea by the recent storms. Billy would be afloat himself in another year or two if he hadn't bought the parcel behind his house. He could move the structure another acre away from the sea and buy himself another ten years at least.

His pug, Dervish, met me at the door, barking furiously. I thought of the Harbor Fuel guy who had been called to repair Billy's furnace a couple of years before. When Billy got home from work, the house was still cold. He called the company and the secretary pulled the work order. The guy had scrawled "No entry. Angry Pug." Billy was still laughing about that one. Dervish was about as dangerous as Pressman's Portuguese water dog. He twirled around my feet now and leapt up to have the back of his ears rubbed.

Inside, Billy was finishing work on a three-story Victorian dollhouse, complete with gingerbread trim. It looked more like Oak Bluffs on Martha's Vineyard than anything you'd find on Nantucket.

When I pointed that out, he shrugged. "Santa doesn't sweat the details."

That's right—Billy was playing Santa, too. Jane's son, Sam, was seven, big for his age and eager to start Pee Wee football next year, but he still believed—warily, suspiciously—in Santa Claus.

This Christmas was Jane's last shot at keeping the dream alive. His questions last year, worthy of her heroine, Maddy Clark, revealed numerous suspicious inconsistencies: "Why do you and Santa use the same wrapping paper?" "Why does Daddy's handwriting look like Santa's?" "How do elves make video games?" "Deer don't fly. How do reindeer fly?" Then there was the chimney issue, and my favorite, regarding those plates of cookies: "Is Santa diabetic? Is Januvia right for him?"

There were definitely too many pharmaceutical ads on TV, and this proved it.

To keep the thin filament of childish belief from fraying entirely, Jane commissioned her old friend Billy to make an authentic elf-based Christmas present. The dollhouse fit the bill, and Sam loved dollhouses, a predilection he had inherited from his mother. But the store-bought plastic items that survived from her childhood had nothing on Billy's masterpiece. He was sanding the cherry-wood floors in advance of a final coat of urethane when I arrived.

He poured us two cups of coffee from his French press pot and we sat down in a pair of big canvas upholstered armchairs that faced the woodstove. Dervish jumped up and burrowed in beside me.

"Police business?" Billy asked.

"We never sleep."

"You better not. We're having a crime wave around here. Gas station hold-ups and all."

"It was just a prank."

He cocked his head at me. "Really? That's not what I heard."

"From who?"

"The surf grapevine, Chief. Everyone knows Stoller's trying to score some drugs."

"And he can't afford Gary Pressman's prices?"

"Oh, yeah. Pressman. That makes sense. I heard he was trying to sell in bulk, turn himself into a middle-man, get out of the day-to-day street stuff."

"But Pressman's clean. I just came from his house."

"Pressman's smart. He always was. Shrewd. Even back in grade school. He was the kind of kid who'd trade Lincoln Logs for treats and corner the market on snack time cookies. Those pills are out there somewhere, trust me."

"Let's say they are. Trying to buy up a shipment like that sounds like Stoller's going into business for himself."

"Well, someone is. Stoller's not that ambitious. You should see him backing off a double overhead wave. I saw him go over the falls trying that last winter. I picked him out of the whitewater and told him, 'You gotta commit, dude.' He just gave me his all-purpose 'Whatever'. No, if he's making a drug buy, he's doing it for someone else. That's my take."

"But who?

"I don't know. Someone he respects. Someone he's scared of. Someone he's sucking up to."

"Like his quarterback."

Billy nodded. "Could be."

I already suspected that Dave Prescott used other people to do his scut work. Like stealing the answer sheet for a test and planting it in my son's locker.

We sat quietly for a while and sipped our coffee. Dervish squirmed his way onto my lap, and grumbled happily as I petted him.

"Dave Prescott," Billy said, finally. "Dave Prescott."

"He'll be a local hero, if he can learn to throw outside the pocket."

"He's a useless little turd, Chief. You can tell a lot about a person by the way they behave in the water. Prescott drops in on people, cuts them off, runs them down. If he tried that shit at Malibu he'd get his ass kicked."

"You should talk to him."

"I have. He knows the rules. He just doesn't give a shit. I'll bet he's a lousy driver, too. And a big talker whose idea of conversation is rehearsing his next line while he waits for you to shut up. Fuck him."

"Wow. Tell me what you really feel, Billy. Don't hold back."

"I'd like to say he was sweet when he was little, but he's always been a punk. I remember him telling some poor little kid, 'Don't even try to be popular. You'll never be popular. Everyone hates you.' I found the kid crying on the beach. Unbelievable. You don't think of some eight-year-old as having such a strong personality. I felt like saying to Dave, 'Stay unformed for a while! I liked you better when you were unformed.' I'm just kidding myself, though. Truth is, he was probably born that way."

I nodded. "They come out the way they come out."

"I'll tell you something about Dave, though. He's never gonna be the engine. He's strictly the caboose."

"Come on—he's a leader. He's the quarterback."

"Right. The quarterback who never argues with the coach, never changes up the playbook. The kid has never called an audible. Ever. That tells you something."

I finished my coffee, set the mug down on the tile floor beside my chair. "So who's the engine?"

Billy sat forward. "Ever hear of a kid called Maxwell Blum?"

"I was at his house this morning. Homer couldn't do Santa this year, so I took over."

"Did you see the Toys for Tots?"

"Why?"

"Just another rumor. Word was some of those toys were stuffed with more than goose down. Homer gives the right toy to the right kid and someone gets a big pay off."

"So the Toys-for-Tots giveaway was rigged."

"Maybe that's why Homer crapped out. If he didn't want to get involved."

I stood and carried my coffee cup to the kitchen, rinsed it at the sink. "That's crazy."

"I thought so, too. That's why I never mentioned it."

"What was supposed to be in the toys?"

Billy joined me in the kitchen. "Heroin? Diamonds? Little gold lightship baskets? There were lots of theories going around. Rolled up hundred-dollar bills."

"And who put the stuff in there?"

He held up his hands. "Hey, I have no idea. It's just kid talk. Like when they decided that the Porter house on Candlestick Lane was haunted. But I was thinking...someone who wanted fast money to buy Pressman's drugs might take the long shot and start cutting those stuffed animals open. Doesn't matter if it's true. It only matters if some knucklehead believes it."

Cut-up stuffed animals—fur flying, that's what Millie Graham had said after she cleaned Blum's house. I reached into my pocket and pulled out the odd-looking marble I'd taken from the bowl on Max's desk. Now it was clear. I turned the little glass ball over in my fingers, that cheesy song from Rocky III turning my breath staccato in a tuneless whistle.

Millie had cleaned up Max's room, scrubbing and vacuuming and, thanks to her, every trace of his vandalism would have been tidied away—almost every trace.

Billy leaned against the counter and watched me thinking.

"Someone wants to take over Pressman's drug business, or at least partner with him. But it's not Dave Prescott."

Billy nodded. "Okay."

"It's Max, but despite that fact that he comes from one of the richest families on the island, he's vandalizing toys for imaginary contraband."

"Okay."

"Tell me about Max."

"I can tell you this much. His father never lets him have a dime. He's always broke, bumming cigarette money from his friends. So that explains the scavenger hunt. And he grew up with those kinds of games. His father organized an actual scavenger hunt on his birthday every year—you'd see groups of kids traipsing around the island, trying to figure out what he meant by 'Go back to square one, and examine a significant milestone in your life' —until one of them figured out that the next clue was buried under the first milestone after the rotary on Milestone Road. I remember gangs of kids digging up our lot on Paddlefish Row. Then one of them went to Fahey's and asked for caviar. That kind of thing. They're a tricky group, those Blums. They say the old man's father won the store in a game of Liar's Poker. Cheating comes natural to them. So selling drugs? The perfect occupation."

"Maybe Max organized the gas station heist."

"Right—he just sent it down the chain of command. Max was Dave's mentor on the football squad, too. He was quarterback in his senior year. He loved those trick plays—the Statue of Liberty, the quarterback sneak. They could have named that one for him. It was fun to watch, though. Unlike now."

It was cold in the kitchen and it was getting dark outside. Billy walked back to the stove and tossed in a couple of logs. I stood by the window, listening to the surf growl against the south shore.

"Any brothers or sisters?" I asked.

"One brother—Martin. He came out as gay and hasn't come home since."

"Sounds like one big happy family."

"Norman Rockwell meets Edvard Munch."

I walked over and sat down. The stove was kicking out a dense solid heat now. The wind wheezing around the eaves made it feel warmer.

"There's girl problems, though," Billy said. "I hear Dave stole Max's girlfriend. Or maybe it's the other way around. Lizza Coddington. That little triangle's been going on for quite a while. It started out isosceles, went scalene, and now it's all the way to obtuse, if you get what I'm saying."

I had no idea what he was saying. "Hey, I flunked math, Billy."

"Even geometry? Most poets do okay at geometry."

"Not me."

"Well, let's just say their little *Jules and Jim* act has gone from bad to worse. It started when Dave was a sophomore and Max and Lizza were seniors. I heard she hooked up with him just to make Max jealous. It worked but the whole thing got out of control. They've switched partners a few times, and things slide a little more every time one of them cuts in."

"So, if they really are in business that might be a weak spot."

"Bigger businesses have broken up for less."

I stood up. It was time to go. "Time to have a little chat with Maxwell Blum."

"Good idea. But try to do it before Pressman sells all those drugs he doesn't have out on Tuckernuck."

"Right."

I had one more question for him. "Say, do you remember what happened to your uncle Brandon? After he died but before the funeral."

"Word was, Ed broke into the funeral home and grabbed the body. Gave the old boy the burial he wanted. It drove Aunt Betsy crazy. She tried to get Ed arrested but nothing came of it. She moved off-island the next year. "

"Did you help Ed move the body?"

"No way, Chief. I never got involved with my brother's hi-jinks."

He walked me to the door. "So what do you think of the dollhouse?"

"It's awesome, Billy. You'd make a fantastic elf."

Chapter Twelve

Eye of the Tiger

Saturday evening, six-thirty, just before the family sits down to dinner—not the ideal time for a visit from the chief of police. As a lawman you get used to being an unwelcome sight. Sometimes a citizen wins the gamble of crossed paths and a cop saves them from a mugging or a murder; more often we catch them doing something they know is wrong and foolish. Driving drunk, most likely—at least around here. No one wants to see those flashers in the rearview and no one wants to see my face at their door after slipping unscathed through one more precarious day.

But I had taken Billy's words to heart, and if bracing Max Blum could help me close down Pressman's drug operation, it was worth a try.

Marjorie Blum opened the door, flooding the front porch with warm light and the smells of a roast chicken in the oven and a fire in the hearth. A blind man would have thought the house was a perfect holiday refuge. But that impression belied what a quick visual inventory showed. It wasn't just the lack of Christmas decorations—no wreath on the door, no tree in the living room; people often left those details until later in December—what concerned me was the look on Marjorie's face. She didn't look as if she'd been crying—more like she had cried herself out a long time ago, and moved on to the immobility of exhaustion.

"Can I help you, Chief?" she said by way of greeting.

"I don't know. Are you all right? Have you been sleeping?"

She stepped back. "What do you mean? Why would you say something like that?"

"Well…there was a pan of warm milk soaking in the sink this morning. That was my ex-wife's trick when she couldn't sleep."

"I—it's…yes. I have insomnia sometimes. It's hard to turn the brain off. I don't expect much sympathy. People assume when you're rich that you don't have any real problems."

I let the loft of my shoulder tilt my head a little to one side in a gesture of fatalistic commiseration. "Different problems," I said. "That's all. No less real."

"Thank you. I wish money was the answer to all our troubles. Sometimes it just makes everything worse."

"It gives you more time to worry, anyway."

She seemed to wake up, suddenly aware of my awkward physical placement. "I'm sorry. Please— come in. It's freezing out there."

"Thanks."

I stepped inside and unzipped my jacket. The house was big and echoey, sparsely furnished, like a show house set up for the real estate brokers. Millie Graham had done her work well. The place was neat and spotless, now. I preferred the mess. At least the jumble made the place feel inhabited.

"How did the Santa day go? All the kids happy?"

She winced. "Oh, yes. Everyone was very happy. I'm sure they're all going to have a wonderful Christmas. All the happy families."

"Well, that's the idea."

"It looks like you resolved the gas station holdup."

"Just a false alarm. Bad timing."

"Yes. We missed you. And Homer Boyce. Poor Homer."

"If you feel bad for the missing Santa, you might mention it to your husband."

She laughed, a humorless little bleat. "I'll be sure to do that. Did you want to talk to Mr. Blum?"

"I was hoping to see Max, actually."

"He's upstairs, working on his video games."

"I had no idea they were work."

"He doesn't play them, He writes them. The… code…for them. Or so he says. I don't understand any of it. Anyway. Go on up, it doesn't matter. Just—we're eating dinner in half an hour, so…"

"I'll be quick."

I found Max in his room, sitting on his bed with a Apple PowerBook on his lap. "Hey, Max," I said. "I've got something of yours."

He looked up and I threw the little glass ball I'd been carrying around in my pocket since the early morning. He grabbed for it, but it bounced off the heel of his hand and hit the keyboard. It must have hit the worst possible key. "Shit! You just deleted two hours' work."

"Always save your material, Max. Even I know that."

He looked at the little green sphere with the dark oval floating in the center. "What the hell—? This isn't a marble. I've never seen this before."

"Yeah, you have."

"What?"

"When you were tearing apart the Toys-for-Tots

stuffed animals. This looks like the eye of a Steiff tiger, to me."

"I don't understand. What are you—?"

"Millie Graham cleaned up your mess, but she thought the eye was a marble, and she put it away with the rest of them, in your bowl. That's where I found it this morning."

"How did you—what did you—what were you doing in my room?"

"Your father gave me the nickel tour this morning. You were in the shower."

He closed the laptop and set it aside. "So, what are you saying?"

"You heard the idiotic rumor that something valuable was packed into those stuffed animals and tore them apart looking for whatever it was. Which was nothing. The question is why? That's a desperation move and you're one of the richest kids on the island."

"I suppose you've figured that one out, too."

"I asked around. Your parents keep you on a short leash. You never have spending money and you have a big expenditure coming up."

"Really? And what would that be?"

"My guess is drugs."

"Drugs, really? I'm trying to buy drugs?"

"Your friend is. And most people agree that Dave Prescott isn't much of a go-getter."

Max laughed. "Yeah, well. Two never made that claim."

"Two?" The single syllable jarred me, like stepping off an unexpected curb.

"You're supposed to be a civic leader in this town. You should start following Whalers football."

"I go to games."

"Ever hear them chanting 'It Takes Two!' when nothing but a long pass will get the team out of a third and fifteen? Two—that's Dave's number, man. Mine was Fourteen."

"It Takes Two"—that was the phrase that popped up on HackAck in the comment stream about the Red Tickets Drawing. There were other connections between the two quarterbacks. "Dave may not be a go-getter, but he managed to get your girl, didn't he, Max? Lizza Coddington, right? You two were quite a couple back in the day."

"Forget it, Chief. We're all good friends. Lizza goes where she wants. And Dave has been picking up my leftovers since he joined the JV practice squad."

"So, what does he want the money for?"

"Ask him. But I can tell you—Lizza ain't cheap. You don't take her for a sub at Stubbys. More like a steak at Pi Pizzeria. And that shit adds up."

"Forget about Dave for a second. What do you want the money for?"

"I don't."

"Good thing. The stuffed animal caper went south and so did the gas station job."

"What? That holdup? That wasn't me."

"It was Mike Stoller."

"So?"

"You like movies?"

"Sure."

"You ever see *The Big Lebowski*?"

"Yeah, I've seen it. So what?"

"I think of you and Prescott and Stoller, you fit the characters. You're the Dude, Dave is Walter. And Mike Stoller is Donny."

He laughed. "Shut the fuck up, Donny!"

"Right. So don't tell me Donny cooked up that gas station heist."

"I'm not telling you a thing. And you can't prove anything, either."

"True." I walked over to the desk, poked a finger through the bowl of marbles. I wasn't quite done with him. "So your mom says you make up video games?"

"Yeah, well. If you have a good game engine and a decent IDE, it's no big deal."

"IDE?"

"Integrated Development Environment. The one I'm using has a good compiler and I work with Python, which helps. That's a programming language."

"But it's all just the means to an end."

"Yeah, I guess."

"The game itself."

"Sure."

I picked up a marble. It wasn't at all like a stuffed animal eye. He should have noticed. "Does your game have a hero?"

He brightened a little. "It has a superhero, dude. He can slow time. He can stop it, too, but that's easy. Anyone born with the Gift can stop time. Learning to slow it down is the hard part. But my game is different because my guy has to deal with real life problems. I mean—having the power is a problem. Being part of the secret guild is a problem. He's, like…alienated."

I nodded. "With great power comes great responsibility."

He grinned. "Or great irresponsibility."

"Just don't fall into the Spider-Man Geek Fallacy."

"The what?"

"Geeks like you get tripped up by it all the time."

"What are you talking about?"

"It's this idea that Spider-Man or—you know, heroes like him—are regular people because they have normal problems. And you can write something meaningful about them because of that."

"Yeah, so what?"

"So it's bullshit, Max, that's what. Spider-Man and your time-shifter guy aren't real people and they don't have real problems. They have the problems a real person might have if they turned into Spider-Man or time-shifter guy. But that's very different. Okay, it's an improvement over Superman, who had no problems at all, except Kryptonite. But still, it's all nothing but nonsensical brain candy. Which is fine. Everybody likes candy. But you'll never say anything worthwhile about life when you go down that route. Which is what I mean by the Spider-Man Geek Fallacy. It's ruined a lot of smart, cool geeks. Look out or you'll turn into one of them."

"Why should you care?"

I smiled. "That's my super power."

"Caring about people? So you're a guidance counselor in Spandex? Sounds like the most boring comic book ever."

"I get that a lot."

Max stared at me. "Anyone ever tell you that you think too much?"

I smiled. "Yeah. Usually just before I arrest them."

"I'll keep that in mind."

"Anyway, game-playing runs in your family. I heard about your father's scavenger hunts."

"Did you hear about the Easter egg hunt when I was eight? No? You missed that one? He kept me hunting after all the other kids went home. In the dark, in the snow. No dinner until I found the last Easter egg."

"Did you find it?"

"He finally gave me a hint. I was half frozen by then. He said, 'When it comes to Easter eggs there's coloration and then there's protective coloration.'"

I got it, and shook my head with mixed admiration and disgust. "He hid a white egg in a snowbank."

"Yeah. It was pitch dark by then, no way I was ever going to find it. But when I figured out the clue, he let me off the hook. He said, 'It's the thought that counts.' Thanks, Pop. What an asshole. Whoo hooo! You fooled a bunch of eight-year-olds. Good for you."

"But you still like the games."

"I like winning."

"We have a big game coming up. Any thoughts on how to win it?"

"You lost me."

"The Red Tickets Raffle on Christmas Eve. People have been daydreaming about rigging that game since it began. The top prize is five thousand dollars. That beats robbing gas stations or pulling apart some poor kid's teddy bear."

"But it's impossible."

"Is it?"

"Hey, if you could cheat the lottery they'd be splitting that billion-dollar Powerball jackpot three hundred million ways."

"But this isn't a lottery, Max. It's a raffle. All you need to win is the right ticket."

"And how could you get your hands on that little item, Chief?"

"I've actually given the problem quite a bit of thought. Because, you know—I think too much. But so do you. It would actually be pretty easy. But it takes more than one person. In other words, to work at all it has to be a criminal conspiracy, with fines up to ten thousand dollars. That wipes out your winnings. Plus you're looking at up to ten years in jail. Conspiracy is considered one of the 'inchoate' crimes because the criminal act consists of preparing to commit the crime, even if you chicken out and do nothing. Then there's 'attempt,' where you bail in the middle and walk away. Oh, and don't forget 'solicitation.' That's getting other people involved. Multiple counts mean multiple sentencing guidelines. And that's before you actually do anything."

"Good thing I'm not planning to."

"Yeah. Because you'd need someone who works at a participating store to palm the winning ticket instead of putting, in the bin with all the others. Once you have a matched set, you need the right person drawing the ticket on raffle day. Normally, that would be the Junior Miss winner, who happens to be Lizza Coddington this year—your girlfriend. Ex-girlfriend, I mean."

"Which wrecks your theory, because the Town Crier's daughter, Alana Trikilis, is drawing the tickets. I'd take a long look at her, Chief. And her dad. That garbage man pulled some serious strings to get her the job instead of the Junior Miss winner who usually does it. Change the rules, get his daughter in position to make the switch. And it just so happens he's about to lose his house. What a coincidence! Five grand would come in real handy around about now. I'd call that motive and opportunity."

It was an absurd accusation. Sam Trikilis was no criminal. In fact, he was the opposite of a criminal, as unthinkingly virtuous as a Buddhist monk or a Labrador retriever. But even as I was thinking that, I could sense the stress fractures in the analogy. Buddhist monks were killing Muslims in Myanmar; and our old Lab knew exactly what he was doing when he snagged the Christmas roast beef off the table just before the guests arrived for dinner—why else would he have been cowering behind the toilet afterward?

So, no one was above suspicion. That's what my old pal from the LAPD, Chuck Obremski, always said. Even saints—"They get canonized for not getting caught." That was Chuck's viewpoint.

But if someone planned to rig the Red Tickets Drawing, as the anonymous posters on HackAck seemed to think, then I'd put my money on Max Blum any time.

I turned to go. At the door I said, "Lizza's still the first alternate for the drawing. If anything happens to Alana Trikilis."

"So?"

"So let's hope nothing does."

Chapter Thirteen

Wild Geese

Back at the station, my cold case was heating up. Haden Krakauer was waiting for me in my office, staring out the big picture window with his binoculars.

"There's a Townsend's solitaire in the trees over there," he said as I walked in. "My first one ever. I thought it was a flycatcher at first." He handed me the binoculars when I walked over. "Take a look. About almost at the top of that big elm tree. They like to perch up high to advertise their territory. Just like certain Selectmen I know. But much prettier."

It was a lovely bird, pale gray with darker gray wing accents and a white ring around the eye like a monocle. It took me a few seconds to locate it, and as I watched, it lifted off in a thrashing of wings and disappeared. "Gone."

He took the binoculars back. "You're my

witness. A Townsend's solitaire! Right here in front of the police station."

"Any other news?"

"We picked up the kid who stole Paul Healy's tools off that Squam jobsite. Your pal Mike Henderson dropped the dime on him. He wondered how a twenty-five-year-old kid came to have all these antique tools—Disston handsaws, wood-molding planes, some old scraper with a wooden knob handle. At the other end of the scale, the kid was using a Festool sander with the vacuum dust-catcher. That's expensive shit. And Healy had been at the Muse the night before griping about the robbery. Mike put it together and made the call. It's tough being a thief in a small town."

"Snoops and gossips."

"Yeah."

"Or you could call it community policing. I'll call Mike and thank him."

"Good idea. Oh, and the soil sample from the Madaket grave came back."

"So fast?"

"I told the boys to skip the State Police lab. They're backed up two months, and that's for active cases. I have a pal who teaches at UMass, in the Ag. Department. They have a brand new defracting laser and he had to tell me all about it. But I

FedExed him the sample and he did the tests at lunch. You were right about the formaldehyde."

"So, case closed? And Brandon Delavane found."

"That's what I thought."

"But?"

"Kyle Donnelly tracked down old Ben Tillotson. We used to call him 'choppers.' He was our family dentist until he retired. Kind of a crazy old guy. He worked out of his house on Cliff Road and gave kids candy if they behaved in the chair. You called him on it, he'd just laugh and say, 'Job security, laddie!'" I remember he had the biggest Novocain needle I ever saw. Scared the crap out of me. I hadn't seen him in years. I heard he moved to Florida. Turns out he sold the house when his wife died and moved into Academy Hill. But he still has all his files stored at Sun Island. Kyle took a couple of uniforms and spent three days going through the X-rays. It wasn't as bad as you'd think. They got to skip the women and the kids, and Tillotson retired in '04, so that meant only seven years of material to search."

I felt my pulse spike. Haden was grinning.

"They got a match?"

"They did. Fella named Ted Coddington. Ted Bainbridge Coddington the Third, to be precise. Old money. Four generations on the island. He was Jackson Blum's partner until November 1997, when he disappeared."

He had to be Lizza Coddington's father— Anna must have been pregnant when he died. I thought of Max Blum's evasions about the girl. One way or another, the Blums and the Coddingtons were still intertwined.

"No one could ever figure out what happened," Haden continued. "They never found the body, obviously."

I tucked a Keurig pod into my coffeemaker, and pushed the flashing blue button. "Well, now we know."

The next moves crowded into my mind like rock fans at a festival seating concert: call Ted McGrady again, talk to the Coddingtons—all the relatives. I'd need a list. And if the body wasn't fresh from the funeral home, what was formaldehyde doing in the grave? I needed the complete soil sample ASAP. And I was going to have to talk to Blum again, too. I needed to know what exactly had been—

"You might want to put a mug under there, Chief!"

"I—what? Oh, shit!"

A thin thread of Starbucks Pike Place roast was pouring into the tray. I grabbed a mug and salvaged about half the coffee as Haden shook his head and raised his eyebrows—universal body language for

"What a nut!" At least he was kind enough not to say anything.

I sipped the coffee. It was a little late in the day and the brew tasted bitter without milk. I set the mug down, thinking.

"Here's what I need," I told Haden. "A list of Coddington's connections—family members still on the island, friends, business associates, anyone who was around twenty years ago who could shed some light on this. Schedule a call with Ed Delavane at FMC Devens." That was the Federal Medical Center—a prison for convicts with mental health issues, which described Billy Delevan's brother perfectly. We'd need to get in touch with the Special Investigating Agent at the prison. "Set it up with the SIA. I have a couple of questions for him. Also I want a complete ballistics report on the bullet we dug out of Coddington's skull. Cross reference it against gun permits and everyone who successfully completed the certified safety course, 1967 to '97 and the voter registration rolls. That covers the thirty years Blum was on the island before the crime was committed. I don't see him registering the gun after that—unless it was with the cod and the haddock in the Great South Channel. I want to know the location of any gun on this island that could be a match, on the off chance that it's still around. People are funny about guns. They get sentimental. Plus your friend's soil sample analysis, and an appointment with Blum."

Haden was scribbling in his notebook. He had actually taken a shorthand course after college and he still swore by it. He looked up with a grin. "Is that all?"

"Not quite. Get someone with patience and a good attention span to go over all the public records from 1997 on—newspaper stories, arrest records, blogs, published memoirs, organizational minutes. I want to see if we can place anyone at the site in Madaket in the right time frame. Maybe they remember something."

"You're looking for witnesses?"

"It's worth a shot."

"I'll put Karen on it. I'll tell her we've spotted a lot of wild geese at the west end of the island. She can chase some of them."

"She might not get a birding joke."

"That's not a birding joke, Chief. That's a crazy long-shot desperate police work joke."

"I hope she gets a chuckle out of it. And tell her I'll scrape a bonus out of the budget for her if she finds anything."

He put the notebook back in his pocket. "Okay. First thing in the morning."

I nodded. It was quitting time. "Thanks, Haden."

As he left the office, the phone rang on my desk. Barnaby Toll said, "Some guy wants to talk to you, Chief. He won't give his name. I told him you were probably gone for the day, but he says it's urgent and I wasn't sure exactly what to do, so…"

"Thanks, Barney. Put him through."

The voice was familiar but I couldn't quite place it. "You get one warning, Chief. Stop harassing people. Keep off Tuckernuck and mind your own business."

"Thanks anyway. But if by people you mean Gary Pressman, and he is in fact selling drugs out there, harassing him is more than my business. It's my job description."

"One warning. Back off. Or you'll be sorry."

Caller ID showed it as a blocked number. "Who is this?"

But he hung up. I can't say the call didn't scare me, but it also piqued my curiosity. Gary Pressman was getting nervous, which I took as an encouraging development. Of course, the caller had been careful not to mention Gary's name, which would allow the hipster to plead both innocence and ignorance. I could just hear him: "Maybe it was one of my neighbors, Chief. They're touchy about trespassing."

I'd been threatened by real criminals during my time with the LAPD. These were professionals, with the personnel and firepower behind them to inflict real damage—and the disregard for all known statutes of civilization to do so without a flicker of conscience or a moment's pause.

This call felt more like a shove from a schoolyard bully. Still, you had to be a little crazy to make menacing phone calls to the police chief in a town as small as Nantucket, and I had never met a trained officer in the military or law enforcement who wasn't scared by crazy.

Crazy schoolyard bully.

I made the connection and recognized the voice. There was nothing I could do about it now, but at least Pat Sauter wouldn't have the element of surprise if he came at me again.

I hung up the phone, straightened the papers on my desk and went home to cook the first dinner for my new compounded family in our new house.

Chapter Fourteen

A Hidden Clue

I didn't mention Sauter's call. But I did break the skeleton news as I served out the pesto tortellini. The kids were all fascinated by the mysterious bones.

"I knew the Coddingtons," Jane said, digging in. "The mother and the aunt. I had the daughter Lizzy in a creative writing class I taught a few years ago. Sad girl. All her stories were about orphans adopted by pirates—"

"Ocean pirates or space pirates?" Tim interrupted.

"Sorry, they were boring old ocean pirates. She had one about a street urchin who turned out to be the daughter of some eccentric millionaire."

"Sounds like Dickens," I said.

"Except Dickens could write. She described a Nantucket blizzard as a 'wild and wondrous winter wonderland of white.'"

I nodded. "Much better than those regular old winter wonderlands of white."

"She had potential, though. I made her think of some specific detail and she said, 'everything's wearing a hat of snow. Even the garbage cans.' Hey, it was a start."

"Did you go out to Tuckernuck, Dad?" Caroline asked.

"Yeah, but we didn't find anything."

"Pressman's stowing those drugs in plain sight somehow," Jane said. We were camped out at the Darling Street house, surrounded by boxes of books and newspaper-wrapped dishes. The transitional chaos was confusing, but spirits were high. The kids loved the new house and seemed utterly blasé about moving in with Jane and her little boy. The only thing missing was a dog, but Tim and I had exhausted that topic on the way home from school. The problem was, he didn't really want anything else for Christmas. I hated to play Scrooge, but I couldn't afford to buy him a dog, the ones at the MSPCA looked weird and mangy, and I doubted our new landlord would appreciate having all those wide, soft-gloss white-pine boards scratched up by canine claws. Mike Henderson made it clear when he refinished a floor: "Dogs void the warranty."

Everything else about the change of address looked good, and I wasn't the outlier in this stage of divorce—Miranda had moved in with her fellow real estate broker, Joe Arbogast, more than a year ago, and they were talking about getting married, though it was still just talk. I had a huge advantage because the kids liked Jane and found Joe tedious at best. He was one of those salesmen who love to tell you that everything is about selling—even friendship, love, and child-rearing. "You gotta sell yourself," he told me at some drunken party when Miranda first met him. If he was right, he was doing a bad job. My kids weren't buying.

He treated his own son Jimmy with a ludicrous favoritism, teaching him how to make a sauce Béarnaise while he banished my kids from the kitchen. Jimmy got an eight-hundred-dollar bicycle for his birthday. My kids got socks. They didn't care. They thought it was funny. And it certainly made Jane look good.

Tim liked her idea of Pressman hiding his drugs in plain sight. And I liked thinking about the small aneurism his mother would have if she heard us talking about drug trafficking at the dinner table. It was Miranda's firm belief that if you didn't talk about something, it ceased to exist. Expecting that trick to work with drugs on Nantucket was borderline crazy, like refusing to discuss coal dust in Kentucky.

"So, where would he put the drugs?" Tim

asked now. He had finished his meal and taken out his hacky-sack bags. He had two of them going, but it was an accident waiting to happen

"Not at the table," I said.

"Okay, sorry, I—aaakkk!"

One of the bags dropped into the middle of Caroline's plate, scattering mesclun greens and salad dressing onto the table and into her lap.

"Shit!" she screeched. "What are you doing? What is wrong with you?! Omigod, you are such a useless little freak. You ruined my shirt! And my jeans! These are my favorite jeans."

"I can get the stains out," Jane said.

"It's olive oil!"

"You just pre-treat it with dish soap and wash it in cold water. It'll be fine. Come on, let's get this stuff in the wash and get you changed."

When they came back, Caroline was mollified, wearing a Regina Spektor sweatshirt that said, "I'm the hero of this story, I don't need to be saved" and a pair of "destroyed" jeans—yes, you pay extra for the wear and tear. Jane had saved the day. Carrie was happy to take a slice of the Bartlett's pumpkin pie I'd picked up for dessert.

But Tim could never let a subject drop if he was interested. He was like a dog with a buried bone. He always found his way back. "So Jane..." he began again now, the bone clamped firmly in his jaws. "You were saying before? About hiding drugs?"

Jane took a sip of coffee. "Right. Sure. There's lots of places. You could hide cocaine in a sugar bowl, for instance. Or marijuana in your spice rack. I heard some geology teacher in Ohio camouflaged his meth with some rock crystal samples. The big chunks look just like quartz."

"You're making this up," I told her. I turned to Tim. "She's spinning ideas for her next book. Real people aren't that clever. Especially real people who deal drugs."

He nodded. "I guess."

I had one more question for Jane, though. "Do you know anyone who wears a New York Giants hooded sweatshirt? I seem to recall we noticed someone dressed that way at a Whalers game a few weeks ago, and I saw someone in a Giants hoodie bolt from Pressman's house as the boat was docking."

"A drug dealer?" Tim asked, wide-eyed.

"More like a drug customer. He definitely didn't want to deal with the police, though."

"I know," said Jane. "It's that Arnold Sprockett, whose kid got hurt in the West Bridgewater game. Maybe he wants painkillers."

"Or he's going into business with Pressman so he can afford some expensive treatment. He could have lousy insurance, and the school's indemnified unless there's total negligence involved."

"Which there wasn't."

"I think I'll have a talk with him tomorrow."

With her pie hoovered up to the last crumb, Caroline said, "Did you finish the Christmas poem for Mr. Springer, Dad? Because Mrs. Gumport wants to use it in my English class."

This was getting out of hand. "How does Mrs. Gumport even know about it?"

"I guess teachers talk. They have a lounge."

"It's the least you can do, Henry," Jane said. "I wrote a whole play just so my son could be an elf."

Caroline turned on her. This had obviously been building up for a while. "And he has one line and he can't even learn it!"

"I'm trying!" Sam said.

"He's only seven years old," Jane added.

"Yeah! I'm little!"

Caroline turned on him "I hope you're not trying! Because if you're actually trying, that would be so totally lame."

"He'll get it," I said

"We open this week!"

"You have to be patient."

"We. Get. Our. Own. Christmas. That's five words. He's an elf, he's been making Christmas for a zillion kids since forever and he's finally getting a tree and a stocking and some presents—all because of me. It's not like it's a stretch. He's standing right in the middle of the first elf Christmas ever. All he has to do is say it! Ugh! Yesterday at tech I gave him the line, I said, 'You got your own Christmas, remember that, Sam?' You just stared at me like I was a rattlesnake and I was going to bite you if you moved."

"I was scared! You're scary."

He had a point there.

Jane said, "Sam has stage fright."

Caroline sniffed. "We all have stage fright. It's part of the job."

I bit down a laugh. Her impression of the haughty professional diva was pitch-perfect— Maggie Smith dismissing some neophyte walk-on.

Caroline glared at me; she knew exactly what I was thinking. "It's true!"

Time to change the subject. "Want to hear the poem?"

"Yes!" Tim exclaimed, pulling his fist to his shoulder and driving his elbow down.

I launched:

"From the age of fifteen
Christmas was a lost cause for me.
A spending spree,
A lot of presents I didn't care about

Commercialization, cheap decoration
Nothing mysterious or sublime
Just tinsel
And cards from people you'd never hear from
Any other time.

It meant less and less as I got older.
I got married, my wife loved trimming the tree
But I told her
It meant nothing to me—
Six weeks of bad music in the grocery
And mercenary corn
And then my children were born.
Without a moment's transition,
Without a break or a pause—
I was Santa Claus.
I was orchestrating the delight
On those tiny faces,
Making the holiday happen
In their eyes.
Well, time flies
They're growing up now.
But this is still the finest gift under any tree:
My kids have given Christmas
Back to me."

"It's great!' Tim crowed.
"Are you insane?" Caroline shrieked. "It's horrible! You weren't supposed to write a poem about

us! Omigod! This is a total nightmare! You can't let anyone see this! Daddy, please. I am so dead if people hear that."

"Well, I like it," Tim announced. "And Mr. Springer will, too. Besides," he said turning to Caroline, "you don't have to give it to Mrs. Gumport. It wasn't an assignment."

"But everyone will know!"

"I think they suspect we're related anyway, Carrie."

"I can't believe this."

"So what were you expecting? Some generic poem about sleigh bells and reindeer?"

"Yes! That's exactly what I was expecting! Why couldn't you just do that, like any other dad would have?"

"Christmas is about family. You're my family. Sorry."

She gave up. "Whatever. I've got homework." She got up and left the table.

Tim patted my arm "She's just being a bitch." I squinted at that word, and he backtracked: "A fink, a rat, a meanie…who cares? But the poem's really good, Dad. Thanks."

"Any parent will get it," Jane said.

"I liked it," Sam offered.

"Thanks, kid."

"And Mr. Springer has three kids," Tim added.

"It's not too cheesy?" I asked Jane.

"Hey, don't ask me—I wrote a play where Santa's daughter makes peace among the reindeer and takes over Christmas. Total cheese patrol."

"But fun."

"I hope."

I turned to Tim. "I've been thinking about your other problem. I have a theory about the fingerprints on that test answer sheet. I'm going to test it out tomorrow. All I need is a football."

"I have a football."

"I know. Let me borrow it for the day and we may get some answers, thanks to the miracle of modern forensic science."

"Cool."

He cleared his plate and went upstairs to wrestle with his own math homework. He knew better than to ask me for help. Sam took another slice of pie and Jane squeezed my hand. "Thanks for dinner."

"It was great," Sam said. "Mom's the worst cook in the world."

"The whole world? I hear there's a really terrible cook in Yugoslavia somewhere."

He laughed and said, "She's worse!" through a mouthful of pie.

I sat back, contented. I had to rate our first

family dinner a success. It was like we'd been eating together for years.

Now perhaps I could find a murderer, close down a drug ring, stop the raffle rigging, and generally carry over a little of that winning record to my police work.

The first order of business—clear my son of cheating.

Chapter Fifteen

Fun with Forensics

The Nantucket Whalers were using a modified form of the West Coast offense, and the coach had given me a couple of tight-end pass plays to call. Hector Cruz knew them—he knew the whole playbook—but this would be the first time he'd gotten a chance to actually run one of them—even if it was only in the high school parking lot.

I saw him open the rust-acned door of his old VW Rabbit and climb out. His jacket was unzipped and he wore no hat or gloves despite the thirty-degree. temperature and the sharp east wind: he was too macho for all that sissy cold weather gear. That might drive his parents crazy but it suited me fine this morning.

"Hector," I shouted. "FB West, Right Slot!"

He turned. "What?"

I mock threw the football. "Come on! 372 Y Stick!"

He took off parallel to the playing field fence and then broke for the right side line as I chucked the ball. Not a perfect spiral but he snatched it out of the air and ran a few more steps.

"Good one!" I called out.

He flipped the ball back to me. "Tell that to the coach."

"I will."

• • ● • •

I took the football back to the station and gave it to Monica Terwilliger to scan for prints.

"Is this the deflated one?" she asked me.

"I thought no Patriot fan believed that story."

She shrugged. "He's a cheater. But he's my cheater."

I wondered if she felt the same way about her husband, whom the Nantucket rumor mill had long convicted as a serial philanderer. But I wisely kept my mouth shut on that score, and brought things back to the job on hand. "This one is personal."

"Then I'll make it a priority. Come back after lunch. I'll have a full report."

Gusto and enthusiasm—that's what I was looking for. And it was about to get better, with last night's modest prayer for some progress answered emphatically when I got upstairs to my office. Things were shaking loose. Not an avalanche yet, but I could sense it was coming—the snowpack creaking in the early spring thaw.

Haden Krakauer had set the soil sample report in the middle of my desk, and formaldehyde was the least of it. The list of chemicals was astonishing and scary: cyanide, arsenic, benzene, and lead. Was the Nantucket earth this toxic everywhere on the island? Or just near the dump? No, no, no—it couldn't be. The well water would be undrinkable with this stuff seeping through the ground. We'd all have been poisoned long ago. Anyway, you'd know it on your tongue—the tap water in places as diverse as Washington, D.C. and Montpelier, Vermont, had the same unmistakable chemical tang, like drinking from a swimming pool. Nantucket's water—from a glacial moraine single-source aquifer—was the best I'd ever tasted, one of the great quiet luxuries of life on the island, like Bartlett's Farm's tomatoes or the clean Atlantic air.

So what was going on?

I made myself a cup of coffee, sat down at my desk, and called Haden's friend at U. Mass — Professor Lawrence Haas, professor of plant, soil, and insect sciences at the Stockbridge School of Agriculture.

He was teaching a class. His secretary said he'd call me back within the hour.

I turned to Karen Gifford's preliminary report. She had gone through the names listed by the *Inquirer and Mirror* as participating in the annual Christmas bird count over the years—it took the enthusiasts to the area of Madaket where Coddington's skeleton was found, at roughly the correct season. She had gotten in touch with fifteen people, none of whom recalled anything unusual beyond rare sighting of a Bullock's oriole or a Western kingbird.

Karen had ten people left to call, but didn't offer much hope. Birders were a sociable lot and if any of them had discovered a newly dug grave, all of them would have known it. She had also started on the police logs for the area—DUIs, deer-jackings, gun target practice, used appliance-disposal arrests, illegal disposal of toxic chemicals, two runaway kids found at the west end of the island. There had been search parties; she was tracking down the names.

Her final note: "I'll keep looking."

I was setting the printout aside when Professor Haas called back.

"Chief Kennis! Sorry I missed your call."

"No problem. Thanks for calling back. I was hoping you could clear up some questions about the soil sample Haden Krakauer sent you."

"Chewing tobacco."

"Excuse me?"

"Or chaw, as its devotees call it."

"I'm not sure what—"

"That's what we found in the soil, Chief Kennis. Residues of chewing tobacco."

"All those chemicals are in chewing tobacco? Lead? Cadmium? Benzene?"

"Don't forget cyanide. But the giveaway is the N-nitrosamine. It's formed during the curing and fermentation of plug tobacco."

"But there was no nicotine in the sample?"

"It's water-soluble. Five good rainstorms would wash it away. But these other compounds have staying power. Except the polonium-210—it's a radioactive isotope commonly found in these products. But it has a short half-life and decays to lead. Which explains the lead in your sample."

"This is nuts."

"Well, it explains a lot of mouth cancer."

"Yeah. So…how much of this stuff would have to have been mixed with the dirt for it to still be there after all these years?"

"Well, I don't want to go all 'inside baseball' with you, Chief, or put you to sleep with technical jargon, so the term I'd be most likely to use is—a shitload."

I laughed. "But why?"

"Not sure, but the most likely idea is preserving the grave. You have a rat problem over there?"

"I—uh, no. Not a problem. But we do have rats. Especially at the dump. And—"

"And this guy was buried nearby."

I nodded. "Less than a mile away."

"There you go, then. The government tried to do animal testing on tobacco back in the fifties, but no animals would touch this stuff. Rats were the last resort, they'll sample most organic material to see if it's edible. But they wouldn't go near this crap. Which is actually a pretty good test all by itself."

"Yeah."

"So now what?"

"Now I find out who was selling snuff on the island twenty years ago, and see if they remember any bulk sales in November of 1997."

He let out a whistling breath, almost a laugh. "Sounds like a long shot."

"I guess. But they pay off big when they come in. My dad won the trifecta at the Preakness in 1991—Hansel, Corporate Report, and Mane Minister, win, place, and show. Twenty-two hundred bucks on every two-dollar bet."

"Do you mind if I ask—how much did he…?"

"Just two hundred dollars. But we went home with more than two hundred thousand. Three cops escorted us off the Pimlico grounds through a secret tunnel under the track. It was quite an afternoon for a nineteen-year-old boy."

"Wow."

"So, anyway…I like long shots. Especially when all I have to do to win them is work."

"All right, then. Good luck, Chief. Let me know how it all turns out."

My intercom buzzed: Haden had put a call in to FMC Devens, the federal medical prison, and he had Ed Delavane waiting on the line. The last time I dealt with Billy Delavane's brother, two years before, he'd helped me catch the men who were planning to bomb the Boston Pops concert at Jetties Beach. That day he told me a bizarre, twisted story of rage and retribution that stretched all the way back to the first Iraq war. The case was a complex jigsaw puzzle, and he'd held a few key pieces, though he gave them up grudgingly.

Now I heard his familiar, grating rasp. "Howdy, Chief. How's it hangin'?"

"Pretty well, Ed. Thanks for asking."

"You looking for another war story?"

"More of a crime story this time," I said.

"Haden gave me the heads-up. So you finally figured out who was buried in that grave."

"Fella named Ted Coddington. You know him?"

"I shoplifted from him a few times. Candy

from a baby? Fuck that. Try golf clubs from a trust fund baby. Didn't bust me on the course, either. You'd never catch him dead at Miacomet—he was more of a Sankaty Head Golf Club type."

Miacomet was a shabby nine-hole public course near Bartlett's Farm. The rich summer people and local gentry preferred the two lavish, members-only eighteen-hole swaths of greenery, with their luxurious clubhouses, at the east end of the island. Sankaty was the old money sanctuary, with a decade-long waiting list that left it unavailable to the washashore dot-com millionaires and hedge fund managers. They had to make do with the less exclusive but more luxurious Nantucket Golf Club.

"You hear anything about Coddington back then? I mean…was he involved in anything shady?"

"How would I know?"

"You'd know. It's a small town and it was even smaller in 1997. If I wanted to know paint gossip, I'd talk to Mike Henderson. Real estate? I'd ask Elaine Bailey—"

"And for crime, you come to me. What an honor."

"Think back. Anything? Gambling debts, drug use, feuds, infidelities?"

"Well, everyone was fucking everyone back then and he was always fighting with his partner and his neighbors, but who wasn't? Everybody wants a bigger share, nobody wants the asshole next door to put in a hedge or build that ugly guest cottage. Same old same old. You're digging out a dry gopher hole, Chief."

I blew out a breath. I still had one more gap for him to fill in. "Say, Ed—what really happened to Brandon's body?"

"Good question."

"Come on. It was a misdemeanor. You're already serving twenty to life. No one would bother with this, even if I told them—and I won't."

He laughed; or maybe he was just clearing his throat. "Bran was a fisherman, Chief. Worked a sixty-foot Eastern rig dragger, the *Jean Marie*—all seasons, all weathers, east of the moors to the Grand Banks. We gave him a proper burial at sea."

So that was it. I should have guessed. "Thanks, Ed."

"You just love getting all the answers, don'tcha? All the boxes filled in, nice and tidy."

"Pretty much."

"Looks like you've found a home, then."

"Yeah. Any message for Billy?" The two brothers hadn't spoken for years, but there was always hope.

Or maybe not. Ed's voice was flat when he answered. "Sure, Chief. Measure twice, cut once."

My next call was to Ed's old nemesis, ex-Police Chief Ted McGrady. I figured he'd know which stores sold chaw back in the day; and I had a few other questions to ask him.

"Well, let's see now," he said, talking on his cell phone as he walked the stony beach near his house, the wind a low static roar behind his words. "You had the Hub, of course, and Island Value—we always used to laugh at that name! The most over-priced general store on the Eastern Seaboard calling itself 'Island Value.' That's Nantucket for you. Land of bizarre store names. Hell, we even had a shop that sold sneakers called itself 'The Athlete's Foot.' Who else? Ahhhh—Cumberland Farms and Lucky Express. Oh, yeah, and the Smokehouse, on East Chestnut Street, across from the old police station. That place is long gone now. Fella named Hugh Tabor ran it, but he left before the towers fell."

"Any idea where he might be living now?"

"Someplace warm, I'd bet. He's got to be in his seventies and nobody complained harder about a Nantucket winter. I could tell him a thing or two about that! My heating oil froze two years ago February. Right in the tank! Now that's cold, son. Anyway, if you're looking for old Hughie, I'd start in Florida. He told me once, 'I used to laugh at those pathetic old people retiring to Miami Beach to get away from the snow. Now I understand.' I'd peg him for more of a Key West man, though. He loved his Hemingway."

"Thanks. This is a good start." I finished scribbling a note, took a sip of my cooling coffee and changed the subject. "We identified the skeleton," I said.

"Brandon Delavane?"

"No, actually it's a guy named Theodore Bainbridge Coddington III. Ever run across him?"

"Sure, I knew Ted. Knew the whole family. Old-time Nantucket. I think one of his ancestors bought the island from the Wampanoags."

"Did he have any enemies?"

"You mean did anyone hate him enough to put a bullet in his skull and bury him out in the moors? No. Not that I knew of."

"So he was a popular guy."

"He was a rich guy who kept to himself. He didn't drink, he didn't abuse the waiters at the local restaurants. Married, member of all the right clubs. Brought his wife's sister over from Eastern Europe somewhere. I asked him about that once. The whole immigration thing moved so quick. He said 'Money solves problems, Ted.' What else? Supported the Boys & Girls Club. On the board of the NHA and the Basket Museum. Pretty standard stuff."

"Come on. There must have been something

askew somewhere. He didn't end up like the rest of the Yacht Club fork-lifters." It was a phrase I had learned from Jane Stiles, whose grandfather had started the Nantucket Yacht club in 1906, and served as its first Commodore. It was an old salts' dismissive term for members who didn't sail, and only used the club for its social cachet, hosting dinner parties or taking afternoon drinks on the patio.

McGrady chuckled. "You're learning the lingo, son. And I guess you're right. Fact is, I figured Ted took a powder, you know? He wouldn't have been the first one to drive onto the boat, drive off at Hyannis, and just keep driving. All the way west like Lewis and Clark."

"But why?"

"Well, the rumor was he'd been having an affair. Maybe he got found out. Maybe he took off before he got found out. His wife was pregnant at the time. And there'd been some kind of falling out with his partner."

"His partner?"

"He and Jackson Blum owned Blum's Sporting Goods in those days. Maybe Blum bought him out. Or forced him out."

"Or killed him."

"Well, that may look like a possibility now, but back then it would have seemed a little far-fetched.

We hadn't had a capital murder case on the island in, oh, more than a decade. Things were quiet."

"So…he disappeared and no action was taken?"

"Whoa, down, boy! We took action. There was an island-wide search that weekend, must have been hundred and fifty people walking the moors till all hours. Funny thing—Pat Folger was out there, pacing out the moors east of the dump. But it took him twenty years to dig up the skeleton. Yeah, I heard all about it. I still have some friends on the force."

I didn't like leaks, but I could hardly complain about some old-timer, probably Paul Quimby, talking things over with his ex-boss. I finished my coffee, set the mug aside. "So reopen the case with me. It's a murder now. Who are your suspects?"

"Hmmmm…well, there's the jealous wife. She'd be on top of the list. That Anna Coddington was a tough customer. Fought off a burglar with a fireplace andiron one time. He dialed 911! The poor guy couldn't wait to get into a jail cell where it was safe! What a dame. She got the Blums into the Yacht Club, you know. All she had to do was hint at it and the membership committee jumped. Hell, she was the committee. But I think she wound up regretting it. Some scalloper was living on his boat one of those summers, with a mooring near the club. Lots of loud music, pot smoke, party noise. Plus the skiff was an eyesore. Then it sank one night. Twenty two caliber bullet hole just below the waterline. Anna was out in that Boston Whaler of hers. Putt-putting out to Coatue, supposedly. No law against that. Anyway, it was August and the harbor was busy that night. No witnesses, never found a gun. And Jimmy Turpin—that was his name...Jimmy had plenty of enemies, poaching peoples' special spots, dropping his dredges on their tows, crossing lines. We never proved Anna did sink his boat, never even filed charges on her. But everybody knew she could have. You know what I mean? That was one tough broad. I can see her blowing her husband's brains out, easy."

"How did she react to his disappearance?"

"She was frantic, but she managed to organize the search. She was beating the bushes with the best of them. But then she would, wouldn't she? If you've just shot your husband you don't tell the world 'good riddance.'"

"How about the girlfriend? Do you have any idea who that was?"

"I have no idea if there even was a girlfriend, Chief. I'm spit-balling here. Playing the odds. Love and money, that's what it usually comes down to— unless you're talking about some whack-job serial killer. Love and money."

"So Blum's on your list."

"Oh, yeah. I seem to recall the store did very well after Coddington disappeared. Moved to a bigger location—one of those Winthrop properties on Main Street. Coddington hated the Winthrop people. 'They're wrecking the island,' he used to say. And I'd tell him, 'Someone's been wrecking this island since Thomas Mayhew sold his stake in the place to the first settlers for thirty pounds and a pair of beaver hats.' I seem to recall Ted and Jackson Blum had quite a little dustup at 21 Federal, just before Ted vanished. But Blum brushed it off. They fought all the time, so he said, but they always shook hands and worked it out in the end. He was pretty upset himself that Coddington was gone."

"So—it just blew over."

"Pretty much. With no murder weapon, no witnesses, and no body…"

"Did you run down the other theory? That he walked away from his life?"

"As a matter of fact, we did. Not much to check—boats and planes. No one remembered him leaving at the Steamship or the Hy-Line. But we hit paydirt out at the airport. Several guys matching his description flew off that morning—tall, Waspy, well-dressed, impatient. Two of them paid with credit cards—round trips to Boston. One of them paid cash—one-way to Hyannis. Bingo. Elvis has left the building."

"Did his ID match up?"

"This was pre-9/11, Chief. That long lost idyllic once-upon-a-time when you could just pay cash for a plane ticket and walk on board, no ID required, no questions asked."

"But you figured the one-way ticket was him?"

"Girl behind the desk IDed a photograph. Shot in the paper from the last Daffy Day—him and his wife, posing in front of his tailgate picnic."

"The girl was certain?"

"Guess it shows people don't pay much attention. Then, again, Ted was a type, you know what I mean? Dime a dozen on the Rock, especially back then. Nantucket reds, blue blazer and all."

"Topsiders with no socks."

"You got it, washashore. You're turning into a regular local. Be complaining about the new people next."

I had to laugh. "I already am."

"Never fails."

"I wonder who that other guy at the airport really was."

"Probably just some big shot doing his Christmas shopping. Took the boat back. Most likely."

"Or he really was someone running away from home."

"Nah, he'd have been missed. Small island."

"Okay, thanks, Ted. I have my new call list."

"Sure, no problem. Just keep me in the loop, Chief. I kind of miss the loop out here."

I took a shot. "Paul Quimby a little soft on the details?"

He laughed—bull's-eye. "Paul's a little soft, period."

"He's a plodder, but he gets the job done."

"Always was. Always did."

I disconnected and sat back, contemplating another cup of coffee. But I was already too wired. I needed to move. Blum hadn't returned Haden's calls, but that was just as well. I wanted to surprise him, anyway. I had some questions for his clerk, Arnold Sprockett, too—if he was still wearing a New York Giants hoodie.

It was definitely time for an ambush. But that would have to wait. First, I needed to pick my kids up from school.

Chapter Sixteen

Boys and Toys

By the time I got to NHS, I was ready to make my move. Monica Terwilliger had been as good as her word, and the news was better: Hector's fingerprints on the football matched both the set on the test paper and the ones on the box of chocolates from Caroline's mystery suitor.

I caught the kid as he was coming out of his last class, and took him to the dining hall, which was empty at that hour before various after-school activities used the space.

I sat him down at a metal-edged table. "Here's what I know, Hector. You're a talented athlete in a tough situation. Money's short and your family doesn't exactly feel welcome here. It's like starting a drive at your own one yard line. I get that. I also know you have a crush on my daughter, and that can't be easy. Right now she has no idea who sent her those chocolates and I'm not sure she even knows you exist. My son, Tim, likes you, though. He told me you read some Lorca in the original for the class the other day and then three kids signed up to take Spanish class. It should be a required course, as far as I'm concerned. But I pulled your fingerprints off that test answer sheet, so I know you planted it in my son's locker."

He started to speak. I held up a hand to stop him.

"I also know who you did it for, and I'm pretty sure I know why. So I need you to give me the name. Then we're done. I won't rat you out—to Bissell or to my daughter. Or to Dave Prescott. You're a good kid. You deserve a break. But you have to help me out here."

Hector looked down at the soda puddles and crumbs on the Formica tabletop and I had a moment to notice how much my job had come down to coaxing teenagers to talk to me without ruining their lives. First Mike Stoller, now Hector—and Dave Prescott would be next.

"If Dave flunked the poetry class they were going to bench him for the first two games next season," Hector finally told me, eyes still on the leftover lunch mess.

"Then why take an AP English course?"

"He thought, you know—read some poems, copy some bullshit from Sparks notes or Wikipedia—done."

"Then he met up with Ted Springer."

Hector looked up. The smile lit his face like headlights. I thought—you should try those high beams on my daughter. She might notice you after that. "Yeah," he said, "Mr. Springer's a badass. A poetry badass. Just like you!"

"We exist, Hector. A rare species, but not quite extinct. Now get home. I have to talk with your quarterback."

I found Dave Prescott hanging out with some friends by his car. One of them was my son's old nemesis, Jake Sauter. It looked like he'd grown four inches and packed on fifty pounds in the last couple of years. As left tackle Jake had protected Dave from many blitz attacks this season. I was glad to see his natural aggression channeled in a useful direction. His father's natural aggression was a much different problem, especially since he seemed determined to channel it at me.

I walked up to the group. "See ya, kids. I have to talk to Dave. Go. Now."

They shuffled off, Jake eyeing me as if he was contemplating the relative advantages and disadvantages of an assaulting-a-police-officer felony conviction. Like father, like son.

"What?" Prescott said when they were out of earshot.

"Don't you mean 'How can I help you, Chief Kennis'?"

"Right."

"Then say it."

He rolled his eyes, blew out an exasperated breath. "How can I help you, Chief Kennis?"

I didn't answer immediately—I was distracted. I had stepped back, my eye drawn to the asphalt under his car. One more connection—but it would have to wait. "Well, first of all, you can walk with me into Superintendent Bissell's office right now and admit that you cheated on your AP poetry midterm, and planted the answer sheet in my son's locker."

"You can't prove that."

"Actually, Dave, I can."

"Yeah? Like how?"

"You don't want to know. Because if you behave, confess to Bissell, take your two-game suspension, and confirm Mike Stoller's confession about trying to buy opioids from Gary Pressman, I may be able to keep you out of criminal court."

He stared right into my eyes, no doubt because he had read somewhere that liars tend to look away. In fact it's just the opposite. Liars overcompensate.

They stare. He said, "I have no idea what you're talking about."

"Then why were you parked at the Jackson Point landing?"

"I wasn't."

"Don't force me to make you lie under oath, Dave. Your car was identified in that location."

Well, maybe not the car itself, but the leaking oil under his car right now was a good circumstantial fit, and I knew I could match the brands if I took a sample.

"Look—" he began

"Are you telling me you have any friends besides Pressman on Tuckernuck?"

"He's not my friend."

"I'm glad you understand that. You boys didn't buy the drugs because he was selling in bulk and you couldn't afford the price of the shipment. But you can testify against him and help us find his stash. Where is he hiding it?"

"I never saw the stuff, Chief. But I mean—he's Gary Pressman. It wasn't like he was bullshitting us."

"That's a start. So you'll testify?"

Two kids approached the car, Dave waved them away. I took that as a good sign. "Can it be…like…anonymous or secret or, you know, in chambers or whatever?"

"I don't think the Selectmen would have it

any other way. The suspension's going to be tough enough for the town. They don't want their golden boy tangled up in a drug case."

"Maybe they could give me some community service. Like…cleaning the beaches or something."

"Maybe. But first things first. Come clean with Bissell and Springer. And apologize to my son."

"Okay, okay."

"And if you have any other schemes for making money this season, forget about them."

"Uh—okay."

"In other words, stay away from Maxwell Blum. He'll just get you in trouble."

"Yeah, I guess. Okay."

"Okay. Here's a question that wasn't on the midterm. You read *Ballad of the Red Earl* this semester, right? Well here's a stanza of Kipling for you:

> *"You have cast your lot with these, Red Earl*
> *"Take heed to where Ye stand*
> *"You have tied a knot with your tongue, red Earl*
> *"That Ye cannot loose with your hand.*

"How does that relate to your current situation, Dave?"

"Uh…"

"Think about it."

"I'm…it's—the opposite?"

"Exactly. Ted Springer would be proud of you.

Now go untie some knots with that silver tongue of yours. I'll take care of the rest."

By the time I got back to my cruiser the kids were waiting for me and the war was on. I had read about sibling rivalry during Miranda's first pregnancy, when the concept of a new human being arriving between us seemed baffling, and the prospect of two was beyond my grasp. Still, I did my homework. I was intellectually prepared to experience some jockeying for position, some struggle for power and attention between a pair of healthy kids. But this was different. This was a relentless blood feud that seemed like it would go on forever. I knew that probably wasn't true—my brother and I get along pretty well now, though we don't see each other much. And we'd fought like tomcats. But the dry, abstract assumption that my kids might grow up to be good friends was scant comfort in the trenches of their childhood.

I stood back for a few moments, waiting for a lull in the combat.

Carrie was texting while Tim practiced with his hacky-sack bags again. He actually had all three going at once—for a few seconds.

He dropped one, and Carrie snapped.

"Can you please just stop that! You look like an idiot. And a spaz!"

"It's cool!"

"It's lame! You're pathetic. You want to grow up and be a clown? You already are a clown! All you need is big floppy shoes and a red nose. No, seriously. You should, like, totally get the whole outfit. Then you'd have an excuse when everybody laughs at you."

"No one laughs at me."

"Omigod! You are such a delusionoid. Debbie Garrison laughs at you."

"That's bullshit!"

"Tim!" I intervened.

"Sorry." He bent over to pick up the dropped hacky-sack bag and started working them again.

"Why do you think she avoids you? She pretends she doesn't know you! You embarrass her!"

"I do not!"

Maybe it was the shouting, but Tim lost concentration and one of the bags spun out of control. It hit Carrie's hand and knocked her phone loose. It hit the sidewalk and the cover popped off. This was one hacky-sack attack too many. Carrie cried out, "Ugh! I hate you!" and stamped on the bag. It burst and dozens of little pellets squirted into the street. I gaped at the ruptured scrap of cloth.

The kids finally noticed me. "Dad! Carrie wrecked my hacky-sack bag!"

"Tim broke my phone!"

Their shouting scattered around me like wind.

I wasn't listening. I was paralyzed by that sense of retroactive stupidity you get from the obvious answer to a difficult question. Carrie had done a lot more than break one of Tim's juggling toys.

She had solved a case.

Jackson Blum and Arnold Sprockett would have to wait. If Blum had committed a crime, it was twenty years old and it could wait another day or two; if Sprockett was involved in dealing drugs on the island, I'd be rounding him up soon, anyway.

Two hours later, I had dropped the kids off at Miranda's house, tracked down Sal Pereira, and was headed across Madaket Harbor toward Tucker-nuck, search warrant in hand. I was alone this time. I didn't want to alarm Pressman, Karen was buried in her research, and Pereira and I were getting along fine, thanks to her introduction.

Judge Perlman had bent the rules a little to grant the warrant, and he wagged his finger at me as I left his chambers, with a chastising "Don't be wrong about this."

That was okay. Because I wasn't.

The wind was high and the water was choppy on the fifteen-minute crossing. I was cold and wet by the time Sal let me off at Pressman's dock. It was a clear day and I hadn't thought about needing a raincoat. I did have my other supplies, though.

He turned the boat around with a curt "Call

me when you're ready to back. I got things to do," and put-putted away.

Alone on the pier, I pulled a ping-pong ball out of my coat pocket and pushed it into the gas tank of Pressman's outboard motor. It's an old harmless trick to temporarily disable an outboard—the ball gets trapped by the intake and stops the motor. I had patrol officers watching Jackson Point and the Madaket Public Landing, but a few extra precautions couldn't hurt.

Bailey was snoozing on the porch when I walked up from the beach. He lifted his head and thumped his tail a couple of times in greeting. I bent down to ruffle the fur behind his ears.

I had the warrant in my hand when I knocked on the door. Pressman opened it wearing a U-Mass hoodie and sweatpants and an old pair of Reeboks. The house was warm—he had fired up the wood stove.

"What?" That was his greeting.

I handed him the warrant. "Read that while I look around."

I pushed past him into the house and crossed the living room to the bean-bag chair. He was right behind me. "Hey, I told you about that chair—"

"Yes, you did. No sitting on the museum piece. But you didn't say why."

"What are you trying to—?"

"Stop it, Pressman. How do you open this thing?" I picked it up—a giant, misshapen hacky-sack bag. I felt up and down the length of it and found a flap of leather covering a Velcro closure. I twisted the bulky leather chair around to show him. "This little addition would ruin the chair's integrity as an art object, Gary. Don't bother taking it on *Antiques Roadshow* now. It's worthless. But that doesn't matter, does it? It's what's inside that counts."

I yanked the Velcro loose and cascade of round white pellets avalanched out of the chair...along with thousands of dollars' worth of oval blue pills: oxycodone.

I expected him to ask me how I'd figured out his cunning little hiding place. The answer would have been mildly embarrassing, but it never came up. Pressman had a different, less thoughtful response to the growing mess on his living room floor.

He ran.

Chapter Seventeen

High and Dry

In five seconds Pressman had sprinted to the back door, leapt across the deck, and charged into the moors beyond his house, breaking for the line of low trees in the middle of the island.

I took off after him, awkward in the big rubber boots I'd worn for the boat ride, feeling the absurdity of the chase but badly wanting to tackle him anyway. Pressman could run into the swampy oak and grapevine forest ahead of us, but Tuckernuck was small, his boat was disabled, and unless he had a personal gyrocopter stashed somewhere nearby, running wasn't going to help him much. I heard occasional gunshots, as well as distant ATV motors. Pressman and I weren't wearing orange vests. The most likely result of this absurd footrace would be one of us getting mistaken for a deer and shot by a hunter.

I was winded and panting when he disappeared into the low dark interior forest. I stood bent over with my hands on my knees, catching my breath, assessing the situation. Pressman must know all the trails and paths through this marshy woodland—he'd lived on Tuckernuck most of his life. There was no chance I'd be able to catch him in there. His best move once he lost me would be to circle back and try to get to his boat.

I walked back to Pressman's house. A noise from inside made me freeze on the back porch. I was alone, Pereira was gone. If someone had been in the house before, they must have been hiding. I drew my gun and stepped inside.

Jim Prescott was standing in the living room in a drift of opioid tablets. He looked like his son, but heavier, with that rawboned face filled out by middle age, and his hair thinning on top.

"Where's Gary?"

"What are you doing here?"

He just shook his head. "You ruined everything."

"How's that?"

"You don't understand. You don't get it."

I re-holstered my gun. "Enlighten me."

"You think I buy drugs from this piece of shit? You're right. That's why I'm here right now. The most secluded spot on the Eastern Seaboard, and some goddamn cop blunders in like it was the airport on poker night. Jesus Christ. Anyway, yeah. I buy the drugs from him because the Mexicans won't do business with me anymore because their end-user pool dried up. Guess that makes me the worst middle man ever. Me and my group."

"Your group?"

"There's a few of us. We pool our money and buy the drugs. But we don't sell 'em. We burn 'em."

I stared him. "You've got to be—what does that cost you?"

"It doesn't matter. I watched Pat's son, Doug, go down to this shit—"

"Pat Folger is part of your…group?"

"I'm not saying that. But Doug is gone, Chief. He's at the bottom of a hole and he's never climbing out again."

"He went to rehab! He was fine."

"He went to rehab three times, thirty grand a pop. And it didn't make any difference. They can't stay away from the stuff, Chief. This isn't a bunch of desperate inner-city kids. It's regular kids. It's your kids and my kids. You know how Doug got into it? He and my son and a few of their friends were sitting around somebody's house while the parents were off-island. They watched some PBS documentary about the drug scene in Boston that showed kids lighting up oxy pills and smoking them. It looked like fun, so they found some of the stuff in the mom's medicine cabinet and tried it. Boom bang done. End of story. That's all it takes to ruin a life and wreck a town. Some random well-meaning TV show and an open medicine cabinet. That's when we started buying from the MS-13 boys, but they got pissed off when the drugs disappeared. Lots of unhappy customers. They told us to back off and we did. Those guys don't fuck around, Chief."

"So, the next move was Pressman. What happens when he figures out what's going on?"

"He'll be in jail, looks like, so who cares? Someone else'll grab the business and we'll be there."

"Until they find out. It's not sustainable, Jim."

"Yeah? Well, maybe not. But at least we're doing something. We're trying. That's more than the DEA ever did."

"They're stretched thin. They can't cover every little town in America."

"That's why you're here."

"Exactly. That's why I'm *here*. In Pressman's house, busting him. It's my job."

"What about MS-13? You going after them?"

He was talking about the Mara Salvatrucha, a West Coast gang that had started franchising itself in New England. They had begun in El Salvador, and I'd heard that "Salvatrucha" was a combination of "Salvador" and the Caliche term "trucha," which roughly means being sharp-witted and on your toes. I'd dealt with the gang in L.A., after they merged with some local groups and added the 13 to their name—M is the thirteenth letter of the alphabet. These were tough, ruthless criminals, and I thought I'd left them behind when I moved to Nantucket.

No such luck. "Yes we're going after them, Jim. We're working with Immigration Customs Enforcement and we're making progress. A lot of arrests, a lot of drugs and weapons confiscated. But it's a slow process. There's a whole Hispanic community who have nothing to do with this shit and I don't want to target them. I want to protect them—they're the main victims right now. It's tricky and it's slow and there's not much margin for error. That's why I need you to stay out of our way and let us handle this."

"You going to arrest me?"

"No. But I want the names of your friends. I need to talk to them, too. This has to stop. It's well-intentioned, it's enterprising, but it has to stop before one of you gets caught in the act and busted or beaten up by these gangbangers—or killed."

He stared at the sandy, pine-plank floor. "All right. But I've got to talk to them first."

"Do it soon."

"Okay. Sorry, Chief. We're all getting a little crazy around here."

I let him go—he had a Boston Whaler tied up at the other side of the island. I wanted to call Lonnie Fraker at the State Police headquarters and State's Attorney Dave Carmichael in Boston, but there were no landlines on the little island and my cell phone had no reception at all.

I blew out a breath. There was no rush now. This was going to be a big bust, finally one with no ICE involvement, especially if we could get Pressman to roll over on his supplier. I knew Dave would want to get out in front of it. He'd be writing the press releases as soon as we got off the phone.

I let Bailey in and sat down on the couch. He jumped up to join me, circled his pillow a few times, and then settled in with his head on my lap. I stroked his neck and he snuggled closer. What an excellent dog! Pressman was going to jail. What would happen to Bailey?

I had a brainstorm about that just as I heard an outboard engine kick to life. It wasn't Jim's— this was the heavy snarl of a four-stroke engine, not a Boston Whaler two-stroke. And the sound wasn't coming from Pressman's boat, obviously. My ping-pong ball had taken care of that. Gary must have grabbed a neighbor's boat, and known where to find the keys. Tuckernuck people trusted each other—maybe too much.

I had the Madaket Landing points covered, but Pressman could head around Eel Point and along the north shore into town; he could even cruise to the mainland if he had enough gas in the boat. The wind had died down. And Sal Pereira had left me stranded.

My simple arrest was turning into a nightmare.

I eased Bailey's head off my lap, stood up, and went outside. On the porch, with my head cocked to listen, I must have looked a little like a dog myself. In the clear, still air it was easy to follow the sound of the outboard engine. It was coming from the direction of North Pond. I started along the dirt road that looked the most direct route and after a hundred yards or so I got a break. A hunter driving some sort of modified golf cart offered me a lift.

"Great day for the race!" he boomed as I climbed aboard. I could smell the rye whiskey on his breath.

"Which race?" I asked, knowing the answer but giving him the satisfaction of pounding the old joke into the ground—call it cab fare.

"The human race!" he shouted, clapping me on the back.

"Right—of course. The human race."

He stuck out his hand. "Ted Stackpole. Remember me? I was at a town meeting, shouting down those goddamn 'Sconset plutocrats and their geotubes."

"I do remember that."

"This is the place," Stackpole said, sweeping of his arm to embrace the empty moorlands and the scattered houses. "This is my Nantucket."

"Do you own a home out here?"

"My grandfather sold our family place in the fifties. Bought and sold a few times since then. The new people just finished a big renovation—they brought in some architect from Boston to trash the house. But here I am anyway, keeping the deer out of their flower garden! And they say I hold a grudge. Chasing the bad guys today?"

"Just one."

"Gary Pressman, am I right?"

I shouldn't have been surprised. Nantucket was a small island and Tuckernuck was even smaller. I shrugged and said, "Yeah."

Stackpole tipped his head forward. "No surprises. Little Gary always was a problem. Getting girls in trouble. Joyriding cars. He drove one off the bluff at Cisco his senior year. Thought that was hilarious. Just a nasty little person."

When we reached the beach at North Pond,

Stackpole started laughing. "That boy must be doing too many of his own drugs!"

Pressman's outboard motor, small in the distance, whined at a steepening pitch. But the boat refused to move, caught in the narrow inlet that led to the waters of Madaket Harbor.

I glanced over at Stackpole. "What's happening?"

His laugh had collapsed into a cough. He paused and pulled in a deep breath. "What's happening? Low tide is happening, that's what's happening! The little punk is high and dry."

Pressman had run aground.

"Now what?" I asked.

"Now we borrow one of Pee-Wee Ottinger's two-man kayaks, and you paddle out to the rescue."

"How is Pee Wee going to feel about that?"

"Well, Pee-Wee spends his winters in Key West, so he ain't around to make his feelings known. But it's a neighborly sort of a gesture, in aid of the local constabulary, so I'm sure he'd be happy to oblige. Not to mention, anything that rids this place of Gary Pressman will be cause for celebration come Memorial Day."

We drove to the Ottinger house, its windows boarded up against the winter gales, and found the kayak around the back by the garage. Stackpole helped me carry the bulky vessel back to the shore, and pushed me off when I got settled, bobbing and rocking on the water.

He lifted his binoculars as I started to paddle. "I'll keep an eye on you, Chief. He's still in rifle range!"

It took ten minutes to cross North Pond and by the end of the trip, I was seriously considering buying a kayak of my own. The splash of the paddle, the quick spurt of movement over the still water, the sense of gliding across the face of an untouched world—it all shifted me into a state of almost supernatural calm.

Pressman was sitting in his boat, tense and miserable, like a kindergarten miscreant banished to the corner and missing recess. I felt bad for him, turned back on himself like an ingrown toenail, failing to appreciate the New England winter day arching above him. It would take a week of monsoon rain to create this kind of icy clarity in the Los Angeles air. Here it was so ordinary you forgot about it.

"Do I need to read you your rights, Gary?" I asked.

"You might as well."

I Mirandized him, and then said, "I got a call from Pat Sauter yesterday."

"So?"

"He was calling on your behalf, Gary. As you know perfectly well."

"He does what he does. I can't control Pat Sauter."

"Come on. Why not use real thugs, if you wanted to scare me off the case? Your supplier must have an army of them. Old School Dorchester leg-breakers."

He looked away. "I would never threaten a cop. Or ask anyone to."

"All right, look…I don't want to nail you for obstruction. I have enough on you with the oxy. I don't want to arrest Pat over a deniable phone call. I just want to know what's going on in my town."

"Well, okay. First, off, it's not your town and it never will be. But…whatever. Pat and I go back to high school. I tutored him so he could stay on the Whalers and he was my bodyguard. We weren't exactly friends, but…he was part of my life and vice versa and that's the way it is around here. When his kid got into the opioid thing, Pat came to me." he caught my look. "For help, Chief. For help. Pat wanted to keep it secret, so, you know—no time off from school, no rehab. The idea was, I'd keep a stash and string the kid out, taper the dose for him, until he was clean. And it worked. Then Jake got hurt last year playing football, he threw his back out and they put him on painkillers. They didn't know not to, because nobody told them and nobody was going to tell them, either. So Pat came to me and we went through the whole withdrawal dance again—and it worked again. Happy ending, so far. Jake is back on the field and nobody knows what happened except me and his dad—and now you. So if I asked Pat to help me out, he would. Not that I did."

"Okay. Thanks, Gary. It's hard to get to know a place when no one tells you the secrets."

"These secrets going to be used against me in a court of law? Just wondering."

I gave him my best dopey bland innocent stare. "What secrets?"

He grinned and I helped him into the kayak. We almost capsized it. I gave him a paddle. He could have attacked me with it. But I knew he wouldn't. Part of it was the new intimacy between us, but I could see that the hushed noble beauty of the day had affected him, too.

Climbing ashore, he said "I really love this place."

I couldn't let him off the hook. "Act that way, then," I said, "if you ever come back."

Chapter Eighteen
The Grinch

I had a good guess about at least one of Prescott's cohorts and I decided to brace him while I still had the element of surprise. I'd put off my visit to Jackson Blum's store, but my talk with Pressman justified the delay. I needed to brace Blum, too, but once again, my cold case could wait. I had much more reason to suspect his clerk, Arnold Sprockett, now, as my view of the sprinting wraith in a New York Giants hoodie, glimpsed on my last visit to Tuckernuck, clarified.

I hadn't mentioned Sprokett when I called Dave Carmichael and Lonnie Fraker on the drive back into town. I wanted to keep my options open—and Sprokett's. He could tell me so much: the other members of his Quixotic conspiracy, and their sources; perhaps I could even turn him as an undercover agent and let him strike a real blow against the drug dealers who had taken advantage of his son's injuries to create one more customer, probably a customer for life. I had other concerns, too: buying these drugs only to destroy them was an expensive proposition. Where was a retail clerk getting the money to pay for his portion of that investment?

My first thought was embezzlement—Blum was a fat target for such a crime, and the daily temptation must have been overwhelming. In fact, Blum and Sprockett were going at it when I slipped into the store, which was open, despite the CLOSED sign in the window. The voices were coming from the stockroom beyond the cash register desk.

I paused, just inside the door, listening.

"—and you've only yourself to blame," Blum was saying.

"I don't get it. What difference does that make? This isn't about me. It's about my son. It's—"

"Of course it's about you! It's about your reckless negligence and your small-minded, short-sighted penny-pinching stupidity. You gambled with your son's future and you lost."

"But I had no idea—"

"Grownups don't predict the future, Sprockett. They plan for it. They hope for the best and prepare for the worst. They don't just stagger ahead blindly until they step off a cliff. But that's what you did. And now you're falling and you've dragged your family along with you. You're all taking the plunge together. You're in freefall and when you and your wife and your little boy hit the ground you'll be shattered. You'll be broken beyond repair. But that's not even the worst part. The worst part is—you know it's your fault, and so do they. There's got to be a lot of rage in your house right now. A lot of anger. Anger at life, anger at the world, and especially…anger at you, for not keeping them safe from that big bad world out there. That's your whole job, Sprockett! Protecting your family. And you failed!"

"I know, sir. I know that. Which is why—"

"Sir? You're calling me sir now?"

"Yes, I—uh, I thought—"

"You thought I'd appreciate the show of respect."

"I—"

"You thought I'd preen myself at the first note of flattery, and never wonder why I'd never heard you call me that before."

"No, no, I just—"

"Why not go all the way then, Sprockett? Get on your hands and knees. Kiss my shoes. Beg! Grovel and beg and debase yourself for an amount of money so sad and tiny I wouldn't even notice if you stole it from me! Crawl for the spare change rattling around in my clothes dryer. Plead for my pennies. Go ahead, do it. Do it or get out."

I heard some sort of shuffling, and stepped closer. Was Sprockett really going down on his knees?

Then: "Please, sir? Mr. Blum…I'm begging you. I have nowhere else to turn. And like you say… it's not for me. It's for my son. He never hurt anyone. All he wanted to do was play football with his friends and be happy. He has his whole life ahead of him. I don't want him to live it as a cripple. I couldn't stand that…knowing, like you said, that—that it was my fault—so please…if you could only—"

"Lend you the money?"

"Yes! Just for a while, just until—"

"I loaned you money before, Sprockett. And you never paid me back."

"But I did! I gave you—"

"The principal, but not the interest. Almost three thousand dollars in interest, compounded quarterly. Two thousand eight hundred and forty dollars, to be precise."

"I've tried, but my rent went up and I have back taxes that—"

"So you haven't paid the government either. I call that downright unpatriotic, Sprockett. Some people would call it treason."

"No, no, I worked out a payment plan—"

"Which is more than you did with me. Do you remember what I told you on that occasion? Because I do."

"You said…you told me—"

"I pointed out some salient facts. And I laid down the law. Your credit was nonexistent—I checked. I pointed out that in an actual crisis, I'd be your bank of last resort. I told you—pay the money back on time, Sprocket! Every penny, including the interest I charged you, so that I wouldn't have to pay a gift tax on my generosity. Because if you don't, I told you, and I made it very clear, if you're a day late or a penny shy, when that day comes you'll get nothing from me. I'll watch you go bankrupt and hope it teaches you a lesson. Do you remember that?"

Sprockett's voice was almost too quiet to hear: "Yes."

"Did you think I was joking?"

"No, sir."

"Did you think I was bluffing?"

"No, sir."

"But perhaps you thought I'd forget. Forgive and forget! Well I've never done either and I never will."

"But I just hoped…"

"What? What did you hope?"

"I mean, I thought…because it was Christmas…"

"But I don't care about Christmas, and you

know it. I care about the number of shopping days until Christmas thirteen of them as of today. And I care about the day after Christmas! That and the day after Thanksgiving are my biggest days of the year. Christmas is money in my pocket, and that's all it is."

"No, no, sir—it's more than that! It's—"

"It's a way for parents to dope their children with chocolate and bribe them with useless toys they'll be taking to the landfill before the next round of spending starts. It teaches children greed—you've heard them whining for their overpriced baubles on Santa's lap. It teaches them cunning, when they sniff out the hiding places and debunk the imbecile mythology, the elves and the reindeer and the fat man in their chimneys. The holiday turns them into ravenous little consumers and that's the best thing about it! But don't pretend you fall for the treacle, Sprockett. Or maybe you really do believe in all that love and generosity propaganda. In which case you're a sucker as well as a fool."

"So…you won't help me…at all?"

"I'd rather take the money you need and set on fire in front of you. Would you like that? I might consider that."

There was a long silence as the weight of the truth settled on the little clerk. Finally, he said,

"You're the Grinch. There really is a Grinch. And it's you."

"Wrong again, Sprockett. I don't have to steal Christmas. I own it already. Now get to work or get fired."

I spun and light-footed my way to the door and outside into the icy breeze. The last thing Arnold Sprockett needed was to know that anyone had overheard his humiliation. There was one plus side for him, though. I knew now that he couldn't be part of Jim Prescott's drug-buying scheme. He simply couldn't afford it. Sprockett couldn't afford takeout coffee.

I'd missed the first part of the conversation but I could piece it together without much trouble: Sprockett's kid required knee surgery, and for some reason the clerk's insurance didn't cover it. If Sprockett was really broke, a wealthy boss might well be—what did Blum call it?—the bank of last resort. But not this time. I felt bad for Blum's clerk, but there was nothing I could do for him except suggest a Kickstarter campaign. Unfortunately, that process was uncertain at best and took time. From the sound of Sprockett's voice, time was running out fast.

The good news—Sprockett was no drug king-pin. I was happy not to make the poor man's life more difficult, but with him eliminated from my suspect list, I couldn't help wondering as I climbed into my cruiser, who the mystery man in the New York Giants sweatshirt might be.

• • ● • •

It was Prescott himself, I found out later that day—Pat Folger's coconspirator in the opioid destruction scheme. It turned out that everyone but me knew he was a lifelong Giants fan, washed ashore from Massapequa Long Island in 1997, when he came to visit a college friend. Like so many people who came to Nantucket for a honeymoon or a weekend, he had simply never left. A salesman for a discount furniture chain in his mainland life, he applied for a job with the Maury People, and the real estate firm stuck him in their new sleepy 'Sconset office, figuring it would give him time to learn the trade while he studied for his license. The first walk-in wound up buying a six-million-dollar house in Quidnet. And Jim was on his way.

"It's like picking up money in the street," he had told Jane once. They had dated briefly before he met his wife and settled down. Of course they had—everyone knew everyone on this little island.

Pat Souter ambushed me as I was leaving my house on my way back to the station after a quick late lunch. I was distracted, concentrating on work, tying up all the threads of Pressman's indictment—we had to seal off and fingerprint the Tuckernuck house, confiscate the drugs, get started on the subpoena for Pressman's credit card bills, phone records, and bank accounts. It was delicate because I wanted to catch Pressman's supplier and also shield the hapless islanders who had gotten tangled in his schemes, both the do-gooding parents who had bought the drugs to keep them off the market and the kids who had been lucky enough to have their business with him delayed. With any luck I could turn their brush with criminality into a teachable moment instead of a life-wrecking catastrophe.

So I had a lot to think about, and I felt safe on Darling Street. It was the kind of lull in the action my old LAPD pal Chuck Obremski used to warn me about, quoting seventeenth-century tactical genius and samurai Miyamoto Musashi's *Go Rin no Sho* or *The Book of Five Rings*, one of his favorite survival handbooks:

"When the battle is over, tighten the straps of your helmet."

I was actually looking down at the pavement when I literally walked into Sauter, and more or less bounced off his chest. He had just stepped out from the side of the next house down. I looked up, about to apologize, and saw who it was. The adrenaline jolt yanked me back into the present moment: fight or flight.

Or both? Or neither. I heard Chuck's voice in

my head again: "We don't do fight-or-flight, 'kay? We don't have that luxury. We do balk-and-talk instead."

Balk and talk—stop the action, de-escalate, argue them down, chill them out.

"I told you to leave Gary alone."

First mistake, Pat. "Actually you were smart enough not to mention his name. And you did it on the phone where I couldn't positively identify you."

"Yeah, well. Problem is, once you're knocked out you can't remember shit about the last five, ten minutes before it happened. The brain don't have time to store it cause the brain is fritzed out. That's why we're gonna wait a little while before I beat the shit out of you, Chief. Because I want you to remember this part."

"Looks like you thought this whole thing out. Or someone did it for you."

He grunted out a laugh. "You think you're a nail set, and you're nothing but a lousy pot hook."

"What?"

"That's tradesman slang, Chief. You'd know it if you ever worked a real job."

I was interested in spite of myself. "So…a nail set is—necessary? And a pot hook?"

"Just something to attach your paint to your ladder. Nothing special, lots of guys use a twisted up coat hanger."

"So, I could say…you think you're a stainless corner trowel and you're just a plastic putty knife."

He shoved me but I was waiting for it and twisted a little to deflect the blow. He stumbled forward, off balance, and I took a step back, ready to catch him if he tripped. He got his balance back, but now I was making him mad. I almost expected him to say it—the classic bully's answer to victim resistance.

He got to the point instead. "For the last time…drop the charges, close the case down."

"Too late, Pat. It's already been turned over to the Staties and the Mass AG's office."

"Bullshit."

Another thought occurred to me. "How do you know I didn't drop the case already? You expected your phone call to work, but it didn't. And you found that out somehow, and now you brace me on the street. So who's talking to you, Pat? Who's your friend on the Nantucket Police force?"

"I don't need a spy. People talk, people hear things. You say you called in the State Police? All the more reason to get out to Tuckernuck and dump those pills. Lonnie Fraker might be headed out there already! So the race is on."

"Not going to happen, Pat."

He grinned. "Good. That gives me an excuse to fuck you up."

I held up a professorial hand, index finger pointed to the sky. "Hold on. Before we start, I need to explain a few things. Bear with me. First of all, you may have wondered why it seemed so easy to rough me up when we were fighting two years ago at the Delta Fields. I mean apart from your obvious first ideas, that I'm a weakling and a fag."

Another piggy laugh. "Something like that."

"In fact there were two other reasons. First of all, I was pretty well beaten up already. I was a mass of burns and bruises. But that's not even the important part. See, I was trained to fight. Actually trained. It wasn't the kind of fighting you're used to—playground push and shove. All I know how to do is disable and kill. Shatter the knee, close the thorax, drive the nasal bone up into the brain. It's a last resort. Don't drive me to it."

"You finished?"

"Not quite. Beyond that, there's the legal problem. You raise a hand to me and no matter what I do I'm justified and no matter what you do you've committed felony assault against a police officer. I get a medal. You go to jail."

"If there was a witness. But there is no witness."

"Yes, there is."

It was a woman's voice. Karen Gifford stood up from behind a big four-door Jeep and stepped into the street.

"So some girl's gonna fight your battles for you?"

"I don't fight," Karen pointed out. "I watch. And film things on my iPhone 8." She held it out to frame the scene properly.

"There's another alternative, Pat," I said. "Walk away. Forget about this idiotic little game. Go on about your business. Take care of your son. I won't press charges but I am putting you on probation. The next time you step one baby step out of line I will come down on you like the trash avalanche at the CD building. And all you tradesmen remember the trash avalanche."

A toxic slide of construction and demolition debris had killed a worker at the dump a couple of years before—a horrible way to go.

The three of us stood there on the quiet tree-lined street. Finally Sauter caved. "Fine. You win. But the game is rigged so the cops always win."

"Right. It's called 'civilization.'"

Walking into town with Karen on Fair Street—Pat had retreated in the opposite direction toward Pine Street—I asked the obvious question. "What were you doing there?"

"I've been following you in my spare time. Everyone knows about Pat's phone call. I was worried."

"Well, thanks."

"I guess I didn't need to be, with you knowing all that killer karate stuff."

I laughed. "That was bullshit, Karen. My game is poker, and I love to bluff."

Everything fell into place after that, like a jar full of coins dumped into a sorting machine, spinning into neat stacks of quarters, nickels, and dimes, ready to wrap. I talked to Pat Folger and the other would-be vigilante drug squad; Pressman was arrested and booked, his dog taken to the MSPCA for adoption, the drugs confiscated. I gave David Trezize the story—a small early Christmas present—and he ran it on the front page of the *Nantucket Shoals* that week, impressively scooping the *Inquirer and Mirror.*

"I'm a petty and vindictive little man," he told me. "But I love this kind of shit."

Dave Prescott confessed to Bissell without betraying Hector Cruz, who confessed in turn to my daughter and got what would no doubt be the first of many "Can't we just be friends?" rejections (though she was happy to eat the chocolates).

At my suggestion with some gentle pressure from the Selectmen, Bissell offered Dave the chance to work off his two-week suspension in community service, so no scandal tarred the town's sacred Nantucket Whalers football program.

The last coin dropped into the last tube when

I ran into our new sheriff, Fred Lowry, on his way to deliver an eviction notice to Sam Trikilis.

"Can it wait until after the holidays?" I asked him, as we walked out of Fast Forward with our coffees.

"It won't make any difference, Chief."

"But it's a nice gesture. And I'll remember it."

The stall would only buy Sam a few weeks, but he had a pile of past due invoices to collect, and a small inheritance that might rescue him if it cleared probate by January. So it was worth a shot. And I knew that Fred didn't relish the job of kicking a family out of their house this time of year. He was a strident believer in the Fox News "War on Christmas"—this was his chance to take up arms for the beleaguered holiday.

So all the coins were wrapped up and ready to deposit. Carrie's play was going well, she had made her peace with Jane's little elf—apparently he had finally learned his one line—and we were mostly moved into the new house.

Crime on the island had hit at an all-time low. It looked like an easy slide into the New Year.

And then Alana Trikilis came down with food poisoning.

Part Two
Christmas Eve

Chapter Nineteen

The Ghost of Christmas Future

Max Blum hadn't always hated his father. He could remember walking on the beach with the old man, talking about whatever came into their minds. They discussed Max's fear of the ocean—in some book he had seen a looming storm swell referred to as a "motherless" wave, and his dad wanted to know why the phrase stuck with him. "Maybe because…a huge wave is so, I don't know. Not human? Uncaring? Everything Mom isn't."

"Good boy," his father had said that afternoon. "Very shrewd. And your mother will be pleased to get the vote of confidence."

Shrewd: that was his father's favorite compliment. Max understood the significance of that now. But on those long walks he had just been drunk on the smoky elixir of his dad's undivided attention. Dad spoke to him as if he was an adult already (well, of course; children bored him), with no subject out of bounds. Politics? His dad was a Libertarian and thought the only remaining example of American democracy was Nantucket's annual Town Meeting. Sex? "Remember this for later, Max: never let a girl leave a single personal item at your house. Not a shirt, not a hairclip. That's the beginning of the end." Religion? "Fairy tales for fools afraid to die." They both loved puzzles—crosswords and Sudoku, puns and plays on words ("Be it ever so crumpled, there's no plate like chrome") anagrams, oxymorons ("soft rock!"), palindromes (Horses say "Yahoo! Hay!").

His dad had laughed at his jokes, frowned at his concerns, clasped his shoulder with an easy camaraderie that attached him to the world. His dad had been his anchor then, holding him tight against the tides and currents, the chain dropping straight into the dark water, the barnacled metal resting in the silt.

How had it all changed? Maybe it was just puberty. But Max started to see things differently. Discrete observations that hadn't even seemed to register, collected and organized, random strangers forming a mob, a lynch mob jazzed at the hate they had in common.

Max remembered getting his first pair of glasses—putting them on and looking around, the world leaping into a bright caustic unwelcome clarity. The dust on the furniture, the pores on his father's face, the flaws in his father's character.

His father was cruel and mean-spirited. He treated his employees and his friends and his family badly. He was abusive. Max recalled the night Dad had made Martin rewrite some stupid English paper over and over, starting from scratch by hand each time he found a misspelled word, a missing comma, or an improperly indented paragraph. Max felt absurdly protective of his older brother. Martin was flimsy, porous, sad. He needed TLC, and he got that cold rage, that shiver of disgust, that bottomless dismissal. It was midnight before Martin completed the paper to Jackson Blum's satisfaction.

"So, you finally managed to do something right!" Dad had sneered. "Amazing."

Maybe Dad had sensed something even then, something off about Martin, some physical failure to conform, like a limp or a tic. Martin had something much more incriminating, from around the age of ten: a sense of style.

When he was fourteen he spent the summer at Nantucket Sailing. The organization offered the kids free Crocs, as part of some corporate promotion. By the time it was Martin's turn to choose, the only ones left in his size were pink. He politely declined.

"Don't want to look like a fag?" his father had asked, when Martin told the story at dinner that night.

"Oh, because they're pink?" Martin had shot back. "It's exactly the opposite, Dad. No 'fag' would ever be caught dead in those grotesque rubber clogs. Fags have style."

And he did. He spent his allowance on tight-pegged jeans and fancy sunglasses; on a family trip to Manhattan he had slipped off to Trenton, just to buy some "cute" shirts at DD's Discounts. He was amused when hip-hop artists started adopting his style. Eventually the kids who'd been beating him up at school copied the rappers and wound up dressing just like him.

But Martin had already moved on—to crewneck cashmere sweaters, slim-fit chinos, bright-patterned dress socks, and Baldese sneakers. Few fifteen-year-olds referred to themselves as "fashion forward." Even at ten years old, Max knew that much.

And it was clear that their father had been in denial about Martin for a long time. No single trait was conclusive, after all. Jackson Blum enjoyed show-tunes just as much as his oldest son did, and had in fact introduced the boy to the pleasures of the American songbook. Appreciating Jerome Kern and Harold Arlen didn't signify anything but good taste. Max remembered the two of them performing a Frank Sinatra singalong to *The Lady is a Tramp*—and the sophisticated gusto with which Martin belted out the lyrics.

"I'll take Lorenz Hart over Oscar anytime," Martin had remarked that night, cutting another facet into the rare gem of his father's approval. Of course it turned out to be cubic zirconium, but for that one evening Martin glittered with the pride of being seen and appreciated, unable to sing a wrong note or say a wrong word.

Of course it didn't last. Things added up. All the refusals: Martin wouldn't try out for Whalers football, or support the conservative candidates his father financed. He preferred Al Jazeera and Democracy Now to Fox News. Worst of all, he wouldn't take a girl to the prom. In fact, Martin never had a girlfriend at all, though he had many friends who happened to be girls. No one could twine a French braid like Martin, or pay such sincere undivided attention to the melodramatic reconfigurations of cool-girl friendships and rivalries.

And his makeup tips were impeccable.

The girls Martin surrounded himself with confused his father. The old man just didn't get it. One day he said, "You should stop shaving, Martin.

You've got a good heavy stubble, just like me. Let it grow in! You'll look like a real man with a beard."

Martin had laughed. "But I already have Marissa."

Dad's baffled look was priceless.

The evidence kept accumulating. Martin got into Oberlin, turning down Boston College, his father's preferred institution of higher learning. He left home for the wilds of Ohio, and came back every vacation more flamboyant and less interested in putting on the show his father required.

"If I'm going to stay in the closet," he said to Max two Christmases ago, "I'm going to need a bigger one. Too much clobber—all those batts and kaffies." That meant clothes and shoes and trousers in British Polari slang. Martin had started using Polari after listening to old Marty Feldman BBC comedy tapes and classic Morrissey albums. It annoyed and alienated their father; it cut and chewed at the thread binding them together, like all the other details had before, but nothing had quite managed to sever that coarse familial twine.

Until now.

Martin always came home for the four-day "reading period" between the end of classes and final exams. He didn't need what he called the "Oberlin courtesy cram." He generally knew the class material inside-out, and often moved beyond assigned texts to primary source material. This semester, for instance, supplanting the Zeiler and DuBois *Companion to World War Two* with Winston Churchill's six-volume history, from *The Gathering Storm* to *Triumph and Tragedy*, along with Nazi diaries and collections of American GI letters home.

So when classes ended, his time was pretty much his own.

He had always returned to Nantucket by himself. This year he brought a friend, a tall shy slim redheaded boy with freckles and heavy black glasses named Connor McKenzie. Martin despised public displays of affection, so there was nothing obviously outrageous about the two boys together. Max could read the occasional shared smile or raised eyebrow, the quick secret brief touch, hand to shoulder, fingertip to cheek. But Dad was oblivious, and Mom didn't care. She was just happy that her spiky difficult son had found a friend he liked well enough to bring home.

Connor was charming. The youngest of six siblings, with five older sisters who tormented him amiably from toddlerhood, dressing him in their clothes, teaching him to cook so he could serve them breakfast in bed, showering him with nicknames ("Grommet" was the one that stuck), demanding that he communicate entirely through gestures and facial expressions. He was a genius at charades, after a lifetime of practice.

He was a vegetarian, and quite an accomplished chef, and after a day featuring a lunch of quinoa burgers and a dinner of orcchiette with rapini and goat cheese, Marjorie declared that she could attempt a vegetarian diet with Connor in the kitchen.

Blum laughed. "Marjorie has been trying to get me on one cockamamie diet or another since the first George Bush administration. She seems to think everything I like to eat is fattening."

Connor shrugged. "Nothing's fattening if you exercise."

"But I don't exercise. And the only people who do are obsessives and body-fetishists."

"What do you obsess about?" Connor asked. "Or fetishize?"

"Money," Martin answered for him.

Blum turned on his son. "And it's lucky for you that I do. Unless you'd rather have nothing."

Martin was about to answer, but Max saw a look pass between him and Connor, as if Connor knew Martin was about to blurt something bad and possibly unforgivable. A fractional shake of his head blocked Martin's rebuttal instantly, Martin's face shifting in less than a second from a sneer of rage to a baffled frown of insurrection to a half-smile of defeat. And all he wound up saying was, "You're right, Dad. Sorry."

Max wasn't the only one who caught that silent exchange. Marjorie Blum saw it too, and her quick smile was the seal of approval Martin had been longing for.

It went on, from the ilex berry and pine bough centerpiece Connor picked in the moors for the dining room table to the easy way he helped with the housework. He made his own bed and did everyone's laundry. He slipped coasters under errant glasses and fluffed flattened couch pillows. He even found a set of reusable Keurig pods at Stop&Shop to use with the pound of George Howell Terroir single source Caturra coffee he had brought with him from Boston. Marjorie summed it up on the second day of his visit, and even her husband had to agree.

Connor McKenzie: best house guest ever.

That was how things stood on the morning it happened.

The night before they had attended a performance of *A Christmas Carol* at the The White Heron Theater and argued about it amiably afterward over a Gambella and a Rustica at Pi Pizzeria. Blum had always thought Dickens' tale was sentimental claptrap, and the clumsy dramatization had done nothing to change his mind. Martin agreed.

Max and his mother took the other side, touched despite themselves by the spectacle of Scrooge's redemption.

Everyone retired early, congenially drunk after sharing two bottles of wine with dinner.

Blum woke up just after six the next morning to the sounds of a scuffle. At first he thought there had been a break-in—that Max or Martin, or possibly both of them, were subduing a prowler.

He sat up in bed, thinking about weapons. The Ruger was locked away in the gun cabinet downstairs. The andirons were standing uselessly beside the great room fireplace. His cell phone was charging in the kitchen. He held his breath and listened.

A new sound, an unmistakable one: his son's laugh. And another voice, mingled laughter and some sort of grunting then silence and the groan and squeak of the bedsprings, all coming from down the hall—Martin's room.

Had Martin sneaked a girl in there? The waitress at Pi had been flirting with him outrageously.

Then that other voice again, no words this time, just a keening sigh dropping down the registers, landing in the baritone pit with a groan, then jerked up again into a little bleat of pleasure—not a female voice. Not a girl.

Something in Blum's chest clenched. He

couldn't breathe for a second or two. He pulled air in through the constricted passages, his childhood asthma coming back to haunt him. For years he had felt stress and fear and worry in his guts. But this moment was crushing his lungs.

It couldn't be possible. He had to be wrong. There had to be another explanation. There were always other explanations, things were never exactly the way they seemed, were they? People made mistakes, they jumped to conclusions! That's what he was doing right now, jumping to conclusions. When you make an assumption you make of fool of—no an ass, you made an ass of—how did that go? Yourself, the other person, something, everyone. He couldn't remember. But it was bad.

He couldn't afford to assume anything now. He had to know for sure. Even as the thought formed in his mind he was swinging his legs off the bed, setting tender feet on the cold oak plank floor, crossing the room as the sounds went on, spiking and subsiding.

Marjorie rolled over "Jackson—?"

But he was already out the door.

Ten steps down the dark hallway, and the sounds from Martin's room suddenly stopped. He was at the door and through it before he could control the impulse. He was moving too fast, with a swarm of emotions held primed but still inert vibrating in his throat, explosives set to detonate at a signal waiting for the lethal transmission: fear, rage, despair, embarrassment, relief.

But at the moment the door flew open he felt nothing. For the moment his capacity to react was overwhelmed, a power surge that blew all the breakers. His brain went black.

All he could do was stare.

He clutched the doorknob as if it were the only thing that could keep him from hurtling through the ceiling. On the bed, Martin and Connor lay naked, entwined in a position of mutual pleasure generally named with a number, a date, the year of Woodstock and Manson and the moon landing. They were in fact at the moment of perfectly timed release as Blum stepped into the room, thinking, this is Hell. Literally, Hell. If the floor had opened up and showed him the malignant playground of devils and satyrs from his childhood nightmares, with Satan himself grinning bloody-toothed, beckoning him down down down into an eternity of agony and despair, it couldn't have been worse

He had laughed at those grotesque images. Even as a kid. He didn't believe in any afterlife. But he didn't need the afterlife, now. Hell didn't need to wait. Hell was right in front of him.

Finally the boys sensed his presence. Martin twisted around to see him. His son seemed eerily calm. Perhaps he hadn't fully grasped the horrific moment either. All he said was, "Don't you ever knock?"

"What—what are you…? What is going on in here?"

"Are you serious?"

"It—you—"

"This is me—coming out."

Connor sat up in bed, pulling the covers over them both. "Martin, don't—"

"I'm gay, Dad. Now you know."

"You—the two of you—"

"We're in love."

Connor said "Please, sir, if you could just—"

Martin's voice was cold. "Stay out of this."

"But—"

"Just—shhhhh." He turned back to his father. "I can't believe you never figured it out for yourself, Dad. I posted a rainbow bagel on Instagram. Hello—I do a perfect Streisand impression! I know every Sondheim tune by heart. So I won't be getting married, today or any other day. Even though it's legal now. For us. Your example is too fucking scary."

"Watch your mouth!"

"So bad words are the problem?"

"Put some clothes on. And get this…boy out of here."

"He's a man. And he's staying."

"Don't make me laugh. I want him gone, he's gone. This is *my house*."

This seemed to knock Martin off balance for the first time. "You…it—where is he supposed to go?"

"He has a home. There are five boats a day off the island right now. And a dozen plane flights."

Connor touched Martin's shoulder. "He's right. I'll just…"

He stood, covering himself with a pillow, grabbed his clothes off the floor and picked his way to the bathroom, closing the door behind him. The sound of the latch clicking reset the moment.

Martin took a deep breath in the ventilating silence. "Jesus, Dad."

"You make me sick."

"What? How can you—?"

"Physically sick! I feel like I'm going puke right here, right now, standing here."

"Dad—"

"Fouling those sheets. Seven-hundred-dollar Porthault sheets, tainted, ruined. I'll have to burn them now."

"This is absurd. Look—"

"How could you choose this?"

"What the fuck? I didn't choose anything! Did you choose to be right-handed?"

"They chose for me! You never knew that, did

you? I was born left-handed and they made me change at school."

"No wonder you're so fucked up. They say it gives you headaches too. Because they should never have tried to rewire your brain that way. It's child abuse."

"So, I was abused? Is that it? And I suppose you were, too."

"No, you didn't care enough to abuse your kids. You save that for your employees."

"Enough!"

"No, I—"

"Shut up, you little shit. You know nothing about my business! And this has nothing to do with me. Get up and put some clothes on. I want you out of here, too."

"What—so you're kicking me out of my own house?"

"It's not your house! It's my family's house. You're not my family anymore. You're…something else. You're a stranger. You're trespassing."

"Come on, that's just totally—"

"You've fouled your own nest!"

"That's crazy. I didn't—"

"You commit sodomy under my roof but I'm the crazy one!"

"Look—"

"Go! Just—go."

"Jackson."

Marjorie was standing in the doorway behind him, her dressing gown tied hastily, her hair tangled, her face indented from the pillow. The sound of her voice was like something breaking, something precious he had knocked off a table, flailing his arms around. "Please, Jackson…"

This was too much, too many people, too many opinions, too much confusion. "Go back to bed. Or make coffee. Do something useful. I'll handle this."

She didn't move. "Martin is my son, too, Jackson."

Martin had taken the brief lull to stand and start pulling on his clothes.

"Mom…"

"No, I can't stand this."

"You didn't see what I saw!" Blum's voice squealed out raw, high-pitched, crazy. He sounded like an hysterical child, even to himself. He had to slow down, take charge, master this moment, master himself.

"I didn't need to see anything. I've known for years, Jackson. Since he was ten. Maybe before that. It was obvious to anyone who cared to look."

"And you never saw fit—"

"I knew how you'd react. Or at least…I was

afraid of how you might react. Now I see I was right."

"So you've been in this with him all along."

"Yes. That's right! I'm 'in it' with him. I'm in everything with him. I'm his mother."

"Fine. You handle this, then. But make sure he's gone, him and his…boy toy in there. I don't want to see either one of them ever again."

He pushed past her and stalked out of the room. Martin and his mother stared at each other like two survivors of an earthquake, bereft but unscathed, standing in the rubble.

"Martin, I'm so sorry."

He stepped closer, reached out to take her hand. "Don't be, it's okay. It's just him. He can't help himself."

"But I married him."

Martin allowed himself a crooked little smile. "And had kids with him, Mom. I can't totally regret that."

She took his hand in both of hers and squeezed hard. "That's the one thing I don't regret either, Martin. But sometimes I wonder if you—I mean, it seems like you're not really happy to be here, like…you feel…."

"I was happy to be home. I was happy to be here—this morning. I was. Until five minutes ago."

"I can handle your father. I can fix this."

"Mom—"

"We want you to be happy."

"You do. He wants me to be him. And I'd rather die."

Blum charged back into the room. Marjorie stepped sideways, releasing Martin's hands, shielding him. The gesture was unthinking, instinctive, but it stoked Blum's rage. "How dare you say that, you ungrateful little freak—?"

Martin stepped backward, but his tone was fearlessly cruel. "You were eavesdropping? Are you kidding me?"

"I—"

"You're pathetic. You're the freak, you big fat fucking—"

The bomb went off, an engulfing bloom of hate. Blum heard the slap before he felt it on his palm, before he understood that his arm had moved. The impact jolted him to his shoulder, and Martin stumbled backward, shocked to silence. Blum advanced on him, but the boy made no effort to retaliate or even lift his arms to defend himself. They stood panting and furious, staring at each other.

Blum spoke first. "You'd rather die than be like me? Well, I hope you do. I hope you get AIDS and die. I could kill you myself right now."

His wife's beseeching irrelevant voice, from somewhere far away. "Jackson, don't do this…"

"No," Martin said. He seemed to be answering both of them "Do it. Then you'll have to live with it for the rest of your miserable shitty life. I could die happy knowing that. Plus you'd go to jail. You might make your own gay friends there. You're old and ugly but there's someone for everyone."

Stricken, Blum raised his arm for another blow but his strength or his resolve or his certainty, his understanding of the world and his place in it… everything fell away from him at once. He was weak, swooning with disgust for everything in the world, everything in his world, including himself. All he could finally say was: "You're not worth it."

"Coward."

"Get out. Never come back. I never want to see your face again."

He walked out of the room for the last time, leaving the door open. Martin and his mother looked at each other, mute. There was nothing left to say. She couldn't help, she couldn't change anything. Even if she put her marriage on the line and he knew she didn't have the force of will for that ultimatum. It would have been a bluff and they both knew it.

She was wondering how she could possibly explain Martin's departure to his brother, what desperate positive spin she could put on it. But there was no point in thinking that way. The boys talked to each other. They actually communicated, which was some kind of twisted miracle in the Blum family. Max would know everything soon enough. She mustn't make everything worse by lying. At least the boy hadn't had to witness this horrible scene. He would learn about the grotesque banishment of his brother secondhand. That was a blessing, if a small one.

But it wasn't the case. Max had been crouched behind the door of the upstairs hall bathroom the whole time, listening to every word, to the smack of flesh on flesh, to his father's retreating footsteps fading down the hall. When he slipped back to his room ten minutes later, he knew exactly how he was going to spend his share of the Red Ticket Raffle money, and it was a much finer commodity than Vicodin or oxycodone. Maybe revenge was a drug, too—he craved it like a drug.

But he would only need one hit.

Chapter Twenty
Fracking

It seemed like a slow three weeks, that annual lull between Christmas Stroll and Christmas morning, but pressure was building gradually, like the slabs of the Earth's crust grinding against each other, silent and secret and still, until force overcomes friction and the rock lurches and the earth quakes.

Maybe I was drawn to plate tectonics metaphors because of my years in Los Angeles. Though our human temblor was a modest one, it held the same sense of a moment unpredictable but inevitable, a shock that failed to surprise. But like the hydraulic fracturing that was partly responsible for the new earthquakes in Oklahoma, there was a vital element of human meddling here, too—mine. I wanted to force water into the buried fissures and release the trapped gases, the hidden truth. If the placid lives around me felt a seismic shudder afterward, fine.

Put it this way: I liked shaking things up. It was my hobby. Unfortunately for Jackson Blum, it was also my job. I knew the story of his crime. All I needed was the proof.

Karen Gifford had confirmed Chief McGrady's story about the confrontation between Blum and Coddington at 21 Federal. She had found a mention of it in the *Inquirer and Mirror*'s "Here and There" column:

> *As the year-round population grows, public decorum declines proportionately, even among community leaders who should know, and act, better. Rather than setting an example of civil discourse, two prominent members of the Chamber of Commerce involved themselves in a violent argument this week at 21 Federal restaurant, complete with raised voices and unseemly epithets...*

Whatever the subject of that quarrel—love or money or both—I knew where it had ended up—with a gunshot and a hasty burial, the grave protected from curious animals by a layer of tobacco.

I tracked down three of the vendors, one of them still on-island, living at Our Island Home, another retired to North Carolina, the third one settled in a guest cottage on his daughter's Truro property. One of them remembered no special purchases, another one never even sold chaw. The third had a dim recollection of getting cleaned out of Copenhagen, Skoal, and Red Man one afternoon. But he didn't recognize the customer.

That itself might prove useful. "So he wasn't a regular?"

"No, that's right. Guess he wanted to start with a bang. Like the stuff was going out of style." The old man chuckled. "Which it was. By the way. Hardly no one takes snuff these days."

I hit pay dirt with Hugh Tabor, the one storeowner McGrady had mentioned by name. He was indeed living in Key West, selling real estate and renting out a few properties of his own along Front Street in Old Town.

"This takes me back," he said in a wheezing Boston drawl, after I had introduced myself and explained why I was calling.

"So you remember the sale?"

"I remember that whole crazy year. Everything got cleaned out. The cops confiscated all the marijuana plants on the island, you couldn't find Lagavulin scotch anywhere—the Japanese had discovered the stuff and bought every bottle on the market! It was a terrible year for scallops, and some crazy old rich broad tore out her whole garden, the landscaper had put in too many pink flowers. I'm talking something like two, three acres now. They cleared out Bartlett's and every other nursery just to replace the plants. Tough year, 1997. And then the man who spent the better part of a decade at Town Meeting trying to get smoking banned, even outside, even on the moors, even on the deck of the steamship in a gale…this guy comes into the store and cleans me out of chewing tobacco. Every can! I guess he figured it was okay if you didn't smoke it. Or maybe he was trying to keep the stuff away from everybody else. But he ran a store. I expect he knew that we restock items, time to time."

I thought of our own little anti-drug cartel scooping up the opioids and destroying them. The idea was Quixotic and futile but it was also civic-minded. But Prescott and Folger, however misguided, were mounting a crusade. My suspect was no crusader. "This was Jackson Blum?"

"That's right. And I wasn't the only store he hit that day. God help you if you wanted some weed, a hydrangea bush, or some good single malt and a plate of scallops that winter! Or chaw. I didn't restock until April."

"Thanks, Hugh."

"Does this help?"

"Absolutely. One more little jigsaw puzzle piece."

"Like one that's partly treetops and partly sky, and it fits right in the middle?"

"Exactly. Sounds like you love puzzles."

"Sure. I always have one going."

"Me too."

I thanked him again, hung up the phone, stood and stretched. Then I walked over to the door and grabbed my coat off the hook. I needed to talk to Jackson Blum, but I had one more person to interview first.

I met Anna Coddington at Brotherhood of Thieves for lunch. She drank a Navy Grog and ate a basket of bay scallops and spiral fries, the restaurant's signature dish.

But she wasn't happy about it. "This place isn't the same anymore, since the fire," she complained, lifting the frosty copper mug and starting in on her second drink.

"The fire?"

"May of 1999. Very sad. Fire spoiled the Nobby Shop, too. The town smells smoke and instantly everything has to be brought up to code, with lots of renovation money for all the local vultures. Oh, my dear, those sacred, inviolable building codes! Which I decrypt as—remove all charm and history from any targeted structure! The Nobby Shop used to look like a Vermont country store—all those floor-to-ceiling shelves. Now you might as well be in the Cape Cod Mall. Very sad. Of course…people take advantage. The Brotherhood used the renovation to put in this awful bar. That's where the money is. And they added the television, of course. We can't have any public space without a television! I don't even call it the Brotherhood anymore. I refer to it as the 'Otherhood.'" She chuckled at her little joke and took another swig. I was drinking iced tea.

"But you still come here," I pointed out.

"They kept the old Navy Grog recipe. And I do like the fire on a winter afternoon."

I took a spoonful of lobster bisque—my favorite menu item, and said, "So your late husband and Jackson Blum were feuding at the time of Mr. Coddington's death?"

"I wouldn't call it a feud."

"A long-running argument?"

"They had different visions about the future of the business. Ted was happy with the way things were. Jackson wanted to take over Main Street." She offered a cold little smile. "And, possibly, the world."

"Well, that didn't work out very well."

"Thank goodness. At least he never decided to run for President."

"Was he capable of murder?"

"Of course not! Why should you even ask such a question?"

I took a breath, and chose the formal approach. Law enforcement jargon often calmed people down. "We have reason to believe foul play may have been involved."

"Nonsense. Ted killed himself. Simple as that."

I set my spoon down, push away the bowl of half-finished soup. "Why would he commit suicide?"

"Despair? Bi-polar disorder? Drugs?"

"Please, Mrs. Coddington. Everyone says he was cheerful. He wasn't seeing a psychiatrist at the time of his death. And he had no outstanding prescriptions of any kind—not even blood pressure medication."

"Very well. Suppose he was having an affair with my sister and was terrified that the truth might come out? Terrified with very good reason, I might add. The scandal would have destroyed all of us. That's why I have never discussed this with my daughter and I never will. There isn't much in this life I can shield her from. But I'm happy to include the foibles of her departed father on that short list."

"Are you just speculating about the affair, or—?"

"Oh, it's true, Chief Kennis. I'd known about it from the start. Ted was never much good at keeping secrets. Especially from me."

"But…you never said anything to him?"

"Really, my dear, how old-fashioned! The situation worked out very well for everyone."

"Until someone else found out."

"Or his conscience just got the better of him. He was even more old-fashioned than you, I'm afraid. Though still ruled by his…nether regions. I'm sure that created quite a conflict."

"Your husband was buried, Mrs. Coddington. What does that suggest to you?"

"A good Samaritan?"

"Coming across a body in the moors, burying it, and never reporting anything to the police?"

"A crazy person, then. Why not? We have plenty of those."

"The soil was mixed with chewing tobacco to keep animals away from the grave. Your good Samaritan with the handy shovel in his car didn't want that body found."

She finished her drink, and signaled to the waiter—one finger curled down toward the empty tankard, eyebrows raised. "So it was murder, then."

"I'm afraid so."

"And you suspect me?"

"The wife is always considered the most likely perpetrator. Statistically."

"And you investigate…statistically?"

"No."

She smiled. "Well, thank you, Chief Kennis. But then again…if you were indeed 'looking at' me, as the television detectives like to say, you'd be foolish to let on."

"True."

"Excuse me for not wilting under these innuendoes. I know I'm innocent. Ted and I had gone our separate ways by the time of his death. But we were still good friends—boon companions. He could always make me laugh. I still miss him."

"So who do you suspect?"

"My sister? Irena left the island soon after Ted disappeared."

"The jilted lover, the moment of passionate rage?

"I suppose."

"Do you think she was physically capable of burying him?"

"In a panic, I imagine…"

"Did she own a gun?"

"No. Well, not that I knew of." The waiter brought her third drink and she took a delicate sip. "It could have been my father. There were outstanding debts, and no love lost. Father felt that Ted represented all the worst elements of my adopted country: entitlement, weakness, arrogance, ignorance, sloth. I suppose he was right. But I liked those things about him."

"Did your father ever visit America?"

"He never left Lithuania. But he was a powerful man. He could have made a phone call, wired some money…the deed would have been done. And at modest expense. Murder is quite a bargain in the demi-monde. So I'm told."

I watched her as she took a healthier slug of the fresh Navy Grog. "But you don't believe that."

"Let's stop dancing around it, Chief Kennis. We both know it was Jackson Blum. And neither of us can prove it."

"Did he own a gun?"

"I have no idea. Probably. He did keep a shovel and a tow rope in his car. It's the law, if you want an over-sand driving permit. But of course you know that. Being a lawman."

I nodded. "So he had motive and opportunity."

"And no moral compass at all."

I pulled a twenty out of my pocket and set it between us. "That should cover my half of lunch."

"You're leaving so soon?"

"I have a wasp's nest to poke."

She drained her mug. "I can guess which one."

"I'd rather you didn't."

"Be careful, Chief. These little creatures can be astonishingly vindictive when you rile them up. And they move fast! I saw a swarm chase a carpenter for fifty yards once. He barely made it to his truck."

I pushed my chair back, and stood up. "I'll keep it in mind."

But Jackson Blum's house that squalling December afternoon seemed more sad than threatening. It was unlocked when I tried the knob, a lapse that seemed more careless than indifferent—as if no one could be bothered to keep track of ordinary household details anymore. Stepping inside, the place reminded me of nothing so much as a long ago-smoking-permitted truck stop motel room in eastern Pennsylvania.

I know that sounds strange. Blum's mansion displayed brass table lamps with Fortuny shades, gleaming cherrywood floors, and elegant furniture upholstered in striped silk, while the motel room offered nothing more than a chipped desk, overhead lighting, and a lumpy mattress. But I didn't recoil from the shabby furnishings in that distant exhausted evening, halfway through some ancient cross-country drive. No, it was the smell. It was the raw, invasive tang of nicotine. It steamed off the walls, draped the air like poisonous cobwebs. I remember staggering back and slamming the flimsy door, grabbing a cup of coffee, and hitting the road again.

But I had to step into the miasma that smothered Blum's house. It was my job. Still, I almost fled. It wasn't a smell, there was nothing you could touch, not even a film of dust, no sound, nothing to see. The house was silent and buffed, ready for an *Architectural Digest* photo spread. But toxic—something awful had happened there, you could feel it. Then I understood: it was like my own house, before my divorce, when the unspoken animosity between me and Miranda slimed every surface, as dangerous for the children as peeling lead paint.

I had checked with Milly Graham before I arrived, looking for her take on the state of the household. But she had been given the month off with pay. "They don't want me around there, Chief," she had said on the phone that morning. "They don't want nobody there."

And yet the house was almost supernaturally clean and tidy. Milly was more casual. She'd fluff the couch but not line up the throw pillows with such precision. The books, too—they were pulled out to the edges of the shelves, soldiers on dress parade. This was a vindictive housecleaning.

I remembered Miranda avoiding me by banging around in the kitchen, scrubbing the stove as if to scratch any evidence of me off the ceramic surface, refusing my help or suffering it as a pathetic charade of solidarity.

But there was more. Blum's older son was spending a few days home from college with a friend. I knew because Haden Krakauer had run into them at the airport when he went out to audit a TSA orientation session, and mentioned it in passing. He had always liked Martin Blum, though he had no such warm feelings for Martin's younger brother.

College kids were messy. Even the neatest ones left scat behind—rings on the counters from cups and glasses, coats draped over chairs, magazines on a coffee table, crumbs on a couch. I saw none of that. The kids were gone, early, abruptly, mid-weekend, Saturday morning.

"Hello?" I called out. I got no response, but I heard domestic sounds from the kitchen—a kettle placed on a burner, the rattle of cups, a cabinet door closing. I moved through the broad living room into the dining room. The long dark oak table was set for five. The fire in the fieldstone hearth had burned down to ash.

"So you're just going to read the paper?" Marjorie Blum said.

"Why not?"

"I can't stand this."

I stepped forward. She turned off the fire

under the kettle and started for the door at the fire side of the big sunny kitchen.

"What about your coffee?"

"Jackson."

"I could bring it up to you."

"Stop. Just—stop."

She walked out.

I stepped into the doorway. "Mr. Blum?"

He set his paper on the kitchen table. "What are you doing here? How did you get in?"

"The door was open. I need to talk to you."

"The children's day with Santa went very well, despite all the desertions. Thanks for your interest."

I moved into the room, leaned my forearms on the chair back across the table from him. "I'm here to ask you about Ted Coddington."

"He was my partner. He was a good man. His disappearance was a mystery that haunted his friends and family for decades. We're all glad to finally have closure."

I smiled. "Does that conclude your prepared remarks?"

"I resent your tone, Chief Kennis. Ted's suicide was a tragedy that—"

"I think he was murdered."

"You—"

"Someone shot him and buried him in the

moors. Have you ever purchased or registered a twenty-two caliber handgun?"

"Certainly not!"

"Not even for home protection?"

"Don't be ridiculous. This is Nantucket."

"The island is changing."

"Yes, well—but this is twenty years ago you're talking about. The Irish were establishing themselves, the hardworking Brazilian carpenters and painters had just started to arrive. We had not yet been overrun with the swarm of immigrants we see today. The social fabric of the town was still intact."

"So, no gun?"

"Certainly not."

"A search of your house would reveal nothing incriminating?"

"You'd need a warrant for that."

"I can get one in an hour."

"Do I need my lawyer? Am I under arrest?"

I pulled out the chair, stepped around it and sat. "Let's calm down. You're welcome to have a lawyer present. You're not under arrest. I'm just trying to figure out what happened to Coddington. It was a long time ago and there's not much to go on."

"So you're poking around a twenty-year-old cold case. Don't you have any real work to do?"

I ignored that remark. "I understand you and

Coddington had been fighting in the days before his death."

"We argued. We were partners. If we agreed on everything, that relationship would have been meaningless—a mere financial arrangement. A leader and a silent partner."

"So, Ted wasn't silent."

"No."

"The patrons at 21 Federal certainly attest to that."

He blew out a contemptuous breath. "Ancient gossip."

"Not really. More like—eyewitness reports of a near fistfight in a crowded restaurant. Apparently, it was quite a memorable evening."

"I argue with many people, Chief Kennis. If I murdered them all, I'd be Ted Bundy or the Zodiac Killer."

"Are you?"

He glared at me. "I won't dignify that with a response."

"Sorry. Let's back up a little. You don't smoke, do you?"

"Excuse me?"

"In fact you campaigned against public smoking all through the uh-ohs."

"The what?"

"That's what I call the first decade of this century."

He tried to smile but gravity won the battle and his face settled back into resting arrogance. "Very clever. Very apt. In fact, I did lead the crusade against that vile habit. And we won."

"So maybe you could tell me why you bought out every shop that sold the stuff in December of 1997. Four stores, something like thirty or forty cans of it."

He stared at me, carefully expressionless. "I have no idea what you're talking about."

"Think."

"I don't see the point."

"Snuff can be very useful—keeping rats away from a newly dug grave. And we just happened to have one of those that week, out on the old Coddington property in Madaket."

"Of course," he said. "I remember now."

"Tell me."

"It was for one of the parties."

"Burial parties?"

"Very funny. No, Marjorie and I used to throw theme parties—scavenger hunt parties, costume parties. Once instead of flowers we staged the house with dozens of different kinds of sausage. Genoa salami, sopressata, ciauscolo, fegatelli, fellino— Vermont farm sausage, Greek sausage, chorizo, linguica, yun chang—that's a Chinese duck liver sausage—Vietnamese lap xuong…a virtual trip around the world. Of course we had a house full of the stuff afterward. And we ate it all. We speculated about how long a healthy human being could survive on a diet of nothing but cured meats!" He chuckled. "Quite a while, as it turned out. Another time there was a collector's item baseball card at every place setting. And I recall now once we decorated the house with cans of chewing tobacco. The labels are little masterpieces of midcentury design."

I had to admire the audacity of his lie. "You bought the chaw for a party."

"Everyone laughed. They all knew my views on the subject, of course. Someone said, 'It's like a Baptist buying booze!' The alliteration was memorable. How could I have forgotten that?"

"Good question. How could you?"

He stood and carried his plate to the sink, rinsed it, and slipped it into the dishwasher before he turned back. "I see you don't believe me."

"Someone added tobacco to that grave. It looks like you cleaned out the town. Where did this other person find it?"

"Figuring that out is your job, not mine."

"Any guesses, though?"

"Amazon?"

"All they sold was books back then."

"Chief Kennis, we're talking about premedi- tated murder. One would assume premeditation includes procuring the necessary supplies before committing the act. The 'chaw,' as its devotees call it, could have been purchased anywhere, over any period of time, by this diabolical creature you've conjured up."

"Still, it's quite a coincidence."

"I can give you the names of a couple of party guests. Would that help settle the matter? Some of them are still kicking around. Clifford Marks, Rafe Talerian."

"Do you have contact information?"

"I'll e-mail it to you at the station."

I stood. "I guess we're done, then. For now."

He inclined his head, in a dry parody of hospitality. "Thanks for dropping by. You can see yourself out."

I walked back through the house and out into the late autumn drizzle, pulling on my coat against the wind. Marjorie Blum was waiting for me. She sat behind the wheel of her Range Rover, parked at the curb. She gave the horn a single bleat to catch my attention, lowered the passenger side window and said, "Get in."

The inside of the SUV was warm and dry and perfumed with scent of leather. Marjorie Blum looked haggard and red-eyed. She obviously hadn't slept, and she could have used that cup of coffee she'd been preparing.

"My husband is worse than you think. Worse than you can imagine."

The windshield wipers, set on intermittent, swept the rain-speckled glass and came to rest again.

"I have a pretty good imagination, Mrs. Blum."

"Is that so?"

"I'm not sure what—"

"You're looking in the wrong place. Talking to the wrong people. If you want to know what happened. Back then."

"Of course I do. But—"

"The truth is in the laundry hamper, Chief Kennis. You'd be surprised how often that's true. Talk to the person who does the laundry. That's my advice."

"Milly Graham?"

"Milly Graham was living in Jamaica twenty years ago."

I took a breath. "Look, Mrs. Blum…if you have some information that could be pertinent to a murder investigation you are obliged by law to come forward. You can be charged with obstruction of justice, and compelled to testify in court under penalty of perjury. You could be charged as an accessory. Whoever committed this crime may have killed again, may be planning to kill again right now. If you have evidence that your husband—"

"No! No, stop it. I don't know anything, I shouldn't have said anything. That was a tasteless remark about dirty laundry. One thing my mother always taught me was don't wash it in public. And there I was, one breath away from showing you every stain! I don't know what came over me. My family is in serious trouble, Chief Kennis. But it has nothing to do with the law. Now, if you'll excuse me, I have errands to run."

"But—"

"Please. I'm very late. And I have nothing more to say."

I climbed out into the windy drizzle, watched the car cruise down the narrow street and disappear around the corner, thinking, laundry, laundry. What might a housekeeper have discovered in the laundry all those years ago? Blood stains? Gunshot residue burns? Tobacco crumbs?

Or the most obvious possibility. Would a housecleaner have shared that discovery with the lady of the house? I doubted it. A comment to her husband that night over dinner, perhaps—with an eye-roll about the craziness of rich people. But that was it.

No, it had to be Marjorie Blum herself. Either they didn't have help in those days or the murder happened on a day off and a tedious afternoon's busywork turned into a revelation which Marjorie had kept to herself for decades. She had almost spilled it today, though, out of sheer spite. She was angry with her husband. But not quite angry enough. And all I had to work with were some deniable and virtually meaningless comments.

That and two names.

I set Kyle Donelly the task of running down contact information on Blum's friends and left to pick my kids up from school. I parked in front of the low-slung, cheerless building and pushed through the big glass doors just as the last class was letting out. Rising above the clatter and jostle of escaping students I heard my daughter's singing voice.

I edged toward the sound against the jagged tide of unshackled teenagers. When I got close enough I could see Carrie and her chubby friend, Patty Whelden. They had dammed off a space for themselves, a still pool in the torrent, and were singing a cappella to what looked like an Abercrombie & Fitch catalog shoot, five perfect girls with perfect hair, fringe-hem jeans, leather vests and jackets over logo t-shirts. One girl wore peg-leg jeans and another one sported a Union Jack t-shirt; the sneakers were different brands and colors. They probably thought they weren't all dressed alike. But to someone not attuned to those subtle distinctions, they looked as similar as Labrador retriever puppies—chocolate, yellow, or black, English or American, it made no difference, even with the more exotic "fox red" or "polar white" variations. Labs all had the same big heads and floppy ears, the same thick coat, dangerous tail, and tendency to hip dysplasia.

And the girls…well, that's where the analogy breaks down. Labs were friendly. These girls were anything but. I knew a couple of them. They had been Carrie's BFFs once. Best Friend Forever? How about Best Friend For Now? The tallest one, Jill Porter, was the unofficial leader of the "Accidentals" and she did have a beautiful alto voice. But today she was listening. Carrie and Patty were singing a Taylor Swift song called "Mean."

They finished to a sparse round of sarcastic applause from the "it" girls, which was quickly overwhelmed by a real ovation by a couple of dozen other kids who had stood still to listen, amid the diminishing outward churn of their classmates.

I clapped with the others and got a happy smile in return. Carrie skipped over and for one stunning second I thought she was going to hug me. In public. With her friends watching. She caught herself just in time. "Hi, Dad," she said teetering back from the incriminating impulse.

"That was great," I said.

"No it wasn't. But thanks."

I turned to her friend. I couldn't help noticing that she was wearing too much makeup—Goth-style black lipstick and way too much eyeliner. I said nothing—her cosmetic choices weren't my problem. Or so I thought.

"Seriously, Patty." I said to her. "That sounded fantastic."

She studied the shiny linoleum. "Hopefully it made them think for a second or two."

"Yeah."

Carrie jumped into the brief silence. "Can you drop me at Patty's house? We have a rehearsal this afternoon."

"And the play tonight."

"Patty's mom can take me."

"Great."

"Are you coming?"

"For closing night? Are you kidding?"

"Dad—"

"Sorry. I'll wear sunglasses and a hoodie. No one will recognize me. Anyway, your mom's going to be there, too"

"That should be fun. She's bringing Joe."

Joe Arbogast had to be one of the most exquisitely boring people I'd ever met. He knew the price of every property on Nantucket, which spec houses were selling, which ones were in foreclosure, which were in violation of abstruse zoning regulations— and he'd gladly pelt you with the details until you fled, as from a boy scout troop's snowball barrage.

Fortunately the closing night of Jane's *North Pole Confidential* would allow him few opportunities to "hold forth," in my mother's pet phrase for the behavior of marathon talkers. "Joe's all right," I said.

Carrie turned to Pattty. "At my house we play the Boring Game—you try to make up the most boring sentence you can. But Joe wins! He has the all-time gold medal. Tell her what he said, Dad."

I didn't like running down Miranda or her fiancé, but Joe had said the words, there was no getting away from that. I glanced around quickly. In the do-it-yourself surveillance state otherwise known as small-town-life, almost anything you said about anybody would get back to them somehow. But the corridor had cleared out. We were alone for the moment. And Joe's line was a classic. 'A girl I went to high school with just got a job with the phone company.' You can't beat that one. But don't think about it too much. It'll knock you right out. Objects will slip through your nerveless fingers."

Carrie laughed; Patty was confused. It occurred to me that I might have had kids just so I could have some people around me who got my jokes.

Outside in the parking lot, Hector Cruz was teaching Tim to juggle. It was a perfect photograph for my personal slide show of sustainable human diversity on Nantucket, and it made me feel better than it probably should have. It didn't mean as much as I wanted it to, any more than Billy Delavane's friendship with Brazilian painter Francisco Silva did. Mike Henderson's relationship with Francisco was more encouraging. Mike seemed to accept that Francisco could work twice the hours he could, for half the pay, and still stand Mike for drinks at the Box when he was done. Mike worked for Francisco sometimes, when the Brazilian needed a fine touch on trim or a window sash.

As to Hector and Tim, Hector had apologized for his part in the cheating business and even defended Tim from Jake Sauter, the fat bully who'd been making Tim's life miserable for years. Hector had ended Sauter's reign of terror, invoking the Nantucket Whalers during a tense confrontation in the dining hall, a few days before. He had stepped between the other two boys.

"You're on my team, Jake. And I'm on his team. You know what that means?"

"I…I'm on his team?"

"Right! It's a syllogism. Just like we learned in math class."

"But with people."

Hector clapped him on the back. "*Es toy orgulloso de ti! Echale ganas.*"

"He's teaching us Spanish," Tim explained later. We were driving to the MSPCA. I had already dropped off the girls, and since I was bringing Tim out to Miranda's house, she asked if I'd pick up her cat from the vet, on the way. In fact, it was out of the way, but I had always liked Ellie, the ancient Abyssinian we had found in a Los Angeles street and tamed with food, long before the kids were born. After a successful thyroid surgery and a night at the animal hospital, she was ready to come home this afternoon, albeit with a lifetime prescription for hormone supplement pills and a bag of weird new food that would probably incite a prolonged hunger strike.

When I was filling out forms at the main desk and listening to the pilling instructions, Tim said, "Can I see the bless you animals?"

Judy, the lady behind the desk, glanced up from the instruction sheet we were reviewing. "The what?"

"The rescue animals up for adoption?" I clarified. "Tim called them that one day when he was five years old and it just kind of stuck. Now it's part of the family language. Like calling Wheat Chex and Cheerios 'surreal.' Or 'casting aspirins' when you say something mean about someone."

"Wow. My family can barely use regular language. Bless you animals! That's so great. We should use that in our next fundraiser."

Tim was getting impatient. "I know the way."

"Sure, honey, go on back." When he had started down the corner she turned back to me. "Bless you animals! Kids are amazing."

"They can be highly entertaining."

"You guys are doing such a great job with them."

"Well…we're trying real hard not to fuck them up…pardon my language. It's like carrying a Ming vase for eighteen years. My advice—don't drop it."

She smiled. "So far, so good."

When we went back to collect Tim, I realized my mistake. He was in the middle of a major love-fest with Pressman's Portuguese water dog, Bailey. The attendant had opened the big cage and they were rolling around on the floor.

"Carlos!" Judy bleated.

"It's okay," Carlos said. "Just for a minute or two? Look at them."

When Bailey was back in his cage I heard the question every parent dreads. "Can we keep him?"

"There's no dogs allowed at the house. It's in the lease." That was a slight exaggeration but I knew the Frakers wouldn't be pleased to have a dog in the place. They were not dog people. They were "Why can't we enforce the leash laws?" people.

"But what if no one takes him and they put him to sleep?"

"Someone will take him. He's a beautiful dog."

"Then someone else will have our dog!"

"He's not our dog. We can't adopt a dog. It's—too much work."

"I'll take care of him."

"No you won't. Which, I mean—that's fine, you shouldn't have to. It's a whole other job and you have a job right now, which is going to school. And Jane and I have jobs, too."

"Lots of people have jobs! And they still have dogs. Billy Delavane has a job and he has Dervish!"

"It's not happening, Tim. Our life is—full. There's no room in it for a dog. End of discussion."

As we were walking out, Judy said, "Good luck with that vase."

I took the words to heart. I was having other child-rearing problems that winter, mostly involving Jane Stiles and the two teenagers who had just parachuted into her life like commandos on a wartime sabotage mission. It had been a successful raid, worthy of the OSS, from the piles of clothes on the floor to the stained towels in the bathroom to the books left on the wet kitchen countertops. No charcoal-smudged team of expendables blowing up bridges and ammo dumps could have done a more effective job. The enemy was reeling.

But she was starting to fight back.

"I'm not sure how we're supposed to do this," Jane said a few minutes later, after I had dropped off Tim and the cat. We had the Darling Street house to ourselves for the night. She was standing at the kitchen sink washing the leftover dishes from a hasty breakfast. I grabbed a Marimekko dishcloth and took a plate from the drainer.

"You wash, I dry, we both put away?"

"Henry—"

"Or—we get a dishwasher, as soon as possible."

She forced a narrow smile. "That would help."

"But that's not what you're talking about."

"No."

"Second thoughts?"

"No, no it's just—how is this supposed to work? Your kids, my kid, your rules, my rules…"

"My rules are pretty basic. Just what's needed for civilized coexistence—inside voices, politeness. Brush your teeth, finish your homework before you watch TV. Chew with your mouth closed, do your dishes—"

"Well, that's what I'm talking about. Nobody did any dishes this morning."

"We were running late."

"Rinse a bowl, put it in the dish drainer. It

takes ten seconds. You spend more time thinking about it. If everyone just does it, like a habit, like marking your place in a book, or rolling up the car windows, then it never becomes a chore, and you know what chapter you're on and the car seats stay dry when it's raining and the mess doesn't accumulate. Doesn't that make sense?"

I put away the plate I was holding. "Of course it does. I'm working on that. We fight about it all the time."

"But they win the fights."

"Not always."

She turned off the water, took a breath.

"Look—I don't want to be the wicked stepmother—or whatever I am. The wicked live-in girlfriend. But it's kind of—it's a sanity question, Henry. Seriously. I'm very sensitive to my environment. I don't think you have any idea how sensitive. Chaos makes me crazy. I can't work with the house the way it is now. I can't concentrate. Carrie rolls in and dumps everything on the floor and makes a snack and leaves everything out on the kitchen table, and—she's like a tornado, Henry. There's rubble behind her everywhere she goes. Sorry. But, I mean…I'm constantly cleaning just to keep up… just to maintain some equilibrium. I know that makes me sound compulsive or something, but I'm not. It's normal. I'm normal. Everyone likes cleanliness and order. They like to be able to find things and not get sick from living in their own house."

"Hey—"

"I'm not saying that. It's not a health hazard anymore. I scrubbed out the mildew. It's just—this isn't some philosophical issue with them. Or some teen political thing—'Neatness is so *bourgeois*' or 'Chaos is my *statement.*' I know kids like that. Your kids aren't like that. No one complains when I pick up their dirty laundry! They just don't want to make the effort. They're lazy! Sorry, but—"

"I know, I know. You're right."

"I guess what I'm saying—asking…is—I want to make sure it's okay with you if I kind of…if I go to war on this. I hate confrontation. I suck at it. But I feel like I don't have a choice right now. If we're all going to live here together."

"Feel free. I hope you do better than me."

"I'm small but relentless. You should see me negotiating a book contract."

"Doesn't your agent—?"

"I fired him. He didn't even understand what a rights reversion clause was."

"Yikes. Come here."

She took a step closer and I pulled her into a hug. "Where do you want to start?"

She kissed my collarbone, pulled away and took my hand. "I'll show you."

She led me into the bathroom we shared with Carrie. Not a classic piece of architectural design, but it was a big comfortable renovation with two sinks, a clawfoot tub and stall shower, with lots of mirrored cabinets and veiny marble tile on the floor, softened (and made safe for wet feet) by a pair of Marlo Jacquard bath rugs in a muted gray pattern that matched the towels. Jane pulled one of the towels off the bar and handed it to me. "See for yourself."

I turned it over and immediately saw the black streaks. I had noticed the marks before but I'd made the half-conscious choice to ignore them, assuming they were temporary.

"These don't wash out?"

"Pre-soaking doesn't work. Bleaching will just ruin them. I tried the miracle products—spots-be-gone, all that stuff. Nothing."

"So we replace them."

"And I'm okay with that. But I'm not doing it more than once."

I knew the culprit. Patty Whelden virtually lived with us these days. Her mother collected feral cats and was kind of a feral cat herself. Half of Patty's clothes had wound up at our house, and on our floor, as Jane had pointed out. Patty slept over every few days, and I got the feeling sometimes that the only square meals she ever got were the ones I served up. She loved my pasta. She wasn't quite moved in yet, but her makeup had started to overflow from Carrie's cabinet. Carrie used very little herself—some pale lip gloss, a jar of foundation, that was it.

But Patty's Goth look required some serious products. I checked them out. She had all the cool brands—Bare Minerals white concealer, Urban Decay black lipstick and dark eye shadow palettes, Rimmel ScandalEyes Retroglam mascara, Smashbox eyeliner, Eve Lom cold cream for cleaning all the gunk off.

I pulled out the narrow eyeliner pen, uncapped it. "I think we've found the weapon, Inspector Stiles."

Jane took it, nodded. "The towel smells like her Eve Lom."

"I'll trust you on that. So…means, motive, and opportunity. I'm not sure any of this will be admissible in court without a warrant, though."

"We'll plead it out. Carrie and Patty help us pay for the new towels and then get some cheap ones they can ruin to their hearts' content."

"Sounds good."

She paused, as you might before opening a suspect closet door, half expecting an avalanche of random junk.

"What?" I asked.

"It's Tim and my books. I don't mind him looking at them, he was great with the move, helping me get them out of boxes onto the shelves here. But…well, I found one of my fore-edge books in the kitchen the other day. On a wet countertop."

"Oh."

We had some history with those books, antiques with paintings on the outer edges of the pages that were only visible when you fanned them out. After a yard sale in September, Jane had briefly suspected Tim of stealing one of them. The culprit had turned out to be our own Town Sherriff Bob Bulmer, but it made kind of a rocky start between Jane and my son. Apparently he hadn't lost his interest in her antique editions.

"It's funny about those books," she said. "They belonged to my dad but they were never mentioned in the will. My two sisters and I just kind of divvied things up in the house before we put it on the market and no one else wanted the library, so I got it by default. Technically, they're still his. I'm just the caretaker. I guess that's not exactly the legal situation. But that's how it feels."

I didn't answer her. I was thinking. She had made a connection for me. There was an answer I needed in what she'd been saying but I couldn't grasp it. It felt like a memory lapse, not a failure of deductive intelligence—like some movie star's name that I couldn't recall. A "senior moment," though I was a few decades shy of that designation, or that problem. So then what was it? How did her ambiguous ownership of her father's stuff tie in with my casework? Because that was how it felt. There was a key to my investigation, to some investigation, in what she had just said. Pressman's drug deals? The Red Tickets rip-off? Coddington's murder?

I gave up, let it go, at least for the moment.

Jane was still talking. "…really think this will all work out. I'm pretty optimistic right now. Henry?"

I jumped back into the conversation. "I— yeah. Me, too. Totally."

"I shamed Tim into taking the garbage out last night. I used a little *Our Town*. I said, 'I saw your dad taking out the garbage yesterday, after a hard day's work. I suppose he just got tired of asking you and decided it was easier to do it himself.'"

I laughed. "That line is a killer."

"And it worked!"

"One time, anyway."

"It's a start. They're great kids, Henry. Don't get me wrong. I love what Carrie's doing with The Grace Notes. They were fantastic at the Firehouse Christmas party."

"Thanks."

"From the 'Hallelujah Chorus' to 'The Hanukkah Song.' Who knew the three stooges were Jewish?"

"Not to mention Drake and Scarlett Johansson."

"Yeah."

"They really were good, weren't they? Much better than The Accidentals."

"Plus they finished with my all-time favorite Christmas carol."

"'Lo, How a Rose e'er Blooming'? Are you kidding me? No one knows that song. I taught it to Carrie because we sang it in chorus at my high school."

She made a small curtsey. "Mine too."

Talk turned to Christmas presents—a new coat for Carrie, an X-box for Tim—and to the fate of Bailey, and Tim's yearning for him. "It's hard to believe Lonnie's family hate dogs so much."

I shrugged. "They're worried about the floors," I said. "Dog claws on the floors."

"Well the floors are in horrible shape, anyway, so I don't see what difference a few more scratch marks would make."

"I could talk to them again. Tim loves that dog."

"Or we could just do it."

"Don't go rogue on me, lady. We've had a lot

of changes in the last few months. Adding a dog
might be a bridge too far."

"I guess."

In a show of solidarity I cleaned the bathrooms
while she vacuumed, and we had time for a comically fast, half-dressed lovemaking session before
we scrambled out to the play.

In the crowded lobby of the Congregational
Church, before we filed into the auditorium, several
teachers came up to me, including Ted Springer,
Tim's AP Poetry teacher and Ida Gumport, Carrie's
English teacher. Apparently my little Christmas
poem had been a hit.

"I see where Tim gets his love of poetry," Ted
told me.

"I cried," Ida gushed. Giving me a breath-
snapping hug. "The police chief! Who knew?"

Miranda, strolling by with Joe Arbogast, wit-
nessed the moment.

"Oh, my God," Miranda said. "You must be
strutting like a prize rooster. The poet laureate of
Nantucket High School!"

"An unpaid position, alas."

She closed in, with an avid smile that told me
she had some choice gossip to impart. "Speaking of
unpaid, did you ever wonder why Mr. J. Hastings
Pell III didn't just cash in the insurance policy on

his seventy-million-dollar boat and carry on with his crazy plan?"

Pell had concocted a scheme to turn Nantucket into the ultimate gated community, through a combination of buyouts, eminent domain filings, and a spectacular land grab. But it had all hinged on leveraging the value of his mega yacht, now resting at the bottom of the Atlantic Ocean, ten miles off the south shore.

"Well, my guess is that he trusted Liam Phelan with the paperwork and Liam let the coverage lapse."

"He—I…it—how did you know that?"

I had ruined her fun. "Just a guess, Miranda. Liam hated Pell long before his daughter died. So it makes sense."

She let out a low disgusted sigh and stalked off with Joe, clasping his arm tightly.

Jane watched them go, then took my arm, echoing Miranda's proprietary gesture. "So how long were you married?"

"Twelve years."

"Me, too."

"And she broke it off. I was the dumpee, Jane."

"Me, too."

"I was a total doormat for the first year afterward."

"Me, too."

"Plus, I can shell a pomegranate in under three

minutes, I believe Billy Joel is tragically underrated, and I refuse to throw away old cashmere sweaters with holes in the elbows."

"Which got there because you insist on sleeping in them."

"They're warm!"

"Exactly! It's like we met on Match dot com!"

"Do they ask questions about this kind of stuff?"

"They should."

"Marcia!" A large woman with an unruly tangle of red hair was loping toward us across the lobby "Marcia! How are you? When did you get back?"

Jane groaned. "I'm not Marcia."

"You—it's…wait, what? How—?"

"Marcia Stoddard. I'm not her."

"Are you sure?"

"Pretty much a hundred percent."

"But—"

"Supposedly, we look similar, but…"

"Oh, my God, you are totally like twins!"

"We have to get inside. Sorry for the confusion."

Jane took my arm and steered me away from the woman. When we found our seats in the auditorium she said, "People just don't see what they're looking at. It used to bother me but I'm over it. Marcia is small and slim with a long face and frizzy hair. She wears baseball caps and clogs and baggy jeans, just like me. She copies my style, for some reason—I started the girls-wearing-baseball-caps thing around here, by the way. But we don't look alike, Henry. At least I hope we don't."

I'd never seen this Marcia Stoddard, so I enjoyed the luxury of not having an opinion.

"I'll point her out to you," Jane said as the lights went down. "You'll see how crazy this is. Which is why you can never trust eyewitness reports, by the way."

I nodded. That much was true. People were shockingly unobservant, as a rule.

The play went well, and the next day Kyle Donnelly had the phone numbers of Blum's two party guests waiting for me on my desk.

The first one, Clifford Marks, had a Facebook page, which must have simplified things for Kyle. A sculptor who designed giant public installations, Marks had more than ten thousand followers and a gallery in Boston for his smaller pieces. The owner gave me the phone number for his house in Brookline.

"Clifford Marks," he said, picking up on the second ring.

"Mr. Marks, this is Chief of Police Kennis, calling from Nantucket."

"Nantucket! There's a name from the past."

"You never come back?"

"I never even look back. I got out when the going was good. Sold my beach shack in Shimmo for the price of the land, packed a suitcase, and grabbed the first flight out. I'm sure there's some hideous palazzo there now. Sad."

"I wanted to ask you a few questions about the old days, if you don't mind."

"Is this part of an ongoing investigation?"

"It's police business, yes."

"But you can't tell me anything about it."

"No."

"Well, all right, I suppose. I have nothing to hide. But I doubt I have much to offer, either."

"I won't take up much of your time. I was wondering if you remembered the 'theme parties' thrown by Jackson and Marjorie Blum—back in the day."

"Sure. There was the 'Catch a Quaker' scavenger hunt. Margie was fascinated by island history. I remember I found Mary Starbuck and her son, Nathaniel, but I got tricked when they took me to Parliament House—that was the Starbuck home in Capaum, back in the eighteenth century. Of course it was gone! Turned out they'd used everything they could salvage from the place to build a new house on Pine Street. By the time I figured that one out, the game was over. Margie was a tricky old girl."

"Do you recall any special party decorations?"

"Oh, yeah   the baseball cards. I hit the jack-pot that night, especially for a Mets fan. Sorry, Red Sox, I grew up in New York. Anyway, I got Nolan Ryan's Topps rookie card, from 1968. I still have it."

"Any others?"

"Well, there was the chewing tobacco party. That was crazy. Just thinking about the chairman of the New England Division of the American Cancer Society buying all that snuff. It was like a Baptist buying booze!"

I sat up, staring out the big picture window of my office, seeing nothing. "Interesting turn of phrase."

"Thanks."

"You thought of it just now?"

"Yeah—no...I don't know. Maybe I heard it back then. I don't really remember. Hits the nail on the head, though, don't you think?"

"Sure does."

I hung up, and called Rafe Talerian in Naples, Florida. Kyle had located him through a quick NDR search. We spoke for less than five minutes. That was all it took. I disconnected the phone, closed the National Drivers Register website and checked the Mass. Department of Criminal Justice Information services, along with Florida's DAVID database. I printed out the information for both men to get Haden Krakauer started, and then took the stairs two at a time down to the second floor. Haden was on the phone when I got to his office, but he hung up as I walked in.

"Whatcha got, Chief?"

I put the paperwork on his desk. "I need to know how these two guys are tied in to Jackson Blum. Outstanding debts he paid for them, loans he made to them, jobs he helped them get, trouble he got them out of, bail he paid—any obligation, any reason they'd lie for him, anything I can use to make them tell the truth."

"You think he got to them?"

"I know it. Unless two people living in different parts of the country and out of touch for decades would spontaneously think of the same phrase remembering a minor social event twenty years ago."

"Same phrase? I'm not sure what—"

"A Baptist buying booze. Both of them said it. And so did Blum."

I left Haden to do the digging on Blum's friends, knowing it would be slow tedious work, but necessary. Like most jobs, the last five percent of a criminal investigation seemed to take fifty percent of the time. I was certain Blum had killed his partner, but so far I had no viable forensics, no ballistic evidence, no witnesses. Even the circumstantial detail of the tobacco purchases had been nullified by Marks and Talcrian. Karen Gifford was still working her way through the historical records, but we both knew that was a long shot. If all my digging had caused even a mild civic earthquake, there was no sign of it yet.

The only effect of my focus on Coddington's murder was that I had let myself get distracted from my present-day caseload. Understandably—no new crimes had erupted, Pressman was in custody, and we had confiscated his stash. Even my speculations about rigging the Red Ticket Drawing had begun to seem absurd and fanciful…until Alana Trikilis got sick, three days in advance of the raffle. With Lizza Coddington set to take over Alana's duties on the big day, it looked like the plan had actually been set motion. The felon I should have been hunting wasn't Jackson Blum at all.

It was Max.

Chapter Twenty-one

Scammers

December twenty-third, and the game was on.

The problem was—how to prove the Christmas drawing had been rigged. More than that, how to convince people the proof was real. In my experience facts just irritate the true believer, and the Nantucket Board of Selectmen believed in the sanctity of the Red Tickets Drawing. So did the Nantucket Chamber of Commerce. I needed to be absolutely certain of the plot before I even approached them.

So, where to start?

How do you solve a crime that hasn't been committed yet? But that was the point. If my theory was right, it had already begun. Getting Alana Trikilis out of the way was a crucial first step.

I was pacing my office. It was ten-thirty in the morning, Tuesday December twenty-third. It was raining again. Everywhere else on the Eastern Seaboard was getting snow, but the blizzards kept missing us, running north and east of the island. The weather was dreary and Nantucket looked as appealing as a wet cat. The chamber of commerce must have been miserable, and for once I agreed with them.

I held a message slip in my hand—Barnaby Toll wrote down my overnight calls and hand-delivered them in the morning. Today's batch featured a panicky call from Sam Trikilis. His daughter had been admitted to Nantucket Cottage Hospital around eight-thirty the night before, with high fever, nausea, cramps, and vomiting. Four other people had also been admitted around the same time, and all of them had eaten at a new seafood restaurant in town called Ahab's. The health inspector, Lou Morgenstern, had closed the place down and spent the morning working the site. I called him.

He answered his cell on the first ring. "Hey, Chief."

"Anything yet?"

"We checked the backflow preventive assemblies on all the plumbing lines—looking for copper contamination. Nothing there. We're looking at the refrigeration levels, but frankly, if they had a problem there, everything would have gone bad and we'd have a lot more sick people on our hands."

Lou was methodical, but I was impatient. I skipped to the obvious question. "What dish were all the victims served?"

"I'm getting to that. They all had the crab-cakes. I sent samples and the victims' blood work to the FDA lab in Boston. They're backed up this time of year and they're slow anyway. I was going to call you a little later, ask you to pull some strings for us. You're pals with the state's attorney, right?"

"I know him."

"This is the last gasp of tourist season, Chief. It's in everyone's interest to wrap this one up as fast as we can. Call in a favor."

"I'll try."

I knew the favor Dave Carmichael would want in return and it wasn't a parking pass on Main Street or a scrubbed DUI ticket. He used a State Police driver and he never drank.

What he wanted was me.

"I just fired two deadbeat investigators, Kennis. You can have both their jobs and both their salaries. We both know you work harder than the two of them put together."

"Fire a third one. I'll take all three jobs."

"Are you serious? Because I'll do it. I have just the Entitled-Generation-What-the-Fuck slacker to dump. His dad's a State Senator. What a coincidence."

"Generation What-the-Fuck?"

"They want to be called Generation C, that's what I've heard. C for *connected*. This kid was connected, all right. Not the way they mean, though. Clueless punk. Together the three of them make around a hundred and twenty grand a year. How does that sound to you? And you know our medical coverage. It makes Blue Cross look like Medicaid. Dental included. Guess the deductible. Zero! You'd have to get elected to Congress to find a plan like this one, Kennis. Plus, I can still shift you into that corner office."

"Dave, please."

"What? You want a license to kill? I can't swing that. Maybe a learner's permit to crack some heads in the interrogation room."

"Very funny."

"I'm serious. People who say torture doesn't work just aren't doing it right."

"You're unbelievable."

"I get it. You won't work for a Republican."

"I can't work for anyone anywhere but here. We've been through this. I can't raise my kids from Boston and I couldn't take them with me."

Hew grunted in disgust. "Family man."

"Sorry."

"So what do you need? I'm guessing this isn't an invitation to the NPD Christmas party."

"We had a case of food poisoning last night. Morgenstern sent samples of the food, and victim blood work to the FDA in Boston. I was hoping you could bump us up to the front of the line."

"Jesus."

"You can do it. You must know a guy over there."

"I know a lot of guys over there, Kennis. And this is the kind of bullshit request that pisses them off and makes them hang up on me when I have a real problem."

"This is a real problem."

"Oooo, someone hacked my Apple Watch! They're cheating me on my frequent flier miles!"

"Now you're just giving me shit."

"You're a bunch of spoiled brats. Did you know that Nantucket Airport gets more traffic than Logan in August? And it's all private jets."

"This is December, Dave. All the rich people have gone home."

"Really?"

"Well, most of them. Can you do this for me?"

"Call me this afternoon. I'll have the results."

"Thanks, Dave. You're The Man."

"Goddamn right, I am. Write an angry letter to the *Herald* the next time they say I'm not."

"Will do."

"I hate it when that happens. Some tabloid

rag telling me I'm not The Man. Now hang up the phone and let me get some work done around here. Before I change my mind."

I put my phone away and resumed pacing. I had to admit, it was nice to finally have an office big enough for pacing.

I had a few hours before I could call Dave back, and I wanted to use them productively. I deconstructed the scheme, according to my original theory. They needed Alana out of the way, so that Lizza Coddington could draw the winning ticket. But first she had to have that ticket in hand.

The mechanics of the raffle were simple. On Christmas Eve, three uniformed cops would collect all the tickets from all the participating stores, and bring them under guard to the Pacific Bank building on Main Street where they would stay until two more of my officers, some bank personnel, and someone from the chamber hauled the big bags out to the steps and dumped them into the bed of a shiny new Don Allen Ford F-350 parked right there at the top of Main Street. Then, at exactly three o'clock, Lizza Coddington would draw five tickets—four separate thousand-dollar prizes, and the final five-thousand-dollar grand prize.

There was nothing for a computer genius to hack; it was done old-school, off-line, with a physical ticket no one on the island had the skill or the resources to counterfeit. If you were going to cheat the system, it had to be done in person, by hand. That meant that somewhere on the island some clerk in some store had palmed a ticket instead of throwing it in the collection bin. All that clerk had to do was get the purloined ticket to Lizza Coddington. After that, it was up to Lizza. If she could fake it successfully, and "pull" that ticket—obviously it had to be in her hand already—then whoever was standing in the crowd on Main Street holding its twin would collect the grand prize.

I turned and headed back down the length of my office. A stiff wind rattled the icy rain against the windows, but it made the big room seem warmer. I could hear a phone ringing beyond my closed door, and the steady rush of the forced-air heating. No one would barge in on me now—my standing orders were "Don't even knock when the door is closed, except for emergencies." So, no distractions.

I stalked the carpet and broke the caper down. Who had to be involved?

Lizza, of course.

And her ex-boyfriend Dave Prescott. But neither of them could have dreamed it up.

So that meant Max Blum had to be part of it, also.

Plus someone who worked at one of the stores.

Someone at Ahab's to expedite whatever they did to Alana's dinner.

And a final person, with no obvious connection to Lizza or the target store, to actually claim the prize on Christmas Eve.

Many businesses on the island had installed security cameras in the last few years, and a surprising number of them trained at least some of their surveillance on their own workers. "Nine times out of ten, shoplifting is an inside job," Jackson Blum had told me the year before, when I had turned down a request to monitor his video feed at the police station. I couldn't spare the manpower—or the cloud storage space—to indulge his paranoid fantasies.

But I knew he wasn't alone.

I sent Kyle Donnelly and a couple of uniforms around to start collecting digital tapes from those who used them and getting permission to download footage from the rest. That was the easy part. Going through the hours of insanely tedious video streams would be the real challenge, made even more frustrating by the likelihood that the single golden moment we were looking for might not have been captured at all, either because the clerk was too deft, the camera was pointed elsewhere, or the whole thing took place at one of the many retail outlets that had never installed cameras.

As a detective bringing this quixotic search to my chief, I would have expected to be turned down flat, but I was the chief now, so I could do as I pleased. It was grueling work, with little prospect for success, but in a slow crime month I could afford to play the odds.

So I did. And I had an ambitious patrol officer named Patty Stokes who jumped at the chance to do some real detective work, however menial.

Meanwhile, there were people I wanted to see. And before that, meetings I had to attend. With the Selectmen, and with Lonnie Fraker. After his drug enforcement unit cleared out the Pressman house on Tuckernuck, and—based on some harebrained cold call source—the State Police had dug up most of Pressman's yard, including every square damp, cobwebby inch under the front porch, looking for more drugs or plastic-wrapped bundles of cash, or both. I think someone just liked the idea of all those shiny, crewcut, gun-toting bully-boys crawling around in the dirt.

I didn't mind the idea myself, though I kept a scrupulous poker face as Lonnie described the futile excavations. The whole expedition was just so clueless, so mechanical and out of touch. Anyone who knew Pressman would know that he would never squirm around on his belly, pawing through the muck under his porch. That wasn't his style.

I didn't say this, of course, and I was more than glad to let Lonnie take credit for the bust. He needed the gold stars on his chart. He was my landlord, now, along with his squabbling siblings. Lonnie was ambitious in his own way, but I had turned out to be a better fit for Nantucket. Lonnie had lived here all his life, but my lack of ambition suited the place. Urgent life goals seemed to stretch out to the horizon here, like the ocean at the South Shore, gilded with sunset. The island dismantled the sense of urgency. Everything could wait. Besides, the world beyond the Sound was so ugly, so dirty, so loud. The air was smoggy and the water tasted bad.

Most of the kids who had roused themselves to shake off the procrastination bug did it because of their native talent and their need to impress that talent on the wider world. They were long gone—the boys who went off to study cello with YoYo Ma, or quantum physics at MIT, the girls who took their PhDs in Marine Biology to the Woods Hole Oceanographic Institute, or went to Nashville with a suitcase full of songs and came back with a hot record and a Grammy nomination.

They were rarities, outliers, and Lonnie wasn't one of them. He wasn't destined to make his mark on the world. He stuck around Nantucket—or was stuck here, more accurately—because he didn't have the talent to leave. But he still wanted to rise. So I was glad to pitch in whenever I could, and help polish his resume. Looking good on paper might get him the promotion he craved.

Turning from Lonnie, I had a list of possible suspects—persons of interest—in my own investigation. First up was Lizza Coddington. I didn't want to alarm her mother, who no doubt hated Max Blum just for his last name and might not even be aware that Max and her daughter's on-again-off-again romance was in full swing again.

We agreed to meet at Gardner Farm, a Land Bank hiking trail off Hummock Pond Road. She arrived late at the little dirt parking area, driving a pale blue MINI Cooper convertible—a birthday present, no doubt.

"Hey, Chief," she said, climbing out of the car.

"Let's walk."

We started across the wide field toward the pitch pine forest. You could hear the low rumble of the surf beyond the houses at the south end of the property. We were less than half a mile from the ocean. "Does your mother have you on a strict allowance?" I began.

"No. It—why would you ask that?"

"So, spending money's not an issue."

"No, I just said—"

"So why rig the drawing, then? Just for fun?"

"I have no idea what you're talking about."

"I can see Max doing it for fun. So you're doing it…for him?"

"I haven't done anything!"

"Not yet. Though, technically, planning a crime counts as conspiracy, which is a Class A felony in the state of Massachusetts."

"I'm not planning any crimes!"

"Do you know anyone who works at Ahab's?"

"What?"

"The new fish restaurant in town. They were hiring part-time workers this fall."

"What about them?"

I spoke slowly, as if she hadn't understood. "I was wondering if any of your friends work there. I'll find out anyway, when I talk to the staff later. But you could speed things up a little."

"I know lots of people who work in lots of restaurants."

"And at Ahab's?"

"No. Not that I can think of right now."

We walked along. "So you're going to give me nothing."

"I have nothing to give. Seriously."

"Okay. Let me just clarify this for you. The only way to rig the drawing is with a group of people—someone to switch the ticket, someone to pick the right one out of the bin. That would be you. But whoever is holding the matching ticket, whoever actually steps up the Pacific National steps to claim the prize? That's the weak link. If they have anything to do with you or Max…whether it's family, friends, teammates, classmates…I will jam them into an interrogation room and get the truth out of them. It won't be hard. They'll fold like laundry."

This got no response that I could see. She actually smiled. "Well, the odds are against that, Chief. I don't even keep track of the tickets. I find them months later in, like, a coat pocket or my sock drawer or whatever. And I've never known anybody who won. I've never even known anybody who had more than three numbers in a row out of seven. So a pal of mine winning is, like, the last thing I'm worried about."

As I drove back to town, a couple of small wrong notes stuck in my head. Call me paranoid, or just bored, looking for crime where there was none, a big-city cynic with no real work to do, ginning up bogus conspiracies, but I had to wonder how many people knew off the top of their heads how many numbers were used on a Red Ticket— especially someone who thought the whole lottery was "stupid" and never bothered to keep any tickets of her own.

Also, Lizza's utter cool when I mentioned the

suspicion that might fall on the winner suggested to me not that she was innocent, but the exact opposite—that she had the glitch covered. They had found someone to pick up the prize that no one would connect with her. But who? I needed a new direction if I was going to pursue this scam.

Fortunately, one was waiting for me on my office desk.

Chapter Twenty-two

Methomyl Blues

When I walked into my office, on top of the morning pile of message slips hand-scribbled by Barnaby Toll, I saw this masterpiece of brevity:

CALL DAVE CARMICHAEL

So Dave had come through for me, as expected. I had his number on speed dial. He picked up and started talking without salutation, as if we had just been interrupted for a second or two. "Ever hear of methomyl?"

"Is it some kind of meth?"

"Nice try. It's an RUI—restricted use insecticide. Registered for field, vegetable, and orchard crops. In small doses it can produce cramps, nausea, vomiting, blurred vision, headache, diarrhea. Sound familiar?"

I ticked off Alana's symptoms in my head. "Very."

"The good news is—no long-term health effects after the stuff wears off. So it's the perfect product for taking someone out temporarily without doing any long-term damage. Just what the doctor ordered. If your doctor happened to be Fu Manchu or Hannibal Lecter. Speaking of which, I'm amazed those guys never got sued for malpractice."

"I think the plaintiffs were too busy being skinned alive or eaten."

"Yeah, that shit slows you down. Anyway—all five victims had trace elements of methomyl in their blood and urine. So you're good to go."

"Thanks, Dave."

"They're painting the corner office this week. Any particular colors you like?"

"You're insane."

I got off the phone, ignored the rest of my messages, including three from Chief Selectman Dan Taylor, and drove back into town. The dinner rush would be starting soon at Ahab's.

Norman Quint, the owner and chef, was standing outside in the alley smoking a cigarette.

I walked up to him and stuck out my hand. "Mr. Quint? Police Chief Kennis."

He shook it. "No need for introductions.

I've been to Town Meeting. This about the food poisoning? We got a clean bill of health from Morgenstern."

"I heard. Good news."

"Yeah."

"It's tough for a new restaurant in this town."

"Yeah…well. Straight Wharf and the Lobster Trap are closed for the season. And the Seagrille's in the mid-island. So I get the walk-ins."

"Quint. You should have named the place after yourself. I mean—Quint's our Ahab."

He grinned. "Tried that. Got tired of people saying 'No shark on the menu?' and 'You're gonna need a bigger store.'"

He took another drag. The wind off the harbor kicked up and I wished I'd worn my coat. Quint seemed comfortable in his chef's whites, no coat. He'd grown up here. After the better part of a decade as a washashore, I still felt my thin Los Angeles blood on these damp winter evenings.

"So what's up?" he asked.

"We know what happened, Mr. Quint."

"Norman, please."

"Norman. There's a pesticide called methomyl. Someone put it in your crabcakes."

"They poisoned my crabcakes?"

"Sorry."

"That's more than a crime, Chief. That's a sacrilege."

"I'm sure."

We just stood there for a few seconds, chilled and outraged.

"Damn. So who did it?"

"That's what I'm trying to figure out. Do you have a list of everyone who was working the night it happened?"

"I got a list and I got better than that. All of them except Trudy Vesco are working tonight."

"And Trudy?"

"She's the bartender, and I don't serve food at the bar this time of year. She was strictly drinks, so she's off the hook. Feel free to talk to any of the others. But, hey—try to make it quick. I got a business to run here."

I was quick, all right. I immediately eliminated two Ecuadoran bus boys, a Jamaican dishwasher, and the Brazilian sous chef. I didn't see them running in Lizza Coddington's crowd. Ditto the two older waitresses, sisters named Pam and Dorothy Glover.

That left Ingrid Cole.

She fit the profile perfectly: a high school girl with short brown hair and clear braces, plain and shy in her black dress and white apron, probably working to help her family make ends meet, long-ing to be part of Lizza's cool-girl world.

Helping out the NHS royalty would be a crime of aspiration for a girl like that—a rite of initiation.

I found her in the back dining room, setting tables.

"Take a break, Ingrid," I said. "We need to talk."

"But Mr. Quint wants—"

"Quint gave his permission. This is police business."

She set down a handful of cutlery. "Oh."

"I'll try to be quick. I know you're busy. Let me tell you what I know, and you can fill in the gaps."

"Uh—okay."

"Yesterday during the dinner rush you sprin-kled some methomyl on a batch of crabcakes. You couldn't be sure who was getting served which cake so you poisoned all of them to make sure that—"

"It's not poison! It just makes you sick for a little while."

That was progress. I took a breath and let her realize the implications of what she'd said. Then I pushed on. "A total of five people got sick, includ-ing Alana Trikilis, who was supposed to pick the Red Ticket for the drawing on Christmas Eve. That's tomorrow. But Alana should be too sick to stand outside in the cold for a least a week. Which clears the way for Elizabeth Coddington, who put you up to this."

"It's—she—I didn't know about that."

"About what?"

"About anything! Lizza just asked me to do it and so I did it. She promised no one would get hurt. And they didn't! I mean—everyone's going to be okay."

"But they didn't know that when everything they'd eaten for the last three days was coming out of both ends simultaneously just as the headaches and the cramps began."

"That's awful."

"It wasn't much fun for them. I hope Lizza made it worth your while."

"Nobody paid me! It wasn't—I'm not—"

I held up a hand. "I'm not talking about money, Ingrid."

"Then I—what?"

"I'm talking about the real currency. I bet you're getting lots of likes and comments on your Instagram selfies lately. Probably even some shares. Those shares are huge."

She looked almost comically shocked. "How did you—?"

"I have a daughter."

She looked down, studying the half set-up table and the white tablecloth. "Oh."

"It feels good to be popular," I said. "It always has. Long before smartphones."

She glanced up ruefully. "But you couldn't measure it with such…"

"Precision?" I filled in for her. The word made her wince.

She nodded. "Everyone knows exactly where they stand these days, Chief Kennis."

"Yeah."

"So…what's going to happen to me?"

"You'll testify when the time comes and you'll get a tongue-lashing from Judge Perlman and a year's probation. You're a minor so those records will be sealed."

"I can't do that."

"It's your best option."

"But—it would just be my word against Lizza's."

"If it were just the two of you. But I'm building a case and your testimony will be one small part of it."

"Omigod. I can't believe this."

She started crying. I reached out to comfort her, saw her tense up and let my arm drop. I offered a grain of hope instead. "There's another possibility. The victims may choose not to press charges.

Your lawyer should investigate that. He'll have the chamber of commerce on his side. And Quint will try to make things right without going to court."

"You really think so?

"It's a possibility."

"Oh, thank you, thank you so much!" She threw her arms around me. I patted her shoulders like an awkward uncle.

I had what I needed. She might not have to testify, but I could use the threat of her testimony as leverage with the others. First, I had to identify them all.

I extricated myself from Ingrid's embrace, left her wiping her eyes, thanked Quint on my way out the door and headed for Bartlett's Farm. The methomyl had probably come from there, courtesy of the next conspirator, whoever that might be. Time to find out.

My cell went off as I turned down Surfside Road. It was David Trezize looking for a quote on the food poisoning story. He already had his headline: "DEATH CRAB FOR CUTIE."

I asked him to hold off on the story and corrected his *Daily News*-style screamer. No one died, it was a crabcake not a crab, and Alana would hate the term "cutie."

"Right," David said. "So I should change it

to…'Mildly debilitating crabcake for feminist.' That really swings."

"Don't run the story at all. It's a nonevent."

"Like the gas station holdup?"

"Exactly."

He sighed. We both knew I'd always come through for him when it really mattered.

Bartlett's was open until six in this final run-up to Christmas. I drove the winding route out along Hummock Pond Road toying with various approaches and strategies, but in the end I didn't need any elaborate plan. Devon Flynn was working in the greenhouse, and he was wearing a *TimeDraggers* t-shirt.

TimeDraggers—that was Max Blum's embryonic video game. Of course. And how typical that he had his brand registered and his logo designed before the work was done.

Max had to be in the center of this, writing code for his own real-life multi-player video game. What could be more fun than virtual reality? Actual reality—as long as Max was in control.

I found Devon setting out pots of paperwhites. He knew instantly why I was there. He extended his wrists for handcuffs.

I said, "I might just be here to pick up some flowers."

"Nope. Uh-huh. The way I see it, you're not

the last-minute type. Too methodical. If you were into paperwhites, you'd have planted the bulbs at Thanksgiving. Actually…I've kind of been waiting for someone to show up. I didn't expect the chief of police. And out of uniform. But it makes sense—low profile. Everything hush-hush for the touristas."

"Something like that."

"So they found the methomyl and that led you here."

"And I recognized your t-shirt. From Max's video game. This would be a good moment to stop time."

"Or just slow it down, so I could get away without setting up any mental dissonance in your brain. Like the Fourth Circle masters do."

"Max really thought about this crazy idea."

"Oh, yeah. It's awesome."

I hated that word. "Are you talking Fukashima tsunami awesome, or Adele's new single awesome?"

"Somewhere in between, Chief."

He set the pot of flowers on the long trestle table, and rubbed his palms over his jeans. "Okay, so you know Max told me to do it. But he didn't tell me why and I didn't ask."

"You just do whatever he says."

"More or less."

This was the heart of the matter. "I don't get it. Why?"

Devon shrugged. "He's Max."

"Well, Max just got you fired."

He shot me a sly little grin, a full-face shrug. "I thanked him in advance for that."

"You may have to testify against him in open court, in front of your friends and family. Have you thanked him for that, too?"

"No need to. It's not gonna happen."

"We'll see."

There was no further point to this conversation. Devon wasn't going anywhere. Despite his bluster, he'd testify as required. Like Ingrid Cole, he was an arrow in my quiver if I decided to mount the hunt in earnest. With only one day left until the drawing, I had to make my move soon, if I made it all. I knew Ingrid and Devon might try to warn Max, but my reading of the kid was that he was too cocky to worry about it. Jane had summed him up perfectly when she said, "He's smarter than himself." And he might have outsmarted himself permanently.

It was time to confront my quarry.

Chapter Twenty-three

Odd and Queer but Not Peculiar

I stopped by the hospital on my way into town. I wanted to check in on Alana Trikilis. She was recuperating in a big sunny room on the second floor. When I walked in her parents were sitting in chairs pulled up to the bed. Alana looked pale and gaunt. I suspected she had lost some weight during her ordeal. But she smiled at me.

"Hi, Chief."

"Hey."

Sam Trikilis stood up, shook my hand. "Good to see you."

His wife, Jen, twisted around in her chair. "Thanks for coming."

"How's she doing?"

"She'll be okay." He walked me a few steps away from the bed. "I'm hearing this was no accident."

"We're looking into it, Sam."

"If someone did this to my little girl—"

"Then I'll catch them and they'll be punished."

"And I'll pick up their trash, same as ever."

"First of all, you don't have a monopoly on garbage. And you've been helpful before, picking up the trash." The previous summer he had found a significant clue in a customer's garbage. Sam was an inveterate snoop, but on the side of the angels.

He shrugged and changed the subject. "I quit as Town Crier."

"Sam! You shouldn't let—"

"I just don't have the heart for it. With Alana in here."

"They're going to give the job to Dan Taylor. He's been trying to land that gig for years," I reminded him.

"He'll be fine."

"He might not want to give it up, if you want to come back next year."

"I might not even be here next year."

"Things will work out."

"Really? My dad always used to say, 'You can't win them all—but you can lose them all.'"

"Well, I'm going to pray for you."

"Says the man who never goes to church."

I pointed an admonishing finger at him. "There are no atheists in the residential foreclosure process."

I walked back to the bed, patted Jen's shoulder, gave Alana a cool limp-hand squeeze and fled. There was nothing I could do to help them and we all knew it.

• • ● • •

Ten minutes later I was walking into Max Blum's room in the big house on Pleasant Street.

Max was working at his computer, talking to Dave Prescott in a Skype box open in one corner of the screen. "Here's another one, Dave. John Lennon and George Harrison—but not Paul McCartney."

Prescott's voice was faint and tinny. "Uh— John and George wrote in minor keys and Paul didn't?"

"Annnggghhh," Max made a game show "wrong answer" noise. "Here's a hint. Put this one together—look for the connections! Ferrari and Cadillac but not Toyota."

"Luxury cars! John and George are classy, like Ferrari and Cadillac."

"No, no, no—you're missing the point. Here's another one. Guinness Stout, Beefeater Gin, but not Absolut Vodka."

In the tense cogitating silence, Max went back to working on the computer, jabbing the keys. He hit them hard with two fingers and they made a low thumping sound in the quiet room, like rain on the roof.

Finally Prescott said, "I've got nothing, give me a few more."

"This is so simple. Fine. Let me think. Daal and vindaloo but not masala."

"Are those Indian foods?"

"Yes, Dave, but that's not the point. The Eiffel Tower, The Colosseum, but not Big Ben."

"Fuck it. I give up."

"Good. I have to go anyway. The cops are here."

"The police?"

"The coppers, the fuzz, but not the constabulary. Get it now?"

"What are the police doing there?"

"Bye, Dave." Skype made its electronic bubbling disconnect noise and Max swiveled in his chair to face me. "Sorry, Chief, didn't mean to be rude. That's a little game I play with Dave called 'Odd and Queer but not Peculiar.' All he has to do is figure out the common identifier that connects the first two words but not the third. We've been playing for weeks, but he still doesn't get it. He hates the game but it's fun for me. He's still trying to figure out how Hillary Clinton, Maggie Thatcher, but not Carly Fiorina connect to E.E. Cummings and Edna St. Vincent Millay, but not T.S. Eliot."

"And all of them with three brands of vodka, Indian cuisine—and the Beatles."

"Exactly."

"He's not very bright, is he?"

Max lifted his shoulders with an amused fatalism. "Turns out even playing football *with* a helmet can scramble your brains."

"Sad. Because the answer is obvious."

"Really? This is my new favorite game—'Match Wits With Inspector Kennis.'"

"Too bad it has to be such a short one."

"Really?"

"Yes, Max. The answer is obvious. You have the poor idiot going on one wild goose chase after another. It has nothing to do with the subjects, does it? It's the words themselves. The first two have double letters. The last one doesn't—like…assault and battery, but not fraud."

"What an appropriate example."

"I thought so."

"You must know this game."

"Never heard of it. I've heard of all kinds of fraud, though."

"Like cheating on the Red Tickets Drawing."

"Right."

He blew out a weary breath. "You have to let this go and concentrate on real police work, Chief. Due respect. Someone dug up a skeleton with a bullet hole in its head! Plus, we have drunk drivers terrorizing the island. And a terrible drug problem."

"Thanks to your friend, Gary Pressman."

"He's not my friend. And he's the least of the problem, as you well know. He's one branch on the trunk of the tree. It's the roots you have to dig up."

"We're working on it."

"Good, because this raffle tickets hobby of yours is getting out of hand. Let me lay it out for you. You have some goon at Bartlett's—"

"Devon Flynn."

"Whoever—and he says I asked him to steal some sort of industrial pesticide—"

"Methomyl."

"Whatever. Then you have some worker bee at a local restaurant—"

"Ingrid Cole, at Ahab's"

"Fine. She supposedly put the stuff into some tainted food—"

"Crabcakes."

"Crabcakes, right. She implicates Lizza Coddington, this Devon person implicates me…but it's all hysterical hearsay and none of them have any idea of what's really going on…assuming anything actually is! I could have wanted that insecticide for my aunt's garden, assuming it really was me that wanted it in the first place. Lizza might have a grudge against any of the five people who got sick—if it really was Lizza, if this Ingrid Cole doesn't have her own grudge against Lizza. Or maybe she's just using Lizza to cover her own tracks. It all sounds very suspicious to me."

I was listening for holes in his argument, and there were plenty to choose from. "How do you know it was five people? How do you even know there was a poisoning incident? There's been nothing in the news or online about it."

"I know people, Chief. It's all anyone is talking about at the hospital. The point is, it's all a bunch of disconnected he-said-she-said chatter. The only thing lashing it all together is your wing-nut fantasy—no offense—about the Red Tickets Drawing. I don't see a case there."

I shook my head. "Well, it's hard to see yourself. Unless you look in a mirror, and even then the image is reversed."

He grinned. "That's deep. I like that. So, let's say it's all true. I'm the mastermind of a diabolical plan to rig this stupid raffle. What's the big deal? Someone's going to win, and everybody who loses *fully expects to.* You have to be there in person, right? And every year, without fail, someone with a winning ticket happens to be off-island or home sick or something, and they call out the numbers and wait…and wait—and then they move on. That person lost their chance. Tough luck. But here's the thing—if you skip the drawing, you think—Oh no! What if that was me? What if I had the winner?

And I blew it! On the other hand, if you show up on the day, and you're standing there with your ticket or your list of ticket numbers in your hand with everybody else, you *know* that unclaimed winning ticket *wasn't yours*. It doesn't haunt you. That's why people show up. Not to win. To be sure they lost."

"But you're making sure everyone loses. That's the difference."

"If I'm actually doing this."

"If you are."

"Look, Chief—no one gets hurt. That's the point. Everyone has fun. It's a victimless crime. I don't see why you care."

"It's the principle of the thing, Max. I don't like cheating. And I really don't like cheaters. Neither do you. What if people find a way to cheat at your video game?"

"They won't."

"It's impossible?"

"Pretty much."

I thought of Jane's comment. "You're too smart for them."

"Something like that."

I cocked a finger at him. "Well, I'm too smart for you."

"We'll see."

I let him have the last word. I wanted him to remember it.

Chapter Twenty-four

Honor Among Thieves

Dave Prescott's family had just finished dinner when I appeared at their front door. I was getting hungry for my own dinner. Miranda had the kids for the night, which meant a frozen flatbread pizza and a salad for Jane, Sam, and me. A humble repast, but I wanted it badly.

I told myself this would just take a few minutes.

Jim Prescott came to the door, still wearing the rumpled gray suit from his office hours at the town building, where he served as chief clerk.

Jim was no fan of mine, but the situation between us was delicate. True, I had revealed his son Dave's cheating, but I had also helped cushion the blow, and anyway the sneaky underachieving side of their son was something they should have noticed long before I showed up. That was the real chastisement of my presence. But Jim owed me one for looking the other way about his group's drug-purchasing-for-disposal scheme. He had made good points in Pressman's living room, that day on Tuckernuck, and I think he respected me for acknowledging them.

That was a separate issue. I still had to talk to his son.

Dave emerged from the house a few minutes later, zipping up a down parka. "What's going on, Chief?"

"Take a walk with me." I stepped off the deck and started down the driveway toward the road. He hurried to catch up. When we had struck a good stride I said, "I need your help."

"I'm not sure what you—"

"Come clean about what's going on."

"Hey—"

"I helped out with Superintendent Bissell. I made sure he knocked your suspension down to community service. I'm on your side."

"Okay. So?"

"So tell me about the raffle. For instance— who switched out the winning ticket? Where do they work? What are the exact logistics? How is Max going to pull it off?"

"I don't know what you're talking about. Seriously, dude."

"Dude?"

"Chief Kennis. Sorry. But I can't help you. I got nothing."

We walked along. A line of cars forced us to stand on the shoulder. "I'm puzzled, Dave. I understand why you got involved originally. You wanted the money to buy Pressman's stash. But that stash is history now. You have no reason to put yourself at risk anymore. Is it just loyalty?"

"What do you mean, at risk?"

"Come on. You know how it works. If you don't help us, and we bust the others, and they implicate you…which they will, if only to get a break in the sentencing phase…then you're as guilty as they are. This isn't cheating on some poetry test, kid. This is felony conspiracy and fraud and possibly money laundering, which is a mandatory five-year term."

"Money laundering?"

"Lottery winnings are the perfect cover for a drug dealer. It's cash you don't have to account for. It buys the product and hides the profits. You're covered at both ends. It's kind of brilliant, until you get caught."

He started walking again. I fell into step beside him, caught in the glare of a car's headlights. When darkness closed over us again, he seemed to have organized his thoughts. "I can't be caught. I haven't done anything. No one's done anything."

"Not yet."

"Right! So what does it—?"

"You helped plan this, Dave. That's what the others will say. Backing out doesn't get you off the hook. Only one thing gets you off the hook—helping me catch them. Otherwise, you're looking at obstruction of justice charges on top of everything else. Not a great way to start your senior year next fall. That's supposed to be the best year of your life. Don't wreck it."

"So—what—I'm supposed to testify against my friends?"

"It probably won't come to that. But, yeah—maybe. You have to be willing, at least."

"Forget it."

I decided to play my ace—I just hoped it wasn't a joker. You never knew anything for sure in the topsy-turvy Grand Guignol world of Nantucket gossip. "You're very forgiving," I offered.

"What is that supposed to mean?"

"It's admirable. Not wanting to betray your friends. Too bad they don't feel the same way."

"This is bullshit. No one's betraying anyone."

"So Max and Lizza aren't back together? That was what I heard."

"No way."

"You're sure about that?"

"I know Lizza. She would never it's like… been there, done that. Nice try, though, Chief." He stopped walking and we faced each other at the edge of the road. "Look, whoever palmed the ticket can't use it. Max got the original, he bought something at some store, and whoever was working behind the counter that day gave the duplicate to Lizza, so she can draw it out of the truckbed on Christmas Eve. Who's got the winning ticket? Who did Max give it to? That's the key. That's the real question, and no one knows the answer but him. The problem is…he's hiding out somewhere right now, and no one can find him. Yeah, he called me after you left his house. You freaked him out pretty good. He said, 'I'm going under until the drawing. If you need me my location's on the books. Whatever that means.'"

"Another puzzle."

"That's Max." We started back toward the house. At the door Dave turned to me. "There is one more thing, though. He said something about—you know, the girl who's holding the winning ticket: 'Someone from my lonely-hearts fan club,' that's what he said.

"Do you know who he was talking about?"

"No idea. But it's a clue. Right?"

"It is, indeed, Dave. Thanks."

We left it at that and I drove home. All I could really think about at that point was getting my frozen pizza into the oven and opening a bottle of wine. But it was not to be.

I got home to find Jane and Sam had given up on me. Her note said they'd gone for burgers at Crosswinds. But I wasn't alone. Chief Selectman and new Town Crier Dan Taylor was sitting in my living room. He had let himself in—like most locals, Jane and I never locked our door. Dan jumped up when he heard me walk in. Offhand, I couldn't think of anyone I less wanted to see at the end of a long frustrating day.

"Dan," I said by way of greeting, "you could have called."

"I've been calling all day! Check your messages! You can ignore the phone all you want but you can't ignore me. You can run, but you can't hide!"

"I'm not running and I'm not hiding. I live here."

"Really? You'd never know it."

"Can this wait until tomorrow? I'm officially off duty."

"Tomorrow will be too late! And, according to you, a cop is never off duty! Or is that just hot air like everything else you say?"

Clearly he wasn't going anywhere. "Try to

calm down, Dan. I'm opening some wine. Have a glass with me while I get dinner started."

"I don't drink and you know that."

"I didn't, actually. Has it been a problem for you?"

"You're my problem, Kennis. You're like that little pissant newspaper punk crapping all over the new Dreamland Theatre, or those kids who toilet-papered the Main Street Christmas tree last year. You just want to spoil this place for everyone."

I remembered one key phrase from David Trezize's "Dreamland" editorial:

"The old theater got sold to the first hustler with a wad of cash. He gutted the interior and stormed off in a huff, leaving the rubble behind. Well, the new theater is certainly an improvement on rubble, but that's setting the bar low, even for Nantucket."

The column went on from there, but to Trezie's credit, he printed Dan Taylor's furious response in the next week's issue.

With me, Dan's response had to be private, and I had a pretty good idea why. It didn't matter. He could badger and annoy me but he couldn't ruin my appetite. He glowered at me as I opened the wine and half-filled a plain Italian jelly glass. I took a sip, turned on the oven and pulled the pizza out of the freezer.

"So, what's the problem, Dan?"

"You know very well what the problem is! That's insulting! Asking me to lay it out like it wasn't the most obvious goddamn thing in the world! We both know the problem! I'm here to give you the solution."

I took a sip of wine and set the glass down on the counter. "Be my guest. Or more accurately—be my intruder."

"Very funny. Get a lock for your door if you want to keep people out."

"Not 'people,' Dan. Just you."

Believe it or not, I had talked Dan's son, Mason, down from a suicide attempt just a couple of years earlier. The kid was doing well. You'd think Dan might have retained some residual gratitude. Or maybe not. I thought of Jim Prescott, just this evening—furious at me for showing him a side of his son he should have seen himself. I'm sure Dan wanted to be the one to help Mason. But, as usual in Dan Taylor's life, he was the problem not the solution. And I was the reminder of that. "No good deed goes unpunished," that was the old platitude. It struck me that there might be a very good reason. Jane Stiles had recently cleaned up her ex-husband's apartment—out of concern for her son, Sam, who had to spend half his time there. Phil wasn't grateful. He took the long day's work as an insult and an accusation. Jane's efforts made him look like a slob, and I made Dan Taylor look like a bad father. No one likes to see themselves clearly. That's why we turn away from the dark glass of the computer until the screen lights up and hides our reflection.

"Here's how it's going to be," Dan said. "You are going to stop investigating this supposed plot to fix the Red Tickets Raffle. You're going to stop talking to people, and bothering people and rocking the boat. This is the biggest shopping season of the year on this island. We've built it up from nothing over the twenty years, turned it into a month-long event. The raffle is the centerpiece of all that. I'm the new Town Crier and I'm going to make sure the drawing goes off without a hitch. It's our biggest communal celebration, it's the crown jewel of everything we've been trying to accomplish here since the nineteen eighties."

"That's why I don't want to see it trashed, Dan."

"You're the one who's trashing it! You're pissing all over it. Everything was fine until you came along!"

"Actually—"

"So here's the deal. You back off. You know nothing and you like it that way. If someone comes to you and confesses, you ignore it. So everyone has a wonderful Christmas and goes back home smiling to Summit, New Jersey, and Greenwich, Connecticut, or Houston or wherever they live and Nantucket stays their pristine paradise, and they come back in the summer and they tell their friends and contribute to the new hospital fund and everyone's happy and you keep your job. How does that sound?"

I unboxed the pizza and slipped it into the oven. "That sounds okay. I've hit a brick wall on this one anyway. No one's talking to me, and even if they did, there'd be no way to know anything for sure. Talk is cheap."

"So you're giving up."

"I guess it's my civic duty."

"It's your job security. It's your professional survival."

"Well then, I guess I'm lucky the investigation failed."

"Yes, you are. Now make sure you keep it that way. And have a nice dinner. I'm late for mine."

I ate my pizza and salad with a second glass of wine, alone in the quiet house after Dan stalked out. The silent TV, the absence of bickering children and One Directions songs created a resonant sense of peace and quiet. It was like sliding down into the bathwater until your head is submerged and you can hear the warm silence chiming in your head. This was one of the great advantages of divorce: the nights off. I sipped my wine as the Unitarian Church bells rang eight o'clock in the distance and a car rolled past the house heading for Orange Street.

I had lied to Dan. I wasn't ready to give up. Dave Prescott had given me a lead and I was determined to follow it. I wolfed down my meal and headed out to Max Blum's house. I knew Max wouldn't be there, but something in his room might lead me to his hideout.

Chapter Twenty-five
The Geodesic Dome

Marjorie Blum came to the door when I rang the bell. I don't know who she was expecting but she looked irked and disappointed to see me standing in the winter drizzle. "My husband's not home," she said by way of greeting. "And I already told you everything I have to say about—"

I held up both hands, palms out, to staunch the flow of words. "I just wanted to take a quick look around Max's room, if that's okay. I know he's disappeared."

She seemed to refocus. "Can you find him?"

"I can try."

"Well…all right. But wipe your feet and be quick. Jackson wouldn't like finding you here and he could be back any minute."

Up in Max's room I concentrated on the bookshelves—two of them, about five feet high, holding maybe three hundred volumes. I started pulling them out, fanning the pages, checking for slips of paper or cutout centers, but there were no obvious leads in the boy's library—just science fiction by Kim Stanley Robinson and Ted Chiang, a doorstop volume of Westeros maps, texts on computer coding, and works by Borges and Calvino, Nabokov and Tim O'Brien.

Max never met a metatext he didn't like.

I thumbed through a copy of Paul Park's *All Those Vanished Engines*, with a smile of surprised respect. It wasn't a book you'd find in every library, though it deserved to be. Max was obviously as thorough and relentless in his reading as he was in every other area of his life. But I wasn't looking for clues to his character. I needed some ingeniously coded hint that could reveal Max's hideout—the equivalent of a treasure map. I was almost finished before I found it.

Max had a lavish leather-bound fore-edge-painted book sitting on his desk. It reminded me of Jane's collection and I recalled her mentioning that Max's father had bid against her for some oversized collectibles at one of Rafael Osona's auctions a few years before. Despite Max purloining this tome, it would never be listed in any inventory of his possessions, maybe even after his father's death, if there was no specific bequest in the will. It would never even occur to an estate agent that...

I set the book down on the desk and stood very still, as if a careless movement could jar the thought loose. I had just made the connection.

I pulled out my phone and got Haden Krakauer on the line. "Do me a favor," I said. "Check the deceased gun license rolls for firearms where no one filled out an FA-10 form to transfer ownership."

"How far back am I supposed to go?"

"Mid-forties—just after World War II. But you can optimize the search. I have a couple of terms you can use: 22 caliber Ruger and Blum. It shouldn't take long."

"So it's the father's gun."

"Could be."

I put the phone away and picked up the heavy fore-edge book again. I opened the cover and spread the pages, revealing the picture hidden on the page ends: a geodesic dome with blue ocean and sky behind it. The title page announced it was part of the Old Nantucket Collection. I had never seen a geodesic dome on the island but I was hardly an old Nantucketer. I did know a couple of them, though, and I had one of them on my speed dial.

"*Nantucket Shoals,*" said David Trezize.

"Don't you have secretaries at that newspaper?"

"I'm lucky to have paper, Chief. And I wouldn't mind a little news from time to time, either."

"I do my best for you. The Lomax murder? The Pops concert bomb scare? The mega-yacht sinking last summer? You scooped everyone on every story. Thanks to me."

"Those papers are landfill. What have you got for me today?"

"You're incorrigible. Today, I have a request."

He sighed. "Shoot. And I say that with a little anxiety, you being a cop and all."

"I have never shot a journalist. But I'm starting to rethink that policy."

"Now you're scaring me. What's the question?"

"Do you know anything about a geodesic dome on Nantucket?"

"Sure. There was a Buckminster Fuller house out on Cliff Road for years. A crazy old biddy owned it. Rode her bicycle to the Yacht Club every day. Some big Hollywood types bought the place, leveled the structure and put up the usual McMansion. This was like ten, fifteen years ago. Summer people. Couple of years ago, the kid got into trouble. Illegal firecrackers or something. He and some local pals kind of ran wild on the property, lived in the guest cottage, called it the bat cave. One of them hacked into the NPD computers and voided out a bunch of parking tickets. Sound like anyone you know?"

"It certainly does. Can you dig up that address on Cliff Road?"

"I can do better than that. I can send you some Google Earth screen grabs. It's the dirt road just before you get to Tupancy. No one's around this time of year. They're strictly one-week-in-August types. Miller or Mahler, something like that. Mohler, that's it, Kenneth and Francine Mohler. He produces that reality show about people who work at Home Depot."

"Thanks."

"I'll text you the info. Think you'll be able to find it on that newfangled phone of yours?"

"My daughter gave me a tutorial. I'm thinking of starting a twitter account. @copshop."

"To send out words of wisdom?"

"And to chastise my enemies!"

"Next stop, the White House."

I found the house easily. It was hard to miss, even tucked in far away from the road on the brink of the cliff overlooking Nantucket Sound. The place was absurdly, comically huge for two parents and one child. It must have had ten bedrooms at least. I remembered a kid I knew during my Hollywood summers growing up. His house was so big they used an intercom system to talk to each other from distant ends of the mansion. He got a BMW two-seater convertible for high school graduation, but he still stole cars for fun. He got bombed on his parents' booze every night, and died of a drug overdose at age twenty-six. It never seemed like a healthy parenting strategy, giving your kids everything they wanted whenever they wanted it, dipping the ladle over and over again into an inexhaustible ocean of money. I was glad I couldn't do that. I couldn't afford it. I was a sterling and recondite parent—by default. I suspected that if I had the Mohlers' money, I'd be spoiling my kids just as badly. So, lucky for them.

I drove down the winding narrow direct track and the massive shingled palazzo loomed slowly into view. Three chimneys, six dormers, and a widow's walk. Beyond the four-car garage, along the path to the wooden steps that descended to the beach, I found the guest cottage, modest and inviting, just like the image David Trezize had sent to my phone. I climbed out of my cruiser and stood leaning into the steady north wind for a minute or two, listening for some sign of life, watching for any movement.

I pulled out my phone and spread my fingertips on the screen to enlarge the black-and-white photo of the geodesic dome that David had sent me. The weathered boards, cracked glass, and rusting framework had a weather-battered homemade look that stood, or perched, at the edge of the precipice as a stern New England rebuke to the ostentatious pile behind me. But the rout was clear. The cranks had lost and the cronies had won, the eccentric bought out and brushed off by the extravagant. Money would always win those battles, but I found the triple chimney triumphalism disheartening.

The property was deserted, the main house windows boarded up. But the cottage showed signs of life. The outdoor light was on, the shell driveway showed fresh tire tracks, and spying in the windows I could see a sweater draped over a chair in the living room and dishes in the kitchen sink. On the wall visible from the sidelights of the front door I could see the alarm, turned on but unarmed.

The door was locked but I always kept a set of Peterson lock pick tools with me—the fancy one with the rubber handles. I had been trained by a paroled burglar back in Los Angeles, though I rarely needed to use my modest skills on Nantucket, so I was a little rusty with the pick set, and the Schlage lock was stiff. It took me almost five minutes to get inside.

The house was warm, with a comfortable-looking old couch and a pair of armchairs arrayed in front of a working fireplace still showing a pile of ashes from the last blaze. Hooked rugs softened the wide-board pine floors and tall bookshelves stood between the windows. The view of the Sound made the house feel airborne. The big kitchen was messy but Ikea modern with the required six-burner Wolf range, granite countertops, and Sub Zero fridge.

Upstairs I found two bedrooms, only one of them in use, bed rumpled and unmade, clothes on the floor, papers strewn across the desk—a plank laid across two filing cabinets. I counted an Apple PC, two Asus laptops, a Sony PlayStation, a Samsung flat-screen TV, and an iPod among the electronic clutter.

This had to be where Max was living—the central chamber of the bat cave.

Someone was living here with Max, or at least staying over often enough to leave her clothes in the closet. I checked the sizes—a big girl, not normally Max's type. So—a secret romance, with a girl no one would suspect he liked? That would be a perfect candidate for the final member of his team. The sex to bind her to him, the secrecy to make her win look clean. But who? I set the question aside and continued the search.

I checked the papers—notes for his video game, scratched-out lines of computer code, drawings, nothing connected to the Red Ticket Raffle. Was I hoping for some notebook in which he gloated about his accomplices and laid out his plans? If there was such a thing it would be on one of those computers, in a file hidden by numeric pin numbers and firewalls. I did find a stash of Red Tickets, along with a standard printout of the ticket numbers, listed in order. One of them might be the winner, but I had no way to tell which one; and in any case Max could already have handed it off to Lizza. I needed to find the person with its twin—the little red jackpot someone would be clutching in their hand tomorrow afternoon.

But who?

I found a solid clue in the medicine chest.

The girl kept a collection of cosmetics here, and they were all too familiar—the Rimmel mascara, the Smashbox eyeliner, Urban Decay black lipstick. I was sure most of it would match the stains on my towels.

Hello, Patricia Whelden.

I put everything back, suddenly hyperaware of my police cruiser sitting in the driveway. I didn't want to be caught here in uniform, for a lot of reasons. I was committing a crime, first of all, several crimes, in fact: criminal trespass, illegal search and seizure, though I hadn't seized anything yet, and of course the familiar old standby, breaking and entering. But beyond all that I didn't want Max to know I'd been here. If the plan I was putting together succeeded, Max's heist would vanish without a trace, a seagull into a fog bank—no one would know it had ever been there and not even Max would understand what happened.

In the end I couldn't arrange the papers on Max's desk exactly as I'd found them, but mess was mess and I doubted he'd notice. Five minutes later I was gone, heading toward Madaket, where I knew Patty lived, with not a single car in sight.

I punched the name Whelden into the cruiser's database and got the exact address, down Ames Avenue, across Millie's bridge and on to Massachusetts Avenue, via Rhode Island Avenue. The west end of the island was closed down and uninhabited, with just a few hardy locals hanging on through the winter.

The Wheldens owned a sagging saltbox with a priceless view of Madaket Harbor. The cottage had probably been in their family since the nineteen-twenties. The warped shingles, peeling paint, and rotting windowsills told a story of neglect, but not necessarily one of poverty. Old school Nantucketers seemed to take neglecting their houses as a matter of pride, with a Yankee contempt for throwing money away on frills and trifles. After my brief tour of the Mohlers' pleasure dome, I could start to see their point.

I drove past once, saw that no one was home and then parked in a driveway a few houses down.

I walked back, pulling my coat closed against the cold.

I looked around once and slipped through the unlocked door. I moved through the low, dark kitchen—chipped porcelain sink and rusting stove, cupped grease-stained pine floors—through a narrow living room with torn armchairs, a sprung couch, and an incongruous forty-one-inch Samsung flat-screen TV, into the pink-accented bedroom that had to be Patty's.

I felt tense and uncomfortable violating her privacy, but it was better than arresting her. I glanced around the tight little room—double bed with too many pillows, dresser, closet, desk with a laptop computer. Where would she have put the ticket? It wouldn't be an elaborate hiding place. She wouldn't play games as Max did. It would be somewhere personal, near at hand but safe.

I saw the locked diary on her dresser and knew it had to be there. I picked the lock in ten seconds, rifled the pages and saw the little Red Ticket instantly. "Happy Holidays. From Us to You. Buy Local & Win." I slipped the ticket out and replaced it with one from my wallet. No one would be alarmed, and the plan would move smoothly until it failed, Patty waiting in vain for her ticket number to be called.

Plot foiled.

I closed and locked the diary, set it down in the rectangle of dust I had revealed when I picked it up. I hadn't read one word of her private thoughts or touched any other object she owned. But my presence in Patty's house still felt wrong. It was wrong, and it would stay wrong until I made it right. I wasn't sure exactly how to do that, although switching out the tickets and thwarting Max's scheme felt like a decent start.

Haden Krakauer called me as I drove back into town—he had found the gun registration in the old records: a twenty-two-caliber Ruger, belonging to Dexter Blum—Jackson Blum's father, listed at the same address on Pleasant Street. The gun that killed Ted Coddington was stashed somewhere in that house, and Haden had taken the initiative to get a warrant. Finally, the blow I'd been waiting for—the hammer hitting a hairline crack. And the case was splitting open.

Chapter Twenty-six

Circumstantial Evidence

We were on our way out of the station to serve the search warrant on Jackson Blum when I solved the last piece of the Pat Sauter problem. It was a lucky break. Haden wanted to stop in the operations room to get a Twix bar from the vending machine. His nephew, Byron Lovell, was in there talking on the phone, and I heard him say "—that guy? He's a total plaster button, man."

The odd little slang term sounded ominously familiar. After my confrontation with Sauter, I had asked my friends in the building trades if they had ever come across the "small tool" slang that Pat had used. He claimed it was universal, but as far as I could see it hadn't even gone viral on the local jobsites. Nether Billy Delavane nor Mike Henderson had ever heard of it, though Billy was amused.

"I know one guy who's definitely an allen

wrench." Maybe the jargon was going to go viral after all.

Meanwhile, Byron's dad installed granite countertops and Pat Sauter had worked for him off and on since the nineties. The connection was obvious and making it gave me a small but distinct pleasure, like setting out an eleven-letter word on a triple word score in a Scrabble game, with the "F" in "infiltrator" sitting on a double point square.

I told Haden to warm up a car, and took Byron to a desk at the far end of the big room.

"I understand why you did it, Byron," I said. "You were scared."

"It—I…what?"

"And I understand that. Who wouldn't be scared? Pat Sauter is a scary guy."

"Hey, wait a second, I don't know what—"

"But here's the thing. I can't have official police business spread around town like gossip—information directly pertaining to ongoing investigations. It's sloppy and unprofessional, and it can also be dangerous. There's no specific law against it—we don't issue security clearances. But the police photographer who released his own pictures of the Boston Marathon bomber lost his badge over it."

"Wait a second! I never—"

"Obviously, this is very different. But the policy makes sense. Sometimes we take an investigation a down a dead end. No one needs to know all our mistakes. Sometimes we just like to have the element of surprise. Either way, I can't have leaks. They're bad for morale."

He could see further denials were pointless. "Listen, Chief—I'm sorry. I didn't mean to do anything wrong. It was—I mean, I was so…"

I patted his shoulder. "I get it. So I'm not going to fire you. I'm going to suspend you for a week, put you on probation, and let you work with the summer specials this year."

"Writing parking tickets?"

"If everything works out, I'll reinstate you next fall."

"But—"

"Call it a do-over. It's my Christmas present to you."

I left him standing there and joined Haden in the parking lot. "Byron screw up again?"

I shrugged. "Nothing he can't fix."

Jackson Blum answered the door when we arrived with the search warrant.

"What the hell is this?"

I handed him the document. "Read it."

He unfolded the papers and skimmed the text, blocking the entrance, shifting through all four pages, pausing to study Judge Perlman's signature. "I'm getting Alan on the phone. He'll cancel this."

"No he won't."

We stared at each other. Blum played golf with Alan Perlman. More importantly, they played poker together. Perlman was a shrewd cardsharp who rarely bluffed and possessed an unerring instinct for "leveling"—predicting and outguessing his opponents. Haden had sat in on some of those games, back in the day, before the stakes got too high and he started losing his beer money.

Blum handed me the warrant. "So you're going to tear my house apart on the day before Christmas Eve?"

"There's no need for that, Mr. Blum. All we want is your father's Ruger."

"How could you possibly know about that gun?"

"We still have your father's registration on file," Haden said. "You never renewed it."

"I never used it!"

Blum had stepped forward. I raised a hand. "That's what we intend to find out."

"This is outrageous. Nantucket is turning into a police state!"

I sighed. "Not really. In a police state I'd rough you up, arrest you, and look for the gun later. No warrant, no worries. No, actually, in a real police state? Someone like you would 'own' the cops and be untouchable. But this is still a democracy, where we follow the rule of law. Sorry."

"I'm not letting you in."

"You don't have a choice. Except this one: ten cops searching your house, or you peaceably surrendering the weapon. Right now."

He looked away first. He knew when he was beaten. "Fine. Stay here."

Twenty minutes later I was in the basement of the police station in our small but effective and well-equipped SID lab, handing the gun in its plastic evidence bag to Monica Terwilliger. She had cut her hair and lost a little weight. I wasn't sure whether to mention it, and she smiled at my discomfort.

"Eight and a half pounds, Chief. I'm on the longevity diet."

"What's that?"

"One day I eat what I like—the next day, six hundred calories. It's the diet you're supposed to break! That would be my slogan. I appreciate eating on the days when I can, and, frankly, it's a relief not to think about food on the days when I can't. Which, I mean—I still eat. Toast and black coffee for breakfast, vegetable soup for lunch, and a big spinach salad with a hard-boiled egg for dinner. All I have to do is keep a pot of soup going and remember to buy spinach. But at least I actually eat the stuff now, instead of letting it turn into a science experiment in the vegetable drawer."

I nodded. "Sounds pretty good."

"It's like a little cleanse. It gives your organs a rest from the constant avalanche of food. Not that you have that! I don't mean you. But for me…anyway, the point is, it works! Plus no more headaches and my eczema cleared up. Too much information?"

"Maybe a little. I like your hair, by the way."

She did a little twirl. "R.J. Miller. He's the best. Now what have we got here?"

She pulled on a pair of latex gloves and removed the gun from the bag.

"Twenty-two Ruger? This could be it."

"Yeah."

"I'll have to test-shoot it. Then we can look at the two fired ammunition components under the comparison microscope and check the rifling. Shouldn't take long."

"Fired ammunition components? You mean bullets?"

"Spoilsport! Jargon is fun."

"Do you run the data through the IBIS BulletTrax?" The town had paid a lot for that ballistics identification system, but like the disabled-access elevator at the Nobby Shop (which led to the work clothes department!), it had never yet been used.

"Funny about the IBIS, Chief, even when the 3-D imaging finds a match, it still has to be verified by a human expert."

"And that would be you."

"Oh, yeah. That would totally be me. Wait here. I'll be back in a sec."

The bullets were a perfect match.

I had my murder weapon, but still no compelling evidence that Blum was the one who used it. I thanked Monica and took off.

I was halfway home when I got a call from Karen Gifford. I hadn't spoken to her about her dusty search through the files and documents, and had left her unsupervised to comb through the historical records for a bystander who might remember those twenty-year-old events in Madaket. I had pretty much forgotten about the plan, but Karen was relentless, like all good cops, and this time her persistence paid off.

"Get back to the station, Chief. I found an eyewitness."

Chapter Twenty-seven

The Osprey Nest

"Who and how?" I asked Karen, standing in her first-floor cubicle, five minutes later.

"Let me do the 'how' first," she said.

"Go."

"Well…I found a story in the *Inquirer and Mirror* from December of 1997. A police helicopter located a marijuana grow house on the Land Bank property donated by the Coddington family. That was what caught my interest. They used thermal imaging to identify the shack, which had originally been used as some kind of hunting blind in deer season. But they also documented the find with regular photographs. The actual case was a dead end, at least for me. I tracked down the growers and the cops who made the bust back then. No one remembered anything about a murder or a burial on the property. I still wanted to look at the photos, so I tracked down the case file but apparently the pictures were filed separately when the archive was sealed. I filled out a release form and threw your name around a little."

"Did it work?"

"It took a day or two, but I got in there. One of the pictures happened to show an osprey nest being erected on the property. What they call a V platform. There was a decent-sized group in the picture, but of course I couldn't identify any of them. So I went to the Maria Mitchell Association and checked their newsletters. The ones from 1997 are still on microfiche, so that took a while. Turned out the nest was a school project they had sponsored. There was just a little squib about it. So I went to the high school and started digging out old issues of *Veritas*. Hard copies, stacks of them, in the basement. They've been meaning to get back issues onto the computer, but…anyway. Some years the paper is really well-written and sharp. Nineteen ninety-seven—not so much. But I found the story. Two local boys, recent NHS graduates home from college on Christmas break, helped out with the project. One of them was Haden Krakauer! I talked to him but he didn't really remember much. He was always volunteering at Maria Mitchell, helping with bird walks and things. He even built a few osprey nests, but he didn't have much to do with the Madaket project. He was never on-site. The other helper was Billy Delavane."

"You're a genius."

"Well, it's supposed to be ninety-nine percent perspiration. I have that part covered."

"Did you talk to him?"

"I left a message. Then I called you."

"I'm headed out there now. Thanks, Karen. That was great work."

I was halfway out the door when she stopped me. "Chief?"

"What?"

"I just wanted to say something. I worked at lots of jobs around here before I decided to join the force. The Basket Museum, the NHA, the Theater Workshop. I worked for the Lifesaving Museum and the Town Clerk. And in all that time, in all those jobs, no one ever thanked me for anything. It was like some kind of zero-sum game for them… if they praised me it made them look bad. It was always the same—overpaid people at the top ignoring the people who did the work and taking all the credit. I started to think that's just the way things worked. The way of the world! But not with you, not in your world. So, just…thanks."

She was right about the normal functioning of the world. Things worked the same way in the LAPD, and I had watched the dynamic play itself out when Homeland Security took over a case on-island a few years before. People on top didn't even want to know how the work got done or how much how much of it was involved in a project or an investigation. The thought of other people working made them feel lazy, and the intelligent people under their command made them feel stupid. Mostly they were, in fact, lazy and stupid, but watching their betters make half their salary added guilt to the mix and the combination was toxic.

I had always vowed—not in my police department.

Karen's awkward gratitude made me think I was on the right track.

I pulled out of the lot and headed for Billy Delavane's shack in Madaket, squinting against the glare of the setting sun.

"I remember that day," Billy said when we were settled in two chairs facing his wood stove, his pug, Dervish, anchoring my lap. "It was weird."

He had offered me a Whale's Tale ale and since my day was officially over, I'd taken him up on it. I set the bottle down on the flagstone floor. "How so?"

"The nest was badly made—no predator guards, no drain holes, and the post wasn't set deep enough. Building a nest like this...it's like framing a house, because the birds do all the finish work themselves. We just have to give them a good base. Which on this particular day meant starting over from scratch. Lots of digging. But here's the bizarre part. I had a little preview on my way over. As I was driving into the property I saw this older guy I knew—Jackson Blum? He was coming out of the pine trees, covered in dirt…just the way I was going to be. He even had a shovel in his hand! I remember thinking—that's weird. And then I got caught up in the job, we were there for like five hours, and I had a date that night and I was late and…I don't know, I never thought about it again. Until Karen Gifford left that message today. The laundry I had to do that night was more memorable than some random guy I saw standing by the side of the road. I wound up throwing away my shirt."

Laundry—that's what Marjorie Blum had been talking about. She must have washed her husband's clothes that night. She had known something terrible had happened and she either chose not to find out what it was or she had kept her husband's secret all these years.

Billy was putting things together, also. "The skeleton Pat dug up in Madaket. Blum was burying the guy that day. Coddington! It was Coddington land—or used to be. Until they sold it to the Land Bank and the Land Bank sold it out. Did the Land

Bank make the deal with Blum? Sure, but they had to get Coddington out of the way first! Another real estate murder."

I waved my hands across my face, as if I was trying to stop an oncoming truck. "No, no, no. The Land Bank is clear on this one."

"So it was…the Main Street store! Coddy didn't want to do the Winthrop deal. So—" He flicked the edge of his hand across his throat like a knife. "Bye bye, spy guy."

"Looks that way."

"But you're finally going to nail him."

"Thanks to you."

"Wow."

"You don't mind testifying in open court?"

"Against that guy? I'd re-cobble Main Street by hand to testify against that guy. And Main Street could use some re-cobbling."

"You may get your chance. To testify."

I shook his hand and pushed back out the door through the small screen porch into still, frigid air. It was full dark, now. The surf was rumbling beyond the dunes, and I was late for dinner. I had the kids tonight, and that meant Jane was alone and badly outnumbered.

Like the last-minute five-dollar donation that secures the funding for a fifty-thousand dollar

Kickstarter project, I got a final contribution as I drove back to town.

Kyle Donnelly had been researching Clifford Marks and Rafe Talerian, the ones who supported Blum's story about using chewing tobacco tins as party decorations.

As I suspected, they both had deep compromising ties to Blum. Kyle's search through the real estate filings and tax records revealed that Blum had paid off a giant tax lien on Clifford Marks' house three years ago and now held the paper on it. Marks was three months behind and Blum could foreclose on him at whim.

Talerian had a more complicated story. His daughter Eliza had gotten involved with an immigrant guy that her parents disapproved of—a Jamaican landscaper five years older than she was. He earned a good living, with a crew of six and three trucks complete with rattling trailers packed with riding mowers, weed whackers, and leaf blowers. His family was as distraught as hers and David Trezize had run a long piece about it in *The Shoals*. "Diversity and Division: Romeo and Juliet on Juniper Hill Road." Juniper Hill was a wealthy subdivision tucked behind Moor's End Farm, off Shimmo Pond Road. Talerian had overextended himself to buy one of the bigger houses there, and so he took the low-bid landscaper, who happened to be Bradon Edwards. His daughter started chatting with Bradon one August afternoon, and things moved quickly from there.

Talerian's solution: pack Eliza away to a pricey boarding school and let distance do the rest. The school was Northfield Mount Hermon, where Talerian had met his wife-to-be back in tenth grade. They both worked on the alumni committees, organizing fundraisers and even helping with the annual newsletters. They had pull and influence, but they couldn't afford the tuition, which was topping fifty thousand dollars a year. Eliza had worked in Blum's store and there was a shoplifting charge Blum had dropped around the same time. Store video of the crime was mentioned in depositions but never offered in discovery before the case was dismissed.

So Blum chose not to prosecute, and helped pay for the school. Bursar's office records showed an LLC that Kyle traced to Blum's Pleasant Street address. As it turned out, Eliza met an extraordinary African-American young man named Marshall Stackhouse in her second year there, and married him right after graduation. She supported Marshall through Tufts medical school and his internship and residency at Brigham and Women's. Recently he had opened a practice in Burlington, Vermont, and they were, by all accounts, living happily ever after.

According to an article Kyle dug out from the *Burlington Free Press*—Eliza worked as a features editor there—meeting some actual black people had tempered her father's racism somewhat and he had entered a state of what she called "useful confusion."

All of which begged the question: Why had Blum helped these two men and their families? Was he a much nicer guy than anyone suspected? I was skeptical, and Kyle had some tentative confirmation of my doubts. Blum's son, Martin, had transferred to Northfield Mount Hermon after a disastrous two years at NHS, marked by ostracism, bullying, and bad grades. On the phone, Talerian had admitted to "twisting a few arms" to make that happen. He was glad to do it. He owed Blum "big time."

Talerian had been a general contractor based in Concord back in the day, and even though it meant shipping his materials across the sound by boat and flying his crews on and off the island every day, he did all the renovation work on Blum's house and store for free. Kyle's combing through both bank accounts showed no invoices or payments.

So Blum took his pound of flesh.

"My reading?" Kyle said. "He just likes having

the power. These guys are terrified of him. That's sweet, you know?"

I nodded. "Like the smell of a bakery."

"Yeah. One of those all-you-can-eat bakeries where you never gain a pound."

"So why did they talk?"

"Well, no one wants to be an accessory to murder, Chief. And I kind of promised I'd keep their names out of it. Is that a problem?"

"Probably not. Don't worry. I've bent the truth a few times getting a suspect to talk. Once I kind of purposely forgot to Mirandize this guy before he incriminated himself. I knew he wouldn't talk if he thought he was a suspect. I was waiting for a reprimand or a suspension, but we got a solid confession and a clean conviction. He's doing ten to twenty-five at Corcoran—and I got promoted. Obremski said to me, 'Here's an LAPD poem for you, K-Man—'Liar liar, pay grade higher.' Not that I approve of dishonesty in general terms, but in this case—good work."

"Taught by experts, Chief. Merry Christmas."

I ended the call as I pulled into Darling Street. So that was it—no chewing tobacco tin party decorations. Blum had bought the snuff for one reason and one reason only: to keep the rats off Coddington's grave.

I thought about my quarry for a few seconds

before I climbed out of the warm car. For a man who hated the holidays, this was a drastically ironic turn of events.

Jackson Blum was about to have the worst Christmas ever.

Chapter Twenty-eight

The Drawing

I slipped into the house just in time to catch the end of Jane's first battle in her war on teen chaos. I had no idea what the exact flash point had been. I stopped in the front hall to listen.

"I don't want to!"

"No one wants to! Are you a baby? We all do things we don't want to do, most of the time."

"So I should do everything around here?"

"You do nothing! Start with doing something! Once! We'll talk about you doing everything after that. Look—if you clean the mess when it happens, it never turns into this."

"I was going to clean it up."

"No you weren't."

"I was! But you can't wait! Everything has to be *this second!*"

"Yes! Because that's all you have. Life is this

second. Everything else is nothing. The past is gone, the future is rushing at you and meanwhile it's *this second*, and it always will be."

"I don't even know what you're talking about."

"I'm talking about taking care your own life now, not waiting for someone else to do it."

"I can't believe this. You have no right to say this shit. You're not my mother."

"No, I'm your roommate. And I won't be the last one, either. You're going to have roommates all your life—in college and in the city when you get your first job and eventually when you get married because your husband will be a lot of wonderful things but he'll also be your roommate and he's probably going to be a shitty one and you'll be having this exact conversation with him when you finally get sick of cleaning his crusty cereal bowls and picking his wet towels off the bed. Believe me, I speak from experience. Learn to be a good roommate now. You'll have a much better life."

"You're not the boss of me."

"Good thing. Because you'd be fired."

Tim laughed. It was the first sound I'd heard him make. "She's right," he said.

"Shut your stupid mouth, you zit-faced little suck-up. I'm out of here."

"I have one pimple! One!"

Carrie wasn't listening. I eased up the stairs

out of sight as she stalked into the front hall and slammed out the front door. It was a cold night and all she had was a learner's permit. She'd be back soon.

I came downstairs and walked into the living room. The tree Jane had bought at Moors End Farm almost touched the ten-foot ceiling. She had bought extra ornaments and strung the tiny white lights perfectly. She had hated Christmas until Sam was born, but once he got old enough to care, she hurled herself into the holiday with typical tireless abandon. Jorma Kaukonen's acoustic Christmas album was playing softly in the background.

"That was intense," I said.

Jane walked over and hugged me. "She'll come around."

"I did my own laundry today," Tim said. "I even cleaned the lint tray in the dryer."

"I helped," Sam chimed in. "I folded!"

I could imagine how that turned out, and I could see Tim start to speak and pull back. I guessed he was enjoying having a younger brother too much to spoil it with a mean-spirited remark.

Carrie came back an hour later, and ostentatiously hung her coat up on a hook in the hall.

"Sorry," she said to Jane. "You're just like Gramma." She meant my mother. Miranda's mom was an unreconstructed troll straight out of

Grimm's fairy tales—the original German version, too intense for younger children. Carrie went on: "You're always the most infuriating and annoying when you're—the most right. Okay? You're right. I don't want to be a bad roommate."

Jane put an arm around her shoulders. "You might turn out to be one of the best roommates."

It looked like there might be another roommate on the scene a few minutes later. I got a call from Jacqueline Talbot at the MSPCA. The place was closed, but she wanted me to know that Bailey, Pressman's Portuguese water dog was due to be put down the next morning. No one had wanted to adopt him. He was miserable in his cage and growled at people. "That's not the real Bailey but it's hard to convince people. Anyway…just thought you should know. In case…"

I made a split-second decision. No one was going euthanize that lovely dog. If we had to pay for the floors to be refinished when we moved out, so be it. Maybe Jane would have a best seller and we'd be able to buy the place ourselves!

"We're picking Bailey up from the vet tomorrow morning," I said.

"I knew it," Carrie said.

Tim's whole face seemed to widen, not just the eyes. "Really?"

"No one wanted him but us."

He flung himself at me and I caught him in a hug, staggering backward a few steps. "This is so great!"

Sam was grinning and Jane nodded a quiet assent. She was a dog person, though her family had preferred aloof little terriers. It was decided.

Or so I thought.

• • ● • •

Christmas Eve started out off-kilter. I put one foot wrong getting out of bed and I wound up sideways all morning. I wanted to get to the station early so I could prepare the probable-cause materials for Judge Perlman. I wanted an arrest warrant in hand before lunch. Alan had been working with us on the case, so I knew he'd expedite the warrant if I gave him a solid affidavit—probably even a writ of capias, but I had no worries about Blum fleeing the scene. A mad dash for the airport would just confirm his guilt.

Billy Delavane had signed a statement, as had Marks and Talerian—faxed signatures, to be followed by the notarized originals sent registered mail. I had the ballistics report on the Ruger and Marjorie's Blum's (reluctantly signed) statement to back up Billy Delavane's testimony. The written narrative of the evidence clearly showed a man who had used his father's gun to kill his partner, after quarreling over the business, and then protected the grave from rats with several pounds of chewing tobacco. We had him buying the snuff, we had an eyewitness who had seen him holding a shovel on the day in question, with the dirt from Coddington's grave all over him, soiled clothes the wife had laundered without demur but with worried suspicion, that same evening. He had no alibi, and he had failed to dispose of the weapon, apparently for sentimental reasons relating to his father.

The document needed to be clearly written and I was a writer. I wasn't used to deadlines, though, and I wanted the maximum amount of time to make the chain of evidence clear and the story convincing.

I submitted the affidavit just before lunch and Judge Perlman said he'd have an answer—and most likely, a warrant—by five. "Best to wait until after the drawing anyway," he told me. "We wouldn't want to disrupt our quaint annual festival of greed and disappointment."

"Right. I don't want to end up in the Star Chamber."

He laughed. "Don't flatter yourself, son. No secret tribunals for you. They'll just vote to cut your pay, or run you down with one of those giant new Jeeps they drive."

The upshot was, I didn't get to the MSPCA

with Tim until twelve-thirty, and by the time we showed up Bailey was gone. Not put to sleep—adopted. Someone had slipped in there before us.

"No!" Tim started crying before the vet had gotten the words out.

"Wait a second, I told you—"

"You didn't give us a verbal commitment. It's first come, first served, Chief. Sorry."

Tim turned on me. "You didn't tell them we wanted Bailey?"

"Yes, I did, I said—"

"Well, they didn't get it, Dad! And now he's gone!"

"Sorry, Chief—they just left twenty minutes ago. I kind of expected you first thing this morning."

"I don't believe this," Tim moaned.

"I was writing a murder warrant affidavit," I said.

"So what? Who cares? You could have written it after we got Bailey."

"Tim—"

"I hate you!"

I reached for him but he flinched away from me. "I'm going back to the car."

I watched as he slouched out of the big glass doors and crossed the parking lot to my cruiser.

"Sorry, Chief. I guess we got our wires crossed."

"Yeah, I guess so. Merry Christmas."

I followed Tim outside through a swirl of snow flurries, and climbed into the car.

"At least he's going to a good home," I offered.

Tim looked away, out the passenger side window. "Yeah, just not ours. Thanks, Dad."

We drove home in silence. There was nothing more to say. Both of us knew I had blown it. I had always sworn I wouldn't turn into one of those fathers who put work ahead of family.

This was why.

• • ● • •

The Nantucket Christmas Eve Red Ticket Drawing represented more than sixteen million dollars in sales this year. Of course the results were skewed away from pure gift-giving, since Stop&Shop started to participate. It was a good change. It turned the drawing toward a more egalitarian note, and gave an immigrant family with lots of kids, who spent most of their disposable income on food, a better chance to win. Though obviously the gloating one-percenter with a roll of tickets and a ten-page list of numbers from buying a new Jeep Grand Wagoneer would always have the edge. But that was Nantucket in a nutshell.

Still it was good to see the crowd.

Main Street was packed, curb to curb, sidewalk to sidewalk, storefront to storefront, with thousands of people and they were all in a party mood. The temperature had dropped into the twenties but the weather had cleared and no one seemed to mind. People were greeting old friends, patting each others' dogs, hugging each others' kids. Bundled toddlers were riding their fathers' shoulders and there were faces at every second-story window overlooking the street. My police were out in force, ready to quell a riot, but I had given strict orders to leave people alone and join in the spirit of the afternoon.

Raised in Manhattan and Los Angeles, my concept of crowds was formed by throngs of crazed fans in front of the Pantages or the Kodak Theatre on Oscar night, the Macy's Thanksgiving Day Parade and New Year's Eve in Times Square. Those, and the big political rallies, the angry marches, like the giant nuclear freeze demonstration the summer I turned ten. The idea of people gathering in such numbers just to be together struck me as bizarre and quaint and wonderful.

No one really expected to win the drawing, but everyone would be happy for the person who did. It felt like a giant surprise party, thrown by everyone for everyone else, and no one was really surprised but me. This wasn't Shirley Jackson's New England, with grim squinting Puritans cleansing their collective sins through murderous rituals of atonement.

These locals were going to throw money and kisses, not stones. If their sin was greed, it was a festive, self-mocking version of that transgression.

I saw most of my friends and acquaintances as I pushed the crush of people toward the bank steps. I embraced Mike and Cindy Henderson, twirled their two-year-old little girl, shook hands with Pat Folger and Billy Delavane and the Graham family, hugged David Trezize, air-kissed Elaine Bailey, and lifted a hand to greet a dozen others.

When I noticed Sam Trikilis, he was clutching a cardboard box full of plastic bags stuffed with tickets organized numerically. For reference he had the familiar printout of numbers, running to six pages.

He jammed it all between his left arm and his side, freed up his right hand and shook mine.

"How is Alana doing?" I asked him.

"On the mend. She'll be out of the hospital tonight and home for Christmas. We hope. It might be her last Christmas in the house, so…"

I checked out the bounty of Red Tickets, and he saw the perplexed look on my face. "They're all from my friends, Chief—the tickets," he said. "And customers, and teachers at the school. All donated! I couldn't believe it."

"People love you, Sam."

"Well, I love them right back, and it was a

great gesture and I'm so grateful to everyone but…I mean—it's not going to do any good. The raffle's still a million-to-one shot. It's a great way to say good-bye, though."

"Sam—"

"Hey, let's face facts. It would take a miracle to get my family out of this one, Chief."

At that moment I remembered the Red Ticket in my pocket, the one I had taken from Patty Whelden's diary.

Lizza Coddington was still going to palm its twin when the five-thousand-dollar ticket was drawn, and Patty Whelden no doubt thought she was going to drive the conspiracy home by claiming the money.

But that wasn't going to happen, and no one knew it but me.

I reached into my coat pocket and felt the flimsy stub against my fingertips, slipped it into my palm, closed my fist as Sam Trikilis talked about having to give up his business when he left the island, trying to figure out where he and wife could go without becoming a burden on his family.

He had no choices and no prospects.

"Once you leave Nantucket, there's no coming back, you know what I mean?" he was saying. "You can't afford the rent even if you could find a place to live, and you can't. You cross that bridge, it's burnt. Forty years building a life here and you're just a homeless bum. You don't have the big bucks? You have to win the lottery just to get a house you can afford to live in around here! I was talking to a couple of kids yesterday. They won the drawing for one of those covenant houses on Old South Road. 'We get a house! We get a house!' Yeah, built on the cheap, smack dab against ten other crappy little houses, but it beats moving away. I felt like telling them, 'When I was your age, I started a business and bought a house here. No games of chance required, just hard work.' But that was back in another century. Now I have to play the goddamn lottery, too. But that's life, I guess." He lifted his box of tickets with a morose little smile.

Sam was right—he needed a miracle.

And I was holding one in my hand.

I pulled the ticket out and handed it to him. "Take this one, Sam," I said. "It could be the miracle you're looking for."

He gave me a bewildered smile. "You only have one ticket?"

"One is all it takes."

I pressed it into his hand. "Come on. It's my contribution."

He took it and pulled me into an awkward hug, half-pressed against his box. "Thanks, Chief. I'll keep a special eye on this one."

"You do that."

I eased away into the crowd. I had crossed a line but I didn't care. I'd been given the power to do something good for someone, and I took it. It was a crazy fluke, but a happy irony—Max Blum's nihilistic, cynical scheme would now serve to save a family's home and allow a beloved member of the community to remain. I couldn't imagine the Red Tickets Raffle serving a better purpose.

I was on the steps above Lizza when she drew that last ticket. I saw the sliver of red in her fist before she plunged her hand into the pile. No one else saw anything and I studied her face when she handed the ticket to Dan Taylor and he read off the numbers into his megaphone. She was looking off to the left where Patty was standing and I took a moment's pleasure in the look of bewilderment on Lizza's face when the crowd in the middle of Main Street around Sam Trikilis erupted into cheers and applause.

"Looks like we have a winner," bellowed Dan Taylor. "Come on up!"

Sam could barely make it through the crowd. People were slapping him on the back, hugging him. Someone had a bottle of champagne in a shopping bag—they popped the cork and handed the foaming bottle to Sam, a clear violation of the municipal open-container laws which I had absolutely no interest in enforcing. Sam lifted the bottle took a huge swig and handed it back, to a new round of cheers and applause. There was a brief scuffle and then two big guys lifted Sam up on their shoulders like a winning quarterback and carried him through the crowd. The mass of people parted like fabric ripped along the seam and Sam opened his arms to them all.

They had all gathered in the center of town on a frozen afternoon, glad to participate and happy to lose. Now, unexpectedly, all of them had won.

Sam shook my hand again when they let him down and he climbed the stairs of the bank, pulling me into a bear hug. "A miracle!"

I set him back at arms' length. "I told you one ticket was all it takes, Sam. Merry Christmas. And many more to come."

Sam was laughing and crying at the same time. I slipped away before I started crying, too.

An hour later I stood in front of his house with Jane, listening to Carrie and Patty Whelden and the other Grace Notes sing "Good King Wenceslas" to Sam and Jennifer and Alana, the latter wrapped in a big blanket against the cold.

Jane touched my arm. "That's her."

I turned. "Who?"

"Marcia Stoddard. My supposed look-alike. In the full-length down jacket and the Santa cap."

I glanced over. Dusk was settling in but I could see her clearly. Jane was much prettier but I could see the resemblance. It's a verifiable fact of human nature, that if you tell someone they look like someone else—even if that other person is much better looking—they'll be insulted. No one wants an accidental twin. It's like hearing your own voice on tape, your full-throated baritone reduced to a nasal tenor. It constricts your self-image.

Of course, I didn't say any of that. This was not the moment for nuance.

"She's your height. That's it. Hey, people used to tell me I looked like Phillip Seymour Hoffman."

"Before he got fat, I hope."

"And before he died. I look much better than him now."

She elbowed me in the side but I got the smile I was looking for.

When the song was finished another group appeared out of the growing darkness. It was Jill Porter, Bessie Trott, and the other Accidentals, out on their own rounds of caroling. Jill approached Carrie. They looked like two mountain lions at the same watering hole.

"That sounded pretty good," Jill said.

"Thanks."

"I had no idea we had so many good singers in school."

"Well...we do."

"Yeah..." She brightened. "Take a selfie with me? I have FaceLight Flash. We'll get a million shares."

"Cool!"

They took the picture and Carrie said "Let's sing one together. How about "Adeste Fidelis"?"

"In G major?"

"Perfect."

They were singing, all twenty of them sweetly in tune like some Viennese church choir, when my phone went off. I checked the screen—Judge Perlman. He had the warrant ready for me in his office.

It was time to arrest Jackson Blum.

Chapter Twenty-nine
Three Spirits

Jackson Blum was drowning in his own life. The telephone call from Mass. General had tumbled him into dark water. When the police arrived, five minutes later, he felt fingers gripping his ankle, pulling him down. He couldn't breathe. He had done this to himself. This was suicide. He had been committing suicide for years and he hadn't even known it.

He'd read somewhere about a man who jumped off the Golden Gate Bridge and survived. As soon as he started to fall, this man knew he had made a catastrophic mistake—the last mistake in a life full of them. None of them could be corrected, none of them could be taken back. Yet he had survived somehow, with his ankles shattered, his knees and hips broken, his shoulder dislocated, and his vertebra crushed. He had been pulled out of the bay, hauled aboard a fishing smack, and lived to tell his tale.

Blum would not be so lucky. You could survive the real ocean, the real fall, but not the one inside, not the one you made yourself. There were no happy accidents on that ocean, no convenient fishing boats, no helping hands, no blankets, no doctors, just the cold currents and the grasping fingers clawing you down.

They had been having drinks in the living room, anticipating a rack of lamb and Marjorie's garlic mashed potatoes for dinner, followed by coffee and key lime pie and the annual viewing of what his son Max regarded as the finest holiday movie ever made: *Mickey's Christmas Carol*. "You're Scrooge McDuck, Dad," Max had laughed last year. "Own it!" What could you say to that but "Bah, humbug"? So he had. Max had just shaken his head. "Making my point for me. Just like always."

This year was more tense, but Max seemed reconciled to his brother's banishment, and apparently chastised by the day's events. Something bad had happened, but Blum chose not to pry. As for Marjorie, she just wanted to salvage what was left of her favorite holiday. Everyone was making an effort. The line was narrow, but they were all walking it together, single file.

Until the phone call.

Blum set his drink down and hurried out to the front hall, listening to the muffled "Ride of the Valkyries" ring tone fanfaring from his coat pocket. He dug out his iPhone and answered.

"Hello?"

"It was you! It's your fault! You did this."

"Hello, who is speaking, please?"

"He's dead, are you happy now? That's what you wanted and you got it. That's your Christmas present, you miserable, rotten, fucked up—" The voice broke into ugly, heaving sobs.

Blum pulled the phone away from his ear a little. "For the last time, who is this?"

"It's Connor! Connor McKenzie! Your son's gay lover! Who loved him! Who loved him more than you could ever even imagine loving any one. And he loved you, that's the sickest most fucked part of the whole thing, he loved you so much. All he cared about was your opinion. What will Dad say, Dad would love that. Dad should read this, Dad should hear that, I can't wait to tell Dad whatever the fuck it was. Dad, Dad, Dad! Well, he finally told you something—he finally got up the nerve to tell you the most important thing in the world—he gave you trust and love and you gave him hate! You threw it in his face. You rejected him and kicked him out and disowned him and now he's dead!"

"He's—he…what? I don't—"

"Your son committed suicide tonight! Understand? I'll send you the note! It's all about you. Dad,
Dad, Dad, just like always. I kept telling him you
could change, you'd come around, there was still
hope, even Dick Cheney supports gay marriage
now, but he didn't believe me. I was on your side!
Isn't that fucking hilarious? But he wouldn't listen.
He knew better. He laughed when I tried to pull
that Mary Cheney stuff. 'Do you think Dick would
adopt me?' That was what he said. And I told him
Mary said she was Darth Vader's daughter and he
said, 'I'll take it! At least Darth admits he's on the
dark side! He calls his weapon the Death Star! Dad
would call it the Peace Moon!' He was so funny. I
don't know where he got his sense of humor from
but it wasn't from you. He said he'd never seen you
laugh, not once, not ever. Until now. You have the
last laugh now because you did everything you
could to make his life a living hell and now he's
ended it. You might as well have stuffed the pills
down his throat because you killed him and you'll
have to live with that for the rest of your life."

"Wait, I—"

But Connor was gone.

Blum stood in the front hall, gasping for air,
choking and panicking, the dark water closing over
his head, listening to Max and his wife laughing

about something, some trivial moment in their separate world, in these last moments before he destroyed that world forever with his news.

He stood there for a long time, listening to their bright chatter, taking shallow panicky breaths, trying to hold back the moment, trying to stop time, but it was futile and he knew it. He walked back to the dining room door.

"Martin is dead," he announced, with someone else's voice. "He committed suicide this afternoon. Connor called from the hospital."

The two faces gaped at him, blank with disbelief.

At that moment they heard the pounding on the front door, and the vices bellowing from the other side.

"Police! Open up!"

He stumbled back down the hall, cravenly relieved not to face his own family, and opened the door. Chief Kennis was there, and Assistant Chief Krakauer, and three uniformed cops.

"Jackson Blum," Kennis said. "I have a warrant for your arrest for felony first-degree murder in the death of Theodore Coddington. You have the right to remain silent. If you choose to speak, anything you say can be used against you in a court of law. You have the right to an attorney—"

"Wait—"

"If you cannot afford an attorney, one will be provided for you by the state."

"Chief, listen—"

"Do you understand these rights as I have read them to you?"

"Chief—"

"Do you understand these rights as I have read them to you?"

"Yes, yes, but—"

"We're going to take you into custody now, Mr. Blum. As a courtesy, you won't be handcuffed, but I'm going to have to ask you to—"

Blum's mind finally caught up with the moving train of this new outrage. He swung himself onboard, assembled the words he had always known he might have to utter someday. He started to speak but the words caught in his throat like acid reflux, the irony burning his esophagus.

Suicide.

Within the space of an hour, the mortal sin that had just destroyed his life was now going to save it. Now he had to be thankful for suicide! Suicide to the rescue! He had driven Ted to the act, long before Martin. Blum was toxic. He left death behind him, like a worm in an apple—everything in front of him fresh and white, everything behind him brown and rotten.

"Mr. Blum?"

He still hadn't spoken. Some atavistic lust to survive fought free from the paralyzing self-hatred. He croaked out the words: "Ted committed suicide! I found him—I buried him…he killed himself with my gun. I knew what it—how it would look, if the body was ever found. I can prove it! I have the note."

Kennis squinted at him. "You kept your friend's suicide note for twenty years?"

"Yes, because—"

"And you never showed it to anyone. His widow, for instance. Didn't it occur to you that she might want to know what happened to her husband?"

"That he killed himself? Over an affair with her sister? No! I thought she should never know that! I hoped she would never find out. Better the mystery, better not to know."

"But you knew. You and no one else."

"What are you saying?"

"Private remorse rarely pushes a man to kill himself, Mr. Blum. My guess is you were blackmailing him."

"That's ridiculous! You can't prove that. The note says nothing about that. Let me show it to you and we can end this nightmare."

"All right. Go get it. I'll come with you. And

just so you know, I have men posted at your back door."

"You think I'm going to run? You think this is some crazy trick?"

"I keep an open mind." He stepped forward. "May I?"

Blum stepped back, turned and strode back past the dining room, through the great room and his office. Out of the corner of his eye, he saw Max rising from the table. Marjorie sat still, stricken—a waxwork impression of herself, a pale statue of grief and horror.

In the office, Blum crossed to the closet, pulled the old tobacco humidor off the high shelf and set it down on the desk. He pulled it open.

Empty.

He stared at the blank interior, the faint smell of cedar and cigars drifting up to him. He thought of the day his car had been stolen in Manhattan years ago—walking to the empty parking space, double checking it, unable to process the obvious facts.

"It was here," he mumbled. "It was right here. I put here, that day. I—it…this makes no sense. Someone—someone took it!"

"But no one knew about it," Kennis said quietly. "That was your whole point."

"They must—someone must have found it, someone must have been snooping—"

With the tingle at the back of his neck that had alerted animals to silent predators since the dawn of time, he twisted around to see his son, Max, smiling, ever so slightly, just a tiny lift at the corners of his mouth, gone as soon as Blum caught his eye.

Max.

Some rabid snarl of accusation died in his lungs. What was the use? Max would deny everything, he had probably destroyed the note long ago. To attack his son, now, in the caustic shadow of Martin's death and his own culpability...it was impossible.

Kennis was glancing from father to son, studying the moment. Did he suspect something? How smart was he, really? Smart enough for this. But he did nothing. Blum saw it all so clearly. No one was going to help him. And that was how it should be. He had dug his own grave. All he had to do now was climb into it and let the first spadeful of soil hit his face. Eat the dirt, gag on it, let it block his throat. A different kind of drowning, a more appropriate one.

Let the punishment fit the crime.

He turned to Kennis. "Let's go."

● ● ● ● ●

They put him in a cell in the basement of the new police station and left him alone. The claustrophobia of the cage surged and receded. He didn't ask for a lawyer, he didn't care about bail. He didn't want to talk to anyone or see anyone. He couldn't bear the thought of anyone looking at him, judging him, seeing him for what he was.

He sat on the hard bunk, clasped his knees with his hands. He was bad. He was a bad man. Everything everyone had ever said about him was true. Kennis had seen through him, recognized him as a blackmailer. Was there a lower crime than that? A more despicable sin? Using someone's weakness against them? In Ted Coddington's case, using the purest feeling the man had ever known, the true love that Blum himself had always scoffed at, the most vulnerable fold of a man's hardened heart, to destroy him with the threat of shame and disgrace? And all for money! All to close a deal. But it wasn't just money, it was power, influence, prestige, making himself more important. He had to be the biggest fish in this ridiculous little pond. A guppy in a bucket. And why? So he could strut and preen and lord it over people like poor Arthur Sprockett and Homer Boyce? All Homer needed was a break on his rent. And Arthur, what was Arthur's emergency request? Three thousand dollars? Pocket change! Money that meant nothing to

Blum. Sprockett might as well have asked for the pennies and dimes. Three thousand dollars! He spent more than that on a set of Hermès boxers and a pair of Berluti loafers! And he'd never ever worn those shoes. Where was he supposed to wear them on Nantucket? What a joke. And now that poor boy was going to be crippled for life because Blum cared more about feeling superior than lifting one finger, one pinky to help someone else.

The kid wasn't real to him. That was the fact. No one was real to Jackson Blum but Jackson Blum. He was a plague. He was Ebola. But they had found a vaccine for Ebola. There was no cure for Blum.

He leaned back, let the back of his head press against the cinder block wall. His past and his present were lost, but it was the future that haunted him tonight.

He had lost Martin in the Cape Cod Mall once, years ago. The boy had been six years old. Marjorie had left him in his father's care for a few minutes while she did some Christmas shopping at the toy store. Blum had looked away for a second, distracted by one of those shiny new cars they parked in the middle of the concourse. When he looked down Martin was gone.

Bewilderment turned to fear and fear turned to panic as he ran from store to store, asking everyone, "Have you seen a little boy with brown hair wearing a blue down parka?"

He remembered standing still among the rushing crowds, feeling a dark door opening, showing a view of his future, a future without Martin, where he had let his son disappear forever because of a moment's inattention. It had been the most frightening moment of his life. It lasted fifteen minutes.

The security people found Martin wandering around the Sears store at the far end of the mall, chatting with a clerk in the luggage department, happily oblivious to the uproar he had caused.

This was so much worse. Martin was truly gone now, he was never coming back and the guilt and the misery would never end. Connor McKenzie was right. He would have his whole life to contemplate the unbearable vileness of his behavior. Jail would be a holiday cruise compared to that.

Past, present, future—all gone.

He found himself crying and he couldn't stop and he hated his self-pitying sniffles most of all. He finally fell asleep, curled into the fetal position, hands caught between his legs, knowing that sleep was the best he could hope for now, and dreading the morning.

He was awakened near dawn by his cell door opening. The young policeman who processed him out of custody explained: apparently Marjorie

Blum had called his lawyer, who had swung into action and awakened Judge Tobias Renninger. Something extraordinary had happened, but Blum couldn't discover what it was. The judge must have found it convincing, though. He had rolled out of bed, gotten dressed, and driven down to the station personally to expedite Blum's own-cognizance release, pending a bail hearing on the following Monday.

"This man is no more of a flight risk than I am," the judge had told Barnaby Toll, the Christmas Eve duty officer. "And good God, man, it's Christmas."

Toll called him a cab, and Blum staggered out into the icy clear dawn to wait for it. He had no coat and he was shuddering with the cold when the cab finally pulled up. A fat grizzled islander, working on Christmas morning. The man probably had no family, no one to go home to. Welcome to the club.

The house was dark when they pulled up on Pleasant Street. Blum gave the driver the last of the cash in his pockets—a fifty-dollar bill, twice the cost of the ride. Normally, he would have stood on the frozen street shivering while the man counted out the exact change. Giving a tip was letting yourself be taken advantage of, it was legalized theft, it made people weak and lazy, dependent on handouts, expecting something for nothing. How many times had he given that dreary lecture?

Not anymore.

"Keep it," he said now, and let himself into the warm dark house, with no sound to greet him but the low roar of the furnace.

"Max? Marjorie?"

There was no response. The house felt empty. He checked the bedrooms. He was alone. Where were they? Where had they gone? What was happening? He pulled his cell phone out of his pocket. It still had some charge but he found he was afraid to make a call. He didn't want to know where they'd gone, or why they had deserted him this morning. He didn't want to hear the bitterness and accusation in their voices. Maybe it was better this way.

He walked into the living room and lowered himself onto the couch. He had slept badly in jail, a ragged shallow nap, nothing more. He was exhausted but he dreaded the sight of his own bedroom. It was a ghoulish museum of a life gone extinct. The couch was neutral territory.

He sat staring straight ahead, while the light grew outside the big windows and morning advanced on the broken world, waiting for a reason to get up.

• • ● • •

His family was flying home from Boston.

Ten minutes after the police had taken Blum

away, the landline in the kitchen had rung—an actual ring from an earlier decade, just like the old rotary dial phone itself, kept on a kitchen counter for emergencies only, for the moment when power lines and cell phone towers came down in a hurricane or a war.

Marjorie picked up the bulky handset and heard Connor MacKenzie sobbing with joy.

"They brought him back! They brought him back! He was dead for three minutes but they brought him back!"

At first Marjorie couldn't absorb the news, any more than she had been able to absorb the news of Martin's death less than half an hour before.

"Martin…he's alive? How—it…I don't understand."

Max was at her side instantly. "What did he say? What's going on?" He grabbed the phone. "Connor? Is that you? What happened? Is Martin okay?"

"They used the defibrillator. He threw up over all of us, but he's okay. He ran outside after he took the pills and collapsed in a snowbank. He was, like…frozen, basically, and the doctor said that may have saved him. I don't know, I just know he's okay. He's asking for you and your mom. Can you come here?"

They booked a private jet on zero notice for

close to twenty-thousand dollars. On the way over, Max confessed to his own crime. He and Lizza, belatedly investigating her father's death, had found and stolen Ted Coddington's suicide note. They had kept it as a secret they might use, or weaponize, someday. And that day had come. Bitter and furious, Max had said nothing when the police dragged his father off to jail.

But Martin was alive and whatever else Jackson Blum might be, he was not a killer.

The reunion at the hospital was tearful, the flight back was jubilant.

Jackson Blum was still sitting on the couch when he heard the car doors slam and the steps outside and the front door swinging open. He stood to face the delayed judgment of his family, ready for the full force of their sorrow and their hate, bullets from a firing squad. He had been justly convicted, he deserved the execution. All he could do now was accept it with dignity.

He turned and saw his older son, weak and pallid, standing in the hall, leaning against the door casing.

Martin attempted a crooked smile. "Hi, Dad."

"Martin?"

Was he hallucinating? Had he finally gone mad?

"They saved me, Dad. The doctor said, 'Good

thing you weren't living in the nineteenth century. Or in Roxbury.' They shocked me and pumped my stomach and gave me saline and I don't really know what else. They wanted to keep me overnight but Mom was like "No way! My boy is coming home."

"Oh, my God."

Blum lurched across the room and gathered his son into a crushing hug. "I'm sorry, Martin. I'm so sorry." He was crying, soaking Martin's shirt. The boy held him tight.

"It's okay, Dad. It's okay."

"I can change. I can be better. Please…give me a second chance."

"Well…technically, it would be like your fiftieth chance. But it's the first one you've ever taken, so—sure."

Blum pulled himself together. "Is Connor here? I want to see him. I want to welcome him into our home, wish him Merry Christmas, tell him I'm sorry, let him know—"

Connor appeared behind Martin, smiling. "Merry Christmas, Mr. Blum."

"Jackson, please—Jack. Anything you want to call me, but not Mr. Blum."

"Jack. I like the sound of that. Merry Christmas, Jack. Marjorie tells me the dough is in the refrigerator, and we should get started on the sticky buns."

Max and Marjorie joined the hug and Blum said softly to them, "There's so much I can't fix, so much I've done wrong to so many people—" He stopped short.

Max pulled away a little. "What?"

"I have to go!" Jackson announced. "I'll be back soon. Before the sticky buns are out of the oven. Just—wait for me."

He lurched out of the living room, grabbed his coat off the hook in the hall, snatched his car keys off the little table by the front door and flung himself outside into the bright cold empty morning. No one was out and about. Everyone was indoors, opening presents.

He stopped for a moment, taken by surprise. Snow had started to fall. He tilted his face up to the sky and let the cold flakes touch his skin. Snow! He walked to the car feeling an absurd extravagant elation, climbed in, gunned the engine and pulled out into Pleasant Street. He slowed down—no rush. He had actually been arrested for speeding on Christmas morning a few years ago, driving to his store to pick up a forgotten present. The last thing he wanted to see now was police flashers in his rearview mirror. Staying under the speed limit, it still took him under five minutes to reach Homer Boyce's cottage off Fairgrounds Road.

Homer was eating cold cereal in his bathrobe

when Blum knocked. Homer opened the door and gaped at his visitor, speechless. He couldn't have been more surprised if it had been the newly elected President standing there. But he had some choice words for POTUS. To Blum all he could say was, "How…it…what are you doing here?"

"I won't stay long, Homer. I just wanted to ask you to stay on at your store. I'm lowering the rent, and I'll be paying the utilities this year. If you'd consider the idea."

"But—I don't…why? Why would you do that?"

"Nantucket needs your shop, Homer. You said it yourself—where else can someone buy a thimble in this town?"

"You rented the space to some jewelry store."

"I'm breaking the lease."

"They'll sue you."

"I'll sue them back."

"You'll lose."

"Probably. I'll have to pay them some money. I can afford it."

They stared at each other.

"Are you serious?"

Blum clasped his tenant's hand and gripped his shoulder. "I have never been more serious in my life. And yet I feel positively giddy. Merry Christmas, Homer. And a very happy New Year."

The next stop was the most important one. He drove further on Fairgrounds Road toward Surfside Road. He had the streets to himself. His mind was a blank. For once he didn't want to organize his thoughts or "prepare his remarks"—that was how Chief Kennis had put it.

He reached the little house on Third Way, parked in the dirt by the front door, climbed out of the car and knocked hesitantly. No response. He knocked louder and finally a tousled-looking Arnold Sprockett came to the door, with a mug of coffee in his hand.

"Arnold! Merry Christmas!"

"Mr. Blum?"

Blum saw the flash of fear and guilt on Arnold's face. Of course! He had demanded that the poor man work at the store this morning, and now he'd been caught playing hooky!

"I'm going in to work soon, sir, I just—"

"No, you certainly are not! Not on Christmas morning."

Blum pulled him into a clumsy embrace, and it was all he could do not to spill his coffee.

Blum squeezed his shoulders, moved him aside, and strode into the house. "Nat? Are you here?" The boy was sitting on a chair in the living room, his leg in a cast. "You're having surgery, Nat. Tomorrow! As soon as we can schedule the operation."

Arnold had followed him inside. "But you said—the loan—"

"Forget the loan. I'm paying for everything—the operation, the rehab, everything. And we're getting the best orthopedic surgeon in New England! Price is no object." He took his clerk by the shoulders. "Can you forgive me, Arnold? Can you forgive me? I said horrible things to you, unfair, mean-spirited, dreadful things. And I've never given you the credit you deserve. I couldn't run the store without you, and everyone in the world knew that but me. I'm doubling your salary next year and I want you to think about a partnership. A real stake in the business. Anyway…I'm sorry. I didn't mean to intrude on your morning. But I wanted to see you and let you know about the operation…and—I guess…just say Merry Christmas. And Happy New Year."

Nat looked up from the gift book he was reading, pulled away from Bob Cratchett, Tiny Tim, and the Christmas turkey, feeling a delicious shiver of recognition as life and art twined together and his future opened in front of him like the last door on his Advent calendar.

There was only one proper thing to say. "God bless us, every one."

"Yes, indeed! Well put, young man! God bless us, every one."

Chapter Thirty

Christmas Morning

It was our first Christmas Eve together in the little house on Darling Street and I had been a little nervous about it—Sam in a new house with a new family, my kids dealing with a new step-sibling (for lack of a better word), and a new woman in my life. It could have turned into a nightmare, especially since this was my year to have the kids on Christmas morning. My kids adored Sam and were at least getting used to Jane. Carrie and Tim had even done the dishes after Christmas Eve dinner, though with a little too much ceremony. I thought of my old LAPD pal Chuck Obremski, laughing about some recent Academy graduate's unnecessary overtime or exhaustive prep for a two-minute court appearance—"He's gotta be the hero!"

But we all knew that Jane was the hero of this little story. Sam cleared the table and wiped down the countertops, and the three of them working together finished the chores in less than fifteen minutes.

"Many hands make light work—that's what Grandma always says," Carrie pointed out.

"Just for the record," I pointed out, "She also says 'Fuck the neighbors' and 'Dream girls don't go to the bathroom.' Hey, she didn't want me to be embarrassed about the kids on the block seeing her teaching me to ride my bike, or their parents sneering at the peace stickers on her VW bug. And she knew my tendency to…idealize my infatuations."

"Do you idealize me?" Jane asked sweetly.

"I try. But you always exceed my fantasies."

"Awwww," Carrie said.

"Ick," Sam said.

"I think it's nice," Tim said.

"Omigod, just stop!"

I lifted my hands. "Enough. Please. It's Christmas Eve."

"And I was Santa's daughter."

"In a play," Tim pointed out.

"I lived the part. I patted a big dog with reindeer antlers yesterday and I even asked a little boy what he wanted for Christmas."

"What did he say?" I asked.

"He wanted one of those remote-controlled fire trucks with a siren, Dad. You would have been so proud—I told him it would make his parents crazy. He just grinned. It was scary."

We watched my all-time guilty pleasure holiday movie, *White Christmas*, and went to bed early, the corniest song still running through my head.

"We'll follow the old man, wherever he wants to go…"

I sometimes fantasized about my own troops singing that song to me at a retirement party, but I was no Dean Jagger. I did get my White Christmas, though. Show was falling steadily when I woke up and the world outside my window was frosted like a cake.

Sam led the charge waking us up and we were all downstairs attacking the presents by six-thirty in the morning. The plate of cookies he had left for Santa showed one discreet bite taken from one cookie, with a note: "More than a million cookies tonight! I only nibble the best ones. Thanks, Santa."

"Mine was one of the best," Sam crowed.

"Hello, I helped a little," Jane said.

"Yeah, just the recipe and the mixing and the baking parts," Carrie added.

"I mixed!" Sam protested. "I creamed the butter and sugar together."

"I've always loved the sound of that," I said.

"Want to try one?" He brought over the plate.

I took a half-moon of vanilla shortbread, chewed thoughtfully and nodded. "Santa has good taste."

Only Sam had a stocking—Miranda insisted on filling the ones for my kids, on which her mother had embroidered their names. They never left her house, which was fine with me. I didn't have her microscopic eye for detail. She collected for the stockings all year—miniature high-bouncing superballs and china animals, exotic candies and cast-iron toy cars, sets of French colored pencils and packets of paper-thin beef jerky from some Midwestern farm. I'd hear about the new batch of treats tomorrow. For now we attacked the big stuff—Billy Delavane's Victorian dollhouse for Sam; a stop-motion animation kit for Tim, with weird creatures sporting flipper feet and propeller hands, complete with miniature camera and software; a full-length quilted down jacket in black for Carrie, who was always cold in the winter. This one was rated for sub-arctic temperatures and also looked great on her. Jane found them cool lunchboxes—vintage Gilmore Girls for Carrie, classic Beatles for Tim. Jane gave them smart wool socks; I found them good lined gloves, hoping winter would eventually arrive. I got Tim a clear fiberglass sled; Jane got Carrie the earrings she had been coveting from Le Souk. As for the grownups—I'd found a complete set of Jane's beloved Nancy Drew books, which she matched with the new Lee Child and a full bells-and-whistles *Breaking Bad* DVD collection. I got a cashmere turtleneck; she got the flannel PJs she coveted.

The kids pooled their money together to buy us a deluxe edition of *Clue*.

We made coffee and pancakes and enjoyed the drifts of wrapping paper, settling in for seconds all around when the doorbell rang.

We gave each other the "Are you expecting someone?" look, then I shrugged, set my mug down and waded through the mess of paper to the front hall. When I opened the door, Max Blum was standing on the front stoop, holding a manila envelope in his hand.

I stepped back. "Come on in. Merry Christmas. Coffee?"

"That would be great."

I led him into the kitchen and poured him the last cup out of the Chemex. He hesitated. "We were just about to make more."

"Uh, okay. Thanks." He took a sip, set the cup down on the counter. "That's Ted Coddington's suicide note in there," he said, tilting his head toward the envelope. "I took it a long time ago. I thought I could use it against my dad someday. I liked the idea of owning his Get Out of Jail Free

card. I guess I wanted to hurt him and I thought…
well, you never know."

"But you're here."

"Everybody deserves a second chance, Chief.
Like Sam Trikilis. That was really great—him winning the drawing like that. And my stupid little
prank turning out so well. And…I guess…no one
getting in trouble over it."

"The Selectmen wouldn't have liked that."

"I guess not. So…everyone gets a second
chance. Even you."

"I'm not sure what—"

"I heard coming to Nantucket was kind of a
second chance for you. Getting to start over."

I nodded. "I think it was."

"Looks like you made the most of it."

"I hope so. You do the same. Maybe your dad
will, too."

"He's off to a pretty good start."

And speaking of do-overs, Max hadn't been
gone for more than ten minutes before the doorbell
rang again.

"Jeez, you're popular," Jane said.

"But I'm not."

I opened the door. Jacqueline Talbot, the vet
from the MSPCA was standing there. Bailey was
sitting next to her, tail thumping the deck, wearing
a big red bow.

I was stunned. "Jackie…"

"Turned out when the mom and the kids adopted the dog…the father didn't want him. There was a big fight and Dad won. So Bailey came back and I thought, since it was Christmas…"

"Come on in. Let's get that leash off him."

As soon as I unclipped it the big wooly dog bounded into the house and I heard Tim shriek "BAILEY!" That was all he had time to say because the dog leapt halfway across the room and knocked him down. By the time I got into the room, they were wrestling on the floor and the big dog was licking Tim's face in a frenzy of canine infatuation. Needless to say, the feeling was mutual.

"Can we keep him, Dad? Can we?"

"I guess we know whose dog that is," Jane said.

"I thought he liked me best."

"Sorry."

"So we can keep him?"

"I think he's keeping us."

Carrie was petting him now, too, and the big dog was rolling on his back, soaking it up. "He'll be a good friend for Dervish," she said.

Billy Delavane's pug was a little huffy around other dogs, but it was worth a try. "Absolutely."

Driving them out to 'Sconset later, with the big dog lolling between them, his head in Tim's lap and his tail slapping at Carrie's leg, I asked them about their mother's fiancé, Joe Arbogast.

"He's okay," Carrie said. "He's nice to us. He tries a little too hard. But I like that about him."

Tim piped up: "Mr. Newman, the guidance counselor? He told me I come from a broken home. That's a horrible thing to say, isn't it? Besides, it's not even true. I used to have one home and it was broken, but now I have two and they're both put back together. He thought I had half and I really have double, so he flunks math, too! Which he supposedly teaches."

"Did you tell him that?"

"Should I?"

"Probably not."

They both hugged me as they got out of the car, and Tim whispered in my ear. Driving home with Bailey riding shotgun, his muzzle in the breeze, halfway out the open window, heading back to a lazy afternoon with Jane, eating chocolate Santas, matching wits over a game of *Clue* and reading our books (Sam's dad had him for the night), with all the small worlds I was responsible for, improbably but happily in order, I couldn't help but agree with Tim's sober and thoughtful assessment.

This was the best Christmas ever.

To see more Poisoned Pen Press titles:

Visit our website:
poisonedpenpress.com/

Request a digital catalog:
info@poisonedpenpress.com

CPSIA information can be obtained
at www.ICGtesting.com
Printed in the USA
BVOW03s1244251017
498629BV00001B/3/P